DECEPTION AND DESIRE

"Ignoring our problems won't make them go away, Richard," she protested as they moved through the crowded dance floor, speaking in a voice so low it could barely be heard beyond the compass of her elegant fan. "After this ball I will still remain a prisoner of the one man who most wants to expose us — and who is most capable of doing so. He watches me all the time."

Richard lifted an eyebrow quizzically. "'Tis only fair. So do you watch him.?"

"What?" Jenny looked up in surprise.

"He fascinates you," Sir Richard accused. "He has done, I verily believe, from the beginning."

"He terrifies me," she contradicted. In her heart, though, Jenny had to admit Richard was right. Wolf did fascinate her. He was a mystery, a man composed of paradoxes — equally ruthless and kind, cold and passionate. . . .

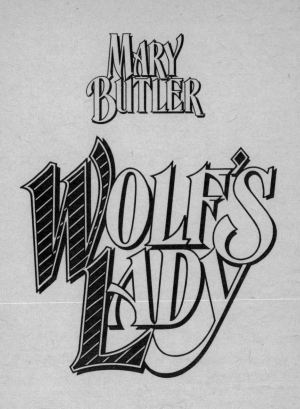

MARY BUTLER

WOLF'S LADY

LEISURE BOOKS ⬛ NEW YORK CITY

A LEISURE BOOK®

February 1992

Published by

Dorchester Publishing Co., Inc.
276 Fifth Avenue
New York, NY 10001

Prologue

"Thief!"

Despite the seriousness of the charge, the girl's warm hazel eyes reflected only amusement. She gave her accuser an ironic glance, more annoyed by the tickling of a curl that had escaped from beneath her cap. By what accident the brooch had arrived in her market basket could only be conjectured. But theft? How utterly ridiculous! It was a hideous piece, glaringly vulgar like the mistress who owned it. Like her it too was false, a clever copy but not one to fool the educated eye.

The liveried youth at her side pointed an accusing finger. "So you're the one that's been lifting all those trinkets! The mistress is so forgetful, you said. She must have misplaced it, you said." His voice was raised so that everyone could hear, raised loud enough to attract more listeners among the idlers and customers outside the chandler's shop. "You could have cost us all our posts."

She still did not understand. "What trinkets? James, what are you talking about? I don't know how . . ."

"Save your speeches and innocent looks for the beak."

The word was not a familiar one to her, but she guessed from the approving murmurs of the gathering crowd that the footman referred to a magistrate.

"Don't be foolish," she said. "You won't be thanked for making a fuss over mere mischance. I'm sure everything can be investigated to the master's satisfaction as soon as we bring the bauble back home."

The calm reasonableness of her voice did not influence her listeners in her favor, however. A hired companion was just a servant, after all, and had no right to the authority and airs of the gentry.

Heartened by signs of support, the footman grabbed her viciously by the wrist. At this unexpectedly violent act the girl took a long, clear look at her accuser. For the first time she began to understand what he intended, if not why. James knew perfectly well what he was doing, and he was deriving immense enjoyment from it as well.

The crowd was pressing close, too close. Now, all at once, she felt she could not bear the footman's sneering attitude, the sweaty grasp of his hand, one moment more. With her free hand she swung the basket at his head and leapt free as he instinctively released her to raise his hand in a protective gesture.

His howl was echoed by the crowd. Looking around her, she suddenly realized that she was surrounded by strangers. James had insisted on going out of the way to a different shop where, he assured her, better-quality silks and ribbons could be had for a lower price.

There was no time to worry about why the footman should wish her harm. Or to think about her mother's warnings against giving in to what she called "Jenny's wild starts." No time to do anything but drop the basket and run.

The wind pulled her cap off and within minutes had loosened her thick auburn tresses free from its pins. She was hampered by her panniers and full skirts, but sheer willfulness as much as fear lent speed to her long limbs. If she could but reach the house before the malicious James caught up with her, if she could only gain the master's ear for a moment . . .

The footman was as determined in his pursuit. Moreover, he had now unleashed a most terrible weapon against her—the mob. No force on earth could stop them now. With every step, more and more people—shopkeepers, idlers, servants, and masters—joined the chase. The cry of "Stop, thief" seemed to draw them irresistibly and to rob them of humanity.

She couldn't seem to shake them. They followed her as unerringly as the hound who scents his quarry on the very breeze. The girl dodged in and out of the alleys behind the shops. In only a few turns the streets had changed from rows of respectable shops and businesses to a series of disreputable taverns and tenements. The denizens of the area—whores, drunks, and beggars—might have scant respect for the law, but they joined the hunt with relish all the same.

Passing by the kitchen door of one of the grog shops, the girl slipped in the filth and fell. She was up again immediately, but her small lead over her pursuers was lessened. In desperation she tried darting into the next drinking establishment, but realized her mistake as soon as she entered. Even marked by contact with the slop pail, she was still indisputably a lady, and as such entirely out of place in surroundings like these.

The room stilled at her appearance. No wonder—she must look like a madwoman. Her hair hung loose about her shoulders now, looking darkly red against the clear pallor of her skin. One of her panniers had broken, giving her a lopsided appearance, and the cotton print gown was torn and besmirched.

While every eye was on her, however, every ear could hear the approaching horde. This was neither the time nor the place to beg for pity or assistance. In the proprietor's bloodshot eyes she could read her doom. Drink made him slow, however. Before he could grab her shoulders, she pulled a chair out from under an unsteady customer and thrust it in his path. She made her exit out the rear while the landlord was still picking himself up from the floor.

Already the mob was entering the gin shop. She hoped that some, at least, would be lured away from the chase by the abundance of cheap liquor. Surely they must be hot and thirsty by now.

Her own throat was dry. One of her stays poked

into her ribs; her breath came with difficulty. Secure in her innocence, she had no real fear of the law, but she was now terrified of the mob. Clearly, the crowd no longer remembered the purpose of the hunt. Some other, more primitive, instinct drove them on.

Clutching her side and trying simultaneously to hold up her skirts, she hurried through the next yard and into the street. She had now worked her way back to the principal road. Impervious to other perils, she darted out between an elegant barouche and a grocer's cart, causing the team of the latter equipage to buck and sidle in a dangerous fashion.

A sensation of triumph filled her as she realized she was only a few short steps from home. Then she'd be safe, then justice would prevail. Then . . .

The mistress herself answered the frenzied pounding at the door, hurriedly, as if she had been waiting for someone, something. Her large figure, extended in width by her wide panniers and up by the fashionable height of her wig, completely filled the doorway.

"Ma'am, I must see Mr. Ransome at once. James, the footman, has gone mad. He tried to . . ."

"Incompetent fool! I should have known he couldn't be trusted."

"Then you know he took your pin? Oh, you ease my mind considerably. If you please, ma'am, he'll be here any minute—with a mob behind him. Permit me to enter and catch my breath. I think Mr. Ransome should be here to deal with this as well."

"Mr. Ransome will be of no help to you, miss."

She raised her eyes slowly, hardly able to credit the rage she heard in her mistress's voice.

"Did you think I wouldn't notice?" the horrible voice continued. "My husband? In my house?"

The veneer of gentility Mrs. Ransome tried to maintain was beginning to crack. "Thought you was different, did you? His own class? He found out soon enough class don't mean a damned thing without brass behind it. And now you're going to find out the same for yourself."

The girl shook her head in disbelief. Her ears were filled with a terrible roaring.

"You?" Her mind tried to grapple with this strange twist. Not James, but Mrs. Ransome had done this to her. By design. Unwilling to accept the truth, she protested, "No, oh no."

"Oh yes, my girl. And don't think he'll speak up for you. He may not like it, but he'll do as he's told. He always does . . . in the end."

The anger that had fueled the girl's escape resurfaced for a moment. "Do you truly believe that anyone will credit your accusation? That I would risk my position and my character by stealing an ugly piece of . . . of paste?"

The mob was upon them now, physically spent and taken aback by Mrs. Ransome's imposing figure, but triumphant nonetheless. James and a few confederates grabbed at the girl, pulling at her arms until she cried out in pain. Still she had the satisfaction of seeing her parting shot hit home. An angry flush settled over her mistress's coarse features. She hadn't known! The venal Mr. Ransome must have sold or pawned the original in secret.

Her sense of victory, however, was shortlived.

"It won't be paste by the time you come to trial," Mrs. Ransome taunted as she shut the door in her face. "I promise you that, Miss Jenny Wilde. If you live long enough to be tried!"

Chapter One

Jenny shivered against the cold stone wall of the Women's Hold and wondered how long it would take to die.

Death would be preferable to madness or . . . No, she would not become like those others—animals, women who had sold themselves so often they had nothing left.

She had thought she was no innocent before this. She had seen too much of war and its horrors to be easily shocked. But nothing she had seen or heard could have prepared her for the ugliness, the very real evil, of Newgate.

In the days that followed her painful initiation into prison life, Jenny had learned a great deal. It had taken her a little while to understand. Everyone seemed to speak another language here. But one thing soon became clear: you could have anything you wanted—for a price. Call it chummage, call it garnish, it was money they wanted, all of them, from the jailers to her fellow prisoners.

Jenny had nothing, no money nor even any possessions to barter. Without the protection of even a few pence, she was fettered by the jailers and beaten by the prisoners who stole every last stitch of her clothing. If she had not been able to grab the dirty rag of a shift discarded by the woman who stole hers, she would have been left with nothing to protect her body from the cold and the filth.

That was Newgate's first lesson to all prisoners. The second was that the worst of prison life was not the cold and the filth, not even the unhealthy stench and the obscene language in the air, but the boredom, the complete lack of purpose or activity. This it was that drove the others to fight, to drink, and to gamble. And to go mad.

Jenny learned too what it was to have an enemy in Newgate when she refused Caleb Deems, the jailer.

He was smiling as he came strutting through the hold toward the corner where she huddled near the fever victims.

"Well, if it ain't the high and mighty Miss Wilde. I didn't hardly recognize you in your becoming new costume." He smiled still as he fingered the deep cut that ran across his cheek. No, he'd never forget Jenny's refusal. His face would bear the reminder for the rest of his life.

Jenny tried to pull the ragged cloth more closely about her and put a brave face on. "What do you want?"

She shouldn't have said that. She knew what he wanted. He wanted her—to use her for his pleasure and to sell her for the pleasure of others.

"Me? Not a thing. I gots anything I want."

Jenny watched the swish-swish of his whip warily. "How fortunate for you."

"Aye, I'm a man who makes his own fortune, his own rules."

His rules were that no one was to buy from her or sell to her. If she wanted anything—straw to sleep on, better food, drink, anything at all—she had to deal with him. And pay his prices.

"I only come, like a considerate landlord, to inquire about your well-being, so to speak. Accommodations up to your hexpectations? Would there be anything I could do to see to your ... comfort?"

The whip swished closer for a moment. Jenny flinched. That small movement changed her field of vision by the merest fraction, but it was enough. Behind Deems she could see that most of the women were involved in the business of getting drunk on the bottles of gin he had delivered. A considerable row had broken out over the proprietorship of one of the bottles. No one had their eye on Deems but Jenny—and one other. And that other, Jenny could see from the corner of her eye, was expertly picking his pocket.

It was beautifully done. Had Jenny not watched for hours the practice of the younger girls in the art of removing articles from each other's pockets, she would never have guessed.

Deems certainly had no idea. Laughing, he seemed satisfied he'd made his point, and was ready to go.

Except the pickpocket wasn't finished.

"Yes," Jenny said quickly, surprising them both, "there is something you can do."

Deems smiled. "Ahh. Is there now?"

Jenny felt a fool, but she could not resist the urge to assist in his humiliation. "You can reduce both the vermin population and the stench of the hold by removing yourself immediately," she answered, "before I become violently ill."

"Why, you bitch."

Yes, that got him, she thought, refusing to consider that she might be creating her own doom.

"You're adding to the score, miss," he threatened, lifting her head up with the whip. "Caleb Deems doesn't forget."

As he turned away, he began to reach toward his pocket—his empty pocket. Instinctively, Jenny thrust out a foot to trip him up. Deems fell with a most satisfying thud, to the great pleasure of the other prisoners. The noise made upon contact with the floor was loud enough even to attract the attention of the others, who turned away from their drinking and fighting to express their delight in this impromptu entertainment. Jenny's pleasure was no less than theirs, but she knew she would have to mask it if she were to escape whipping.

Clutching at her leg, she screamed. "You did that on purpose, you—"—Jenny struggled to find a suitable insult "—you brute. Monster, you nearly tore my foot off!" She keened softly to herself, swaying back and forth as if in great pain. To her own amazement, she was even able to come up with a few tears.

The jailer looked carefully at her performance,

hate in his eyes, but he evidently saw only the pain and fear he wanted to see. "Just a reminder, miss. If you think it can't get worse than this, I can show you how very wrong you are. Think about it."

He swung his whip casually as he left, ignoring the chorus of catcalls and curses that followed him. With some trepidation, Jenny waited for the jailer's stormy return. Once Deems discovered the theft, as surely he soon would, it seemed impossible he would look elsewhere for a scapegoat. He did not return that afternoon, however. Either he wanted her to experience fully the horrible torment of anticipating punishment, or he was more stupid than she had supposed.

That night she had more than a troubled mind to keep her wakeful. One of the women had reached her time. She faced her labor without patience, restraint, or courage. Her companions surrounded her, offering rough encouragement but little real assistance.

Weak though she was, and terrified of facing the brutality of the chief bullies, Jenny was about to offer what small support she might when she heard the woman loudly dismiss any assistance but that of gin.

"She's all right," a voice by Jenny's ear suddenly asserted. "This will be her eleventh. Drops 'em like a pig in litter, she does. Here. This is for you." It was the girl who had so efficiently impoverished Mr. Deems. In her outstretched hand she offered a piece of bread and cheese.

Jenny hesitated. She had done more than hope for death, she had courted it. When she allowed the others to steal her meager food allowance, when she hovered by the side of the dying, she did so well aware of the consequences. Still, she was tempted.

Despite her resolve, a strong will to live, to survive, yet persisted. Even here, life still had its attractions, its pleasures. Today she had found satisfaction, almost amusement, in confounding her jailer. Now she was being offered friendship with that food. It would be discourteous to reject it, and yet . . .

The pickpocket seemed to sense Jenny's turmoil.

"I seen you. I know what you been thinking. But don't do it, girl. Don't give up."

"Why not?"

"If you die, they win. Don't let the bastards win."

Jenny thought of Mrs. Ransome, of James and Deems. Let them win? No, that would be wrong, terribly wrong. How strange that it should fall to a prisoner here to prick her pride.

"Thank you," she said and accepted the gift.

"I owe you. I didn't dare come forward earlier. That bacon-faced bully, Deems, has put the mark on you. When he says he can make your life a hell, he ain't lying. And he's threatening to do just that to anybody who gives you a hand. That's if he can catch 'em." Even in the dark, Jenny could sense the girl's elfin grin. "He ain't real bright, our Caleb. Too greedy. He ought to be looking out for his own back instead of mounting every bitch in sight and counting his pence."

That could well be believed. "And when he finds his pocket empty?"

"Ah, but he won't. I've been diving since I was

a babe in arms and I knows better. He'll find his pockets lighter, but not empty. And then he won't be able to quite recall how much he had when and where he had it."

And then Jenny did laugh, to her great surprise.

"That's the ticket. You know," her new friend said in a serious tone, "I had my glims on you when you come in. You ain't like the rest of us somehow. But you're all right."

Before Jenny could express her gratitude, the girl held up her hand for silence. A baby's cry rent the stillness. "I'd better go. We'll talk again later."

"Wait! I . . . I don't even know your name. Mine is—"

"I heard, I know yours. Mine's Sukey."

"Sukey. Sukey what?"

A giggle answered her. "Sukey nothing. I'm lucky to have that much of a name. Ta, Jenny Wilde."

In the darkness Jenny smiled. She had always been one to appreciate the bizarre or the unexpected. For the first time since she had arrived in London, she had found a friend, in a Newgate pickpocket.

Sometime during the night the baby's cries stopped. The mother, having procured the spirits she craved, had paid no attention to the insistent wails; she paid no attention now.

The riot only started when the turnkeys came to remove the infant's body and were prevented. Not by the mother, who had succumbed to the effects of the gin, but by a poor unfortunate who no longer had the full use of her reason. The girl thought the lifeless babe well and her own. She hugged the corpse to her breast and refused to release it. Neither entreaties, cajolery, nor bribes would she heed. Force she answered with force, to no small effect. Soon half the women had joined in, for no reason but the pleasure of the fight. It relieved the boredom.

Jenny turned her face to the wall and, for the first time, wept.

"I wish I could cry," Sukey whispered from nearby. "That's when you know you've been here too long—when there ain't no more tears."

Wiping at her face, Jenny turned to her new friend. "Sukey, you told me to fight. But if I turn into one of these, haven't they won after all?"

The pickpocket considered the mass of bodies in turmoil. "They were halfway to being animals afore they come here. Hardly a real craftsman in the lot, 'cept for a few bawdy baskets and a boung nipper who's drunk so often it's no wonder she was caught."

"You were caught too, Sukey."

"Not diving, I wasn't," she answered in heated defense. Before Jenny could ask, she returned quickly to her point. "Anyway, this bunch is about to lump the lighter. Napped a winder, half of 'em. They won't be here long, so what do they care?"

"If I understood even half of what you said, perhaps I could answer you properly. Does London speak a different English than the rest of the world?"

"Part of it does at that. Haven't you never heard pedlar's French?"

"I thought I spoke French very well, but the words you use sound like none I've ever heard."

21

"Not parley-vous. Flash, patter, cant. It's thieves' lingo, dearie."

"I see. But what does it mean?"

Sukey concentrated on her choice of words. "They're sentenced for transportation to the colonies. Half of 'em are sentenced for life. So they're just marking time, see? They'll be going as soon as there's a ship. You'll get the same yourself, I dessay, maybe only seven years if you're lucky. So, you see, there's no reason to fear the hempen fever . . . er, the rope, that is, when they can make a profit on you another way."

"How ironic!" Jenny caught the questioning look in Sukey's eye. "One of life's jests. I might have stayed put for all the good my traveling has done me."

"You mean you been there, in the colonies?"

"I was born in the Americas. It's my home. Why do you stare? Is it so very surprising?"

"No, no. I was just thinking, I dessay that's where you learned the frogs' lingo . . . er, French." The pickpocket sat up straight, obviously interested. "How long have you been here in England then?"

"Six months. My family, all but my mother, died in the fighting with the French. So mother and I decided to come back and seek out her family." She had learned to state only the bare facts, to block out their meaning.

"No luck?"

"No. It was too late anyway." She closed her eyes in pain, remembering despite herself. "My mother did not survive the voyage."

"Ah, isn't that just perfick . . . perfickly awful," Sukey commiserated, but her voice sounded oddly excited. "How the hell did you end up here, then? Somehow, I don't see you pinching a bloody great gewgaw like they say you did. You may be innercent, but you ain't so stupid to get caught with the goods in your hands."

"Thank you for your confidence. No, I'm here because the mistress—I will not say lady—I served as companion felt that the master of the house looked my way too often."

"A put-up job then."

"The funny thing is I would no more have touched her worthless husband than I would her worthless brooch. Well, perhaps I'll be better off home again after all."

"That's right, Jenny dear. Perhaps she has done you a service," she said in a pensive tone, then disappeared into the shadows.

Jenny knew Sukey dared not be seen in private converse with her. It comforted Jenny to know, just the same, that she was no longer alone. When Sukey paid Deems with his own money for a visit to the taproom, Jenny laughed silently to herself. She thought it no wonder Sukey looked so smug when she returned.

It wasn't until Sunday, when the prisoners were herded to the chapel, that the two friends had an opportunity to speak again.

"Look at them." Jenny pointed disdainfully at the audience of richly dressed ladies and gentlemen who came, not for spiritual guidance, but for the titillation of gaping at the prisoners. "With their noses in the air and their eyes avid for excitement. How very bored they must be. Are there usually so many?"

"No, they're here on the odd chance they might

see our latest boarder—the highwayman, Lord Danger. And so they shall. Look!"

Jenny followed her friend's gaze to see a man enter with an escort of turnkeys. He had the carriage of the aristocrat whose title he usurped and the flamboyance of the provincial actor. His costume of scarlet and gold would have been perfectly appropriate at the French court. So too would have been the airs and graces of the court exquisite.

Only in his face did Lord Danger fall short of the requirements of fashion, for his features were entirely hidden in a wealth of mustachios and beard, like a pirate of the high seas rather than one of the land. His black hair was dressed in the style of the last century, curling down to his broad shoulders. From behind all this hirsute growth his eyes gleamed dark and brilliant—directly at Jenny.

"Sukey. Sukey, he's staring at us."

"Of course he is. That's why the nobs come, to stare at wicked women like us."

"Not one of them," she hissed, unnerved by those dark eyes. "That highwayman is looking straight at us."

"Ah? Some say he'll hang. Some say he can't be killed. They never got his gang, you know, he saw to that. Even here he has a lot of power—more than Deems and his lot, believe me."

"But why is he staring like that?"

"Admiring me figger?"

"Now he's waving."

Sukey waved back, smiling broadly. "Must be polite."

* * *

Back in the Women's Hold, Sukey stayed with Jenny, as if it no longer mattered if Deems knew she and Jenny were friends. She seemed nervous and elated all at once.

"We really are mates, ain't we, Jen? I mean, if you could help me, you would. Well, you did help me. If Deems had caught me, I'd be dead. He's a mean bastard is Deems."

"I know."

"No, you don't know. You've seen some hard times, but you ain't got the slightest idea what that man can do to you—what he will do unless a miracle happens."

There was a strange urgency in the girl's voice that alarmed Jenny. "Are you trying to frighten me, Sukey?" she asked.

"Maybe." She turned in alarm as two turnkeys entered the ward, looked around, and walked toward them.

"It's the only way, Jen," Sukey continued in a rush, holding Jenny's arm and watching anxiously over her shoulder. "Deems'd eat up an innercent like you. You'd be dead inside and the shell still walking around. I couldn't let that happen. D'you understand? This is really for the best."

What did she mean? What was the only way? Jenny wondered in confusion. Before she could question her friend, however, she became conscious of a presence close behind her, waiting.

"All right, Wilde," the first turnkey said. "Moving up in the world you be. Cor, I wish I knowed how you pulled it."

"Where ... where are you taking me?" Jenny tried to brush the turnkey's hand from her arm.

In alarm, she turned to her friend for help, only to realize that this was what the young pickpocket had intended.

"Sukey!"

"I tell you, it's for the best, Jen." Sukey's eyes seemed to be begging for understanding.

The turnkeys forced Jenny along. One of them shook his head as she began to struggle in earnest. "Dashed if I knowed what Danger sees in you, but there it is. He's gorn to a lot of trouble to acquire your company, so we'd best not keep the man waiting."

"No! Sukey, what have you done?"

"Made your fortune, love," the pickpocket called after her. "Made your fortune."

Jenny's struggles only seemed to amuse the turnkeys. Perhaps Deems, when he heard of it, would be mollified to hear that Miss Wilde had gone to her new lover as to her executioner.

They took Jenny first to have her fetters removed. The freedom and lightness felt wonderful, but so strange that she had to relearn how to move. As they stepped out of the dark corridor into the Press Yard, a sudden brightness blinded her. Sunlight—and air! After so long in the twilight world of the Women's Hold, Jenny could not bear to open her eyes fully as the turnkeys pulled her along.

"We dasn't let her go, sir." The turnkey's voice was not merely respectful, but humble. "She won't—argh!—stay still."

"Spirited? So much the better. What do you think, m'lord?"

There were two men before her, judging by the

shadows, standing at their ease directly before the glaring sunlight. Lord Danger, she presumed. But who was the other?

"Make her take her arm away from her face. Lud, but she's filthy," the second man said, also in educated tones, but with an underlying sneer that stung her.

"If your influence will extend so far as to improve the service of the abigails here, sir," she responded in an acid voice, "I pray you will use it."

"You're in the right of it, she does have spirit." It was the sneering voice again, but now laced with humor—and a touch of condescension. "That's good. The voice is good too. Sukey tells us that you have been in the colonies."

Jenny tried to open her eyes wider. For all her spirit, she was confused. What interest could her life at home have for Danger? Certainly his approach was different from Deems, but was his purpose?

"It's my home. I was born there," she answered, her voice tinged with suspicion.

"Where? North? South? The Carolinas? Maryland? New York?"

Was that the other one now? Jenny couldn't tell, but clearly one of them knew what he was talking about. Most Englishmen, she had found, spoke of the colonies as if there were but a single lump, about the size of London, on the other side of the ocean.

"New York, in the north of the colony, near the French territory of Canada. And in Massachusetts for a while."

"Near the French, eh? Learn the lingo?"

Sukey had been interested in her linguistic ability, too. Why? Keeping her questions to herself, Jenny told her interrogators what she thought of them swiftly, fluently, and very idiomatically in that language.

"So. Sukey said truly." The sneerer sounded pleased, almost triumphant.

"Aye. What say you, m'lord?"

"I say yes. And you?"

There was a long moment while he—whoever he was—considered. "Yes. Take her to the cell."

Zounds, did they mean to share her body between them? Jenny's arrogant pose, her suspicions over the nature of their questioning, disappeared abruptly as she transformed herself into an enraged maenad. Her fury had no more effect than before, although despair lent her surprising strength. The turnkeys would sooner fail Deems than the powerful highwayman. Only he had been captured; his gang ran free still to carry out any orders he might pass along.

As they toted her bodily away, Jenny caught one last exchange between her new jailer and his friend.

"She may be trouble."

"Oh, I think not. Nothing we cannot handle."

Inside the cell Jenny sensed she was alone, for the first time since her arrest. In a little while her eyes finally adjusted to the light that streamed in through the windows. She kept her eyes to the floor until she could look up without squinting.

At first she thought either her mind or her eyes played her false. It was as if she had returned to the reasonable world again, the world of genteel occupations and pleasures. In just such a room had her grandfather spent his latter days.

Then she saw the bars on the door and the window. No, this was still Newgate, but the Newgate of the very rich. If you had enough money, you could buy fine food and wines, fashionable gowns, lutes to make music with, books to read. Evidently you could buy almost anything, she realized, and shivered.

The books were all in French, Jenny noticed. Recent, too. Was this a test? What significance her fluent use of French could have perplexed her, yet she felt sure that it was significant.

As for the gowns, flamboyant and low cut, that hung over the chair, they made her very uncomfortable.

She tried to ignore them as she waited, but as time passed and Danger failed to arrive, she became bolder. Finding a basin of water, she cleaned the wounds made by her fetters and then ate some of the roast chicken apparently left over from the highwayman's meal. When still no one appeared, she finally opened one of the books, but Voltaire could not hold her interest. Her eyes kept slipping away from the page to the massive curtained bed which took up nearly half the room.

Jenny had finally dozed off in a chair when a number of drunken voices announcing Danger's return startled her into wakefulness. The highwayman gave her a knowing look, and ushered a scantily clad young woman into the room and then into the big bed. Jenny knew then she was safe—for the night.

Sunlight woke Jenny in the morning, but she was left, stiff and undisturbed, in the highwayman's easy chair. A servant came with food, and still Danger snored on.

A knock announced another visitor and the door opened to reveal the perfect gentleman. For a moment Jenny thought she must have drifted off to sleep again. Here was the Greek ideal of beauty, a statue by Phidias come to life. Amid the sordidness and debauchery of Newgate, he appeared an angel come to visit hell.

He was scrupulously clean, which Jenny had noticed many gentleman were often not, and well dressed. The proud carriage spoke more of the aristocrat than the professional man. Was this one of the fashionable world come to gawk at the wicked highwayman? As Jenny pondered how disappointing it would be if it were true, the vision removed his hat and saluted her courteously.

"Miss Wilde, your humble servant. I hope I have not kept you waiting long." There was a questioning lift to the end of his salutation which confused Jenny. Before she could be expected to respond, however, the gentleman realized something was out of order. The host was missing. "Did Dick go looking for me?"

Jenny had never heard the highwayman referred to in so casual a manner, but who else could he mean? Wordlessly, she nodded toward the sleeping area.

"What, still abed? The lazy rogue! And I suppose he simply left you to your own devices until he deigns to take notice of you. Bah, the man doesn't deserve the name of gentleman—no, not even gentleman of the road." He walked over to the bed and set up a clamor, setting the bed rings ajangle. "Hola, m'lord Danger. Get up, you slug.

There's business and a lady waiting."

There was silence, and then a groan issued from behind the bed curtains. The nether limbs of the highwayman appeared for a moment. After making contact with a small uncarpeted section of cold stone floor, the limbs withdrew hastily. Various muffled noises could then be heard. Finally the highwayman appeared, clad in an ornate dressing gown and stockings.

"Alas, I have ever been a slave to business." Danger emphasized the last word slightly. His business of the previous evening was now partially revealed, still sleeping heavily, but he gave no sign of having been rudely awakened or of having indulged in unnamed vices the night before. "Time for me to go to work, m'dear, and time for you to go home." He gave her a shake. "Time to go. But here's a bauble to remind you of Danger."

The diamond he tossed on the bed quickly roused the girl. She grew profuse in her expressions of gratitude until Danger finally pushed her out the door and threw her clothes out after her.

Jenny struggled to appear calm, despite her growing confusion. The highwayman scarce seemed to pay her any mind. Clearly he did not need to go to such trouble for female companionship. Why, oh why, then, had he brought her here? Not, she thought, out of the kindness of his heart.

He was watching her now, not openly but sideways, calculating, rather like a supercilious cat. "Very well," he said, "to business, since you must. We'll talk as I dress."

"Wait!" the other gentleman begged in distress. He lowered his voice to a stage whisper. "What about the girl?"

"What about her?" Danger grinned. "She may watch, if she pleases. Or not. If she's so bashful as you seem to think, she may wait outside—and you too if you cannot keep your mind off trivialities."

"Danger, you know perfectly well we can't . . . Oh, the deuce with you. We'll be back when you've made yourself decent."

"Oh, long before *then*, I hope."

Jenny hurried out before the highwayman's dressing gown hit the floor.

The gentleman followed with two mugs of ale and a plate of cakes. "We could starve by the time he finishes his toilet. You mustn't mind Dick, though. That's just his way. He's really not a bad fellow."

"For a highwayman?" As soon as the words were out, Jenny cursed her reckless tongue. She had meant to appear impassive. To reveal too much of herself might be to place a weapon in her enemies' hands, if enemies they were.

The gentleman laughed, but he reminded her, "You of all people, Miss Wilde, must know that everyone in Newgate is not exactly as he might appear."

"Very true, sir," she conceded, uneasy. Did everyone know her story, or was this the gentleman who had discussed her with Danger the night before? Now that she had heard them both speak, neither voice seemed to fit.

"You speak warily, Miss Wilde, as if you have not yet decided to trust us. Is it Danger's reputation that you mislike or our scheme? Or is my story too fanciful for belief? Lord knows, I can understand your doubts on that score."

Jenny examined the man carefully. He looked sorrowful, and disappointed. "Our scheme" he had said. Well, she would not gain the answers standing mute, but she must try to keep all signs of curiosity from her voice.

"I know nothing of you, sir, nor any scheme. You will know best whether Lord Danger's reputation should inspire trust."

"You mean he hasn't . . . ? Didn't he tell you anything?"

"As you saw this morning, sir, Lord Danger was much occupied with other matters."

"Why, that rascal! My apologies, Miss Wilde. I had no idea. Danger will play his little games. Lud, you haven't the faintest idea who I am, have you? I must have sounded a very idiot. Permit me to introduce myself, ma'am." He look around to find a place to set down the plates and mug. Finding nothing immediately at hand, he set his burden on the ground. "Nathaniel James Walter Beauchamp, Earl of Vickers, Viscount of Quarles, Baron of Tinsdale and Sarn, a fellow sufferer under the law's kind justice, and your most obedient servant." He bowed gracefully, his arm making a delicate flourish of self-mockery.

So he too was a prisoner? Jenny covered her astonishment quickly while the gentleman retrieved their breakfast. She acknowledged the introduction with a slight nod. "My lord."

"Ah, Miss Wilde, my name may mean nothing to you, but it is of the greatest importance to me. It is the reason I am here in this hellish situation. And yes, Miss Wilde, it is why you are here as well. If you will grant me a few minutes of your time, I would like to explain."

Jenny held her head erect, although she was painfully aware of her appearance. In the Women's Hold, she could almost forget how long it had been since she had been able to wash properly, but not now.

"I have no other appointments," she announced with a shrug, carefully holding her hand over the bodice of her torn shift.

He grinned and led her to a corner bench, where he set the plate of cakes within easy reach of both. "You think me ridiculous, Miss Wilde. Perhaps you are right. What use are the airs of the courtier in such a place as this? None, I suppose, but to keep one's self-respect."

Yes, this Jenny understood. Hadn't she, unconsciously, done the same?

"And what I am about to tell you certainly will sound ridiculous," Vickers continued, "like the story of some gothic tale or opera. Lord knows, too, that Newgate is full of excuses, explanations, protestations of innocence ... But what I tell you is true, damnably true.

"I was born to the younger son of a younger son of a very noble family. When my parents died, however, I was taken in by my great-uncle—the Earl of Vickers."

His face warmed with the memory. He was still for a moment, then he met Jenny's eyes with a more lively glance. His whole body was tense with enthusiasm.

"I wish I could convey to you what manner of man my uncle was. I wish you had known him. He was the most generous man I've ever known, and the most understanding. I could talk to him about anything. The only things he didn't understand, couldn't even see before him, were greed and envy. To his cost. But I get ahead of myself. Pardon me."

Jenny relaxed a little under his courteous treatment. This gentleman belonged to the sane and reasonable world she had once known. Although she schooled her expression to remain blank, her heart was touched. She too had known an old man who understood everything she told him when no one else did.

"I can see you regarded him with the deepest affection," she admitted.

"Yes, I loved him. He did not merely take me in, he treated me like a son. And his grandson, my cousin John, was just the same. We were more like brothers. I thought all three of us were brothers then."

"Three?"

"I said my uncle was generous. I was not the only stray he adopted. One of the neighboring estates belonged to the diplomat Lord Yves. His son, Wolfram, was often left there, alone but for a veritable army of servants and tutors until Vickers stepped in. His compassionate heart could not bear to contemplate the boy's loneliness, so he made Wolf part of all our activities—so much so that the lad was more often at Vickers than at Yves. He was ever a strange lad, though. Always tagging along after John and me or hanging on to the earl's every word. Different somehow. But I never would have thought then that he—"

He smiled, sadly this time, then continued. "It was during the uprising of '45 that things began to happen, that I began to suspect . . . It's hard to find the words to describe that time. You probably were not even born then. A child like you could not hope to understand."

Jenny was horrified to find that she was blushing. "I am five and twenty, sir. And I know what war is, perhaps better than you." Here in England it seemed to her that only the merchants had been touched by the seven years of war with France. How should they know the terrors of a war that had been fought far across the oceans, in India and in the Americas?

He looked at her closely. "Yes, I suppose you do. But this wasn't simply war, but revolution. Do you understand what that means? In the north it was madness. The merest whisper of Jacobite leanings could send a man to the gallows. Trials, if they were held at all, were only formalities to be hurried through as fast as possible."

"And your cousin?"

"Someone put the word out on John. That's all it took in those days. He was no Jacobite, but he'd fallen for a girl who was half Scots and half French. It was enough. Between the girl and his reputation for wildness, it was easily believed."

"So he was killed," Jenny guessed.

"No. Fortunately, he was warned in time. And Wolf hurried him out of the country—so fast that the authorities decided he must be guilty. John finally wrote me from New York. His sweetheart had joined him and they were happy as larks."

At the mention of her homeland Jenny raised her eyebrows questioningly, but Vickers was lost in another time, another place. After a moment, he looked up, embarrassed, and went on. "I tried seeking him out through agents. When that didn't work, I decided to find him myself and drag him home if need be. The political climate had finally changed enough to make his return possible—and his grandfather needed him, badly."

Vickers' mouth twisted suddenly at some memory. "I was in New York in 1757 when war was declared. The search had been difficult enough before, but after that it was virtually impossible. I was finally able to trace his travels, but his village was gone by then. Wiped out by the French. One of the few survivors had actually seen them fall—John, his wife . . . and child."

Jenny closed her eyes in pain. It was not Vickers and his young family that she saw, but her own father and grandfather, the servants who had not had time to reach the fort, almost all the people she had known and loved. By the time she had reached the house it was all over, but she did not need the witness of burnt timbers to know what had happened. Her grandfather had taught her of the Indian traditions, their methods of warfare. She knew.

If Vickers noticed her reaction, he was kind enough to ignore it. "Perhaps it was a mercy that I never had to tell my uncle the news," he continued. "His heart finally gave out. Such was the news that awaited me on my return. My memory of this time, I must confess, is not of the clearest. How much I am to blame for what then befell me—" He stopped abruptly. After a moment his face cleared and assumed a sheepish expression. He shrugged. "Much though it pains me to admit it, I was a fool."

Despite herself, Jenny smiled at his wry confession. "Folly is not yet punishable by law, my lord.

If it were, we should be far more crowded here than we are."

"That depends on the type of folly," he countered. "Mine was in not giving proper consideration to the future. To my defense, I would like to say that my uncle would have been extremely insulted had I intimated a need to find a profession. It was only on my insistence that I be useful to him that he allowed me to help with his affairs. He had always made it clear that I would be provided for."

"And you were not?" Given the description of the old earl, such behavior seemed out of character.

"No. Odd though it was, however, it should not have mattered. John, had he lived, would certainly have carried out his grandfather's wishes, expressed or no. And with John dead, the title fell to me. I was my uncle's heir." The muscles around his jaw tightened. "I am my uncle's heir, but I cannot prove it."

"Not prove it?" Jenny asked, no longer able to hide her interest. "How is that possible?"

"Things had changed while I was away. Wolf was now Lord Yves, having succeeded to his father's titles and estates, and was quickly making a name for himself at court. In hundreds of little ways he had also made himself indispensable to my uncle. So indispensable, in fact, that my uncle named him executor of his will. Do you understand how much power that gave him?"

"Yes, but surely—"

"There was no time to remedy the situation. Wolf had obviously prepared for this for a long time. His first act as executor then was to try to kill me. Oh, quite honorably. He challenged me to a duel, practically at my uncle's grave."

"Why? Did he give no reason?"

"He gave an excuse, not a reason. Fortunately, I was not without some expertise with the small sword. I survived. But while my apartment was empty, it had been looted. My proof of John's demise was stolen. What could I do? The war still raged. Wolf had control of the estate. He claimed John still lived. In searching for John, I had all but ruined myself. The lawyers who took my case completed my ruin. Wolf bought up my debts and had me imprisoned here, thus putting a very effective halt to my attempts to prove my claim."

"But to what purpose? What could he hope to gain? Surely he had no personal claim to the estate?"

"No, but there is much advantage to be gained in the administration of so great an estate. You're quite right, though. There must be something more, something I don't understand. I keep trying to think back to those early days. Did we treat him badly without realizing it? I think he may have been jealous—of our belonging to Vickers as he did not. Who can say for sure?"

Jenny could see now what Vickers had meant when he said his identity was the reason for his presence here, but how did it involve her? How could her knowledge of the colonies help them?

Vickers looked as if he were about to say more when a servant came up and whispered in his ear. "Ah, m'lord Danger has finished his toilet. Shall we rejoin him?"

Jenny followed him back to the luxurious cell. The answer was coming soon now and she did not know whether to be glad or afraid. Danger sat at the table and had made some inroads on the breakfast already. Once again he was dressed for a royal levée, this time in peach satin and gold lace. His long curls and beard had been carefully dressed. Jenny realized as she looked at him that Danger's features were hidden more effectively than they would have been by a mask. She had only his eyes by which to judge the real man.

Those eyes, cynical but assured, were now fixed on her, although he addressed the soi-disant earl.

"How much have you told her?" he asked.

"Don't rush the girl, Dick. I've told her my history, no more."

"Hmmmm. Took you long enough. Well, Miss Innocence, you've had a chance to see how the world runs here. You've heard Nate's story. Do you still believe in English justice? That all men are by nature good and kind? And that truth and virtue must overcome greed and cruelty?"

"No, I know better than that." Jenny's voice was very small. She was not proud of the admission. She had been happier with her old blind faith in man's goodness, false or no.

"Excellent. I want you to remember that. I want you to remember your old mistress, and Deems, and Lord Yves if you ever begin to doubt it again. Myself, I'm a romantic at heart. I'd like to give justice a push. And I'd like to make a healthy profit by it as well. I think we can all profit—and right a few wrongs in the process." Danger leaned forward, suddenly not at all languid. "But it can't be done by playing by the so-called rules. The rules put us all here in Newgate. No, we'll have to be a deal more ingenious."

Jenny swallowed nervously. If she hadn't been so determined to put on a brave front before the highwayman she would not even be able to eat. Good or bad, at least now she would know.

"And I would play a part in this plan?" Her voice sounded cool, she noted with relief.

"We all have parts to play, but while his lordship's and mine are primarily financial, yours would require that you, shall we say, perform certain tasks." Danger leaned back again, smiling such a smile even his whiskers could not hide his meaning. His voice caressed each word as his eyes caressed Jenny.

She stood up hurriedly, knocking the chair over as she backed away. She lifted her chin in an attempt to regain some dignity. "I realize well I have little control over what happens to me here, but you'll not gain my consent or my help in that. I'm not that desperate."

"Oh, sit down, girl. And get your mind out of the gutter. You ladies are all alike, minds like the Fleet. If we'd wanted a woman for 'that,' as you so quaintly put it, do you think we'd have looked twice at *you*? SIT! Damned silly wench."

"Really, Dick," Vickers protested. "You cannot blame the girl for thinking the worst when you have made certain the jailers would."

He'd wanted her to think the worst too, Jenny realized. There had been laughter behind his curses. But there was comfort for her, as well. She would not have believed a simple assertion that her virtue was safe. She believed that laughter.

Vickers was still complaining to the highwayman. "You never explained to her what you wanted. All you have done—"

"Enough, enough. If you think you can explain, without offending the lady's delicate sensibilities, please do so and spare me your recriminations." Danger put his feet up on the table and with hands clasped on his chest assumed an expression of rapt attention.

"Miss Wilde, we three all want the same things. First, to get out of Newgate." Vickers paused and shot a warning glance toward Danger, who was muttering beneath his breath. The words were inaudible but the tone was unmistakably sarcastic. "And second, to achieve financial security thereafter. Do you agree?"

"Certainly." Jenny too adopted a sarcastic tone to hide the spark of hope his words kindled. "But how do you propose we should accomplish this? Are you working on a tunnel?"

"Nothing so crude. No, in your case and mine, the simplest means are best. Money, provided by the good and prosperous highwayman, shall open the doors of Newgate for you."

"Don't worry," Danger interrupted before Jenny could open her mouth. "Your Mrs. Ransome will be glad to take the money and let you go. Glad to." His smile boded no good for the jealous mistress.

"I can be released any time my debts are paid, of course," the earl continued. "But to do no more than that is simply to forewarn Wolf, Lord Yves. I would still have to establish my claim. And who is to say that Yves, thus forewarned, will not be able to forestall me?"

And put Danger's investment at risk. Jenny understood the meaning of the sidelong glance at the highwayman.

"But how can your claim be established now?" she asked "You said your proof had been stolen."

"My proof of *John's* death. But the thieves were sloppy or, more likely, ignorant—the child's name could mean nothing to them. By whatever miracle it came about, the thieves left behind the last few pages—the pages that contained the description of the poor child's death. I cannot prove John died. But his daughter, newly come from the colonies, could bring the news of her father's death. And her word would be accepted as proof."

"No, you can't." Jenny shook her head; but it was clear from their expressions that they indeed could. "You want me to pretend to be your cousin's child?" she asked Vickers in disbelief.

"Precisely. I'm glad to see you're so quick to understand. No one ever saw the child. I can tell you all you need to know about John and the family. You know the colonies firsthand. It will be simple."

"Simple!"

"It will also restore me to my rightful position, not to mention saving us both from this hell-hole. As my cousin, you would also be entitled to an income more than sufficient for your needs. You know you'll never be able to work as a companion or governess again. If you must change your name, why not change it to one that will confer good on others as well as you?"

The way Vickers phrased it, the plan sounded so reasonable, but some feeling greater than reason protested against it. "This is too much. I hardly know what to think, what to say," she protested. "Transportation has no fears for me, you know. Why should I not let His Majesty's government pay for my passage home?"

Danger sniggered. "You haven't learned a thing if you think you could survive a few months in the Women's Hold or the sea voyage. Convict labor does not travel under any conditions you would recognize. That's assuming your case ever comes to trial, of course. Major Bernardi waited more than twenty years. But that's here in the Master's Side. Nobody lives very long on the Commons Side."

He was right, of course. Jenny knew it in her heart. Yet the way that they offered her seemed too good to be true. Something had not been said.

"And what do you get out of this, Lord Danger?" she asked, full of suspicion. Danger was no philanthropist. He would expect full value for his money.

"The Vickers estate is large. My investment will be repaid, with interest, never fear."

"And how are you to escape?"

Danger laughed. "Remember the way of the world, my girl. I shall escape no matter what happens to you or his lordship. I will thrive."

He would, too. Jenny and the earl might languish forever, condemned for nothing at all, for the jealousy and greed of others, and Lord Danger would not only live, but live well, off the riches saved over his long career. Such was the justice England had to offer her.

"Well, are you one of us? Or would you prefer to return to the Women's Hold?"

Where Deems waited, where she might hope to ward off the fever until she was shipped like slave cargo back to her home—where Mrs. Ransome could come and gloat over her misfortune.

Don't let them win, Sukey had said.

"All I ask is that you try," the earl urged. "There will be chances to pull out if you think you can't go through with it."

Don't let them win. Jenny looked at the two men carefully—the highwayman, the wronged gentleman. Vickers really had more to lose than she did, yet even now he offered her another means of escape. She remembered all that she had endured, all that had brought her to this point. That was what the highwayman counseled. Remember? She could not forget if she tried.

If you die, they win. Don't let the bastards win.

"What do you say?"

"I say . . ." She made them wait a moment for her answer, although they knew better than she that in the end there was only one answer that could be made.

"I think I should have a bath, at once."

Chapter Two

The man whom the servants referred to as "that odd little bloke" and whom Lord Yves called his eyes and ears had left, silently and without notice. If it were not for the second glass on his lordship's tray in the library, no one would know that he had ever been there.

But Yves was very conscious of the news the little man had brought. He sat in the large wing chair before the dying embers of the fire deep in thought. In his hand he held a single sheet of paper, closely covered with script. The paper seemed to bring him no pleasure. Yves' expression did not change—it never did—but the hand holding the paper clenched convulsively for a moment.

The moment soon passed. Yves carefully restored the paper to its previous shape and read it again, and again until he had it memorized. When he finally set the paper to the candle flame, it was carefully and deliberately, with no hint of emotion behind the act.

The paper destroyed, Yves resumed his mental exercise. Lately he had been much concerned with the calendar. Not because of his advanced age of thirty-five years, as his aunt had suggested. His lordship had no vanity and remarkably little interest in what the world thought of him. No, he looked at the calendar every day and counted the days, months, years it had been since the war with the French had ended.

How much longer could the situation hold? The war had provided the perfect excuse. John lived on the frontier; he could not be contacted during such troublous times; he had had to move on to avoid the Indians. The excuses were without number, but now they were gone, had been gone since the peace treaty was signed in 1763, two years ago.

The solicitors were getting restless. They were intimidated by him, of course. He knew that and used it. Still they were getting restless. How ironic—to think that after all the schemes and plots he should be defeated by the impatience of lawyers. So great an estate should not go without a master, they said. They must think of the estate, of Vickers.

Vickers. That beautiful house, the loveliest country in England, his home—and they wanted to hand it over to Nate Beauchamp.

Well, Nate would not have it. No matter what he had to do. No matter what the cost.

The candle flame guttered out and still Yves sat

in the wing chair, quite still, with his fingertips touching lightly. This was not the first night he had spent in thought in the library chair, and it probably would not be the last. Until the problem of the gentleman presently residing in Newgate gaol was answered, there could be no rest for Wolfram, Lord Yves.

Yves was still fully alert when the slight tinkle of broken glass announced an unexpected presence in the house. The sounds were slight—the creak of a board in the hallway, the scraping sound made by a chair being moved—but Yves was quick to recognize their meaning. His servants did not wander through the house in the dark hours of the night; they knew better.

The sounds came closer, grew more distinct. Intruders. They moved slowly and carefully, but they knew where they were going. They were not after the silver.

Yves stayed where he was. He did not have long to wait for his visitors. A sliver of moonlight peeped through the curtains to show the door slowly opening. Yes, there were two of them, dressed in dark clothes and carrying the tools of their trade, the jemmy rook, the bess and glym.

The two thieves did not even think to look at the chair by the fire. One of them set the glym, the dark lantern, on the library desk and looked around, examining the paintings on the wall.

"The safe's behind one of these paintings. Take 'em all down till you find it. I'll work on the desk."

"Not yet, you don't. I'm going to need some help if I'm to get these blasted things down without waking the whole house. Look at the size of 'em. Blimey, who'd want a picture of a bloke like that one staring down at you? Fair gives me the shivers."

"Quiet, you fool. Do you want to wake the house with your chatter instead?"

"Ah, I'm being quiet. They can't hear. You didn't fall for all that stuff we was fed about his lordship? Wolf, indeed."

"Nobody could be as tough as that. I just don't believe in taking chances. That's how I've stayed clear of the law this long—by being double careful. And I'd advise you to do the same."

The thieves set down a large canvas depicting the family estate of the late Lady Yves. Behind the castle on the Rhine was revealed at last the metal casing of his lordship's safe.

"I really cannot allow you to scratch the paneling, you know," a calm voice announced from behind them.

The two thieves stood as if stunned for a moment, looking at him with horrified eyes, as it dawned on them that they had put down their tools and weapons in order to take the pictures down. Now they clearly noticed that his lordship, although long of limb and broad of shoulder, was also unarmed. And alone.

"Don't," Yves warned.

The tone in his voice caused them to pause, but only for a moment. He could almost read their thoughts. Two men against one. By the time the servants came to investigate the noise, they'd be out of there.

The noise, the thud of furniture being knocked over, the terrible cry of pain did not last long. It was some few minutes, however, before the servants, led by the butler with an antique musket, called up enough courage to investigate.

"Fools. Why will they never listen?" Yves' voice rang through the closed door, encouraging the servants to enter.

"Put that away," Yves ordered. "You'll hurt yourself before you do any damage to the house-breakers."

"House-breakers, my lord?"

"Is there something wrong with my diction? Ah, thank heaven, someone has had the sense to bring some light. Well, what are you waiting for? Two of you can clear this mess up; the rest of you go back to bed."

"But . . . but, my lord . . ."

"Yes?"

"Shouldn't we send for the constable . . . to take the thieves to gaol?"

"Whatever for?"

A footman who had stooped by the fallen thieves whispered the answer. "They're dead. They'll never go to Newgate now."

"No," Yves answered. "But I think I must."

Jenny thought she would never feel clean again. Her co-conspirators had left her to bathe in peace. One of them, most likely the earl, must have realized she would need some time before she felt human, felt herself again.

But I am not myself, Jenny remembered. *I am to be the great-granddaughter of the late Earl of Vickers*. Despite the heat of the water, she shivered. She would be what she was brought up to be, she reminded herself sternly, a lady—not a slave nor an animal.

Solitude might have brought further second

thoughts, but a pleasant surprise came with the refilled hot water kettles—Sukey.

The pickpocket had been a little unsure of her reception. Truth to tell, Jenny felt unsure as well. Was her friend truly her ally, or was she Danger's tool?

In the end Jenny realized that Sukey's sincerity could not be doubted. Her judgment was another matter.

On the matter of Jenny's dress, however, Sukey was wise enough to see the reasons for the flamboyance and the decolletage. "Deems and his lot have got to think you're here for ... well, you know," she reminded Jenny. "And you won't convince 'em looking like her ladyship's governess."

Alas, mere gowns were not enough. Even dressed as a whore, Jenny was still unmistakably a lady.

" 'Sblood, but you even look like family," Nate exclaimed when his voice returned to him. His first sight of Jenny on his return had obviously given him quite a shock. "Your hair ... that color. With those golden brown eyes, too. Most of the Beauchamps look like me, but every once in a while that coloring pops up. And when it does ... nobody forgets the red Beauchamps."

"It's not red," Jenny answered defensively. He had touched an old sore.

"No, not exactly, but the fire's there just the same. Well, I wonder what Wolf will make of that."

"More to the point may be what Deems makes of her." Danger circled the girl and inspected her as if she were horseflesh—that was not up to his standard. "Something still needs to be done. Do you have to stand like you've got a broom up your back? Relax, dammit."

"Obviously, milord, you have never worn stays. I wonder how easy you might find it to ... to lounge decadently if you wore armor like this."

"Sukey does it." Danger leered at the new abigail, his expression clear even behind the wealth of beard and mustachios that hid his features. "She lounges decadently most beautifully."

"What's decadently?" Sukey demanded. "Is it good?"

"It is to me, my love, which means that to stiff-rumped schoolmarms like Miss Jenny, it is most decidedly not good."

'Stiff-rumped schoolmarm' did not sit well with Jenny. "You must consider, milord, that the training which fits me for your scheme is not likely to be very suited to acting the ... the ..."

"Lud, she can't even say the word. Whore. Doxy, prime article, Athanasian wench, blowen, crack, laced mutton, trull, wagtail, woman of the town, of pleasure, of easy virtue—"

"Danger," interrupted Lord Vickers to no effect.

"All right, whore then. If I knew how to behave like one, I wouldn't be here, would I?" Jenny demanded. Cleanliness seemed to have given her added courage.

"She's got you there, Dick."

"Oh, I wouldn't say that. You'd be surprised at the number of well-bred ladies who know how to play the whore when it suits them. But that's usually a private performance, I agree. Very well, Sukey will help you. And you will do your very best to get it right. Make no mistake, this performance is just as important as the one that will follow."

"He's right, Miss Wilde," Vickers confirmed. "This isn't just to allay the suspicions of the turnkeys and jailers. If you've been to service at the chapel, you know we're the most fashionable amusement in town next to Bedlam. Danger here may even put us ahead. We'll have the ladies and gentlemen of the town trooping in and out of here every hour of the day as Danger's trial approaches. The jailers make too much money out of it to stop it. These people must not recognize the Honorable Miss Beauchamp as a woman from Newgate."

"But I'm not likely to meet any of these people while making my claim."

"We can't take that chance," Vickers insisted.

"We'll get a wig for you as well—dark, not powdered. Sukey can help you do something with your face as well, can't you, love? Be liberal with the paints. You'll know what to do, I'm sure." Danger was going out of his way to charm the pickpocket, and succeeding very well by the looks of it.

Oh no, Sukey would not believe anything bad about Danger. However much Sukey valued her friendship with Jenny, she would not under any circumstances distrust Danger.

Lord Vickers met Jenny's eyes and smiled. "I've made some notes for you to study. Here's as much of the family tree as I can remember. On this sheet—"

The highwayman switched from laughing complaisance to attack in a moment. He tore the papers from Vickers' hand and quickly made a small bonfire of them. "You fool, you unconscionable idiot," he accused. "Don't you *ever* put anything in writing, do you hear? Not ever. Lud, this is what comes of working with amateurs. Are there any more?"

The astonished Lord Vickers shook his head.

"Are you absolutely sure? Because if I find that there is even a scrap of paper with a hint of our plan on it, I will see to it that you look upon your time in Newgate as paradise compared to what you will have to endure. Do you understand?"

"Yes, yes. I'm sorry. I didn't realize."

"You didn't realize." Danger looked at the earl with disgust. "If you thought one of the nobs recognizing Jenny here could cause trouble, give some thought as to what could happen if anyone—like Jenny's friend Mr. Deems—found physical proof of our scheme. You might be lucky, of course. Perhaps you would only pay a fortune in blackmail for the rest of your life."

"All right, Dick, you've made your point. I'll be more careful in the future. I only thought that since Miss Wilde is supposed to be your companion, it might appear odd if she spent too much time with me."

The highwayman relaxed again, as if his outburst had never happened, smiling cheerfully. "Of course. I had considered that myself. But I have decided that it will be best if you teach Jenny when we are all of us together. No private sessions. You understand."

Jenny understood if Vickers did not. The highwayman did not intend to give them an opportunity to conspire against him.

"Yes, I understand," Vickers answered in a

voice that shook a little. Jenny doubted that he understood at all, but clearly he had adopted the role of peacemaker as well as that of tutor. "I thought we should begin with Miss Wilde's past first, actually. See how much of her own life can be used for our own purposes."

"Very good," Danger conceded. "But I think that we should start first of all by dropping 'Miss Wilde.' 'Jenny' will serve, but even in private we must all learn that there is no Miss Wilde any more. There is only the Honorable Miss Beauchamp."

The Honorable Miss Beauchamp was expected to behave in a manner which appeared far from honorable for a good part of the day. Sukey taught her provocative cant expressions and how to imitate the inviting mannerisms of the courtesan. Giddy from all the new pressures placed on her from her lessons in how to perform for the visiting gentry as the dimber-damber man's arch dell, Jenny could not help but compare these lessons to those she had learned from her mother. In her mind they seemed very similar in form, if not content.

She had been forced to remember more than was pleasant. At first it had seemed easy, describing the home her grandfather had forged out of the wilderness, her mother's attempts to maintain civilization even on the frontier, the French trappers, the Indians . . . the war.

With skill and great delicacy, Nate drew her out and encouraged her to continue even when it seemed to Jenny that she would collapse with exhaustion before she could utter another word. "Go on," he would say in a sympathetic tone. "Go on, Jenny. Tell me more about your mother...the farm...your escape."

Having chosen the bits and pieces of Jenny's past which were to be kept and those to be discarded, her teacher began to school her in her new family history. The Beauchamps were an old family, and she would be expected to know how their fortunes rose and fell with the kings they supported. For purposes of demonstration, Danger allowed the purely temporary use of a slate to diagram family relationships.

"Now we come to the fifth earl, my great-uncle's father," Vickers told a droopy-eyed audience. "He was a real martinet by all reports. Every one of his children ran away from him, one way or another. Uncle, the eldest, escaped to London society. His brother John—Wild Jack they called him—got involved with smugglers and disappeared at sea. 'Twas he that my cousin was named for, and in truth John shared the same wildness. Then came the Lady Eugenia, who died in disgrace. I doubt John would repeat her history to a young girl," he said with a wink, "except as an object lesson. And this was the baby—my grandfather, the Honorable Mr. James, who married the daughter of a wealthy merchant, who subsequently lost everything in the South Seas Bubble." He smiled ruefully. "It is to be hoped that the family luck soon changes."

Jenny examined the diagram carefully. The same names ran through her family, so she was not likely to slip up there. There was still so much to memorize, but she was beginning to feel that she knew this family, especially the old earl and

his wild grandson. In some ways they'd been mis-
fits, like herself. Jenny liked to think they'd be
glad of her impersonation. She would be a daughter the house of Beauchamp could be proud of.

Her impersonation perfected, Danger began to
discuss further details. "I have friends at sea,"
Danger told them. Smugglers, Jenny doubted not.
"They will take Miss Beauchamp, her maid, and
her escort," he pointed to himself, "to Plymouth.
From there we will journey back to London to
meet with your solicitors."

And he would have to withdraw into the background. He wouldn't like that, Jenny thought.
From then on the solicitors would be in control,
the solicitors and Lord Yves—Wolf. Then she
would be on her own. It would be her responsibility to make sure she was accepted as the sole
surviving issue of John, Viscount Quarles. If she
failed, not only would Vickers continue to be kept
apart from his heritage, but she would find herself
back where she started, in the Women's Hold.

After all they had gone through to reach this
point, Jenny did not know if she could do it. Lord
Vickers had said he would understand if she
wished to withdraw. Somehow she doubted that
Lord Danger would be so understanding.

Although Jenny had not expressed her doubts
to Sukey, she was sure the sensitive girl knew
how she felt. Sukey's decision to teach Jenny to
dive clearly had been an attempt to relieve the
stress of learning one role while performing another.

Jenny was also sure Sukey had told Danger of
her misgivings. The highwayman, after that single outburst of warning toward Vickers, had

maintained an attitude of cynical calm which even the approach of his trial date could not break. His only concern, it seemed, was to put on a good show for the ever-increasing influx of visitors.

To the best of her ability, Jenny tried to ignore them. She hated the avid curiosity in their eyes, the way the women looked at Danger, at her, and then at the big baroque bed. When the highwayman said the high-born ladies could behave like whores, he was probably right. Danger flirted with the women, and engaged in battles of wits with the men. The fools didn't even realize he was laughing at them.

Fortunately, they usually had eyes for no one but Danger. Since Vickers hoped to return to the fashionable world soon, clearly he did not wish to be remembered as a prisoner. So that he could leave, and the others ready themselves, another prisoner had been hired to give them warning of company, but when full of gin, he was not always quick enough.

It was only by chance one day that Nate had stepped outside the cell door to see what was delaying an order for refreshments.

"God and all the saints preserve us, it's Wolf. Get back," he warned Jenny, who stood stunned, watching at the doorway. "Maybe I can lead him away."

Jenny ran back to take her position by the side of Danger's easy chair—his throne, she called it. Her hands were shaking. They would never be able to fool that man. She had only glimpsed him for two seconds and she knew they would never fool him.

Why hadn't Nate warned her? No, be fair. Nothing he could have said would have prepared her for this, for him. Different? He was as different from other men as day from night. Not because he was taller or stronger. Not even because he clearly cared nothing for the opinions of others. No, the difference lay deep inside the cool intelligence that lurked untamed by convention behind those piercing eyes. More than anything else, it was those eyes that had held and frightened her. They were like ice, pale and the color of the cold north seas—all the colors of the sea, green, blue, gray. Nothing escaped those eyes. Nothing.

"You look well, Nate." Yves' voice carried clearly into the cell. "I should have known you would be a success here."

"Come to gloat, Wolf? I'm sorry not to look more pathetic. Had I known you were coming I might have painted hollows in my cheeks so you would not be disappointed."

Though they addressed each other by the names they had used as children, there was nothing of childhood friendship in the air between them. Perhaps it was because they had once been friends that they so patently hated each other so much now. There was nothing worse than the betrayal of friends, Jenny thought, her body tense.

Both Danger and Sukey, she realized suddenly, were looking at her strangely, surprised by her reaction. They had only heard his voice; they hadn't had even that brief glimpse that had frozen her. They didn't know.

"Come, let us go out into the yard," Vickers said, evidently trying to lead him away. "Then you can see better what ravages Newgate has left upon my face."

"Any ravages are more likely to be due to dissipation. No, I've come to see the infamous highwayman, that gentleman of the road known as Lord Danger. Won't you introduce me to your friend?" He pushed his way past Vickers and entered the cell.

Everything about him was cold—his voice, his behavior, even his features. He was pale and fair, his features bold and angular. Despite his coloring, it was not an English face. No, it was too strong, too forceful for that. For all his paleness, there was nothing insipid about Wolfram, Lord Yves.

He moved his head slightly, looking around the prison cell, and all at once the light turned his hair to the same gold as that which embroidered his velvet coat. Jenny had not realized until then that contrary to the dictates of fashion he wore no wig, no powder, but she wasn't surprised. *Wolf was always different*. Wasn't that what Nate had said?

For once Jenny was glad of the protective warmth of Danger's arm. She rested her head on his knee and brought up her arm to cover her face from view as she had learned to do. The idea, she supposed, was to convey utter exhaustion from hours of lovemaking. She was tired enough, in truth, but rest was impossible now. It took all her concentration to keep her body from trembling with fear. Even hidden from view, his voice chilled her to the bone.

"Well, I can certainly see why Nate finds you such a valuable friend, Lord Danger," Yves continued. "I'm sorry, usually his manners are impeccable. I must introduce myself, I see. Lord Yves, sir, at your service."

"Lord Danger, sir, at *your* service. How kind of you to visit my humble cell."

"Not so humble, I think, sir. Were it not for present company, I would compliment you on your taste. Very nice."

"Thank you. One does one's best. May I offer you some refreshment?"

"No, I thank you. I have only come to see how my old friend here does in his confinement. It is so easy to fall into bad connections in his situation. You must be very careful to whom you extend your friendship."

A lie and a warning. Lord Yves had certainly intended more than a simple visit to the man he had imprisoned. But to offer warnings to Danger!

Danger's voice sounded cool enough when he answered. "My lord, in my position, any friendship at all is to be valued. Friends grow scarce indeed in the shadow of the gallows."

"Ah? It may be so. It has been my experience that the one sure end to friendship is an end to the gold that buys it, but I have not found myself close to the gallows—yet."

"No? If you have the opportunity, you should come see me off. It should be most entertaining, if I say so myself. I've been working very hard at my farewell speech."

For the first time, Jenny felt a spurt of admiration for the highwayman. His speech was sheer bravura, of course, and possibly foolish in the extreme. Although the details had not been discussed with her, Jenny knew that the day he was to hang was the day Danger would escape. The last thing he would need would be those observant eyes watching for sleight of hand.

Neither gentleman made mention of the trial which was yet to come. Danger knew better than anyone that his sentence had been decreed the day he was captured.

"I thank you for your kind invitation, sir. But I fear I must decline. The mob at Tyburn has become so outrageous, so I'm told, that it is hardly less dangerous for the spectators than it is for the condemned. Circumstances have taught me to be more careful of my life—and my possessions."

"You do well to be careful, Wolf," Nate answered him, his voice shaking with anger. "For in the fashionable world there are liars and thieves all around you. They may even hide behind the mask of respectability. Or of friendship."

"No doubt but you are correct. Naturally, you would know more of treachery than I."

Jenny heard a gasp—Nate's? Yves' icily smooth voice continued. "But I believe I am not easily deceived."

"I know you *think* you know everything," Nate answered.

"You would have me look for a reason behind every reason, I suppose. For example, a pair of thieves broke into my study the other night. By your reckoning, I should suspect them of searching for more than merely money or valuables."

"And did they take more than money or valuables?" Danger indicated a polite curiosity.

"They took nothing." Yves paused. "And it is too late now to ask them their intentions, I fear."

Dead, she realized with a shudder. They had

tried to rob him and he'd killed them, probably with no more compunction than he would squash a spider. But obviously he did suspect more to it—that's why he was here. He was wrong to suspect Nate, however. This bore all the hallmarks of one of Danger's plans—lack of trust, his criminal contacts, and his carefulness. Except that it had failed.

Jenny could feel a sudden tension enter Danger's body, although only those who knew him well would recognize, and fear, that certain note in his reckless laugh.

"Foolish of you to be so precipitate, sir, don't you think?"

"Why, no," Yves replied. "I am not so suspicious as my old friend, you see. I doubt that two thieves, especially two so untalented, could tell me anything I do not already know."

"And you think my execution will be equally unedifying. You wound me, sir."

"You will have audience enough without me to add one more. But I shall read your final words with interest, I promise you, when they appear in print."

Danger rose, clearly ending the interview. Lord Yves was not quite ready to be dismissed, however.

"Yes, I will be interested to see your confession—no doubt it will be full of excellent moral lessons. Although I suppose you think the moral behind your life story is not that taking up a life of crime leads to ruin, but that one must be more careful in choosing companions that might be trusted, eh?"

Jenny, still huddled by the chair, dared not lift

her head but she had no doubt that Yves' eyes had shown he referred to the earl, not the man who had betrayed the highwayman. Danger chose to answer in kind, however.

"Sadly, even the best of us make mistakes. One can but try to see that they are not repeated."

This time Jenny could not control her shiver. Everyone knew that the man who had betrayed Danger was now dead.

"Your young lady is cold, Danger. Strange, I had thought it was growing quite warm in here. Well, I will leave you to your amusements. Nate's very good at being amusing. Farewell, gentlemen." Yves moved closer to make his adieux, so close that Jenny could feel the feather of his tricorne brush against her gown as he bowed. "Ladies."

There was a long moment of silence before Danger nudged Jenny, more gently than usual. "He's gone now. You can get up."

Sukey, she noticed, was still staring slack-jawed at the doorway. The earl was standing quite still in the corner. His arms were folded over his chest as if he could contain his rage by physical force. Danger was pensive, although he managed to maintain his customary air of nonchalance. But the powerful presence that had just departed had diminished him. If nothing else, Jenny thought, the strange enemy had served to conquer her fear of the highwayman. Danger was not so dangerous as Wolfram, Lord Yves.

And this was the man they had to outmaneuver. *Don't think of it*, Jenny told herself. *Think of how Lord Vickers has been cheated of his inheritance for no reason*. Now that she had met the enemy she had no doubts that Yves could do such a thing from pure malice. His hatred had hung in the air like a fog. He could not even be content with having the man thrown unjustly into prison; he would see that Nate remained without friends or assistance even within the very walls of Newgate.

Yves had not succeeded in turning them against Vickers, though. If anything, he had confirmed the wronged man's claims. From that moment, however, there was no more sense of playing games. They were in dead earnest.

Danger remained the most relaxed. He had the least to lose. As he had told Jenny before, he would escape regardless of what happened to the others. The failure of his private plan to steal information from Yves evidently meant nothing to him in the long run. He had been challenged now, however, and that was something he could not resist. He was no less determined that the plan would work and was much harder on Jenny when she faltered in her answers.

Time did not make the impersonation any easier, Jenny found. She had not realized before how great a strain she would feel in pretending to be someone else. Every time she hesitated, she saw the ice-cold eyes of Lord Yves upon her. Her own identity seemed to have become lost and had no value to anyone but herself. Could she keep Jenny Wilde alive within her until she had won free of Miss Beauchamp?

Between fear and exhaustion, Jenny was less aware of those who observed her behavior, outside of their judgment of her performance. Danger had learned, however, just how far his subordinates could be pushed. He knew when to administer punishment, when to add incentives.

"My man has already dealt with Mrs. Ransome," he told Jenny at last. "You'll be released in a day or two. There's no reason for you to stay after the trial. The crowds will only get worse and will leave no time at all for rehearsing."

This was no boast. Jenny knew it to be a simple matter of fact. Already the crowds gave her too much time to think and worry. Conscience—and discretion—decreed that now was the time to tell Danger of her doubts. Outside Newgate she would be delivered into the hands of his gang, and there would be no turning back then.

Danger was giving her one of those looks, as if he knew everything that slipped through her mind. "Once you're out, it will be easier to get Sukey out."

In other words Sukey would not escape unless she did. "How so?"

"The obvious is often the best way. Once my arch dell has left, I will need feminine companionship. Five whores come in, five whores leave. But not the same whores. Do you see?"

She nodded.

"You appreciate the delicate compliment to yourself, I hope. That while I have you, I lack nothing." Oh, he enjoyed trying to get a reaction from her.

"I think you enjoy masquerades. Surely you could have bought Sukey's way out as well."

"No more than I could have bought my own. You don't know, do you? Sukey is one of the brightest of the canting crew that I've ever met, but she's done two stupid things in her life. She married a great hulking brute who abused her and stole her earnings. And then she killed him."

"No," Jenny cried in protest. Not Sukey, not her gentle friend, the girl so proud of her skill. But Sukey had admitted that she was not in Newgate for diving. "Obviously, it must have been an accident, or in defense of her life."

"Of course. He was going to break her fingers. Do you understand what that would mean to Sukey? She hit him and he fell and cracked his skull open. That won't help her in the courtroom, though."

"They'd sentence her to hang for that?"

"If she's lucky. You see, the murder of someone to whom one owes allegiance—like a husband— can be treated as petit treason. And that means she'd be burned at the stake. But she needn't worry. Because everything will continue as planned."

Slowly his threat sank in. "What if the plan doesn't work?" she insisted.

"It will work. I do not involve myself with failures."

He had never admitted his part in the attempt to rob Yves and never would. Jenny should have known better. There had never been a chance to pull out. There never would be. Her choice had been made and she would have to stand by it, no matter how much she regretted the decision or feared the outcome.

Danger smiled and fingered his beard. Oh yes, he knew he'd won. "Perhaps now would be a good time to discuss your role at my hanging?"

Chapter Three

Jenny shivered in the cold moonlight. Midnight. She was too far away to hear the bell of St. Sepulchre's, but she knew it was tolling now for the condemned as it would again in the morning. Danger was no doubt sleeping the sleep supposedly reserved for the just. Why should he watch and pray when others might do it for him?

But it was not for Danger that Jenny sat, cold and wakeful, staring through a crack in the boarded window out on a bleak rookery courtyard. It was for herself and what she would have to do.

The Covent Garden tenement that had become her new prison had few of the amenities of Danger's luxurious cell. The furnishings were spare and the thin battered walls did little to keep out the cold wind or the raucous noise of nearby revelers.

It served to keep Jenny in, all the same. Even if she had had any place to go, even if she had been willing to risk outwitting the guards placed on her, she would not have dared walk alone through the streets of the rookery.

Danger had been right, of course. There was no problem at all in arranging her release. The charges were dropped; the exit fees were paid. Only Caleb Deems remained unsatisfied, and Danger was not likely to pay him any mind. Reason told Jenny that the malicious jailer could not harm her now that she was free. He had not been perceptive enough to see the lady in Jenny before; he would not recognize Jenny in the lady, Miss Beauchamp. Despite reason, Jenny still feared him. His farewell echoed in her mind during the long hours she spent alone.

"I'll find you. No matter where you run, I'll find you. Your fancy man is going to dangle in the sheriff's picture frame. He won't do you no good after that. And then you and me is going to settle a debt. You've got my pledge on it."

Jenny, plagued by worries and sleepless nights, dreamed of Deems chasing her through the rookeries of London. And always, always there was that greater, all-consuming fear that Yves was on their trail.

Her first week was miserable. It was not that she was treated badly. On the rare occasions that anyone spoke to her, it was with a wary kindness. They made one thing clear, however. Any one of them would give his life for Danger if it were necessary. And should he die, they would make everyone involved pay with their lives.

Matters did improve when Sukey arrived two weeks later. It was the morning after sentence had been passed on Danger. Predictably, Danger's response to the sentence had been to have a rout party.

It was just as he said. Five whores in, five whores out. Only not quite the same whores. Oh, he must have had a lovely laugh over that.

Jenny couldn't laugh, though. What if Danger's plan didn't work? What if the hangman was alert enough to see what she was doing? They would never be able to tell whether Danger was performing, as planned, or dying.

What if Lord Yves decided to take up Danger's invitation and came to the hanging?

By dawn Jenny could already hear the sounds of celebration in the street. Hanging days were the only holidays most people knew. And today, of course, was special. Today the notorious highwayman Lord Danger would dance the Tyburn jig.

A knock at the door announced the return of Sukey. She entered and draped the dress she had been carrying on the bed.

"Did you sleep at all?" she asked.

Jenny turned away from the window and shook her head. "I couldn't. Every time I close my eyes I imagine such horrible things—Danger strangling and none of us able to tell. Deems might be there looking for me." She could hardly bear to mention her biggest fear, the eyes that haunted her even while awake. Neither Danger nor Sukey had seen all that she had seen in Yves. Or at least they would not admit to it, to being afraid. "What if Yves is there?"

Sukey looked at her sharply. "What if he is? Jenny, you're creating a ghostie, a man that doesn't exist. Couldn't. He's a mean bastard, yes, and a clever one to have done for Nate like he done. But he ain't no devil. He's just another greedy nob trying to get his hands on what he's no right to."

"You're wrong, Sukey. You're so wrong."

"So? What can he do? What can he see? Jenny, love, I'm a diver by trade. I ain't fooled easy. If you do just like we practiced, nobody will be able to tell."

"And if I break down? If I don't do it as we practiced?"

"You won't. You're stronger than you know, Jenny."

"I hope you're right."

"Of course I am. You didn't think you could play Danger's doxy, and you did. You just gots to do it one more time."

"Just one more time. I hope so." Jenny turned to see Sukey setting out the paints on the room's only table. "Time to get tarted up?"

"Best to be ready early. They won't call Danger out of his cell until nine, and it'll be some time after that before they leave Newgate, but if you're to get a good position at the church you'll need to start soon."

"Very well, do your worst."

Jenny sat down on the room's single chair and let Sukey apply the heavy ceruse paint and rouge that was part of her disguise.

"Sukey, have you ever been to a hanging?"

71

"Aye, I've seen one. Now turn your head this way."

If Sukey had hoped to dismiss the subject, she had failed. "Well, what was it like?"

"You know what's going to happen. Dick went over it enough times."

"Yes, and chose his words very carefully. I want to know what he wouldn't tell me."

"He didn't hide nothing."

"Sukey, think. If I'm unprepared I could be surprised into doing something wrong. Tell me."

"You can't be unprepared. You do know everything that's going to happen. You just can't know what it's really like till you sees it." Sukey's fingers shook a little as she applied a heart-shaped patch to Jenny's cheekbone. "They likes it, you see. That's the worst of it. The crowd likes it, seeing some poor bloke slowly strangle hisself to death. Sometimes it takes so long . . ."

She turned away, pretending to search for Jenny's wig.

"Well, at least this time we must trust that the man is not strangling," Jenny said.

"Danger won't, but the others—"

"Others? What others?"

"Didn't you know then? Famous Danger may be, but they can't afford to give two holidays so he can have an execution all to hisself. There's three others being turned off with him."

Of course there would be others. How stupid of her not to realize that before. All this time she had been holding on to that one thought for strength—that no one would really be hanged— and now even that small comfort was taken from her.

"Don't look like that, love. Danger'll see that they get some of the drugged wine. Jenny, look at me. They can't be saved. They've been looking toward the gallows since they was born. This may be the greatest moment in their whole miserable lives. For the first and only time, they ain't nothings—they're handsome, brave, and strong. They're heroes on the gallows. Even a thief deserves to die with dignity. Well, this is the best we can expect. You can't pity a man for dying well."

"You're right. Don't worry about me. I'll be fine." She had to be, Jenny realized. But as hard as she tried to concentrate on the part she would have to play, on what she had to do, she kept thinking back to the one person who had the most to gain by their failure.

Lord Yves' eyes and ears had come and gone again, leaving his lordship with another sheet of paper. This time the servant who came in to clear away the tray found his lordship smiling to himself. It was not a comforting kind of smile.

He stopped the servant at the door. "Ferris, am I right in recalling some mention of a hanging today?"

"Yes, my lord. I had given permission to some of the household staff to attend. Young Arthur and Henry have never seen a hanging before, you see. However, if their absence would displease you, I can easily—"

"No, no. Never let it be said that I prevented—Arthur, is it?—from seeing his first hanging. Let them all go, all the servants, if they wish."

"Why, thank you, m'lord. That's very generous of you. I—"

"The highwayman, the one who calls himself Lord Danger, is to be hanged today, I believe."

"Yes, m'lord."

Yves looked down at the paper in his hand. "A very interesting character, this Lord Danger."

"Yes, m'lord."

"With quite a reputation for landing on his feet. I gather some attempt at rescue is anticipated."

"Men have survived before."

"So they have. I wonder . . ." He tapped the paper against his chin a moment before consigning it to the fire. "Yes, I think I must see this hanging myself after all."

It seemed to Jenny that all of London had come to see Danger hang. All along the hangman's route there were mobs waiting, watching from windows, from the rooftops, and shouting their pleasure in the day at the top of their lungs. The noise was almost unbearable and Danger hadn't even arrived yet.

Jenny waited for him, with a crowd of young girls, at the foot of the steps of St. Sepulchre's Church. Waited with them to throw bouquets of fresh flowers to the condemned men.

But when the hangman's cart finally made its appearance, Jenny nearly forgot the reason she was there.

They were just children, two of them. Oh, the third one looked a hardened criminal, but the other two . . . The girl looked almost twenty, but was probably no more than fourteen. The boy was even younger.

Jenny surged forward with the other girls to bestow her floral tribute. By accident she met Danger's warning glance. At that moment she hated him for putting her through this, but she let one of the men help her up to the cart to be kissed by the highwayman.

Danger said it was to establish her as his woman, his arch dell—to the crowd as well as the hangman—so her rights to his body could not be questioned later. Jenny didn't believe a word of it. He wanted to humiliate her because she was the only person who failed to succumb to his charm. He must have taken pity on her at the last moment, however, for although he held her for a long time, he attempted no more than the merest pressure of his lips on hers.

He was watching her with the strangest expression in his eyes as she was helped down. She must have frightened him. Well, she would show him. She would not give way now.

There was one more stop before they reached the place of execution. Traditionally, the landlord of the Oxford Road Tavern presented all the members of the hanging party with a final draft of spirits. It was considered a kindness to help the condemned to drunken oblivion before the execution. Danger had seen to it that all the prisoners would be drugged as well.

Through Hampstead and Highgate they continued until at last the terrible theater could be seen. Jenny, jostled and shoved, felt a rising panic. It was impossible—she would never reach her place by the gallows. The mob was enormous, and growing by the minute. Those who had gained, by money or by force, a fine vantage point were not about to give it up.

Jenny wasn't about to give up either. She dared not. She sidestepped two ballad-singers, each claiming to have Danger's final confession, who glared and proclaimed their superior claims over the other.

As Jenny pushed and wriggled her way closer to the front, she could see the wealthier members of the audience, marked apart by dress and location, but not much by behavior. Mother Proctor's pews were filled with nobles and their ladies, dressed in silks and laces and waving perfumed handkerchiefs to dispel the odors of the lower classes. There was little difference, however, in the way they jostled for a better view or clamored for the attention of the ballad-singer. There was no difference at all in the avid look to their eyes as they watched Danger and his fellow convicts approach the scaffold.

Jenny sighed with relief as she scanned the pews. *He* wasn't there. There was no question in Jenny's mind that she'd have seen him if he were. No matter what size the crowd grew to be, he would stand out. There could be no mistaking any other for him.

Finally, somebody recognized her, perhaps even one of Danger's men, and helped her to the foreground. She had made it, at least this far. The pigeon was released to send the news back to Newgate that the prisoners had arrived safely to the place where they would die. Attention focused at last on the figures in the cart.

Jenny could see the drugged liquor begin to take

effect. Still, each of the other prisoners made some little speech, largely unintelligible to Jenny, regarding their exploits. None of them showed any remorse, not even the children; they were game to the end.

But it was Danger that the crowd waited for. The deafening clamor ceased abruptly as he rose to speak to them.

A provincial actor suddenly given the opportunity to play Hamlet at Drury Lane could not have regarded his audience with a more benign affection. Danger played with them, too, like a skillful actor, letting his gaze roam around the amphitheater, making them wait, hushed and anxious, for his first words.

"My very dear friends," he addressed them. "For I consider you all my friends. A man should not leave this earth at enmity with mankind, so I am determined to regard all with the utmost beneficence. And surely it is an act of the greatest kindness on your part to see a man, a complete stranger to many of you, depart on the greatest of voyages as he travels from this life to the next.

"I see some old acquaintances come to wish me well—Lord Fanshawe, Sir Edward Blount..." Danger cheerfully greeted a number of his noble victims. The list was long. "In our dealings in the past, I had rather the better of you, but I see from your kindly expressions you do not begrudge me my victories."

The crowd howled with joyous laughter. Even those who felt the sting in Danger's wit smiled. This is what they had come to Newgate to see and hear—no tearful repentance but laughing bravado.

"And the ladies—ah yes, the ladies have come to say goodbye. My dears, if I regret anything in leaving this earth it is leaving you, all of you. I have known great kindness at the hands of women."

The audience laughed again, and Danger regarded the crowd with a glint in his eye. "If you're waiting for names again, I'm afraid you'll be sadly disappointed. Those of you who have earned my gratitude must simply take my expression of appreciation as sincerely and personally delivered. Sadly, I can neither say nor do more."

There were probably a few pink faces in Mother Proctor's pews hidden behind furiously moving fans. It was part of the highwayman's now-legendary code that he never took money or jewels from the ladies—only kisses.

As the crowd finally hushed again, Danger straightened his back. The laughter left his eyes and he spoke in tones vibrant with authority and strength.

"In fact, there is a great deal which I am not prepared to say. For those of you who are interested in some trifling tales of those acquaintances I have made upon the highroad, I have given Mr. Jermyn the bookseller here a full and exact account."

Said bookseller stood close to Jenny, as close to the cart as the law would allow. He would make a small fortune from Danger's endorsement of his pamphlet. He was also scheduled to play another part in Danger's exit from this world, Jenny knew, although he did not.

"The gentlemen I have met in such a manner have all acknowledged these encounters so that I feel no compunction in setting down our acquaintance in print—and occasionally setting the matter straight." He shook his head as if grieved by the world's deceit. "Really, gentlemen. Had I received as many musket balls and sword thrusts as I have heard boasted, I should never have lived to entertain you here today."

Jenny suspected that some of the men who laughed at this sally were not, in truth, much amused.

Danger turned serious once again. "These things all men may know. But there are things none may know. Today I go before a higher judge than those in the Old Bailey. There may be crimes enough to condemn me in that court as well, but I shall not be accused of playing Judas. If I take nothing else with me beyond this gallows, I shall take my secrets. Content you with the assurance that the charitable donations of my 'acquaintances' have been put to excellent good use, and that my friends...my friends shall remember that I was truly their friend."

Like the crowd, Jenny had to admire Danger for this. One virtue—loyalty—at least was his. No wonder his friends were willing to follow him so blindly. But Jenny had neither offered nor sought friendship from Danger, she reminded herself. She might be expendable.

Danger turned to look at her now, and Jenny stepped closer to the line of constables holding back the crowd.

"I'll have but one friend by me now, my arch dell, my Jenny. She has stayed by me till the end. To her shall go the final honors. I beg you, as you are my friends, not to hinder her. Trust her to see to what's fit." In other words, Jenny would see if the highwayman could be revived later. True enough, although these people would never know if she succeeded. At a sign from the hangman Jenny was allowed forward to pass a small flask to Danger.

"A drink to my arch dell," he toasted. "And to all of you, my friends and my companions in misfortune." The bottle was passed among the other prisoners, to Jenny's relief. "Ah, none left for the hangman. Well, here's this for you, sir." Danger handed the executioner a hefty purse and then pulled a large ruby ring off his finger and gave it to him. "This suit of clothes is yours as well, as tradition demands. Do your best for me and drink to my memory later. And remember me all of you, if you will, like this—generous and smiling to the end."

And then she saw *him*. The crowd's renewed cheering drowned out the chaplain's final prayers, which were less than coherent in any case. Lord Yves watched from atop his coach, one of a number lined up atop a ridge that overlooked the arena. He was alone, standing somewhat apart from the others. It was that sense of aloofness, that and the way he held his body, that first caught Jenny's eye. The sun shone on his hair striking golden sparks. There'd be sparks from those cold eyes if he saw . . . if he saw.

Jenny dragged her eyes away and turned back to the cart. Whether he saw or not, she had to go through with it. If she was caught she might end up back in Newgate, but if she failed to try, she was sure to be killed by Danger's companions.

The hangman began his appointed business. He

started with the girl, tying her rope around one of the three cross-bars of the gallows and pulling the noose tight around her neck. When that was done, he tied a white handkerchief around her forehead, letting one corner hang down for her to pull as a signal of readiness.

Jenny felt sick with fear. Reason decreed that all eyes—even Yves'—would be on the victims, but still she imagined them, cold and clear as ice, fixed on her alone.

Jenny tried to shut out the conversations around her, but then she was forced to pay attention to what was happening in front of her. The hangman had jumped from the cart and moved to the horse's head. The signal given, he pulled the cart out from under the girl's feet.

Jenny felt the nausea rising in her throat, but dared not turn away. The routine was the same for the others. Friends of the girl and the older man were ready to help pull on their legs to help hurry the process. The boy had no friends and was so slight that the weight of his body did not exert enough pressure to bring swift oblivion. Danger's eyes pinned a man in the crowd, and he moved forward to perform the same service for the youth.

And now Jenny's moment was about to come. The hangman performed his part with the rope and paused. This is what Danger's fat purse and ruby ring had bought her—a few minutes at the cart for what was to look like a final kiss. She launched herself forward and with a little help from the hangman climbed up into the cart. Tears were streaming down her face. The crowd, cheering her on with lewd suggestions, would never know that they were tears of fear and anger rather than grief at the loss of a lover. Her fingers were trembling as they fluttered over Danger's chest, under his flowing beard, feeling for the noose and the hooks of the harness. Hook one, hook two. *Don't think about Yves. Don't even warn Danger. It doesn't matter. In the end, it doesn't matter.*

In her anxiety, Jenny was hardly aware of Danger's lips pressed to hers. Hook three, hook four. It was done. Nervously she felt over each hook to make sure, unable to believe despite all their rehearsals that it would work, that the harness would hold.

Danger was beginning to show the effects of the drug. He must have been more confident than Jenny, for he did not wait for her to whisper a word of assurance. He lifted his mouth from hers and spoke softly to the hangman. "Enough. Take her away."

There was no outcry, no whispers of suspicion between constables. If Yves, watching from the ridge, had noticed anything odd in their embrace, he said nothing, made no outcry. The hangman, clearly inebriated, handed the protesting Jenny to the protection of two constables and walked over to take up the reins. Danger gave one last look around him, smiled with extraordinary sweetness at Jenny, and gave the signal.

The constables released Jenny so that she could help pull him into another life. Danger did not make it easy for her. His body flailed in imaginary protest—or in real agony. Who could tell? It seemed an eternity to Jenny before his body stilled and she could step away.

And wait. It was required that the condemned

hang for a full hour to ensure death. Meanwhile the audience ate, drank, fought, and celebrated in holiday mood.

Eventually Jenny dared look around again, up to the ridge. Yves' coach was gone. There was no comfort in knowing he was no longer watching. He might very well have seen more than enough already.

Yet no one came forward to expose their trick. Part of the crowd tried to break through when at last the bodies were cut down. Superstition claimed that the touch of the hanged criminal had special medicinal properties, and there were many who wished to put the matter to the test.

Jenny could not see them, but she knew that any number of Danger's men were ready now to protect her, to protect him. She was allowed forward to claim the body, and she braced her own slight form to hide his from view. Surreptitiously she felt for a heartbeat. The drug was supposed to slow the heart, but surely she should feel something? A wet drop fell on her hand and she realized that she was still crying. She looked up, trying to find the bookseller, Mr. Jermyn, and found herself facing the mean features of Caleb Deems.

"You," she cried.

"Closed-mouthed to the last, the bastard. I don't suppose you got any idea where all his ill-gotten gains have gotten to? No, he'd not have let you come here if you knew. He was a clever cove, but what did it get him?"

"What do you want?" Jenny tried to put on a bold front, but she knew Deems could see the fear in her tear-stained face, could hear it in her shaky voice.

"You know the answer to that, dearie. And I'll get what I want. See, I'm cleverer than your dimber-damber man. I'm alive and I'll stay that way for a long, long time. I can afford to wait. The nights are cold, love, when you've no place to go and no money to spend. I don't see you taking care of yourself. No, your kind wants a man to pay the rent and buy 'em pretty things."

How wrong he was. Yet his stupidity gave her no comfort. Carefully obscuring his view of Danger, she challenged him, "And you think I can't do better than you?"

"I intend to make sure you can't."

The bookseller appeared at last and stood by respectfully. Deems performed an insolent bow and promised, "I'll see you soon, my dear. Very soon." He ran a dirty finger along the line of his scar and left.

Mr. Jermyn looked somewhat bemused. Jenny had the feeling that this sort of thing was not in his usual line of business. As usual, however, Danger had chosen well. The bookseller had contracted to see to the highwayman's burial as payment for exclusive rights to print his final words and his endorsement. Danger had done his part, Mr. Jermyn would do his, no matter how unpleasant he found the duty.

He had a few of the men from his printshop with him. On his command they took the body to a waiting carriage. Whether from kindness or distaste, he let Jenny ride alone with Danger.

He wouldn't rouse. Jenny knew that the drug was strong, that he should sleep for hours. Still she feared. Drugs were such chancy things. One amount could cure, another could kill, and the difference was often small.

They stopped first at a small inn in Fleet Street where the hangman would hold court and sell the rope he had used earlier at sixpence the inch. Here Jenny could lay out the body for burial and give the hangman his final fee—Danger's flamboyant attire. A small crowd followed them. Some of the revelers were unwilling to see the fun end; they would follow Danger to his grave out of boredom and curiosity.

Danger's second in command met Jenny in the hall and led her up to a small private room where she might prepare the body for burial. A wooden box had been left there, provided by the bookseller. A connecting door, locked, led to another chamber. As soon as Jenny was alone she ran over to open it.

Another of Danger's men slipped quietly into the room and went over to the recumbent form of his leader. He looked at Danger for a long moment and then looked up at Jenny.

"Doctor said as he'd be like this for a while. Pity. Doesn't make our job no easier, but I suppose that don't really matter none. Here, let's shift him quick."

He and the highwayman's lieutenant took Danger into the next room. In a few minutes they returned and presented Jenny with the suit of clothes she must give to the hangman. They went back into the adjoining room again and then returned with an unwieldy bundle wrapped in a shroud. The bundle looked amazingly as if it contained a real body.

"T'other fellow was a hanged today," the younger one told her with satisfaction. "Got it for six bob. Thought we was the surgeon's men. Ah, at least he'll get a proper burial this way, poor bloke."

They were right, of course, but Jenny could not help but wonder what they would have done if that body had not been available. Danger clearly would not risk having an empty casket ever found.

No, there was still too much for her to do to worry about what Danger might have done. At her call Mr. Jermyn's men came and carried out the box to the waiting hearse.

The light had not yet begun to fade when the casket was lowered into the ground in the church-yard of St. Martins-in-the Fields. The ceremony did not last long. Despite a sizable donation, the minister did not feel quite comfortable in per-forming such a service for so notorious a thief.

Those tenacious few who had followed until now began at last to go about their own business. The day was far advanced, and no doubt even the most ragged of them had family or friends who awaited them. The hangman might still be hold-ing court in Fleet Street, and there at least one could find comfort for a dry throat.

Jenny waited quietly until the last of them had finally disappeared. The weather, which had been so fine earlier in the day, had turned cool now. She pulled her shawl more closely about her shoulders and walked to the waiting coach.

It was still too soon to relax, though, as Jenny and her guardians traveled on through the night, first north, then south, but always away from Lon-don and away from the more frequented roadways. She could barely stay awake, yet dared not close her eyes for fear of what she might see in sleep. By now the men who traveled with Danger would know if their plan had succeeded or not, but Jenny would have to travel on and wait for news.

The sky was just beginning to turn pink with the rising sun when the coach at last pulled up in front of a prosperous coaching inn some miles outside the city. Jenny paid little heed to the inn-keeper's garrulous flow of welcome and explanation. She found herself led to a door and entered it, but instead of finding the bedchamber she so ardently desired, she found a private sitting room.

Jenny immediately wished she had paid more attention to the innkeeper's vocal meanderings, because clearly the man had made a mistake. This room was already occupied. A pretty mob-capped servant girl was serving breakfast to a provincial gentleman who was hardly likely to countenance such an intrusion. The severity of his dress bespoke a plain, no-nonsense, country squire. There was a dimple in his chin which might indicate some saving humor, but Jenny did not care to stay and chance it. She turned to try and leave in as inconspicuous a manner as possible. Too late.

"Jenny, love, where are you going?" Sukey asked. "Aren't you hungry?"

The gentleman stood and delivered a meticulous bow. "Ma'am."

Even had she not recognized his voice, Jenny would have known that ironic look anywhere.

The gentleman introduced himself. "Sir Richard Dangerfield, ma'am. At your service."

Chapter Four

Things seemed to happen with remarkable speed after that. Jenny felt as if she were caught in a whirlpool. She was very well aware that Danger—Sir Richard—was taking great care that she should not have time to think.

To her dismay, she was forced to concede that he had succeeded. She *was* off balance. In Newgate she had thought she had learned how to deal with the highwayman. Sir Richard was a stranger, however, a stranger that seemed too like the gentlemen officers she had known in the colonies.

Well, that was what he was supposed to be—a soldier who had sold out of the army upon unexpectedly coming into the family estate and honors. Sometimes Jenny caught herself wondering if it could possibly be true. After all, Nate was not the only younger son of a younger son to suddenly find his fortunes miraculously reversed. And younger sons had taken to the road looking for fortune before as well.

All Jenny knew was that this sense of familiarity made her uncomfortable. She refused to be lured into a false sense of ease. Highwayman or gentleman, Richard was still pulling the strings, still in control, still to be watched.

Jenny missed Nate. Until they left Newgate she had not realized how much his presence had meant to her. He had always been the softening influence, the peacemaker, but most of all he had been the symbol of right. Nate was the living reminder that everything she did, every lie she told, was meant to restore a cruelly wronged man's rights and heritage.

That comfortable sense of virtue was hard to maintain when one spent one's days with pickpockets, smugglers, ex-highwaymen and their lieutenants.

There weren't many moments, however, when she was given the luxury of thought, none when she was given the luxury of privacy. Every day was spent in travel that was invariably tedious and exhausting and usually involved some degree of discomfort. From ill-sprung carriages to ocean-tossed smuggling ships, there were always new masquerades, new impostures, until the final one could begin.

Once Danger's smuggling friends had delivered their cargo to their sister ship from Boston, however, the new order began. Only in Jenny's critical eyes did the highwayman still live. Lord Danger was gone forever. And, as Sir Richard so firmly reminded her, so also must Miss Jenny Wilde disappear. Long live Miss Jean-Marie Beauchamp.

This is what all the planning, all the hours of memorizing, of play-acting had led to. Miss Jean-Marie Beauchamp, late of the city of Boston in the Massachusetts colony, arrived in Portsmouth on the ship *Fortuna* one morning late in the spring of the year 1765. She was accompanied by a maidservant and traveled under the escort of a gentleman recently released from His Majesty's service.

It was all up to Jenny now. If she failed, the entire scheme failed. Sir Richard would lose a sizable investment; Jenny and Sukey would lose their freedom and possibly their lives. Nate, poor Nate, would lose what looked like his last chance to regain his inheritance and would end his days a debtor convict rather than a belted earl. And it all depended on Jenny.

She should have been terrified.

Jenny returned from her first visit to the solicitors smiling. Hardly had she closed the door of the private parlor behind her and Sukey when she burst into laughter.

"I take it all went well," Sir Richard commented.

He had been waiting for them here for two hours. As Jenny had grown to expect, he showed no strain, no worry, only a sudden alertness. His eyes reflected the merriment Jenny knew he must see in hers. She didn't like the fact that he could read her so easily, but even that couldn't spoil her present mood.

"I suppose you might say that, yes. Sukey, do you think it went well?"

Sukey could hardly talk between the giggles.

"Oh . . . oh, Dick, you should have seen that lawyer's face!"

"And the clerks," Jenny reminded her as the maid helped her remove her bonnet and wrap. "When we first went in they were all looking down their noses at us. Who did we think we were, two ladies walking into Mr. Farriday's office without notice. Without an appointment!"

"They changed their tune, all right, by the time we left, though. 'Allow me, Miss Beauchamp.'" Sukey bowed to the floor. "'If we can ever be of service, Miss Beauchamp,' 'Stop in anytime, Miss Beauchamp.'"

"He bought it, then. Well, I think this deserves a toast." Sir Richard poured from a bottle of wine already waiting and offered the two women a glass. "Tell me from the beginning. "No," he interrupted before Sukey could begin. "Let Jenny tell it."

The way Sir Richard lolled back in his chair, at his ease, ready to be amused, was very reminiscent of the highwayman. Even this could not diminish Jenny's good humor today. She put down her glass of wine and paced the floor.

"You know, of course," she began, speaking as Jean-Marie, "I decided I must seek out the family solicitors to discover news of my cousin, Lord Vickers. At first, I met with some disbelief, not to say rudeness," she told him, as if surprised. "I was beginning to question whether this Mr. Farriday even meant to see me, when the strangest thing happened."

Sukey jumped up, unable to contain herself. "Ooh, it was wonderful odd. One of the clerks disappeared for a while and then he comes back hurrying along this poor old geezer who looks like he hardly knows what year it is. Well, this old feller takes one look at Jenny here and goes off his noodle. Starts kissing her hands and muttering about the red Beauchamps."

Nate had said once that there was a resemblance, she remembered. Enough, clearly, for an old man with failing eyesight to take as proof of birth, but it had given her quite a turn at the time.

"Very well, Miss Beauchamp. I will admit that obviously you were right to insist on going unpowdered," Sir Richard conceded.

Jenny smiled. "I was only thinking of colonial styles. Even in Boston, 'tis not used so much as here. But certainly it caused notice." She sat down at the small table and sipped her wine with the appearance of calm.

"Sensation, more like," Sukey corrected.

"That must have thrown you off your stride."

"Not our Jenny, not half. She just sits up straight, like she was the Queen herself, and says—"

"Now, now, Sukey. This is Miss Beauchamp's story. Let her tell it."

Her spirits undimmed, Sukey sat at Jenny's feet and nudged her to continue.

"It was a very moving moment. Clearly this man had known my father and my great-grandfather. He had, in fact, been a clerk of this firm since the days of my grandfather's youth, but had at last retired some years ago to live with his niece and her family."

Sukey hopped up again, unable to stay silent. "You should have heard them. Jenny and this old feller . . ."

"Mr. Arthur Perkins."

"...are having a nice tea-party chat, and while she's listening to him talk about his sciatica and her great-aunt's disgrace, the other gents are getting ready to go to Bedlam. Suddenly, it's 'Wouldn't you like some tea while you're waiting?' and 'Here's a much more comfortable seat,' and finally that Farriday feller comes out hisself and practically throws hisself at Jenny's feet."

"Did he so?"

"Sukey exaggerates," Jenny answered primly. She took another sip of wine while choosing her words. "There was a great deal of confusion in the outer office. Mr. Farriday then appeared and invited us into his private office to discuss our business and take some refreshment."

"What is the solicitor like?" he asked. Clearly, this was important. Much of the success of their plan hinged on what type of man was in charge of the Vickers' affairs. Too timid a time-server could be as hard a nut to crack as the most clever of men.

Jenny gave the question some thought. She closed her eyes for a moment to better recall the image of the man's face, his voice. "A frightened rabbit. Not the man his father was, and evidently knows it too well. Cautious, very cautious," she said, in her own persona.

"Hmmm. He could be trouble?"

The familiarity of that phrase jolted Jenny for a moment, but she could not recall where she had heard it.

"Perhaps. Perhaps not," she told Richard. "Farriday will choose the course with the least risk of blame to him. If he is made to feel that he will be blamed more strongly for waiting, for having waited so long ..."

"I see. Well, go on. What happened in the solicitor's office?"

"Well, Farriday hemmed and hawed and finally got round to asking which branch of the family I came from. So I told him and explained that I had had great difficulty in trying to contact my cousin, the earl."

"And was his face a sight to see!"

"Sukey!" Jenny pursed her lips to keep from laughing. "He was rather surprised," she said, once again Jean-Marie. "Evidently he had never received the communication from me informing him that mother and father had ... had died. My fault, perhaps. I sent it to the only addresses I knew—the Hall and the family house in town."

"Ah well, all the way from the colonies, and in time of war, who knows what might have happened to it?" Sir Richard shrugged.

"Exactly what Mr. Farriday said."

"And what else did Mr. Farriday say?"

Jenny put her glass down and walked to the window where she could observe the busy city street. "Not much that was to the point, actually. I am to return next week."

"That doesn't worry you?"

"No, I don't think so. Farriday isn't the kind of man to commit to a course of action without giving it a lot of thought. He believed me. I am sure of that. Now he merely has to force himself to act on his beliefs."

"Hmmmmm."

"He asked about my present financial situation and said that if I ran into difficulties I should come to him. Honestly, I think that's all we could expect for now."

"If he was willing to proffer some money, then we are doing well indeed. Yes. Yes, well, we will simply have to wait until next week. You might ask around though, Sukey, and see if anybody comes here asking questions, trying to check up on us."

"I'll warn Henry in the stables too," Sukey said, and then immediately jumped up to carry out her plan.

Sir Richard shook his head at Sukey's abrupt departure and helped himself to another glass of wine. "Sukey must learn not to be so precipitate. It will not do for Miss Beauchamp to be left unchaperoned with a gentleman."

"I don't see you hurrying to leave the room," Jenny commented, looking pointedly toward the door.

"Ah, but I'm not much of a gentleman, am I?" Danger rose and joined her by the window. "Lud, but I wish I could be with you when you go to the lawyer's again."

Exhilaration was making Jenny feel brave today. "I'll wager you would. You don't like being on the outside, where you can't control us all and pull the strings yourself, do you?"

"My, you are in alt today, Miss Beauchamp. No, I just wish I could see you in action. See the fun. And it was fun, wasn't it? You enjoyed it. Why, you came sailing in here so elevated your feet hardly touched the floor. I think a life of crime suits you."

She turned to him abruptly. "It's not a crime, it's not! We're not stealing from anybody. We're trying to see that Nate gets what's due to him. That's no offense."

"No, no crime, then. But your eyes wouldn't be flashing like that if all we'd had to do is present a petition to the court."

"All right. Yes, I enjoyed it." Jenny couldn't stay still. She began pacing the room as she remembered the scene. "I looked into that solicitor's silly rabbit face and I wanted to fool him. I thought of Nate in Newgate all these years because this... this idiot wouldn't take the responsibility of facing the truth. And I thought of how they treated us, all those clerks in the office mimicking their master, when they thought we were nobodies. Oh yes, I loved it. I loved watching him swallow every line, watching him jump to attention when he finally saw he'd made a mistake."

"We're not so different, Jenny, my dear. Don't lose that feeling, love. Remember it, keep it close. You'll need it again." It was Danger, not Sir Richard, who faced her across the table. "You know what comes next, don't you?"

"Yves." Jenny kept her chin up and her voice steady, aware that Richard was waiting for signs of distress. Every time Yves' name was mentioned she could feel his eyes on her, measuring, judging.

"That's right. Yves."

"It's not possible," his lordship said calmly. "You've been fooled."

Lord Yves was not one to visit a solicitor's office. No, the legal profession came to him, usually humbly. This time, however, the representative in question seemed to have found a certain amount of courage.

"If I've been a fool, it's in not taking action before this. Lord Quarles left England twenty years ago. There's been no word of him since."

Yves rose from his chair, an action that caused his visitor to become exceedingly nervous. "That's not true. I heard from him."

"Yes, when he first landed in the colonies. But there's been nothing for years. The late earl has been dead now for almost ten years. He was an old man when his grandson ran away."

"John did not run away! And it has only been seven years since my Lord Vickers died."

"In any case, Lord Quarles cannot have thought that it would be many years before he came into his inheritance. However much he might have hoped otherwise," Farriday added to forestall the baron's complaint. "If Lord Quarles cared anything for his heritage, he would have contacted us."

"The difficulties of sending letters from the frontier—"

"No, my lord." For once, Farriday stood firm. "Difficulties in sending letters to the frontier I can easily accept. Had Lord Quarles wished to send a letter to England, however, he could have done so. So, unless you mean to tell me that his lordship might simply have ignored the issue because he cared nothing for Vickers ..."

"No, he cared. My God, how he cared."

"...then I must believe that, unhappily, Lord Quarles died on the frontier."

"You believe this only because some chit of a girl, with big eyes and a simpering smile no doubt, tells you so."

Farriday's hands were shaking but still he met

Lord Yves' cold gaze fully. "I think I have known it for these many years, but I have not dared admit it."

Yves looked the solicitor over, carefully calculating how far the man could be pushed, how far coaxed. What he saw caused him to change his tactics. After a moment he resumed his seat and reached over to a tray of drinks by his side.

"Here, let me pour you some wine, Farriday. Relax. All I'm saying is that we should have proof, good solid proof, before we dispose of a fortune this size. Lud, would you believe any one who came up to you and said, 'The heir is dead, I am the new heir'?"

"Of course not. But this girl's no fortune-hunter, I'll stake my life on it."

"Unfortunately, what you are staking is Vickers', not your own. Risk your life, if you wish, on your judgment of a girl you have known for an hour. But for Vickers, I want proof."

"You want proof? Very well. Old Arthur recognized her at once. He knows more about the Beauchamps than any man living, and he believed her."

"Interesting. Very interesting, but still not proof. If old Arthur's memory and sight were that reliable, you'd not have retired him."

"And there are letters," Farriday announced with satisfaction.

"Letters? From whom? To whom?"

"To her father. From his cousin Mr. Beauchamp. And—" Farriday gave a rabbity smile "—from you. Also a Bible with the child's name and date of birth entered—in your cousin's hand."

"Stolen," Yves answered without a moment's thought.

"Then how do you explain the things she knows? She knew who Arthur was. She knew all about my father." He took a drink and took a cautious glance at his host. "She did not seem to know about her great-grandfather's will, however."

"Really, Farriday, if the girl is an adventuress, she is hardly going to reveal her hand for you to see. Of course, she pretended not to know about Lord Vickers' will."

"If you had seen her face when she told me about the Indian attack..." The lawyer's face clouded with remembered emotion. "No, I am sorry, my lord, but I must insist. I will not accept the responsibility for withholding this young lady's inheritance."

But it was not just a matter of this impostor's claim, but of Nate's. If this scheming girl, whoever she might be, succeeded, Nate would go free. Nate and his schemes, Nate and his Newgate friends. Damn. He'd known this was coming, but not so soon. He was still unprepared. This girl must be very good to have put old Farriday into such a state. But then Farriday didn't know, mustn't ever know, what Yves knew.

"I'm sorry, Farriday. I just cannot believe this tale. It's too...too pat, too fortuitous."

Yves stood up and walked over to the windows overlooking the garden. Nate and his schemes. There was just one thing wrong with them: Nate tended to judge others by himself. He expected others to behave as he would; that's why he could never understand Wolf.

"We seem to be at an impasse, don't we?" For

a moment, Yves stood quite still, then he deliberately relaxed his shoulders and turned to address Farriday affably. "Well, I think the only thing to do is for me to examine this miraculous daughter of my friend John. Don't you?"

This time when Jenny and Sukey went to visit the solicitor's office they were treated like honored guests. They were immediately ushered into the inner sanctum and offered refreshments. How much more the solicitor would offer was yet to be seen.

It didn't take much for Jenny to see Yves' Machiavellian hand behind the lawyer's changed behavior. The man was nervous but apologetic. She read that as meaning he had been ordered not to say or do anything binding, but he obviously believed her story. Which way would he jump?

It was Jenny who jumped, however, startled as the door opened and the cold breeze ushered in Wolf, Lord Yves, looking as if he were ready to eat impostors for breakfast. He moved with the feral grace of his namesake hurrying for the kill. Suddenly the room seemed too small to contain all that energy. The rabbity solicitor shrunk even more. Sukey, who had claimed so long and so hard that Yves was nothing to be feared, grew tense, too. Jenny could see her friend's hands tremble.

And then he looked at her. Through the roaring in her ears Jenny thought for a moment that she heard him speak her name, Eugénie. Those brilliant cool eyes held hers and seemed to examine her very soul. If he had announced her full history, from New York to Newgate, she would not have been surprised. She felt almost as if she were standing naked before him, yet she could not look away.

His eyes were less revealing. For a split second she had almost believed there was a flash of genuine joy, of welcome, in his glance. Then the wariness and the calculation returned. What could he be thinking now? Would he—could he—expose their plan so soon, just when they were beginning to think it would work?

Yves smiled. He laughed. In shock, Jenny heard him say, "Farriday, Farriday, what a fool I was to doubt you. This young lady is without question one of the red Beauchamps—and Lord Vickers' heir."

All Jenny registered was the sudden fact of her acceptance. The last part of Yves' surprising capitulation did not sink in. He was coming forward to introduce himself, and Jenny must try to remember the hardest of Nate's lessons—that John never knew the truth about Wolf.

"Farriday, come introduce me to this charming girl."

The lawyer was completely confused, but he performed the introduction by rote. Having done so, he was ignored.

"Miss Jean-Marie Beauchamp, I am happier than I can express to be able to greet the daughter of my best friend. I only wish I had the chance to see him again, too. Farriday tells me your parents fell victim in one of the Indian attacks."

It took no great acting ability for Jenny to turn pale and quiet at the mention of Indian attacks. His entrance alone had driven all the color from her cheeks. "Yes, my lord. I too wish they could be here with me." Jenny forced herself to look up and smile. "But I am very glad to meet one of my father's oldest and dearest friends. He spoke of you often and always with great affection."

Looking at the broad shoulders and strong hands, the golden hair and clear eyes, Jenny thought how strange and foolish it seemed to be talking to this man as if he were of an age with her father. Even if she had been truly as young as Jean-Marie, she could never look at this man as an uncle.

"John will be greatly missed." Still looking remarkably content, Yves sauntered over to the lawyer's desk and sat down on one corner of it. "He has been missed these many years since he left England. Mr. Farriday has perhaps told you that I have been executor and trustee of your great-grandfather's estate."

"No, he did not mention it. He did say that news of my father's death had not reached you previously. Do you need me to help with some formality? Make a statement?"

"No, no, that won't be necessary."

Jenny saw the lawyer sit up very straight and blink his eyes rapidly. What was Yves up to?

"The details concerning your cousin's accession to the title are easily handled and need not concern you at all."

Easily handled. Nate had spent years unnecessarily imprisoned, and Yves said the details are easily handled. But it was true, she realized. The details would be handled now. It was done. They had won, and Nate would be freed to become Earl of Vickers. They had won.

"However," his lordship continued, "your own

inheritance is another matter."

"My inheritance?"

"The greatest part of your great-grandfather's estate was unentailed. The terms of the will are clear—this unentailed fortune goes to the late Lord Vickers' closest blood relation. That, of course, is you."

But I don't want it, Jenny wanted to scream. A little competence, Nate had said, just enough to keep her, just enough for a quiet cottage in the country.

"That's quite a responsibility for a young girl. I mean to make sure that by the time you come of age you—or, of course, your husband, should you marry—will know how to handle it. You look surprised, my dear."

Jenny felt the need to sit down. "I am. As I told Mr. Farriday, I had thought that perhaps my cousin would offer me some assistance, but this . . ."

"You mustn't be afraid." Jenny could hear him laugh behind the conventional words of comfort. "As executor of the estate, naturally I will continue to supervise your fortune as trustee."

Naturally? Jenny looked to the solicitor and read confirmation in his eyes. Having won Yves' acceptance of her identity, Farriday was clearly happy to accept his assumption of trusteeship.

"You may depend upon me," Yves continued. "Be sure I'll keep you safe from the dangers of London society, especially from all fortune-hunters."

"Society? Oh no, I couldn't . . ."

"Of course, you must take your rightful place in society. I'm not one for the social whirl myself, but I'll see you through, never fear."

Mr. Farriday, silent for so long, finally found the courage to interrupt. "I believe, my lord, that Lord Pertwee's widow is a connection of yours. So difficult for a lady of fashion to make do with a widow's jointure. Perhaps . . . ?"

"Pertwee? Oh yes, she's very close to the Devonshires, I hear. And old Walpole. Yes, she may do very well."

That horrible feeling of being swept up by events beyond her control was back. She'd won, she reminded herself. They had taken the bait and promised the prize. They couldn't do anything to Miss Jean-Marie Beauchamp. Could they?

"My lord, Mr. Farriday." Jenny took a breath and brought her voice under control. "You are both very kind to think of my future, but surely this is something that should be taken up with the head of my family, by Lord Vickers." Yes, Nate would know how to handle this, she told herself. She didn't want to remember that Nate never had been able to handle Yves.

Yves exchanged meaningful looks with the lawyer. "It is true that in the normal way of things you would look to the head of your family to act as guardian—"

"Guardian?" The very word alarmed Jenny.

"—but this is hardly a normal situation," Yves continued. "I have no doubt but that the courts would think it most reasonable that the trustee of your estate should also be responsible for your person in the short time remaining until you come of age. 'Tis unfortunate that you have no female relations still living. Lord Vickers, you know, maintains a bachelor establishment. It would be out of the question for him to take on the care of a young female ward."

The lawyer could be heard muttering under his breath. "I should say it was out of the question. With his reputation . . ."

Clearly Yves had already poisoned the man's mind against poor Nate. No help there. "Well," she said, trying to appear calm, "I cannot say I care much for the idea of someone being paid to take me in." The idea did offer some hope, though. If a woman took her in for money, perhaps she would also look the other way for money.

"Oh, you would not be staying with Lady Pertwee. My aunt acts as my hostess. As she is but newly come from Hanover, she is not familiar enough with the London social scene to act as your sponsor, but she will be most happy to offer you a home with us."

With us? With him? Live in the same house with him? No, oh no.

"All perfectly proper, I assure you," he said. Jenny sat stunned as he smiled at her. "You will feel much more comfortable, I know, to be with friends of your father. We will have so much to talk about, you and I."

Chapter Five

What could she say to stop him? What could she do? Jenny considered one impossible scheme after another before she faced the answer. She could do nothing until Nate was officially installed as Earl of Vickers and freed from prison, nothing but hope and pray that he would be able to get her out of this fix.

If she had been the kind of person to say "I told you so" she might have gained some satisfaction from Sukey's horrified surprise. Well, now perhaps they would realize she was right about how dangerous this man might be. On the whole, Jenny would rather have had them find out some other way.

She was being pushed along by the tide of events again, and it troubled her. A messenger had been sent to Yves' home so that his aunt might be prepared for her arrival.

Another messenger would have been sent to the inn where Jenny and Sukey were staying if Jenny had not asked to fetch her things personally. She did not like the idea of the servants there pawing over her few small effects, she said. And there was one there who deserved to know how she had fared.

Yves had smiled then, and she had shivered at the sight of it. By all means, they would stop by the inn first, if she so desired.

He joined them in the coach so there was no privacy, no chance to exchange a few words with Sukey, whose very stillness was frightening. Even more frightening was the way Yves looked at Jenny. Those cool, clear eyes never left her for a second.

"You look tired, my dear."

"Everything is happening so fast," she murmured. "And nothing the way I expected." That much was safe to admit.

"Not what you expected? Surely your father had something like this planned for you before he died."

"The world turned upside-down when my family died. I did not think anything could ever put it right again." Jenny closed her eyes for a moment. Would the world ever return to its accustomed sphere? "I certainly could never have expected to find myself an heiress. While I rejoice at my good fortune, I must declare I find it a very strange thing for Great-grandfather to have done."

"Not at all. Your great-grandfather was a great and wise man. He never acted without good reason. 'Tis a pity you never had the chance to know him. How, by the way, did you know he had died?''

She tensed for the merest second. Of course, from the very beginning she'd asked for her cousin the earl, not her great-grandfather. Yves didn't miss anything. "I don't know how much of my adventures Mr. Farriday may have told you ..."

"Some."

He'd probably questioned the man until he knew more than Farriday. "When I was in Boston, I overheard a visitor from England mention his death. It was that which gave me the idea to seek out my family here."

"Sad tidings indeed, but we must be glad at least that it brought you home."

"To find my family. Which, my lord, I have not yet done. I would like to meet my—"

The coach jolted to a stop.

"Ah, this is the place? You chose well. I'll settle your account while you pack your belongings. My footman will carry your things down when you're ready."

Jenny forced herself to climb the stairs slowly. Her mind whispered "Don't run, don't run" at every step. Never had she been so grateful for her mother's insistence on the decorum befitting a lady. When she was finally able to close the door of her chamber behind herself and Sukey, however, she was breathing as if she had been running all the way.

"We've got to find Sir Richard, warn him." Jenny didn't want to admit, even to herself, that she desperately wanted Richard's counsel. She didn't trust him at all, but she thought the man who had been Lord Danger might know how to handle this situation, if anyone could.

"If he was in the tap," Sukey said, "he'd have heard us come in."

"He's probably waiting in the private parlor." Unwillingly, Jenny fetched her portmanteaux. "Best help me to put these things away first before you go looking for him. I don't want Yves to realize how badly we want to see Richard."

"How will he know if I go a-looking fer Dick?"

"Oh, Sukey, do you still have to ask? Look outside the door."

Sukey opened the door silently and took a quick peek. "Ye're right. He's got his footman downstairs keeping an eye on us. So what do we do?"

"We do what he says. We've got to. As long as I'm recognized as Lord Vickers' heiress, we're fine. That sets Nate free. And Nate, I hope, can set us free. We're still all right. We have won."

"Then why are we scared to death, tell me that?"

"Guilty consciences."

"My conscience never bothered me none before. I don't see why it should start now," Sukey muttered, but she continued to help Jenny put away her few modest gowns and cosmetics.

They dawdled over their task and listened for some sound in the hall that would announce the presence of Sir Richard, but to no avail. Finally, Yves himself came up and knocked on the door to see if they were ready, and they were forced to say they were.

It was only when Jenny had given up hope, when she was meekly following the footman down the stairs, that Sir Richard at last appeared. He came in the inn's front door as if he had just returned from the day's business, but Jenny could tell from the alertness of his stance and the sharpness of his gaze that he had been forewarned.

"Good day to you, Miss Beauchamp." He allowed himself a gently quizzical look as he stepped aside and bowed gracefully. "I see you are leaving us. Have you been fortunate in your quest then?"

"Well, in a way, I suppose I have, although not—"

Yves had been waiting by the coach, but immediately he was at her side again. Even before he spoke, Jenny could sense him behind her, towering over her. Suddenly the room seemed smaller.

"Miss Beauchamp, will you introduce us?"

Jenny held her breath. They had stood together this close before. Sir Richard looked a good deal different from the highwayman Yves had met in Newgate, but upon occasion he sounded very like him. The way he lounged against the bannister was familiar too.

Yves was regarding him closely, but Jenny did not know yet if such behavior was significant. He seemed to observe everything so carefully.

"Lord Yves, this is Sir Richard Dangerfield, late of His Majesty's Sixth Dragoons. Sir Richard was so kind as to look after me during the voyage from the colonies."

"Glad to be of service, miss. How do you do, Lord Yves. And you would be Miss Beauchamp's cousin then? I am so glad she was able to find you so easily. Funny, I thought the name was something different."

Yves responded with a bow of equal grace, but minus the flourishes.

"I have the honor to be only a friend of the family and Miss Beauchamp's trustee. You may rest easy, however, in knowing that Miss Beauchamp has found the refuge she sought."

"Well, I am glad to hear that. These solicitor fellows can give one such a hard time."

Yves returned Sir Richard's understanding smile. "Indeed."

"Sir Richard has been trying to settle his late uncle's affairs," Jenny interposed hurriedly.

"Ah? In that case, if you mean to make some stay in town, I hope you will visit us in Hanover Square so that I may better express my gratitude for your care of Miss Beauchamp."

"Thank you, my lord. I will certainly avail myself of your generous invitation." Another gracious bow and he was gone.

Feeling as if she had been abandoned, Jenny allowed herself to be escorted to the coach. How ironic—to think she could miss Richard. But he'd be back, Jenny remembered. There was a guarantee of sorts in that promise. Yves knew that Sir Richard would come to see if she was well and happy.

Jenny risked another glance at her host and found that his eyes, bright and inscrutable, were still fixed on her. As she turned her face back to the window, she was uncomfortably aware of a pink flush rising up her throat.

What could he be thinking when he looked at her like that? His face was impossible to read. Did he see an enemy? An obstacle? Or was it possible he saw her simply as a woman, provincial and perhaps shy, but still a woman? Might it even be possible that he might like what he saw?

What was she thinking? *Foolish girl, put your mind to untangling the reasons behind his abrupt change of behavior,* she told herself. It hadn't taken much intelligence to realize that the solicitor's hesitant attitude earlier today stemmed directly from Yves' intransigence. They had expected him to resist the claim; in the end the solicitor would have overruled him. Now he had made that step unnecessary.

Why? He had everything to lose by accepting her claim. Nate would now be freed and would take up at long last his title and estates. Yves should have done—indeed, previously had done—anything to prevent that.

Of course, perhaps he had realized that in the long run he was doomed to failure. At least this way he would continue to have control over part of the Vickers fortune.

And that was a strange thing. You'd think from the way Yves talked that a considerable fortune was involved. Well, considering the size of the Vickers estate and financial holdings, perhaps it could be. Jenny was troubled by the very thought. No, this was not what she had expected at all.

She pulled herself together as the coach slowed to a stop in front of their destination. What she expected no longer mattered. This is what she had to deal with; there was no longer any choice.

Yves' house on Hanover Square was handsome, in a suitably Germanic style, and looked to be about fifty years old. Inside, from the little she was able to see from the hall, the furnishings mixed modern and old with little regard to fashion. It was more austere than she had expected—those expectations again. If greed was part of his motive in holding on to the Vickers' estate, however, it was not revealed in the way he lived.

Sukey was clearly impressed, though. Probably all she had ever known of plenty was Danger's cell in Newgate. In a strange way, it was comforting to Jenny to return to the world to which she was born; now she would not have to depend on others to lead the way.

Perhaps not such a comforting thought after all to know that she could no longer depend on anyone but herself.

There was a sense of flurried activity above-stairs as servants hurried to prepare for their visit. From out of the confusion came a short, matronly woman, dressed in an outmoded sacque gown, who descended the stairs in a spate of unintelligible complaint.

Yves made no attempt to stem the flow of words which poured meaninglessly over Jenny and Sukey. The speech might have continued for a considerable time, since neither breath nor response seemed needed as far as Jenny could see, had not the speaker finally caught sight of Jenny. At once she stopped and reverted to English.

"So. You the girl are?"

Jenny was pleased to see that she was not the only person to find her expectations confounded. Before she could respond, Yves placed a restraining arm on the foreign woman's arm and began speaking in a voice full of warning.

"My aunt's English is sometimes faulty. I fear that living here with me has robbed her of many chances to practice. Tante, this is the young lady of whom I spoke, Miss Jean-Marie Beauchamp. Miss Beauchamp, this is my aunt, Mrs. Mueller."

The aunt looked up at Lord Yves for guidance. She was evidently as surprised by his attitude as Jenny was.

"Miss Beauchamp, welcome. As my nephew says, my English not so good is. Happy you will be here with us, I hope. Let me to your room show the way. After such a day, rest you will need."

Jenny agreed meekly enough. She wanted privacy as much as Mrs. Mueller clearly wanted her out of the way. She needed to hide herself from Yves' probing stare for a while.

At the top of the stairs, Jenny turned and looked. He hadn't moved. His eyes were still on her. After a tense moment of silence, it was Jenny who turned away to find Mrs. Mueller watching the interchange with extraordinary interest.

She and Sukey followed Yves' aunt along the corridor to a spacious set of rooms furnished in a handsome, if masculine, style. A few servants were putting the finishing touches on the rooms. Vases of fresh flowers had been put in the bedroom and sitting room. A kind thought, Jenny noted, and looked at her hostess with more interest.

"I'm sorry that you have been put to such trouble, Mrs. Mueller. This is very hard on you, I am sure, to have to take in a virtual stranger—and on such short notice too."

"Ach, for Wolfram nothing too much trouble is. For years now he tells me of the Beauchamps, of Lord Vickers, and of Lord Quarles, who to Wolf like brother is. Stranger you are not then."

"You are most kind." And Jenny believed she

was. This funny little lady might be utterly mis-guided, but not cruel.

"Ah, phooo. Rest now." There was almost a look of pity in the woman's eyes, as if she knew what it was like to have Wolf rearrange one's entire life in five minutes. Possibly she did. She waited at the door for a moment, silently considering her guest. "Good you will be for this house, I think," she said to Jenny's surprise, and then she left.

"Well," Jenny said, sitting on the edge of the chaise longue. "Well. This is a pretty kettle of fish."

"Ain't it though? Lor, Jenny, this place gives me the shivers."

"Because of Mrs. Mueller?"

"Naaaooww. Because of them servants. Did you see the way that butler feller at the door looked? Lor, oh lor, what am I going to do below-stairs? You can fool the gentry easy, but you can't fool the servants."

"You'll be fine, Sukey. I tell you what you should do—confess to the housekeeper, and to Mrs. Mueller's lady's maid, that you're new to service in a decent house. Don't try to gammon them, ask them how to go on. They'll be flattered, and they won't be as suspicious as they might if you tried to convince them you knew more than you do." Jenny smiled. "They'll learn soon enough that I'm not used to service like this. We didn't have much use for lady's maids on the farm. Even in Boston, people don't live in this style, not even the Royal Governor."

"You're scared too."

"I'm terrified. Sukey, he's talking about pre-senting me to society. I could barely endure what little I saw of Boston society—what in heaven's name will I do here?"

Sukey wasn't fooled. "That's not what you're afraid of."

"No. You can see it now, can't you? He's up to something. And I don't know what it is."

"But we've won, haven't we?"

"Oh, yes, we've won." Jenny smiled bravely, but she didn't think Sukey was fooled by that either.

Lord Yves certainly did not give the appearance of having been beaten as he sat at his desk in the library calmly sanding dry the ink of the letter he had just finished writing.

He smiled. More work for his eyes and ears. But now the way was becoming clearer. And Nate himself would provide the means by which he might at last be destroyed. Perfect.

As for the girl . . .

"Wolfram. Wolfram." His aunt demanded attention by pulling on his queue. "Wolfram, I want to know what you are doing."

"Doing?" He quietly covered the letter with a clean sheet of paper. "I am writing to Lady Pertwee to request her help in introducing our Miss Beauchamp into society." He responded in the language he knew to be most comfortable for his aunt. "You mustn't worry that I mean to impose on your good nature so far. Although I sincerely hope you will accompany Miss Beauchamp as often as possible. It will do you good to get out, meet more people."

She nodded, but with a disbelieving look on her face. "Practice my English. I know. But not here,

116

not now when we might be overheard, *nicht wahr?*"

"Well . . ."

"Ah, I know you. But, Wolfram, this time . . . this time I think you are wrong. That girl upstairs . . . she is not what you said she would be."

"No, she is not." Yves paused a moment, remembering that stunned moment when he had first seen her. "She . . . I confess she was quite a surprise. Not at all what I expected."

"Well, then?"

"But neither is she who she says she is. I think, perhaps, that she does not know who she is."

"Now you talk in riddles."

"I'm sorry."

"What good is being sorry if you do not mean to explain? Ah, I thought not."

"I can't explain. First, because I do not have all the answers—yet."

"*Gott in himmel.* Lord Yves admits he does not know everything. Is such a thing possible?"

Lord Yves ignored the sarcasm. "And most of all because you could never keep a secret."

"I don't like secrets. And I don't like you when you get this way. Don't look at me like that. You know what way."

"Yes, I know. It has to be done, Tante."

"Maybe so. But that girl upstairs now will not be hurt by what you must do. I will not permit it. Remember that. I will play your games only as long as she is safe from harm."

"She is probably safer here than anyplace else. I promise you, she will come to no harm at my hands. And I don't ask you to play any games at all. As far as you are concerned, you need only act

117

as hostess to the daughter of my old friend. I hope, for your sake, that you will involve yourself in her come-out, but I do not ask it of you."

"Oh, you're a sly one. When you get like this you're impossible—just like that wily old diplomat, your father. As if I dared leave her to your machinations."

"As you please, Tante."

"You mean as *you* please. Oh, very well."

"You will help?"

"Yes, I will help. Don't I always, in the end? And I think this time you may need me. There may be more surprises ahead than even you are prepared for," she said, pointing upstairs.

Yves looked up for a moment, as if he could see beyond the wood and plaster straight to the heart of the visitor. He shook his head and returned to his correspondence. His voice was too low to reach his aunt who was already pulling the door shut behind her.

"Yes, I had already realized that."

Jenny dearly longed to avoid dinner, to send a message saying she was too tired or ill and would prefer a light supper in her room. That this was sheer cowardice she recognized. That it would also be rude to treat her hostess in such a manner proved the deciding factor. She left her room and followed a footman to the dining room.

Mrs. Mueller was waiting for her, and for Yves. The woman's eyes lit up as her nephew joined them.

"Already I see how good for us you are, Miss Beauchamp. Wolfram you force to join us. Always he is so busy. Too little is he home."

How much of his present behavior was out of the ordinary? Jenny wondered. He looked particularly fine tonight in a dark gray brocaded satin with Mechlin lace at his throat and wrists, yet Jenny was reminded of the forest predator more than the court exquisite.

He bent over his aunt's hand. "You shame me, Tante. You are quite right, too. I have not been sociable enough. But I mean to reform. You shall see much more of me in the future, I promise you."

To Jenny it sounded like a threat. She marveled that Mrs. Mueller could gaze so fondly at Yves.

They sat down to dine, but Jenny never noticed what was served. It was all she could do to force down a few bites. She knew Yves noticed it at once, but strangely he did not comment on her lack of appetite.

He had quite enough ammunition to fire at her already.

He began talking about the coming season. He apologized that he knew so little about what was necessary, but assured Miss Beauchamp that Mrs. Mueller and Lady Pertwee between them could provide all the guidance she might need. The presentation at court he rather thought he could arrange. There would have to be a ball, too, of course.

Jenny expected some respite when Mrs. Mueller rose to leave his lordship to enjoy his port. He would have none of it. He was determined to be sociable. Why should he sit in solitary splendor and deny himself the company of two charming ladies? No, he would join them in the drawing room as they took their tea.

Tea was accompanied by stories, and questions,

about Jenny's—Miss Beauchamp's—family. And all the time he talked he kept his eyes on her. Watching, waiting for her to slip up.

"Did you know about...? You must have been told about the time..."

Twice she corrected him on small details. Once he waited for her to fill in the end of a humorous anecdote about the old earl. Nate had taught her well, but sooner or later Yves would ask the question for which Nate had no answer.

The question came sooner than she thought.

"Did your father ever tell you how we met?"

Jenny's heart seemed to stop, but Yves didn't even wait for the answer she could not provide.

"No, of course not. He was far too modest. And he would never wish to embarrass me. I will tell you then."

He leaned forward to explain. This story was different from the others, Jenny realized. This was no test, but a message.

"When I could get away from my tutors I used to run over to Vickers. Just to watch. I'd watch the coaches and the people coming to visit. There always seemed to be some activity at Vickers. No one ever came to the manor where I lived."

His voice grew low and quiet as he became lost in the past. Jenny felt lost too. The lonely boy was not a Wolf she had been prepared for.

"I know, it sounds most obnoxious, a boy spying on his elders, but it wasn't really like that. And I paid for my spying after all. There was a *fête champêtre*, a picnic by the lake. I had been watching from a tree. One of the young ladies saw me and let out such a scream that she startled me. Down I fell, straight into the lake. It was deeper than I had imagined, and, of course, I could not swim."

He looked up at Jenny, and suddenly she realized what he was telling her.

"He saved your life."

"He did more than that. He saved me from humiliation. Face to face with those people, I realized how rude I had been. John pulled me by the neck of my shirt, and berated me all the way back to the house. But what he chastised me about was for leaving the party to climb trees when I had been warned not to try it. Not only that, but after I was dried off, he saw to it that my clothes were cleaned and then helped me sneak back. My tutor never knew."

"How kind—and how like Papa," she said. "And he was only . . . how old then?"

He had to stop and think a moment. "Seventeen. Ten years my senior."

Jenny shivered. Something was wrong about his story. The friendship he described seemed too warm, too sincere. Yet it could not be true, not of Nate's enemy. Could it?

"Are you cold? I suppose the climate was much warmer in the colonies?"

"Not where we lived, in the northwest of the New York colony. Winters were very harsh." Jenny tensed. So, the questions had returned.

"You must tell me all about your life there. I want to know about your father, what your life was like."

"And so she shall," Mrs. Mueller interrupted. "But not tonight. Can you not see the girl is tired?"

Frightened would have been a more apt description, Jenny thought, but she was grateful for the older woman's kindness.

"Yes, of course. My apologies, Miss Beauchamp. I must learn not to hurry so. We have all the time in the world to learn about each other. Don't we?"

"Yes. Yes, of course. Good night, my lord."

"Good night, Miss Beauchamp."

As before, Jenny followed her hostess up the stairs and turned to see Yves still standing below, watching her.

Sukey was waiting for her in the room that was to be hers. The room that was to be her new prison.

She tried to keep the anxiety from her face and voice, but Sukey's solicitous behavior made her fear that she was less than successful. It wasn't right that Sukey should worry about her. She had enough to think about without troubling herself about Jenny's ability to carry off the deception.

"How did it go below-stairs, Sukey?"

"You was right, Jen. As soon as I asked fer help, they all stopped staring down their noses at me, even that high-stickler of a butler."

"I'm glad."

"But you, Jen, how did you do?"

"I don't know. I think I said all the right things. But the way he looks at me, Sukey . . . He doesn't believe me. He can't. It's as if he's just waiting for me to make a mistake. He's said he wants to hear all about my life in the colonies."

"Most of that's fer true."

"Yes, I suppose so. But how long can I continue? How long are we to be kept here?"

There was no answer. What answer could there be?

"I'm sorry, Sukey," she apologized. It wasn't fair to inflict her worries on her friend. "I'll try not to be so foolish. It's just that ever since we entered this house, I've had the terrible feeling that I've missed something. Something important. It's as if reality had become skewed. Nothing appears quite as it should."

"I don't understand."

"How can I explain? Well, take Mrs. Mueller for one. She's nice, Sukey. She doesn't belong here."

"Because of what his lordship done? You're wrong there, love. I seen it too many times. Even the worst brutes on this earth got somebody who loves 'em."

"Perhaps. But then there's Yves. He confuses me so. When he looks at me, I feel . . . I don't know what I feel. Tonight he told me the story of how he met my father. I mean, Lord Quarles. You know."

Sukey laughed. "Aye, I know."

"When he talked about him, there was such affection in his voice. As a man might speak of a dearly beloved brother."

"The same way that Nate talked about him."

"Yes."

"Then that's where he picked it up. I didn't believe you when you first started on about this gent, but I'm beginning to now. You should hear the way they talk about him below-stairs. So you just think twice about anything he tells you. 'Cause whether he believes in you or not, 'tis you stands in the way of his plans fer Nate."

After Sukey left, Jenny lay sleepless for a long time. How long would she be trapped here? How long could she stand fast against Yves' probing eyes and questions?

It was a pretty place, this prison. There would be fine clothes, too, and tasty food in plenty. There would be entertainments to amuse her, and young men to court her. All this had Yves promised. And every promise felt like an extra weight added to her chains.

The sound of music interrupted Jenny's unhappy musings. It was Bach, she recognized, beautifully played. She hadn't noticed a harpsichord in the drawing room before. Strange, she had thought Mrs. Mueller ready to retire, but the older woman must have changed her mind.

Sukey was wrong. There was something odd about this place. If she could only find the key ... if she would only have enough time before her mask was pulled off.

Chapter Six

Any faint hope Jenny nourished of delaying Lord Yves' plans for her until she might at least take counsel of Nate was immediately banished the next morning with Lady Pertwee's arrival.

"Since my husband's death," she confessed to Lord Yves, "I have—just for company's sake, you understand—undertaken to help the occasional young lady face the dangers of society. It keeps me from becoming too lonely, gives me an extra interest in life."

The face that smiled at them from behind a painted fan hardly looked on the brink of a decline. The widow was probably no older than Yves. Careful use of maquillage and tight lacing would make her appear even younger in the kinder glow of candlelight.

"I quite understand," Yves agreed smoothly.

"But I am most careful about those whom I choose to sponsor. I would, of course, wish to help a family connection." Lady Pertwee gave an unencouraging shrug. "However, my own reputation is also at stake, you see."

"Naturally," Yves agreed with a smile. "Miss Beauchamp's birth, of course, is beyond question. The Beauchamp family can be traced back to the Conqueror."

"Birth is only one consideration, however, my lord, albeit an important one. Birth alone will not guarantee a successful entrance into society. Something more is needed."

Jenny forced herself not to grimace. Whatever that something might be, she was sure to lack it. Perhaps at least she might be saved from this authoritative woman, who clearly was not willing to risk her reputation as a match-maker, no matter what the encouragement.

"Stand up, my dear," Lady Pertwee commanded. "Let me see you walk."

Jenny walked, uncomfortable and self-conscious, around the drawing room.

"Hmmmm. Not too bad. Thank heavens she doesn't look too healthy. 'Pon rep, some of these colonials seem to carry the stench of the farm with them. No, don't stop. Keep moving, girl. Yes, quite a nice figure. But her stride is far too long. You're in a drawing room, girl, not in the fields. Oh very well, stop. Yes, let me see a curtsey."

With Lord Yves' eyes on her, Jenny did not dare respond as she wished. She curtseyed as her mother, a high stickler for the proprieties, had taught her.

"Very nice, child. Well, I don't know, I'm sure.

She'd need a good dresser, of course."

Do without Sukey? "Oh, no! I couldn't—" Jenny cut herself off swiftly. Too much emphasis would seem suspicious, she reminded herself. "I mean, I would be too intimidated by a fashionable London maid. And the girl who is with me is exceedingly clever with her fingers. And very willing to learn."

Jenny hardly dared to look to see how Yves reacted to this. Had she revealed too much?

Lady Pertwee considered the matter for a moment. "Well, I confess it is a dismal situation to feel oneself beholden to one's servants. Perhaps it might answer." Once again her voice held little reassurance. "Did she dress your hair for you, dear?"

"Yes, my lady, she did."

"Charming. Yes, yes, very promising. Of course, it needs a good cut. M. François is the man to see for that. But properly dressed to a good height, powdered and ornamented, it . . ."

"No."

"I beg your pardon, my lord?"

"No powder. And no maquillage."

"No powder? But, my lord, powder is *de rigueur*. You cannot expect the girl to make a good appearance without—"

"No powder and no maquillage."

Jenny held her breath for a moment. Surely now Lady Pertwee would stalk majestically from the room. She certainly did not appear the kind of woman to accept such treatment without complaint.

Lady Pertwee gave Yves a calculating stare. Suddenly she smiled and relaxed. "It might make a stir. In sooth, the girl would need some extra panache simply in order to survive. She hasn't the beauty to compare to Miss Maria Hervey, nor the wit of Miss Martindale. Although wit is a highly dangerous quality. It is taken amiss as often as it is praised. And to claim it when one has it not is disastrous. Well, well, I don't say it might not be done, with the right introductions."

"Miss Beauchamp's presentation at court has already been arranged," Yves announced in a careless fashion. "I am aware, however, that Society no longer revolves about the court as much as once it did. That is why we look to you for assistance, Lady Pertwee."

Already arranged? Jenny had only arrived the day before. It must be so, if he said it, but how could he have done so much in so little time? Distracted by his claim, Jenny had failed to attend to Lady Pertwee's response.

"...still gives a lady a certain cachet. In itself, it is no longer a guarantee of social success, but one can hardly be considered part of the first circle of Society without it. The correct behavior, knowing how to handle all social occasions, what our French cousins call *savoir faire*, such small details as the use of the fan, matters of dress, these things cannot be underestimated. The matter of dress is especially important. It goes without saying that Miss Beauchamp, newly come from the colonies—" she said the word as if she were referring to a particularly noisome swamp "—will need an entirely new wardrobe. Silks, brocades, laces. Not to mention the small finishing touches—gloves, fans, feathers... These things can add up to quite a large sum." Lady Pertwee raised an eyebrow and looked at his lordship expectantly.

At last. Jenny breathed a sigh of relief as Lady Pertwee finally reached the crux of the matter. Surely now she would be set free of this charade. The competence Nate had led her to expect would never cover the kind of display Lady Pertwee considered necessary.

"Cost is no concern, my lady, only quality. Perhaps I ought to mention that Miss Beauchamp will come into a tidy fortune, left her by the late Lord Vickers, when she attains her majority." He mentioned a sum that left both ladies nonplussed.

Lady Pertwee recovered first. "Well. Well, then no more needs to be said. Miss Beauchamp is sure to outdo the success of the Gunning sisters. I would be most pleased to help her find her way through the London season."

Jenny heard nothing of the following negotiations. Only when her new sponsor had gone did she recall herself. Nonetheless, the first words that issued from her lips came without thought or will.

"But I don't wish to be an heiress!"

Lord Yves turned away from the door and walked to her. He put one hand on her shoulder and held her chin up with the other.

Staring up into those shrewd eyes, Jenny felt lost. She had called upon herself more attention than she wished, more, perhaps, than was wise. It seemed such a long time that he stared at her. And then he smiled.

The smile gave her a shock, for it was the real thing, warm and full of humor. His lips and eyes curved so that she realized for the first time how grim—no, how sad—his face usually looked in repose.

"I verily believe you do not," he said softly. "You are wise. I am glad to see that you recognize the awesome responsibility that wealth such as yours carries. And the dangers it brings. There are those who would do almost anything to win such a fortune as yours. Many will present schemes to cozen you out of only a portion of it. But remember, you have me to help you watch over your wealth now. And soon, perhaps, you will have a husband to help you."

"I don't want a husband," Jenny protested, as Yves' hands released her. "I mean, I had not thought of marrying so soon."

"So soon? You are nearly twenty, my dear. It's more than time to be thinking of marriage. Please, do not look so worried. You are far from being an ape-leader. As you say, there is time to wait. Certainly I will never push a distasteful match upon you."

No, not a distasteful one, but perhaps one that was in all ways suitable—except for the fact that she was not who she claimed to be and had no right to the fortune that undoubtedly would be the real lure. What else was the season for if not to find husbands for unmarried young ladies?

How ironic! At twenty-five, Jenny was closer to becoming an ape-leader than was comforting to think upon. A husband, one who loved her for herself, had been the summit of her dreams at one time. Now she would have to use all her skill to avoid being saddled with one.

Yves was still watching her, with some amusement. He led her to a chair and then took a seat opposite her. Leaning forward, he took Jenny's hands in his.

"What is it that troubles you? The season? It should not. You are not a fool, I think, and will know how to judge what is merely fashionable foolishness and what is not."

Jenny stared at their clasped hands in embarrassment. His were good strong hands, not the pale limp features of the fop. Hands that wielded a sword with some dexterity, she reminded herself. In this comforting attitude, Yves did not appear to be a man who would try to destroy his childhood friend. But he had, he had.

"What then?" he asked. "Does the fortune worry you so?"

"It is just that I don't understand how my great-grandfather came to leave me such a great sum. It is hard to imagine that the whole of the family fortune could be greater than this."

A certain wariness entered his voice. "In good sooth, the late earl's entire estate was not so much more. Your family, I fear, had a long history of filial disagreement. Hence the surprisingly small portion of the entail."

"Do you mean . . . ? My lord, what is my cousin's inheritance?"

His hands dropped hers. The room seemed to grow suddenly cold as he sat back in the chair. Both eyes and voice were changed in an instant. "Your cousin is no concern of yours."

Jenny forced herself to remain calm and to face the anger she could see growing in Yves' tense body. "I beg to differ, my lord. My cousin is the only living member of my family, and hence very important to me. He was brought up by my great-grandfather and spent his life by the earl's side, which is more than I can say. He was also my father's very dear friend. I think I have a right to know how he has fared in my great-grandfather's will. What has my cousin inherited?"

Lord Yves rose abruptly and walked away. "What has your cousin inherited? Far more than he deserves, I assure you. He gains an estate of unparalleled beauty and richness and a title to which he will do no honor. Rest you content, Miss Beauchamp, as long as your cousin moderates his proclivities for vice and debauchery and restrains himself from ruining Vickers with his ill-management, the estate will keep him in comfort, if not in splendor."

"But that's not fair."

"It is what your great-grandfather wished. No doubt he had his reasons."

"No doubt he had, but who can say now whether they were valid or just?"

He whirled round with such speed, such palpable anger, that for a moment Jenny was afraid.

"I would have thought that your father would have taught you better what kind of man the late earl was."

"My father taught me, sir, that no man is perfect. Surely you must see, my lord, that if my cousin is entitled to the honors and titles of the earldom, he ought to be able to expect sufficient funds to support these honors as well. I want to give the money back, all but what I am entitled to by courtesy as a member of the family."

"You have received the fortune to which you are entitled. If you are so foolish, when you come of age, to throw away your heritage upon a worthless rake, then I will not be able to stop you. But as long as I am your trustee, not one guinea of your funds will find its way into your cousin's pockets. I hope I make myself clear."

Although frightened, Jenny met his gaze evenly. "Perfectly clear."

Yves paused a moment by the door. "You would do well to forget that you ever had a cousin."

Too many confusing thoughts were left to plague Jenny in the following days. Far from forgetting Nate, Jenny worried about him even more. Surely he could not have been aware of the terms of the late earl's will before. Could he?

Where was he? She needed to see him, to talk to him. Jenny knew he was free—his accession to the title had been reported in the society journals favored by Lady Pertwee. He had been seen at the opera, at the coffeehouses, and at a score of balls and parties. He had not been seen in Hanover Square.

That, perhaps, was to be expected, Jenny reminded herself, considering Lord Yves' attitude.

Why this attitude should trouble her was a worry in itself. Jenny knew Yves to be Nate's enemy; she suspected that Yves knew her to be an enemy to his plans as well. Yet she found herself haunted by the memory of his face when he spoke of her "father," the sudden brightness of one unexpected smile. Late at night, as she lay in bed listening to the comforting muted strains of Bach being played on the harpsichord downstairs, Jenny pondered those moments again and again. She had felt the warmth of his favor for little more than a moment, yet she was uncomfortably aware now of his displeasure—and her own surprising longing to recapture that feeling of warmth.

It was almost a relief to Jenny to find that she had no time to trouble herself over her various difficulties. From the moment that Lady Pertwee had agreed to be her sponsor, Jenny's time ceased to be her own. It seemed there was not a single moment of the day that she was not being pushed, pulled, turned about, prodded, and tutored, just as she had been in Newgate.

Her wardrobe was the first concern. Lady Pertwee would not allow Jenny to be seen until she was properly dressed. When Jenny thought she could bear no more of looking at fabrics, being measured and stuck with pins, she was allowed to attend to her lessons as a change. All traces of colonialisms must be eradicated. Lady Pertwee was pleased to approve of her accent, as Danger had once done before, but found that her conversation would often revert to subjects that were utterly unsuitable.

"My dear," her ladyship said with fading patience, "you cannot speak of farms in polite society."

"But you asked me about my home," Jenny responded. "My home was a farm, and primitive by English standards. Things are very different there." She looked to Mrs. Mueller, who tatted as she listened, for support, but in vain. The elderly woman hardly dared speak before the fashionable widow.

"Obviously. But you will refrain, just the same, from referring to your home as a farm. Try, if you can, to refrain from speaking of it at all. When someone says 'How do you do?' to you, you answer 'Very well,' whether you are feeling well or not. When someone makes a polite inquiry into your life in the colonies, answer as briefly as possible and change the subject. And do not, under any circumstances, discuss politics, especially colonial politics, with anyone. A girl your age should not pretend to knowledge far beyond the scope of her faculties."

"It would be more to the point, Lady Pertwee, to remind Miss Beauchamp that it is rude to discuss matters that are far beyond the scope of her audience," said Lord Yves.

Jenny turned in surprise at his entrance into the room. She never knew when he would appear, nor how he would appear. His behavior had continued strange since that moment when he had turned cold at the mention of Nate. Yet there were moments like this when he would show a rare sensitivity.

"You will encourage the girl, my lord," Lady Pertwee chided him. But she smirked a little, Jenny noticed. She was, after all, not so very old, although some years a widow.

If Yves saw Lady Pertwee's preening, he ignored it. He leaned over to salute his aunt.

"Good morning, Tante. Ladies, how go your lessons?"

"I fear I make a poor student, my lord," Jenny answered. "I do not mind my tongue well enough."

"Do you not? I am glad to hear it." He watched her keenly. "I would not have you so insincere as to monitor your every word, and to speak only what is pleasing to the hearer."

For a moment Jenny held her breath. When he

looked at her, and spoke to her in such a fashion she was sure he knew. And then ...

Jenny's sponsor did not look best pleased by this speech, but Yves seemed to know the way to mollify her. "On the other hand, one must not be so vain as to think one's every passing thought of interest to others. Fit your conversation to your company, is what Lady Pertwee means to emphasize. Am I not right, my lady?"

"Indeed, my lord, I could not have put it better."

"To those that wish, to those that demand honesty, I hope you will give it."

"But how will I know, my lord, when honesty is called for?" Jenny asked him.

"You will know ... when you must have learned to recognize the false and true in others, I suppose. Well, I must not interrupt your lessons further. Give you good day, ladies."

The lessons never seemed to end. Jenny had thought herself well schooled; now she learned better. Her mother, unable to face the realities of frontier life, had brought up, or had tried to bring up, her only daughter as if she were destined for life at court. Much had changed since Mrs. Wilde had been taught the ways of fashionable society, however. Simply learning to move in the wider hoops of court and formal dress was an athletic feat demanding an incredible sense of judgment and balance.

Jenny practiced getting in and out of a sedan chair and a coach. She negotiated the perils of a drawing room dotted with incidental tables and knickknacks for hours on end. When she had finally acquired sufficient grace to satisfy her sponsor's strict standards, she had to concede that the art of movement was no mean accomplishment.

"You will do very well, my dear," Lady Pertwee was finally pleased to concede. "If only you will remember not to move so quickly. A lady, and a gentleman too, must always move with a kind of studied dignity."

"Lord Yves does not move slowly," Jenny said, more to herself than to her sponsor.

"Lord Yves..." Lady Pertwee sighed. She looked toward Mrs. Mueller for a moment, but that lady's attention had been distracted by a message from the servants' hall. "My dear, you would do well to...to think twice about any counsel his lordship should give you. He means well, of course, but..." Lady Pertwee bit her lip a moment as she decided what and how much to say.

"His lordship is not like other men," she confessed to Jenny. "You will not be able to judge the rest of society by Lord Yves' behavior. He does not move, as is the rule, with that measured gait that is most admired. Although he is marvelous graceful in his movements," she conceded with a smirk. "Nor does he think or speak like most others. But what is acceptable in that most notable diplomat, the Baron of Yves, is not acceptable in a young girl entering society. Do you understand?"

"Yes, my lady." Jenny gave her deepest curtsey. "I understand perfectly."

The single advantage to the constant barrage of tutelage, Jenny realized, was that in her concern over her debut she had very little time to worry about the implications of her continued impersonation. Even Sukey was caught up in the preparations, taking care of the new wardrobe and learning how to survive in the servants' hall.

The date for Miss Beauchamp's presentation at court was approaching rapidly, but it was the date of her first ball that worried Jenny. At the royal levee attention would be naturally centered on the young king. At her ball everyone would be watching her.

She had learned to walk; now she must learn to dance. Lady Pertwee was pleased to commend her natural affinity for the music; she memorized the most intricate steps with ease. Most of the dances, however, were for groups of four. Dancing with a single partner might prove poor preparation for the quadrille.

Jenny had been disconcerted as well when Mrs. Mueller first sat at the harpsichord to play for her practice. The kindly chaperone played competently, but the charm and musicality that nightly so attracted Jenny was quite missing. It must be because, like Jenny, Mrs. Mueller was intimidated by the fashionable Lady Pertwee, whose lessons she attended with great diligence. In many ways this was her debut as well, Jenny realized. Like her, Mrs. Mueller appeared worried about the coming ball. When her nephew made another of his abrupt appearances, however, she immediately became more cheerful.

"Good day to you, ladies. Intent upon dissecting the mysteries of the quadrille, I see. But you look so glum. You should be gay and carefree in the dance."

Yves looked remarkably content, Jenny thought. That frightening tension, the mark of the predator, was gone from his posture.

His calmness seemed contagious. Even Lady Pertwee grew less frazzled.

"We have been attempting a dance for four couples with only one, my lord. Simple arithmetic will tell you the result, I think."

"But there are four of us now," he reminded her. "We can at least form two couples. Tante, come away from the instrument. Give us the pleasure of your voice and your company. Come dance with us."

But it was to Jenny that Yves extended his hand to lead her into the first figure.

The touch of his hand was warm and comforting. Jenny had thought so once before, however, and Yves had turned cold to her within the space of a few moments. Where did she stand with him now?

There was nothing of anger or tension in his appearance this afternoon. Indeed he danced with every appearance of pleasure, not only in the music but in her company. Jenny had always thought him graceful, but she had never suspected he could be so fluid and relaxed in his movements. Somehow she had always suspected that he must find such pleasures as dancing immensely frivolous.

She blushed. He had caught her staring at him again.

"You must indulge in some polite conversation while you mind your steps, you know, my dear. Isn't that so, Lady Pertwee?" he asked as the turns of the figure bore him away from Jenny.

"Quite right, my lord. People will take you for a ninny if you remain speechless."

Returning, Yves took her hand again. "As a gentleman, I should, however, provide you with some opportunity. Permit me to tell you that you dance very prettily, Miss Beauchamp."

"Thank you, my lord." Jenny could feel the warm flush rising in her cheeks. Why did this man provoke her to blushes so easily? Determined to remain cool, she answered, "With so graceful a partner, I could hardly dance otherwise."

Her answer did indeed seem to disconcert Yves for a moment. When he returned to face her again, he spoke of the music that his aunt continued to hum in a reedy soprano.

"Tante tells me that you have an interest in the music of Mr. Handel."

"I enjoy most types of music, my lord. Mr. Handel's work is indeed one of my favorites."

"And who might be the others?"

"Mr. Bach, Mr. Haydn. And Mr. Scarlatti."

"And do you play?" He nodded toward the harpsichord.

"No, my lord."

"I suppose you did not have an instrument."

Lady Pertwee interrupted. "My lord, please, do not encourage the girl."

"Actually we did," Jenny contradicted. Her eyes lit up as she remembered. "It was Mother's most prized possession and she insisted keeping it by her, even though it was hardly ever played. She did wish me to learn, but I could never bear to be sitting down indoors when the sun was shining. Nor, to be honest, when it was not. I was not very restful as a child."

Yves laughed, and Jenny felt a momentary rush of pleasure to know that she had caused it before she realized what she had done. That harpsichord had belonged to her mother—the mother of Jenny Wilde. The story would pass; she had nothing to fear in that. What frightened her was that she had forgotten her role for a few moments. It had been Jenny Wilde enjoying the music and the dance, not Jean-Marie Beauchamp.

"If such sedentary pleasures are less distasteful to you now, perhaps you would like to take some tuition. We must certainly indulge your taste for music. There are a number of good concerts coming up. We might go to hear one of Mr. Handel's oratorios."

"Oh, Mr. Handel's music is quite out of fashion now," Lady Pertwee protested. "Now if that young boy were to give another concert ... What was the name of that prodigious youth everyone was talking about? He gave a few concerts with his sister. You know who I mean."

"Young Mozart. Yes, I am not usually impressed by child performers, but this boy is certainly out of the common way. There are no more concerts planned, as far as I know. But I am slightly acquainted with the family. I believe they remain in Chelsea some little time more." Yves considered a moment, watching Jenny. "We might go to see them."

Yet one more excursion, Jenny thought, pulling her deeper and deeper into the world she had neither right nor desire to live in, involving more and more people in her deception. Her enjoyment in the dance began to slip away.

Mrs. Mueller's gentle humming finally came to

a stop at the last figure's end.

"Poor Tante, it would have been kinder to leave you in peace at the keyboard. But you dance very elegantly, my love. As light on your feet as ever."

"Flatterer," Mrs. Mueller said. "The music to your head has gone."

"The music? Perhaps. Well, I must leave you to your diversions, ladies. Until later."

At the door he paused, as Jenny knew he would. He did not seem to be able to leave a room that she was in without delivering some parting shot to disturb her peace.

"Oh, I almost forgot, my dear. That gentleman who was so courteous to you during your voyage ..."

"Sir Richard?" Her voice showed only the most casual interest, although she felt as if she were balanced above an abyss.

"Yes, Sir Richard Dangerfield. He came to call when you were out. An interesting fellow, I thought. I've asked him to dine with us later in the week."

"Although what good seeing Richard will do me, I cannot tell," Jenny confessed to Sukey as the young girl helped her to dress for that dinner. "Private converse will be impossible."

"Lady Pertwee won't be there to see anything."

"No, but that may not be an advantage. One could at least depend on her trying to attach Lord Yves' interest. He is the one that notices everything."

"He does that," Sukey admitted. "He had the tweenie off to the tooth-drawers before anyone even realized she had the toothache."

The tying of the stays demanded some concentration. When that was finished, Sukey suggested, "Dick could maybe let you know how things're going without being secret about it. You'd think, wouldn't you, that everybody would be talking about Nate getting the title? You said as how it's in the papers."

"What I want to know is how I may be able to escape from this situation. I do not think he can speak openly of that. And I am afraid for him if he dares speak of Nate. The one time I mentioned him to Lord Yves . . ."

"Dick's smarter nor that. Don't you worry none."

Presumably Sir Richard was as intelligent as Sukey said, for the subject of the new Earl of Vickers was never brought up, at least not when the ladies were part of the conversation. Since the gentlemen appeared to be on the best of terms when they rejoined Jenny and Mrs. Mueller after taking their leisure over the port, Jenny assumed the subject had failed to arise then as well.

Her sense of ease departed, however, when she realized that the subject of conversation had turned to Sir Richard's identity and past.

"I hope your travails with the solicitors are in a way to be finished, Sir Richard," Yves said when they had settled before the fire with their tea.

"Very near, my lord. The solicitors are not entirely to blame, however. My uncle left the estate in very sad case."

"That would be the late Sir Everard Dangerfield?"

"Why, yes. Did you know him?"

"Not well. I met him at White's a number of times. He seemed a most sociable gentleman."

Sir Richard laughed. "Too sociable, I fear. I could have wished that he had been found at White's rather less often."

Jenny looked for signs of distress in Sir Richard but found none. Certainly he seemed more secure in his impersonation than ever she felt in hers. Unless . . . No, it was impossible. Ridiculous.

"I notice you do not seem overset by the difficulties you have inherited," Yves said.

"From my youth I had always known that as a younger son I must make my own way in the world. Some men look toward the East; I went to the Americas. I was quite fortunate in my speculations there. This complication does prove somewhat of a setback, but what can one do? Dangerfield Hall is, after all, part of my heritage."

"Well spoken, Sir Richard. The protection of one's heritage is a noble endeavor."

"I make no claims to nobility of character, my lord. One does what one must."

"Indeed one does."

Yves' face darkened for a moment. What did he feel compelled to do? Jenny wondered.

Sir Richard had not been able to secure any private conversation with Jenny that evening. Indeed, he was not fool enough to try. Jenny acknowledged that the attempt would have been folly, but remained annoyed with him for his failure to try. The single advantage gained during the evening was that Sir Richard had charmed his hostess into proffering an invitation to Jenny's ball, the approach of which became ever more terrifying to her. It seemed to Jenny that once she had been presented to the beau monde all possibility of escape would vanish. Once accepted by the fashionable world, her impersonation seemed doomed to continue, with no end in sight.

Nor did her impersonation become any easier with time. While kind attention was shown her by Mrs. Mueller, while every elegance of life was provided her out of the Vickers estate, Jenny could not comfort herself with thoughts of the righteousness of her actions. She could not feel it right to lie to the gentle German widow. As for Yves, he continued to confuse her. While he was present she could find no ease; yet, strangely, there was no peace when he was absent. The days when he had held himself apart from her in anger, over her desire to return her fortune to Nate, had been among the worst she had ever known.

Jenny's presentation at court served only to remind her of the dishonesty of her position. Although the introduction at the royal levee proceeded without incident, she could not forget that she had been presented to her sovereign with a name, and heritage, to which she had no right.

Now she would meet the world as Miss Beauchamp. The holland covers had been removed from the furniture in the ballroom. The austere house had been turned into a floral wonderland. Everything was ready for the great day. Except Jenny.

"Hurry up, Jen," urged Sukey. "That Lady Pertwee will be here any minute. You knows I can't work with her breathing down my neck. There, the stays are done. Let's get you into the hoop petticoat. I will say this, old Peawit knows how to pick clothes."

"Stop, Sukey, you'll make me laugh, and I can't when I'm laced so tight."

"There, now you look better. Can't have you looking so low at your first ball. Got to do me credit."

Jenny reached for the hand Sukey was using to settle the robe over the flounced petticoat. "Sukey, things are going well for you, aren't they? The other servants haven't caused you any trouble?"

"Naaoow. They's me chums now. I like what I'm doing and maybe there's more to take pride in by doing this job well than by stealing a watch fob without getting caught." Sukey looked a little embarrassed. "Truth to tell, I ain't so anxious to leave. Never had it so good afore."

The entrance of Mrs. Mueller prevented Jenny from responding to this strange confidence. Mrs. Mueller was very grand in a gown, garnished with gauze and ribbons, in a color called "prune de Monsieur." Under her arm she carried a small casket which she set on the dressing table.

"So beautiful you look, my dear. No, no, flattery I do not tell. But you need perhaps just a little extra touch, hmmm? Perhaps a little jewelry?" She opened the casket to reveal a hair clip of diamonds and sapphires and a small pair of sapphire earrings.

"Oh, madam, you should not have," Jenny said with great sincerity. She looked at the jewels with horror. What was she to do? She had no right to such an expensive gift; these baubles weren't meant for her. Yet how could she refuse them? Already Mrs. Mueller was watching her reaction with questioning, troubled eyes. "You already gave me my lovely fan. But oh, they are beautiful." Full of guilt, Jenny kissed her chaperone on the cheek, glad the older woman could not see her expression. "Thank you so much."

"No, no, do not thank me. Thanks to Wolfram you should give. He it is who picks these out."

"These are from Lord Yves? For me?"

"But of course. Did you think such an important day he would ignore?"

"No, of course not. I never expected anything so lovely." Nor that he would choose the gift himself. Jenny felt as if the jewels would burn her fingers, but she knew the older woman was watching and waiting. "Come, help me, Sukey. How shall I wear them?"

"I have an idea, miss. May I?"

"Of course. You know I trust your judgment."

Jenny sat nervously before the looking glass while Sukey finished dressing her hair. Where had Jenny Wilde gone? This fashionable young woman certainly was not she.

"Nice it will be to have people in this house. Too little entertaining has Wolfram done before. You are nervous, little one, but you should not be. So relaxed, so easy, the English are."

"Relaxed?" Jenny started to turn her head, but was prevented by Sukey's ministrations. "When I think of all the rules of behavior Lady Pertwee drummed into me!"

"But yes, much more comfortable it is here. Everywhere in Europe I have seen is more formal, more...regulated. To go back into society at home, in Hanover, I could not."

This intriguing statement could not be investigated now, however, for Lady Pertwee had finally made her appearance, elegant in embroidered rose silk.

"Ready? No, don't leave yet, girl," she said to Sukey. "Let me see first. Stand up, Miss Beauchamp. Turn."

Jenny's robe was white silk shot with gold threads. There were royal blue ribbons by the lace at her sleeves, on her petticoat and on her collarette. The diamond and sapphire clip now shone in the auburn hair piled high on her head. A vagrant curl curved around her neckline. In her hand she carried the hand-painted fan given her by Mrs. Mueller.

"Very nice. If only his lordship would permit a little rouge, or a single patch. Well," she sighed, "there's no use repining. Pinch your cheeks, dear. Remember what I have taught you . . ."

"No talking of farms or politics."

". . . and you will do well. I don't know but that I envy you. Oh, to be twenty again. Come, then, the guests will be arriving soon and his lordship is waiting for us."

He was indeed waiting at the foot of the stairs, standing where he had the day he had first brought Jenny to his home and watching her in much the same way. For the first time, though, Jenny was conscious of him not as an enemy or one who was too dangerously perceptive, but simply as a man.

And a very attractive one at that. The eyes that saw too much were beautiful, sometimes green, sometimes blue, sometimes gray. Tonight the blue velvet coat with gold embroidered edging made his eyes blaze with sapphire flames. The gold picked out the lights in his own golden hair. Yet he seemed supremely unconscious of his appearance. Despite his acquiescence to some of the dictates of fashion, he was no fop.

He bowed low over her outstretched hand and brushed his lips against her fingertips. "Miss Beauchamp, words fail me. You are exceedingly lovely tonight, my dear. Lady Pertwee, my thanks, and to you, my dear aunt. You have all worked hard to make this night the success I know it will be."

"Why, my lord, it was a pleasure," Lady Pertwee assured Yves in a manner Jenny found excessively gushing. The attractive widow had certainly taken note of his lordship's manifold attractions. Jenny did not like the way she placed her hand on his sleeve, however.

"You are too kind, my lady. But permit me at least to present each of you with a floral tribute along with my humble thanks." He handed them each a bouquet. As he presented the bunch of white roses and gentians to Jenny he confessed, "I can take no credit for these, however. These are from Sir Richard."

"How kind of him to remember. And how kind of you, my lord, to give me these lovely ornaments."

" 'Tis you who makes them lovely." It was a conventional response, but Yves made it sound particularly sincere. He was not, after all, given to conventional statements. "Ah," he continued, "I believe I hear the sound of our first guests. Miss Beauchamp, will you take my arm?"

"My lord." She rested her fingertips on his arm, conscious of the steel-like strength beneath the velvet. They followed the chaperone and sponsor toward the ballroom. At the door, Jenny hesitated.

"Courage," Yves whispered. "Remember, my dear, you're a Beauchamp."

Chapter Seven

Jenny hoped the shiver of fear that ran down her back would be attributed to nervousness at facing her first ball. It was times like this when she felt sure Wolf knew her for an impostor, knew it and meant to tease and torture her into confession. Was this to be merely another test? Was he hoping that somewhere in this crowd there would be someone who could unmask her, reveal her as a fraud? Reason might insist that he would hardly court such embarrassment here and now—in his own home, where she was sponsored under his aegis. When she looked into those cool, mysterious eyes of his, however, reason all too often fled.

Well, she might not be a Beauchamp but she was very much a Wilde, with all the pride and fortitude her grandfather and father had installed in her—and the stubbornness her mother had tried to eradicate. *Don't let them win,* had been Sukey's advice before, and the wisdom of it still held. She would not fail.

But oh, it was hard to walk into the ballroom and not remember the brief misery of trying to fit into Boston society. The glittering throng here, the splendid apartments, the sumptuous dinner—all these might be different from that other unhappy time. Yet Jenny felt no different. Then she had been lost among strangers, grieving for her loved ones. Alone still, she felt even more alien in these surroundings, with these people, and utterly exposed before their curious examination. Perchance that was the real reason for all the paint, patches, and the powdered wigs—they provided a mask to cover all one's insecurities.

The silks, satins, and brocades of the guests soon made the vista before her glitter and swirl with color. In such a room as this any further decoration other than the few floral additions would be deemed excessive. After the pleasant old-fashioned comfort of the family's living quarters, Jenny had been surprised to find hidden away this Palladian jewel of a ballroom. The rotunda's ceiling, with its *trompe l'oeil* painting of dancing nymphs, rose two stories over the ballroom floor. From where they stood she could see the guests enter on the gallery level, where the orchestra was gathered, and sweep down the long staircase to greet their hosts. Beneath the gallery, supported by Doric columns, classical figures kept guard over the dancers from small niches in the wall.

Jenny looked around at the figures, living and stone, and felt that every one was reminding her that she did not belong here. As she stood in the receiving line with her host and hostess and chaperone, Jenny stole a quick glance at Yves. Where had a small boy fit in such a house as this, one given over to the intrigues of the court and of society? How did one such as he—so different from the common herd—fit in now? Graciously extending his hand to an elderly duchess, he seemed collected as always, the gracious host, yet surely he must feel as out of place as she.

With wealth, power, and noble birth, however, such differences from the norm as they both personified could be forgotten, evidently, just as Lady Pertwee had said. The curious eyes Jenny could feel examining her in painful detail might be the same as they had been in Boston. They did not see Jenny, though, not the real Jenny—and not only because of her imposture. Tonight, they saw first a fortune. Oh, yes, Jenny realized, this time she would be accepted, courted, even feted; but she would be no happier. Foolish, in the present circumstances, but it did make her unhappy to think that no one here could possibly be interested in her.

Smiling nonetheless, she concentrated on remembering as many names as she could while trying to block her awareness of Lord Yves standing close by her side. Without even looking in his direction she could sense his glance upon her, pensive, measuring. Waiting for her to make a mistake? Or perhaps sympathizing with the simple colonial girl thrust so far from her element? With Yves she could never know for sure.

If there was a trap inherent in the guest list, she had not seen it. Most of the names were familiar to her now, thanks to Lady Pertwee's gossip and advice, so she was alert to the possibilities of being tested, but it seemed unlikely. Whatever might be likely to cause her to slip up, it would not be unfamiliarity with colonial life, nor knowledge of French.

She smiled pleasantly and curtseyed to the elderly gentleman next to be presented—the Earl of Chesterfield. Elderly he might be, but Jenny remarked on the elegant air with which he saluted her hand. The charmingly phrased compliment she expected from one of his reputation, however, failed to materialize. Instead, the man looked at her for quite thirty seconds as if he had been struck dumb.

"My dear . . . ," he spoke at last. "Forgive me, my dear Miss Beauchamp. For just a moment, I was returned to the days of my youth. I saw your lovely face, and was once again a lad of sixteen."

Jenny looked at him quizzically. The flirtatious expression she had expected was also missing. The earl was quite serious.

"You are very like your great-aunt, you know," he added to her surprise, then laughed. "I suppose everyone has told you so."

Like her great-aunt? Could his lordship possibly have known some of her mother's kin? But Grandfather had always said she strongly resembled his side of the family!

Despite the sudden hint of danger, she answered in a calm enough voice, "No, indeed, my lord."

"Ah, such are the penalties of old age," he continued, with a wag of his head. "No, I suppose there are few who remember her now, who remember her as she really was, not merely her sad end. She had a great heart, Lady Eugenia, not merely great beauty. I am grateful to you for reminding me of her, and of my green days."

Jenny hid her confusion in another curtsey, and watched Lord Chesterfield bow and move on. So he had meant Nate's great-aunt after all. True, both Nate and the funny old gentleman in the solicitor's office had seen a family resemblance in her. Given her coloring, that was perhaps not unusual. This, however, left her stunned. Old he might be, but Lord Chesterfield had suffered no diminution in the use of his faculties. If he said she looked like the Lady Eugenia, then no doubt she did. But what an odd coincidence that it should be another Eugenia!

Yves looked at her with a quizzical expression. Had she appeared a little too surprised? "Such an elegant gentleman," she commented, quickly recovering her aplomb. "And with such an air about him."

Although she had spoken to Yves, it was Lady Pertwee who responded. Fortunately, she seemed surprisingly unaware of the currents of tension between Jenny and her host.

"You would have to look far to find a man with more refined manners than Lord Chesterfield," Lady Pertwee conceded. "Or worse morals. I do beg you to be careful, my dear. Don't let his years deceive you. If he tries to pull you aside to talk to you about your aunt, you had better be well-chaperoned or you'll follow your aunt's path to destruction."

Poor Lady Eugenia, Jenny remembered, had let her warm heart lead her to ruin in the arms of a rogue who was more interested in her purse than in her person. Jenny spread open her painted fan and hid a smile. Perils enough were scattered on her path to lead her to destruction, but they would not be the lures of love.

Her smile quickly disappeared. No, plausible stories and a handsome face would not take her in. That kind of ruin required a kind of innocence, a lack of suspicion, that she had lost now, lost beyond hope of recapture.

"Thank you, my lady," she answered quietly. "I will remember your advice."

Her spirits rose a little when Richard came to present himself, flirting lightly with Lady Pertwee. Jenny had to remind herself severely that Danger had not changed, that he was still the same rogue who had robbed the rich and controlled a ruthless gang of thieves. Nonetheless, she was glad to see him. Perhaps he did feel some sympathy for her, as only one who had known the horrors of prison could know the pains of lost freedom. With him at least she could feel herself free. The everlasting guard could be dropped, if just for a moment. Despite herself, she smiled brightly in greeting and held out her hands.

"Sir Richard, I am pleased to see you here."

"And I to be here," he drawled. His look told Jenny that he was laughing at her. No wonder! To find her so reduced in spirits as to be eager for his company must tickle his sense of the outrageous. That pose was the one reminder of the flamboyant highwayman. Well, perhaps not the only reminder. While Richard was dressed plainly enough in bottle-green satin, without paint or patches, some touch of the peacock yet remained in his stance, his bow.

The look of admiration in his eyes, however, was direct enough, and disconcerting. Jenny's voice faltered a little as she spoke. "I have you to thank, I am told, sir, for this charming nosegay," she said, indicating the blooms pinned to her waist.

"Your pleasure is my thanks, Miss Beauchamp," he said, taking snuff with a graceful flourish of lace cuffs. "However, I am not so disinterested as to turn aside your gratitude, when I might use it to plead for a dance later in the evening."

It would be their only opportunity for anything approaching private converse, Jenny knew. She turned to look inquiringly, almost pleading, to Lady Pertwee for permission, but it was really Yves to whom her gaze was inevitably drawn.

Was it her imagination, or did he seem more alert, more attentive—not only to Richard but to her reaction? There was a pinched look about his mouth, just for a moment, that made her wonder if he entirely approved of Richard, despite his attitude of camaraderie. When Lady Pertwee indicated her approval, however, he made no move to intervene.

Soon after, they moved within, and it was time for the dancing to begin. Jenny listened to the opening strains with a strange mingling of relief and trepidation. At least the orchestra was good, she was pleased to note, and tried to will herself to lose her anxieties in the music, with some success. Her opening partner, the Duke of Queensbury, another elderly roué, whispered gallantries in her ear and helped her forget her nervousness and her consciousness of the watchful crowd.

Sir Richard, when the time finally came to claim his dance, teased her until she blushed and laughed. With his usual drawl, and a languid approving glance at her decolletage, he complimented her on the elegance of her toilet, then whispered that she had appeared to better advantage in the gowns he had chosen for her. Jenny was beginning to know him better now, though, enough not to take seriously his blatant attempts to shock. Even though she recognized his purpose, she let him distract her, only referring briefly to their private concerns as he led her back to her host and hostess.

"Ignoring our problems won't make them go away, Richard," she protested as they moved through the crowded dance floor, speaking in a voice so low it could barely be heard beyond the compass of her elegant fan. "After this ball I will still remain a prisoner of the one man who most wants to expose us—and who is most capable of doing so. He watches me all the time."

Richard lifted an eyebrow quizzically. "Tis only fair. So do you watch him."

"What?" Jenny looked up in surprise.

"He fascinates you," Sir Richard accused. "He has done, I verily believe, from the beginning."

"He terrifies me," she contradicted. In her heart, though, Jenny had to admit Richard was right. Wolf did fascinate her. He was a mystery, a man composed of paradoxes—equally ruthless and kind, cold and passionate.

As they approached, she could see him standing at the side of the room now, all courteous attention to his aunt and Lady Pertwee as he awaited their arrival. The chaperone was trying desperately to attract his full attention, smirking and tapping his shoulder with her fan, but with less than total success. Yves ignored her attempts as he ignored all the fopperies and fashions of the town, yet without rudeness or cruelty. Toward his aunt, his attitude was one of genuine devotion.

Yet this man who was so careful of his aunt's comfort had deliberately deprived an old friend of his name and inheritance, Jenny reminded herself. Somehow, she felt, there must be a reason, an answer, but for now it was hidden behind his shrewd, glittering eyes and enigmatic smile.

Oh, she was fascinated by him. This must stop, Jenny told herself. Instead of wasting time on useless conjecture as to Yves' motives, she ought to be considering how to escape his sphere of influence. At the very least, she ought to discover somehow what he truly knew or suspected of her, how he felt about her. A movement at her side provided a guilty reminder—she needed to know if he suspected Richard, too.

Yves and the ladies exchanged pleasantries with Sir Richard, who in turn flattered Mrs. Mueller on her performance on the dance floor. When Sir Richard went in search of some orgeat for his hostess, Lady Pertwee resumed her continuing effort at flirtation, an effort that Jenny was beginning to find annoying.

"My lord, I must compliment you," her ladyship simpered. "Your sense of fashion is far better than mine. I confess it now, I had my doubts, but there I see how your quaint notion of presenting Miss Beauchamp *sans poudre, sans maquillage,* has made her stand out from all the rest. Why, all the ladies of fashion will be setting aside their powder boxes tomorrow."

Yves shook his head, and smiled at Jenny, for once with no complex undertones beneath the surface. His expression made her catch her breath in surprise. "I do not look to see it. Few others would profit by such a change."

The subtlety of the compliment was unappreciated by Lady Pertwee, but she obviously had taken note of the warm glance. Her own glance toward Jenny was cool, dismissing. "And to secure the Duke of Queensbury to lead her out. Such a coup!" she continued in a slightly louder voice. "The duchess was cousin to Queen Anne, you know," she said to Jenny, clearly disdaining her as one who would know nothing of such matters. In a more practical tone, she added, "Although I must warn you, my dear, he's very little better than Lord Chesterfield, despite his mild manners."

Of all the things Jenny had to worry about, lecherous older men did not rank very high. Lady Pertwee would no doubt be very surprised at some of the stratagems Jenny had learned from her grandfather to protect herself from unwelcome advances. Her defenses relaxed by her dance with Richard and by the sincere warmth of Yves' compliment, she responded innocently, "Is he so? I quite liked him."

"I don't think you've anything to fear from old Q," Lord Yves said in a tone that was as pointed as it was humorous. "He is, at least, an honest rogue. He does not pretend to be other than what he is."

Before Jenny could respond, he was greeting Sir Richard again, who had returned with the promised orgeat. All her hard-won peace of mind fled on the instant. Although he said no more, but to gently tease his aunt on her beaux, Jenny remained alert.

"Tante, all this talk of elderly roués has me worried for you. I see I must guard you as carefully as Miss Beauchamp," he said.

"So foolish you are tonight, Wolfram," Mrs. Mueller chided him with a fond smile.

"Not foolish at all," Richard added, joining in with a roguish look in his eyes. "Don't think we haven't taken note of all your cavaliers. Miss Beauchamp will be jealous. And so shall I."

Jenny spared a moment to enjoy the older woman's blushing happiness. She agreed with Lord Yves when he added, "It gives me great pleasure to see you enjoy yourself, Tante. You have cut yourself away from the world for too long."

"The world from me did the cutting," Mrs. Mueller corrected him. Softly she added, "My choices I would not change, but I am glad to find new friends here in England."

"Speaking of friends..." Yves lifted his arm in greeting to another friend and gestured him over. "No, don't leave, Sir Richard. Let me introduce you to the one man who knows everything that goes on in London. Selwyn," he addressed the newcomer, "I do not believe you have had the opportunity to meet my ward, Miss Beauchamp. May I make known to you as well my aunt, Mrs. Mueller, and Sir Richard Dangerfield, recently come to town."

The newly arrived guest, a gentleman with

drooping eyelids and a humorous mouth, bowed indolently. "You may make known whom you choose, my dear Yves," he said, "only promise me they won't talk about the colonies. I've just left Burke holding forth *ad infinitum* on that very subject. That's the trouble with attending affairs given by you political fellows. One is so likely to run into people who talk about the most boring subjects, with never a thought about the truly important things in life."

"And what are those?" Jenny asked with an eye on her host. She caught herself at once, and colored up, embarrassed. By his cynical smile, Richard had noticed the covert glance as well. *See*? he seemed to be saying.

"People, of course," Selwyn answered. "And the remarkable things they do."

"In other words," Yves translated, "gossip."

"Precisely," Selwyn admitted genially. "What could be more fascinating?"

The man's reputation came back to Jenny now—a wit, one who made it his business to know everything about everybody. A danger?

Sir Richard faced him with his usual nonchalance—nay, more, with amusement. "Mr. Selwyn, I almost hesitate to admit it now, but both Miss Beauchamp and I are only recently arrived from the colonies. I promise, however," he said smoothly, "not to bore you with accounts of my uninteresting exploits in that far land."

"Miss Beauchamp, of course, may speak of what she chooses," Selwyn responded with panache. "One can never be bored in the company of so lovely a lady, regardless of the matter of her discourse."

"You are gallant, sir," Jenny declared, very much on her guard. "But I will undertake to refrain from such subjects in any case. It would be foolish in me to instruct you, in any case, when by attending to your conversation I might be better instructed regarding this new world—London—that I have now entered."

Despite her resolution not to do so, Jenny could not prevent herself from taking a peek to see Yves' reaction, not that much could be learned from his expression. Surely he could not suspect her of avoiding the subject, she prayed, especially after all Lady Pertwee's strictures. Indeed, Jenny could see that lady heave a sigh of relief.

The wit preened himself. " 'Tis true, I know my world. You, Yves, know only the court and Parliament. Believe me, there is more intrigue to be found in the ballroom than there is in diplomatic circles."

"How true," Yves agreed wryly.

"Now I remember me, I daresay you must be breaking out of your worrisome routine. Did I not see you at the hanging of the highwayman, Lord Danger?"

Jenny could not prevent the instinctive tightening of her muscles. Relaxing her fingers, she cursed her lack of control. Had the terror she felt been visible in her expression?

Selwyn, wearing a beatific smile, certainly seemed unaware of any undercurrents.

"Yes. Yes, I did go," Yves admitted, smiling.

When he smiled like that, Jenny became afraid. There was no sign of anything more than polite interest from Richard, she noticed, but she knew he must be alert to the possibility of peril. Now that he was coming to know Yves better, Jenny could not believe that Richard felt quite so secure in his own omnipotence.

Selwyn was speaking of the hanging with more than common enthusiasm. "Quite one of the finest of this decade, if not longer," he declared. "And I may be accounted something of an expert. Lord Lovat's was nothing to it. From where I sat, you could see the criminal's expression quite clearly—the passionate look he gave his mistress."

Sir Richard coughed. So he was not entirely unmoved. From these words, however, Jenny began to doubt the wit's perceptions. Nonetheless, she flushed with embarrassment. She only hoped everyone was likely to attribute her reaction only to Selwyn's topic. Girls of her station were not supposed to know about mistresses and their ilk.

"I fear, my lord, you were too far off to see anything of value at all," the gossip concluded.

"Not at all," Yves answered, again with that knowing smile. "I was more than content with the view. I was able to see what I needed to see."

Sternly, Jenny tried to arrest the wild speculations surging within her. Reason decreed that if he suspected she had appeared in public as Danger's arch dell, he would not then present her to the public, would never present her to his beloved and respectable aunt. Yet it was hard, damnably hard, to look at Yves and be reasonable.

"The true aficionado," Selwyn was explaining to an amused and apparently fascinated Richard, "must be close, virtually upon the scaffold itself. I have asked to be allowed to travel in the cart, but they refuse."

"No doubt they fear the criminal's escape," Richard suggested as if he had little knowledge of the matter.

"Hardly a reasonable fear in Selwyn's case," Yves mentioned. "Who could have more interest in the capture of a criminal than Selwyn? Why, when thieves broke into Horace Walpole's house, Walpole sent for Selwyn directly, that he might have the pleasure of the capture." He turned to the gossip. "Was it not you, my friend, who secured the confession of Lord Dacres' footman?"

"Indeed it was. You would think the authorities at Newgate would know me well enough by now. I was there no less than five times a-visiting that rogue Danger alone."

No wonder Richard's eyes were lit up with laughter. Selwyn's visits must have occurred after her release. Jenny could not remember him at all, and she suspected she would have if she had seen him before.

"An interesting fellow," Yves said. "I visited him once myself. A gentleman . . . not easily forgotten, I should think."

"No," Selwyn agreed sadly, evidently supremely unaware that he stood mere inches from the very fellow. "It will be some time before we are treated to so remarkable a criminal again. But we most hope for better things." He bowed, recognizing a friend across the room. "Ah, I see Queensbury is still here. You must excuse me. Your servant, ladies, gentlemen."

"Now, what am I to make of him?" Jenny asked, hoping her nervousness would not be evident in her tone. "Is this another gentleman of whom I should beware, my lord?" Or should she simply beware of Yves?

"Indeed you must, but for quite another reason. Selwyn's tongue, as you might guess, is not always so harmless."

"I will remember," Jenny said, taking more warning of his words than the others realized.

"Enough of such morbid subjects," Yves declared. He seemed willing to set aside his teasing threats, as if entirely satisfied by what he had accomplished. Or as if he had meant nothing at all by his cryptic remarks. How much Jenny read into his remarks from sheer sense of guilt, she could no longer tell.

"If you will excuse us, Sir Richard," he continued, extending his arm for Jenny, "the orchestra is about to strike up again and it is time I claimed my dance with Miss Beauchamp. It is the quadrille, and as we have practiced this before, she may worry the less for her delicate feet."

From the corner of her eye, Jenny noticed Richard lead a faintly protesting Mrs. Mueller onto the dance floor behind them, but as their set was full the couple joined another just forming. For just a moment she felt bereft of protection, no matter that there were three other couples in their set, and who knows how many others in the room. Those others were meaningless, however. She was aware only of Yves.

As they stepped forward together to honor the presence, and then salute each other, Jenny too remembered their earlier dance. It seemed an apt focus for much of her confusion regarding his lordship. His attitude seemed to swerve from threat to offered friendship with lightning speed.

Only moments ago she could have sworn that he was needling Richard and her regarding the highwayman's escape from the gallows. Now he looked as if his only concern was minding his steps.

And enjoying her company.

His smile was as warm as the touch of his hand as he led her through the steps of the first figure. Jenny was aware of the quickened beat of her heart, keeping pace with the sprightly tempo of the music.

Breathless, she commented, "The orchestra tonight is remarkably fine, do you not agree, my lord?"

Yves surprised her with a laugh of genuine delight, almost one of affection. "Only moments ago I was wondering who else would truly appreciate the music, and I realized you were certain to notice. I am glad it pleases you," he said.

Flushed, Jenny circled the opposite gentleman. It was true, she realized with a start. Their thoughts were often in tune.

After his turn with the opposite lady, Yves returned to her, still relaxed and gracious. "I hope Selwyn's lugubrious choice of topic did not disturb you. Society has become so used to his vagaries that we forget how they must appear to others."

At the mention of Selwyn's name once more, Jenny became again alert, pretending to concentrate on the management of her wide skirt as she described a circle around Yves. Jenny felt as if her head were turning in circles, too. Yves' expression had not changed, however, she noted. Was she being foolish? Since she had entered into this deception, she found ruin staring out of every shadow. That bizarre conversation might just as likely be the result of chance, rather than his lordship's careful arrangement.

"If Selwyn's conversation follows strange paths," Yves continued, "he is at least probably correct in chiding me for talking politics too much. However, I would like to introduce you sometime to the Mr. Burke he mentioned. Mr. Burke is greatly interested in conditions in the colonies and would be grateful for any information you could give him."

Jenny turned beneath his outstretched arm. The room spun before her eyes; only Yves remained still, the only constant.

"I have heard of Mr. Burke," Jenny said, "and should be pleased to make his acquaintance." She was far from insensible to the implicit flattery of such a suggestion. Was there another gentleman in the room, she wondered, who would so blithely have assumed her interest in such matters? Test it could not be, for most would have considered a lady's ignorance of political subjects to be no more than proper. "Sir Richard has spoken of him with great admiration," she added, "although I believe they have not met."

The mention of Richard caused a shadow to pass over the fair, handsome face. A slight chill entered Yves' voice when he spoke. "Then Sir Richard must meet him as well. I am sure his views as a soldier who served in America would be most illuminating."

There was something in his tone that Jenny could not quite place, something that was not quite suspicion or dislike. Had Richard managed to offend Yves somehow? As the figure of the dance separated ladies from gentlemen momentarily, she stared after him. The sudden breaking of the connection between them disconcerted her. When the figure brought him back to her side again, he mentioned more casually that he had noticed how comfortable she had appeared dancing with Sir Richard. Although he took her hand again, however, Jenny did not feel the same closeness.

"It is comfortable to speak to one who understands one's background," Jenny admitted with genuine emotion, wondering at her desire to reach him, touch him somehow. "I do not need to measure my words so carefully as Lady Pertwee would have me do. Like you, you see, Sir Richard is not put off by references to my home." Did he understand?

"To use the word 'farm' without fear of censure is certainly an aid to comfort," Yves agreed. "Many a courtship has been based on less."

His tone was light enough, and no longer distant, but there was something there that made Jenny wonder if he were serious. She had been very aware of the interest her supposed fortune held for many of the young gentlemen. Would it be a lure for the retired highwayman as well?

"Courtship?" Jenny asked, hoping the stylized postures of the dance would hide her nervousness. "Sir Richard? You must be jesting, my lord."

Her attitude seemed to amuse Yves. No, he was not fooled. "My dear," he said, "you do both yourself and Sir Richard grave wrong to consider such a possibility mere jest. After this evening, I expect he will be but one among many suitors."

Dismayed, Jenny whispered, "Suitors seeking the Vickers fortune."

"Not all," Yves said sincerely. "You must not let the thought distress you. After all, you will be free to do some choosing on your own." The arm he extended to her seemed warm, comforting, strong. Such an arm could protect a lady from any who sought to harm her, she thought.

It was a relief to know that he meant to grant her some say in the matter. But of course he would not push her into marriage, Jenny reminded herself, sternly repressing any dissident thoughts. If she married, the fortune would pass into her husband's control.

He took both her hands for the *tour allemande*. Facing each other, each placed the right hand behind the back, clasping the left hand of the other. The movement brought them so close that she might almost be held in his arms. When Yves spoke again he seemed to be whispering right in her ear.

"What would you look for in your suitor, Miss Beauchamp?"

Jenny looked up at his brilliant blue eyes, so close, so intent she almost expected him to see the answer before she herself knew it. What would she look for? she wondered, examining the elegant chiseled features.

"Kindness," she answered at last.

"So little?" His voice was low, curiously intense.

She shook her head. "I do not consider it a little thing."

"No, of course not. I meant rather that you might demand so much more." There was a hint of some emotion behind the polite mask, an almost wistful quality, very unlike Yves.

Jenny looked away, unable to answer. How could she, in her equivocal position, demand anything? How could she think of suitors, when those suitors knew nothing of who she was?

So close to Yves it was difficult to think at all. She was both sorry and glad when the music ended and he released her. Reminding herself firmly that she needed to keep all her wits about her, especially when near this man, Jenny dipped into her final curtsey.

As she rose, she saw his expression suddenly turn from wistful attentiveness to murderous hatred. The change so stunned her that it took her a moment to realize that she was not the cause of this sudden reversal. Indeed, it seemed that he had entirely forgotten her existence for the moment. All his attention was focused on a solitary figure poised at the entrance—Nate.

Chapter Eight

So taken aback was Jenny that her astonishment gave her time to recollect her position. Miss Jean-Marie Beauchamp had still to meet her cousin—she would not recognize him, she reminded herself. To her this elegant fellow who examined the room through his quizzing glass could be no different from any other that had come to her ball.

But Nate did not look like everyone else. Even among the most beautiful and fashionable of society, he stood out. His costume glittered with silver lace and diamonds. His eyes seemed to glitter, too, with the light of battle.

Lord Vickers had indeed returned, and he meant to see that the world—and Yves—knew it.

The crowd was swift to pick up the tension in the air. Nate's timing had been perfect—almost as if he had planned it. In the pause between dances Jenny could see one person after another stop and turn, looking first to Nate, then to Yves.

No, Jenny decided, it was not her imagination. An awareness of something about to happen seemed to suffuse the room. If Mr. Selwyn was looking for gossip, he would now find an abundance of it. The ballroom grew quiet, as everyone seemed to wait for Yves to make his move. Clearly, the enmity between the two was no secret—nor was the fact that Nate must have come uninvited.

"My lord?" Jenny said hesitantly, feeling that someone must recall him to his senses before there was bloodshed. That violence was imminent was clear. She tried again. "Is aught amiss?"

Thank heaven, the sound of her voice seemed to have reached through to him. "Amiss?" he repeated, startled at this reminder of her presence. "No, just a slight problem with the servants." He shook his head dismissingly. "I fear the porter is not properly attending to his duties." Having been reminded of his own, evidently, by her words, he drew Jenny off the dance floor toward her chaperone. Jenny was aware, however, that she had ceased to hold his attention.

He would have moved away and accosted the figure now sauntering slowly down the long staircase, but Lady Pertwee clearly decided to take matters into her own hands while Jenny was still wondering what to do. Alerted by her social antennae, her ladyship managed to forestall Yves with a nonchalant air belied by the firm glint of determination in her eyes as she stepped between Jenny and Yves. Although she smiled and waved her fan casually for the watching crowd now beginning to resume the dance, her words were blunt and to the point.

"Ignore him, my lord," she told him in a tone that had more of authority than counsel in it.

"Why should I?" Yves demanded. "He's asking for trouble."

Jenny held her breath. Although she could hardly blame Nate for wanting to cause a little mischief, the thought of what might ensue frightened her.

"Yes, and he'll be immensely satisfied if he gets it," Lady Pertwee pointed out. "Tis you who'll look the worse for making a scene, not Vickers. But the one who'll be harmed most is Miss Beauchamp."

Yves had taken a step or two toward the stairs, but this stopped him at once, to Jenny's surprise. Could Nate's enemy be checked by concern for her?

"How so?" he asked.

Lady Pertwee sighed. "You must face facts, my lord. Lord Vickers is accepted by all but you. Do you mean to avoid all the places where he might appear? Or accept only those invitations that exclude him? In that case, my work is done and you may as well immure yourself in the country." She held out her hand toward Jenny for emphasis. "If you bar Miss Beauchamp from his company entirely, hostesses will be put to the choice of whom to invite. That choice will not always run in your favor. There are certainly many mothers of marriageable daughters who will hardly regret the lack of competition provided by Miss Beauchamp."

Without knowing why, Jenny looked at Yves,

pleading silently. She told herself that it was only because her entire future might be at stake here, not because of any concern for Yves. Only through Nate could she see any hope of escape from the prison of Yves' guardianship. If there were no hope at all of meeting him ...

Despite the black look Yves gave her, Lady Pertwee continued. "Proper chaperonage will keep Vickers distant enough, my lord. Do not look for the impossible."

Jenny knew she had to do something, say something, but knew not whether she would advance or sabotage her own cause. They had spoken his name, however, and Yves would expect her to react to that.

"Please, my lord, my lady. Are you speaking of my cousin? Is this he? I don't understand." Her words came out all in a rush, but hardly had she finished when it became clear that the time for decisions was past.

Nate had found them. He approached, smiling cheerfully over Yves' discomfiture. How could she blame him? she thought again. Yves had nearly ruined Nate's life. Yet the odd fancy occurred to her that this evening all roles had been reversed. Tonight it was Nate who appeared cold as the diamonds that winked from the lace at his neck, and Yves who burned with a golden fire. That fire, she knew, was pure hatred, one that would stop at nothing in quest of his enemy's destruction. Why, Jenny wondered then, wasn't she more pleased to see Yves upset?

"Do forgive me, Wolf, for being late," Nate said. Clearly he was enjoying himself, with a vengeance. "For some reason, I never received my invitation. Can you imagine—no invitation to the ball for my own cousin? I knew it must be a mistake. So here I am. And here, an' I mistake not, is she. Come, come, old friend, aren't you going to present me?"

Yves looked as if he would much prefer to introduce his old friend to the amenities of the ducking stool, if not the firing squad. Aware now of the staring eyes of the other guests, he restrained himself, however.

"Miss Beauchamp," he said, his voice burning with fury, "may I present to you Lord Vickers, your cousin. Nate, Miss Beauchamp."

It felt odd being introduced to someone you knew better than the gentleman who performed, with a punctiliousness that was almost alarming, the introductions. Jenny eagerly responded, hoping that Yves would perceive no more excitement than might be expected of a young girl meeting the last remaining member of her family. From his expression, though, she could learn nothing.

"I am very glad to meet you, cousin," Jenny said, with a private smile for Nate. If only he knew how much she had longed for the chance to talk to him, to hear his plans for rescuing her from this situation. "My father spoke of you often and with great affection," she added, emphasizing her role as Jean-Marie for Yves' benefit.

"Your father was a man who inspired great affection," Nate answered with an ease that impressed Jenny. "I am eager to hear all you can tell me about his life after he left these shores. I want to hear all about you, as well. We are the last of the Beauchamps, you and I," he stressed. The elegant motion of his hand revealed the gleam of diamonds and emeralds on his fingers, a show of wealth presumably designed to enrage Yves. "It is up to us to keep up the family histories and traditions. Perhaps, if you have a moment now— I see you have not a partner for this dance—we might take a short walk about the room."

The suggestion was clearly as much a challenge to Yves as it was a request to Jenny for her company. The crowd had begun to lose interest in their conversation, but a single motion from Yves could easily attract it again.

Obviously daring Yves to stop him, Nate offered Jenny his arm with a theatrical gesture probably learned from Danger.

Jenny looked to Yves, too, for an answer and a reaction. The restraining arm of Lady Pertwee stopped his forward motion. Under her breath, the chaperone whispered to him, softly yet audible to Jenny. "What do you fear where all eyes are upon them?"

After an anxious moment, Yves nodded. "Very well. Perhaps it is all for the best." He turned a blazing glance upon Nate. "You will never come to this house again," he said, his voice low yet with an edge like tempered steel. "Miss Beauchamp will accept no invitations from you. Ever. I am told I cannot prevent you meeting in public without encouraging unwelcome gossip that would harm your cousin. Remember, however, that should your attentions ever step out of line, I will do what I must, regardless of the consequences—to Miss Beauchamp, to anyone." He paused a moment before he turned away. "You know, I think, how to value my word," he added and bowed a cold adieu to them both.

As Yves stalked off, Nate laughed. Any feelings of amusement were sadly absent from Jenny's heart, however. Ten minutes ago Yves had been the most charming and attentive of dance partners. Now he had become the enemy again. Jenny knew she should be glad of the reminder, but somehow she was not.

"Cousin, will you take my arm?" Nate asked, giving her hand a little squeeze as he led her around the outer circuit of the room. "You are ravishing tonight, my dear. A real beauty. I'm proud of you."

"Proud of me? How can you?" Jenny forced herself to put Yves from her mind and took the opportunity to draw back a little. For some reason Nate's closeness and the blatant flattery of his compliment made her a little uneasy. "Where have you been, Nate?" she demanded. "Do you know what is happening?"

"Softly, softly, my dear cousin," he cautioned pointedly. "The wolf is still watching." Nate smiled and greeted a group of chaperones, the only denizens of this part of the ballroom. "Where have I been? I have been getting out of prison and starting to reconstruct my life. Surely you knew that." His voice was gentle and reasonable. In fact, he did not seem to understand why she should be upset at all.

The cousinly reminder, surely unnecessary, annoyed her. If Richard had felt secure enough to tease her earlier about her Newgate gowns, Nate should be able to countenance the use of his own name. "I knew you were free only because I read it in the *Morning Gazette*," she hissed more than whispered.

"My dear, how could I have done otherwise? You have seen for yourself how Yves reacts to my presence. We are fortunate indeed that he has promised to be so reasonable for the future. Brazen I may have seemed, my dear, but my knees were shaking every minute, I do assure you."

Nate's teasing had the desired effect. Despite her attempts to stifle it, a hint of a smile played about the corner of her lips. "Fiddle," she said. "You enjoyed every minute."

"Well. Perhaps a little," he confessed. "There's a great debt between Yves and me. I don't mind admitting that I long for the day when I may see him repaid for what he has done to me." With eyes that seemed more shrewd than concerned, he examined Jenny. "He has not been too harsh with you, has he?"

"Not at all," she admitted. "Sometimes he can be very thoughtful. Sometimes..." Her voice trailed off as she remembered the few times she had seen those cool eyes blaze with warmth.

"Yes?" Nate asked. He sounded worried.

"Nothing." Jenny quickly dismissed the subject. She was looking for a way to escape from Yves, she reminded herself. "Nate, there are problems."

"What do you mean? Does he suspect? Do you think he looks to unmask you?"

Of course that would be the first thing to occur to Nate. It was no doubt selfish of Jenny to worry first about her own equivocal position in all this. Still, why hadn't Nate made some reference to her presence in Yves' home?

"I certainly think him capable of it," Jenny finally admitted. "And I think he may still have his suspicions. If he had proof, we would neither of us be here. But, oh, Nate, he says I'm an heiress and I must remain his ward until I come of age. What are we to do? I'm not supposed to come of age for more than a year. Until then I am virtually his prisoner, and can do nothing about transferring your money back to you."

The mention of her inheritance caused a strange expression to cross Nate's face, one Jenny could not read. He became flustered and wasted valuable time seeking his handkerchief—which, once found, he no longer seemed to need. Suddenly Jenny understood.

"You knew! You knew all along about the will and you did not tell me. Oh Nate, how could you?"

"*Plus bas, plus bas,*" he warned her again. "We are still under observation." They walked in silence for a moment, then he resumed in his more usual tone of voice. "I thought it would be all right. That sounds naïve, I suppose, but it's true. After all, I am the head of the family. It never occurred to me that I would not be named guardian, that Wolf would use his court connections to such powerful effect."

"You should have told me," Jenny insisted. Inwardly she could not help but wonder at such naïveté. More than any other, Nate ought to realize what Yves was capable of accomplishing.

"Forgive me, Jenny," Nate pleaded. "I think I was near to going mad in prison. There was nothing I would not do to gain my freedom. From the first, I could see that you would be horrified by the idea of the inheritance."

So he had deliberately deceived her! Well, she too had been willing to deceive to free herself from that living hell, but never to deceive her friends. Had Nate realized, as she had not, that once lured into their scheme she could never escape?

"The money never mattered to me. Although," he admitted with a laugh, "I am not so high-minded that I will refuse the gift if you still want to transfer it back to me. As far as I'm concerned, however, you've earned it, and more."

"You know perfectly well I could never keep it," Jenny said. "Has it ever occurred to you, Nate, that a number of the gentlemen present here to-night may court me for the very fortune I mean to return to you? Has it entered your thoughts that I might feel uncomfortable receiving such attentions, based as they are on a lie?"

"Oh, Jenny, I'm a thoughtless brute." Nate's expression of concern reminded her of their first meetings, when he was the only source of gentility and reason in a brutal, insane world. The look in his eyes grew strangely warm. "You wrong yourself, too, Jenny if you think your fortune the major attraction for suitors. Look about you at this crowd with their paints and perfumes. Do you wonder what is hidden beneath? I'll tell you— nothing. You're alive, Jenny. Any man with life left in him must be attracted to you."

So now she was Jenny again. Uncomfortable again and annoyed, too, she brushed aside the topic. "It matters not. Jean-Marie Beauchamp will never take a husband." Whether Jenny Wilde might marry seemed as doubtful, but that she refused to think upon. Looking up, she saw Mrs. Mueller coming their way, sent, no doubt, by Yves. "We're about to be interrupted," she warned. "When will I see you again?"

"Soon, Jenny, soon," he promised. "Your calendar will be full after tonight. Society has welcomed Lord Vickers back with open arms. Wherever you go, look for me. I will be there."

Perhaps, Jenny considered, but feared that such meetings might prove as unsatisfying as this one. Perhaps she had waited too long, too eagerly for this meeting. Perhaps she had expected too much of Nate, as if he might solve all her difficulties with a mere wave of his hand. She curtseyed her farewell and allowed Mrs. Mueller to lead her to the buffet tables.

No, there was no escape, no possibility of rescue from Nate or anyone. Miss Jean-Marie Beauchamp would remain the ward of Lord Yves until her twenty-first birthday. If, that is, she did not go mad in the meantime.

No, no, somehow she would survive. She was not quite alone after all. There was Sukey, and even Sir Richard, to turn to in times of need, she reminded herself. And Nate, to some extent at least. It seemed, from his words, that Yves meant to allow them to speak and meet casually, at society's balls and routs, at the opera and such events. With these friends she would not have to weigh her words. Now there would be one more person to whom she did not have to pretend to be other than she was.

An errant thought crossed Jenny's mind then as she looked up at her pensive host and guardian who had joined them at the buffet. Except for lying about her assumed identity, she had been more than usually open with Yves. Of all the men she had met, he was one of the few she knew would not judge her for not following the canons of behavior sanctified by society. It was not only the word "farm" that failed to shock or surprise him.

Attempting to put such confusing meditations aside, Jenny concentrated on the music in hopes that the beautiful strains of Haydn would help her regain some measure of calm and enjoyment. To her surprise, she realized she had enjoyed much of the ball, in spite of all her fears. That old rogue, the Duke of Queensbury, had made her laugh during the minuet. There had been pleasure in seeing Mrs. Mueller come out of her shell, the ease of friendship in her dance with Richard.

And with Yves . . . It was certainly not comfort that Yves engendered. Still, she would not have missed that dance for the world.

Almost before she knew it, the ball was over. The last guests finally drifted off, probably to pass on the gossip learned here at some other gathering or at one of the coffee houses.

Lady Pertwee showed a dismaying desire to stay and relive the entire event, prolonging conversation over a last cup of tea, but even she was eventually persuaded to accept the loan of a sedan chair to take her home. Yves gave his aunt his arm as they walked up the stairs together, Jenny following sleepily behind.

"Did you enjoy yourself tonight, Tante?" he asked.

"Ja, ja," she answered, lapsing into her native tongue.

Jenny smiled at this evidence of the older woman's exhaustion. So ingrained was Mrs. Mueller's courtesy that she never resorted to her native language, not even the simplest words, before those who did not understand it. Sleepily she kissed her nephew and Jenny good night and retired to her chamber.

"And you, Miss Beauchamp?" he asked, lighting Jenny's way to her room. "Did you enjoy yourself"

Jenny hardly knew, so much had happened, but she answered, yes, it had been lovely.

Still he stood there, unmoving. They were alone in the hallway now, the darkness broken only by the glimmer of his candle. The light cast warm shadows over his face, catching fire on the gold trim of his coat and the golden aura of his hair. An awkward silence filled the hall for a moment while Jenny searched desperately for something to say, some words of gratitude.

"I was proud of you tonight," Yves said, breaking the silence.

"Thank you, my lord," she answered. She curtseyed, aware that her cheeks had again turned to rose, and started to turn the handle of her door, but suddenly stopped and turned. Yves had not moved.

"My lord, why did you insist I go unpowdered?" Jenny bit her lip as soon as the question issued from her mouth, but it was too late to turn back. Why, she wondered, of all the thoughts that had been plaguing her this evening, should this be the one to find voice? Now that she had spoken it, however, she wanted to know, wanted very much to know, the answer.

Yves leaned back against the paneling, his large frame utterly relaxed, or so it seemed. "There might be any number of reasons," he said. "I might tell you that I find it a filthy habit, and probably an unhealthy one. Or I might tell you that I abhor anything to do with subterfuge, anything that hides the truth."

"And would one of those answers be the truth?" she asked. Certainly she had to wonder sometimes at his professed regard for the truth, when he himself hid so successfully behind a mask of pleasantry, and behind phrases like this which might mean almost anything.

"They might be true," Yves agreed, stepping away from the wall, and standing tall and straight. "And it might be true as well that you have hair that glows in the candlelight and feels softer than down." His fingers rested for a moment on the single curl that slipped over one shoulder along the bodice of her gown. "It would be sin to cover such glorious hair with powder," he whispered, then stepped back and bowed formally. "Your servant, Miss Beauchamp. Sleep well."

Jenny put her hand to her heart, pounding against the stomacher of her gown, now suddenly too tight.

As if she could sleep tonight.

Yves had hardly sat down at the harpsichord when his aunt joined him in the music room. His fingers made not the slightest hesitation, continuing their measured progress up and down the keyboard, but his lips twitched a fraction of an inch. It seemed he was in for another lecture. He looked at his aunt with affection, and wished she had chosen another time to deliver her criticism. The evening had disturbed his calm more than he liked to admit, even to her.

Such vagrant desires were to be banished, however. Nothing but his usual welcome could be heard in his voice as he invited her in. "Tante, how good of you to join me. I thought your expressions of fatigue were perhaps a little insincere. Shall I desert the Italian composers for your Bach?"

"Pho! Bang away as you like, liebling. You will not distract me so easily."

"My dear Tante, I know very well I cannot," he said, suppressing a sigh. "Well, what troubles you tonight?"

His aunt settled herself into a comfortable chair by the fire, but her fingers worried the fringe of the shawl she had thrown over her nightdress. She was not relaxed.

Astute, however, she was. "You, because you are troubled too. And not only because of that man, I think."

That man. Yves wondered briefly how the young lady sleeping peacefully upstairs would feel to hear her cousin described so. And hear it she would. Tante Agathe would never hesitate to pronounce her opinion regarding Nate's uninvited appearance.

"Is it this Sir Richard?" she asked. "I thought you liked him."

"I do like him," he responded at last. That, unfortunately, was part of the problem. "However, I am not at all sure yet how far he is to be trusted."

"And how far his affections have been engaged by our lovely guest?"

"I would have thought that was obvious," Wolf answered with a calm it cost him some effort to maintain, "Tis her affections that remain in doubt, I would say. What think you?"

The question was innocent enough, but he wanted to know, wanted to know with a passion quite out of character for him.

"Is that all you saw?" Tante answered, finally relaxing into laughter. "Men are so blind."

Blind? His hands stilled momentarily as he remembered Jean-Marie (he knew not what else to call her), how she looked coming down the stairs, the sapphire pins in her glorious hair. He had noticed every detail of the girl's appearance, her slightest movement. He had seen immediately how well she carried herself. There was grace in her carriage, a dancer's delicacy of movement, as well as courage. Her courtesy was ingrained, not taught. She might have been a tomboy, as she said, with no concern for the current modes, but whoever she was, she was most certainly a lady.

And whatever her name might once have been, she was now Miss Beauchamp—because he had made her so. After tonight there would be many seeking to persuade her to change that honored name for another. She had seemed unusually upset at the thought of marriage when he had broached the subject before, but might that not be due to having made her choice already?

If so, might she have chosen Sir Richard? Or a suitor he would find even less palatable?

"Enlighten me then, Tante. What should I have noticed this evening?"

"That Sir Richard sighs in silence because he sees no hope, and Jenny does not even notice."

"No hope, you think." He turned around to face his aunt. "What did you call her?"

"Jenny. Is this not right? We are very friendly now, the two of us. No need to be so formal. Jean-

Marie she does not like so well, she prefers the diminutive used by her family."

A small secret smile played about the corners of his mouth. "Is that so? Jenny. It suits her."

This remark earned him a piercing glance, but no reproach. Once again, however, the elderly widow pulled her shawl closer, as if cold. "I am frightened, Wolfram. And so, I think, is Jenny."

"I am glad to hear it."

"Wolfram!" she cried out in protest.

He rose from the piano bench and moved to encourage more warmth from the dying fire. "As long as she is afraid, she will be alert, able to protect herself."

"Then there is danger."

"My dear Tante, where Vickers is involved there will always be danger."

Chapter Nine

Lady Pertwee declared herself positively *aux anges* over the response to Miss Beauchamp's debut. As she listened to her chaperone's raptures the next day in the morning room, Jenny found she could not share that excitement, however. On the contrary, the cards and notes that surrounded her left her miserable.

Half a dozen gentlemen had sent posies, Lady Pertwee announced excitedly to Lord Yves and Mrs. Mueller, while Jenny sat by in silent consternation. The recitation seemed endless. One gentleman had even gone so far as to have orchids sent from his estate's greenhouses. Another had attempted a sonnet to Jenny's Titian tresses, an effort she thought ludicrous, but which was much admired by Mrs. Mueller. The number of gentlemen who had contented themselves by sending notes or simply their cards could hardly be counted.

Nor did her ordeal end with this. She was forced to review the invitations, recited with great gusto by Lady Pertwee. Balls, ridottos, rout parties, drums, visits to the theater, trips to see de Loutherburg's Eidophusikon, or, Jenny noticed with distaste, to see Bedlam and Newgate—all were planned for the enjoyment of Miss Beauchamp.

Jenny listened to all this, appalled, and wanted nothing more than to seek the nearest ship for Massachusetts. Even Virginia would do. Some of her family had lived there once. Perhaps they could still be traced. Nate's inability to think of a solution did not mean she had to resign herself quietly to her fate. There had to be some way she could escape from the future she saw planned for her, some way to escape from Yves.

One look at Yves, however, looking very tall and impressive against the sunlit window, told her that her chances of escape were less than negligible. He had been riding this morning and was very plainly dressed in a brown coat and buckskin breeches. The simplicity of his attire reminded Jenny of colonial gentlemen, but somehow the effect was different. Certainly no colonial gentleman had ever left her so aware of his presence, his every movement.

Yves' mood this morning seemed to reflect the chill civility Jenny had first seen in him. Did he dislike this recitation as much as she? she wondered. Or had she managed somehow to offend him again? His changes of mood disconcerted her when she felt lost enough already. From now on she would never be able to look at him without remembering how quickly his air of disinterest could turn to passionate involvement...or to warm admiration. Having seen that side of him, she could not help but feel the absence of warmth.

His coolness, however, should not be a matter for concern, Jenny reminded herself. Her energies would be far better directed by concentrating on seeking a way to free herself from this situation. Yves was dangerous, to her peace of mind as well as to her imposture. The intelligence that glittered in his cold blue eyes was not to be dismissed.

"No, no, no," Lady Pertwee declaimed, "not Lord John. Utterly charming, of course, but the veriest blackguard in matters of the heart. Not the sort of person to be trusted with a *young* lady."

"A fortune-hunter, I must suppose," Jenny said, trying not to sound daunted. With all she had to worry about, it seemed foolish to let possible suitors bother her, but they did. Every one of the flattering notes before her seemed to be an added link to the chain that trapped her here in this increasingly bothersome masquerade. In the end, it was the Beauchamp fortune to which they paid court, not to her. Not to Jenny.

In this case, however, Lady Pertwee denied the imputation. "No, my dear," she answered, to Jenny's surprise. "One might at least understand that. Lord John simply craves the adventure, the thrill of the chase."

"And is bored by success," Jenny guessed easily. "I see." She had seen the type before. Looking up to find a strange expression on Yves' countenance, however, Jenny realized too late that probably she should not have understood so well or so quickly. So young a girl as Miss Beauchamp was presumed to be would have very little experience of the world's adventures. She would have to mind her tongue better. Innocence, as she was discovering, was the most difficult quality of all to counterfeit.

"These are the fortune-hunters to beware," Lady Pertwee said, tossing aside a few missives, "Finchley, Petherbridge, Berowne . . . They seem to be the only clearly unacceptable names I can see in this lot." Her ladyship turned to Yves with a practiced simper. "As Sir Richard has already been received into your home, my lord, I presume you can vouch for him."

Yves came and leaned over Jenny, so close that the short ruffle extending beneath his cuff lightly brushed against her hand. With two beautifully shaped fingers, he picked up the letter of thanks Richard had delivered this morning. Unnaturally aware of his every move, she wished he would answer and break this tension.

"Dangerfield?" he said slowly, as if still turning the matter over in his mind. "A very respectable parti, I should think," he stated, after a moment that seemed to Jenny to stretch just a bit too long. "His is a very old Devonshire family, highly respected in those parts. The late baronet, I fear, squandered much of the estate, but the success of Sir Richard's ventures in the Americas will easily remedy those losses."

"Ah?" Lady Pertwee grew more interested. "Very pretty manners, I thought."

Jenny looked uncertainly at Yves, wishing once again that she understood him better, could read behind the eyes that glittered alternately with amusement and cutting analysis. How much in truth did he know about Richard? Reason alone told her that a Stuart restoration was more credible than the chance that Yves would blindly accept Richard's own account of his background. That Yves had a spy of sorts in his employ she knew—all the servants spoke of it—and had long ago warned Richard of the man's existence. How much more scrutiny could their conspiracy endure without crumbling to bits?

"Indeed," Yves continued, still unreadable. "At a time when every footpad on the road is laying claim to some title or military dignity, Dangerfield's modesty regarding his career as a soldier impresses me greatly. He served with Wolfe, you know."

No, Jenny had not known. Her tension at the mention of footpads was changed to surprise at this revelation regarding Richard. Oddly enough, the very fact that Richard had never boasted of such service made it all the more believable.

Was his new disguise no less than truth? Had the gentleman with a history of service to his country always existed behind the facade of the roguish highwayman? The idea that she might have judged Richard unfairly made her uncomfortable. It hardly seemed possible, given what she had seen and heard. Yet, she reminded herself, everyone in Newgate was not exactly as he seemed. Of all people, she ought to know that.

With a start, Jenny brought her mind back to the conversation. While she had been abstracted, Lady Pertwee had evidently continued dissecting what she insisted upon calling "Miss Beauchamp's beaux."

Would she never stop? Jenny wondered. Before

a thoughtless word could pass her lips, however, Yves leaned forward again—this time to pick up the single floral tribute that had not been discussed or enthused over by Lady Pertwee. Her ladyship's spate of gossip ceased at once.

"My lord," her ladyship said in a voice that was tense, almost afraid. Unconsciously she reached out to prevent Yves from opening the enclosed card, an effort Jenny saw would be useless.

"You forgot one, my lady," he reminded her, undeterred, holding the card just beyond her reach.

"My lord," Lady Pertwee tried again, but to no avail.

Jenny was not surprised when he announced, "From Lord Vickers. Your cousin is quite punctilious, my dear. Nay, more than that. Why, this is positively amorous."

Nonetheless, Yves neither read the contents nor gave the card to Jenny to read. When he was like this, Jenny had no idea whether he was speaking simple truth or not. And she needed to know.

"It seems your cousin has joined the long list of your suitors, my dear," Yves continued.

"My lord, you jest," she said, anxiously eyeing the note. Had she thought Yves chilly before? His tone now froze her. After his kindness and warmth last night, it seemed unbearable. Was this the real man? she wondered. Were his kindnesses no more than a honey trap to lure her into making a mistake?

It might, she realized unhappily, be safer for her to believe that.

Desperate to discover what Nate had written, she could only watch helplessly as Yves rose and tossed the note into the fire. Two seconds later and it was ashes.

"Lady Pertwee," he said in a voice that made that lady cringe, "last night you persuaded me that to deny Miss Beauchamp any contact with her cousin would do her a grave disservice in the eyes of society. In public, therefore, I have agreed that Miss Beauchamp may recognize Lord Vickers. In *public*," he repeated, pointedly. "Do not make the mistake of thinking that this concession on my part denotes any acceptance whatsoever of Vickers."

The thought that Lady Pertwee's services might be dispensed with brought a momentary glimmer of hope to Jenny's breast, one that was immediately dashed.

"You misunderstand, milord," Lady Pertwee said, hurrying over the words, anxious to restore herself in his good opinion. "Naturally, I will supervise all Miss Beauchamp's correspondence. However, I see no point in hiding such trite expressions of appreciation as this. If Lord Vickers were to ask Miss Beauchamp outright whether she had received his note," she asked shrewdly, "and Miss Beauchamp were to confess she had not, might he not make an unpleasant scene?"

"He would," Yves agreed grimly. "Most assuredly he would," he added almost to himself, then suddenly turned his attention to Jenny. "Miss Beauchamp, you have in the past indicated a rather touching regard for family. I would advise you not to be so foolish as to consider Lord Vickers as such. I can guarantee that he does not view you in that fashion."

* * *

195

Nate as a suitor? The idea was ridiculous, and also surprisingly distasteful. Once the idea had been planted in her head, however, she could not dislodge it. While the staysmaker fitted her for a new corset, she found her mind returning to the subject again and again. She reminded herself how much she liked Nate, even in spite of the way he had deceived her. If she were honest with herself, she had to admit that after a few more months in Newgate she would have resorted to almost any stratagem to be released.

Sukey had been even less forgiving, especially when Jenny told her that Nate said he did not care about the money. "Maybe in Newgate," the pickpocket turned lady's maid conceded cynically. "In Newgate, you could persuade yourself that money don't matter. Nothin' matters there but gettin' out. But he ain't in Newgate now, is he?"

He was not. The reminder of their greatly changed situations gave Jenny pause. Remembering Nate's flattering words at the ball, she had never doubted but that they were such as he might offer, unthinking, to any woman of his acquaintance—not insincere so much as they were banal, meaningless. Yet the simplest compliment from Yves, she realized, a villain if ever there were one, rang with the sound of truth and sent the blood rushing to her cheeks. Absentmindedly she fingered one of her curls.

Sukey said the simplest solution for Nate, for him to regain the inheritance he had inadvertently given up without bringing undue notice upon their conspiracy, was to marry her.

Simple. That word alone alarmed her. That was

how Danger had described his plan in the very beginning. Yes, it had been simple—because he had hidden too many details, had concealed the trap waiting for her. His simple plan had placed her in this situation, where the continued surveillance of Yves kept her every nerve end tingling with awareness. Was it any wonder that Jenny was more afraid now than ever?

Among Jenny's many visitors in the days to come, the former highwayman, whom she hardly dared trust, was not behind in his attentions. Lady Pertwee seemed to perceive him as another suitor; Jenny suspected he merely enjoyed performing a new role. Yet he too was capable of kindness, of listening to her concerns, when privacy allowed, with sincere attention.

Richard had, in fact, gone to such pains to make himself agreeable to the entire family during the following weeks that when he came to call one brisk spring morning, Yves' butler thought nothing of announcing him to the ladies of the household although they were not officially receiving.

"Ladies, how kind of you to be in." He greeted them with a bow that encompassed all three, for Lady Pertwee was with them.

As usual at this time of day, they were gathered in the morning room. Jenny, comfortable in a simple sacque gown, had recently begun work embroidering a hunting scene for a fire screen. As a distraction, it served very well, for she detested needlework, lacking the patience, if not the talent, for such detail. Concentrating on her needle, she could forget Yves and her worries. Nonetheless she gladly set her needle and workbox aside to greet him.

Even Lady Pertwee was not immune to Richard's charm, Jenny observed. "We were just about to ring for some tea," her ladyship observed. "Won't you join us?"

"Thank you. I will and gladly." He took a chair next to Mrs. Mueller and directed his next statement to her. "I had hoped to find your nephew here, ma'am. When I saw him yesterday he said he thought he might be able to put me in the way of a good hunter."

"Oh," Mrs. Mueller said, "missed him you have by only a few minutes. I am surprised you did not see him leave, so close you come after his departure."

Something in his protestation of regret told Jenny that Richard had deliberately avoided Yves this time. Why? She could only hope that he would be able to find a way to tell her.

"You have a card for Lady Wetherby's on Friday, I suppose," Lady Pertwee said. "No doubt we shall all see you there."

Richard shook his head gravely. "I am told on good authority that her ladyship means to induce her company to try their hands at *bouts-rimés*. Now, I will do much for a hostess—I am willing to play whist with dowagers who cannot remember their last bid; I will dance with plain young ladies who cannot remember the figures of the cotillion; I will fetch ratafia, hartshorn, anything you like for a lady in distress—but I will neither compose nor recite poetry in public."

Jenny laughed at his posing. Actor that he was, she suspected Richard would do very well at such a game. "You are not obliged to participate, Sir Richard," she reminded him, glad of the chance to repay him for all the teasing he had subjected her to. "Surely you may stay and admire those braver souls who are willing to exercise their wits in public."

"But then I should perforce also witness the embarrassment of friends who have exposed their lack of wits, which always leads to discomfort," he said as the tea things were set out by the servants.

Somehow Jenny doubted that Richard would be anything other than amused by the performers' embarrassment, but she admired the way he set the ladies, especially Lady Pertwee, at ease. This was just the sort of banter that lady best understood.

"In any case," he continued, accepting a cup from Mrs. Mueller, "I shall probably meet his lordship tomorrow or the next day at Tom's coffeehouse or at Rolandi's."

"Rolandi's?" Mrs. Mueller repeated, questioning. "This is a new place for the gambling . . . the Pharaoh, yes?"

"Not at all, ma'am," Richard answered. "Rolandi's is a fencing salon. The proprietor gives instruction in the fine art of swordplay."

Of a sudden, Jenny felt her cheerful mood disappear, as if the sunlight had been blotted out in a single moment. So Yves was practicing his swordsmanship. Preparing for a fight? He had met Nate once before, Jenny knew. The prospect of another duel between the two sent a cold shiver down her spine.

It was Mrs. Mueller, however, who was most

affected by this news. She set the teapot down with a clatter. *"Gott in himmel,"* she whispered.

Instinctively, Jenny leaned over and reached for the older woman's hands. Cold to the touch, the widow's fingers trembled; her face turned suddenly pale.

"This talk of swords . . . always, from a little girl, they frighten me," Mrs. Mueller offered as an excuse for her obvious dismay.

"There's no danger of bloodshed at Rolandi's, ma'am, I assure you. For practice we use buttoned foils. Besides," Richard added with an encouraging smile, "accidents are very bad for business."

"Is true, I know," Mrs. Mueller said, "but young men—so hot-blooded you are at times."

Hating to see Mrs. Mueller so distressed, Jenny reached out to clasp her trembling hands.

"By the time Rolandi is done with us, ma'am, we are too exhausted to lose our temper," Richard said, trying to offer additional comfort. "Believe me, there is nothing more to it than healthy physical exercise." He seemed embarrassed now, no doubt feeling some compunction for alarming Mrs. Mueller so deeply. "I should hate to think a careless word of mine had distressed you. Lord Yves would never forgive me, nor would I forgive myself."

"No, no, is not your fault," she hastened to assure him. The frightened look, nonetheless, did not disappear from her eyes, although she shooed Jenny away to her own chair.

Clearly Mrs. Mueller feared another duel. With Nate? Jenny wondered. For all she knew, Yves might have a score of enemies eager to cut his throat. Yet she had not, in her brief foray into London society, sensed any such undercurrents. Yves might not be much liked socially, but he was respected, even by those who professed not to understand him.

Yet, as Jenny pictured Yves in her mind, she realized suddenly that perhaps the widow had good reason to fear. She had not previously taken much notice of the fact that Yves always wore a smallsword, a pretty thing with a grip of Meissen porcelain. Richard did the same, she remembered. A quick glance confirmed that he was wearing one now, although the habit of wearing town swords was dying out.

If she tried, she could find plausible reasons for such behavior. Yves, after all, was often called to court, where swords were still *de rigueur*. As for Richard, he had been a soldier (and highwayman); the carrying of weapons had probably been ingrained in him.

No dandy such as Nate, however, would wear a sword. Long, beribboned canes had taken the place of a weapon for that set. Nonetheless, Jenny realized with a pang of fear, she had yet to see Nate without a blade.

She looked at Richard, now trying to charm Mrs. Mueller out of her fright. Very well, he had made his announcement, but what had he meant by it? Had he intended no more than a warning? Or had he been looking for confirmation of his own fears as well? If so, he had it with a vengeance. Jenny only prayed he would be able to explain before he left.

Evidently Richard was prepared. "I must not impose on your hospitality much longer," he said, "but I did wish to bring Miss Beauchamp *au courant* of the latest news from her home. The last ship from Boston was full of messages from mutual acquaintances." From his pocket he pulled a sheaf of papers in confirmation of his claim.

The effect of such an announcement upon Lady Pertwee was easy to predict. Obviously foreseeing a boring account of provincial nobodies, she quickly intervened. "Sir Richard, you will give yourself the headache trying to read letters by this poor light," she said, paying no heed to the brightness of the room. "Why do you not take Miss Beauchamp nearer the window, so that you may both see."

And be seen, Jenny guessed, without being heard. Thereby they allowed the ladies to resume their gossip, probably now centered on Sir Richard himself, undeterred.

Behind the shelter of a letter (which was, in fact, from a Boston merchant), Jenny commented in a low voice, "So you have been improving your skills with the rapier and smallsword, Sir Richard. Do you anticipate needing these skills very soon?"

"Let us simply say that I prefer to be prepared. As, evidently, does Lord Yves."

The look on Richard's face surprised and worried Jenny. For the last two years this man had lived by the sword and the pistol, yet the arrogant self-confidence she had always associated with him was now absent. "Is he good?" she found herself asking.

"Superb. I cannot think of anyone I would rather have at my side in a fight."

Or, clearly, would rather not face in a fight.

Jenny rubbed her arms as if chilled. Quickly she checked to see how much attention their conversation was attracting. It appeared, however, that both Lady Pertwee and Mrs. Mueller intended to be discreetly obliging.

"Richard, am I right to be afraid?" she asked.

"It might even be wise," he answered with no trace of levity.

The very seriousness of his tone alarmed her more than any warning he might have uttered. With an effort, she damped her growing sense of panic. "What is happening, Richard? Have you heard from Nate?"

At the mention of Nate's name, a cloud seemed to settle over him. "Nate...Nate may be in difficulties."

Immediately suspicious, Jenny asked, "Caused by Yves?"

"Caused by Nate, more like." Richard gave a snort of disgust. "If you were hoping Nate would provide some solution for you, I fear you are going to be disappointed."

Jenny sighed. "That is a conclusion I had already reached." Against her will, some of her frustration seeped into her voice. "Perhaps I had expected too much of him, but I hardly see why he must waste time flirting with me when he only does it to annoy Yves."

"Does he now?" Richard was silent a moment, quietly pensive. "Jenny, I know you've never liked or trusted me," he said at last to her surprise, "but...no, don't bother to protest. Considering how we met, that's hardly unexpected."

The image of Danger leading a giggling, much painted woman to his bed intruded. It shocked

Jenny to discover how much she did want to protest, however. Perhaps she did not entirely trust Richard, seeing always some hint of Lord Danger ever present in him, but she had learned to appreciate and like that roguish spirit of his, the spirit that laughed at the world even as he shaped it to his own ends.

"You deliberately made me angry," she argued instead.

"True," he admitted. "It seemed best at the time. When you were angry, you could do anything. Ah, Jenny, with your eyes flashing murder at me, you were grand."

"Richard." Casting her eyes heavenward, she uttered his name half as plea, half as warning. "I've enough of that sort of talk from Nate. Don't you start too."

"No," he said softly. "I know better." His dark eyes were thoughtful as he looked to see how closely they were being observed. "Jenny, thief I may have been, but still I have ever followed a certain code, whether you'll believe it or not. I never stole more from the ladies than a kiss, and I never betrayed one of my own. On both accounts, then, you're safe with me. If your situation ever becomes . . . too difficult, too much to bear, you can always call on me to see you free of it. And if I'm . . . unavailable, go to Sam Harkins at the sign of the Turk's Head on Fleet Street. You'll be taken care of."

This was alarming talk from a man Jenny had always considered unduly confident of his own success in any endeavor. Here was escape offered, but at what risk to the others? If she disappeared, what would Yves do to Nate? "Richard, is there something I don't know, something to beware?" she asked.

He smiled. "No more than there was when we started this coil. Ah, we're noticed at last," he interrupted before she could question him further. Bowing, he said to the company at large, "Now I really must take my leave. The warmth of your welcome and the pleasure of your company always makes parting so difficult. Perhaps I will endure the *bouts-rimés* again after all. Ladies." He bowed again, grandly. "Miss Beauchamp."

As he kissed her hand adieu, he whispered, for Jenny's ears alone, "Whatever happens, remember that you are protected. Two pairs of eyes watch for your comfort, two strong arms are ready to defend you. I am but one of your humble servants."

Jenny continued to mull over Richard's conversation late into the evening—a quiet one for the household. Since Lady Pertwee was committed to friends that night, Jenny and Mrs. Mueller had eagerly snatched at the opportunity to ignore all invitations, stay home, and do nothing.

Nights like this Jenny could almost feel herself at home. Without the supervision of Lady Pertwee, conversation could be natural, almost unguarded. Certainly it could be more interesting when not centered on social gossip. Jenny assumed that it was the fascination of Yves' intellect, the breadth of his knowledge, that made his addition to such quiet entertainments so enlivening.

Tonight he had returned early from the coffeehouse, and seemed content to relax and listen to the sound of Jenny's voice as she read aloud (in French, in deference to Mrs. Mueller's preference for the language of the European courts) from Marmontel's *Contes Moraux*.

The depth of Mrs. Mueller's content was, after a while, evidenced by a gentle snore. Letting her voice grow ever more quiet, until at last it faded into silence, Jenny closed her book.

"You read beautifully," Yves complimented her, "but I fear your Moral Tales have failed to capture Tante's interest."

"So it seems," she said breathlessly, suddenly aware that they might as well be alone for all the chaperonage his aunt now provided. "Perhaps I should have tried *The Castle of Otranto*."

"Heaven forbid!" he said lightly. "We should then be unable to sleep all night." Yves rose and left his place next his aunt to stand, leaning casually against the mantel, close to where Jenny sat in the grandfather wing chair. Tonight he seemed very approachable, she thought, hardly formidable at all. Relaxed, he seemed to be sensitive to her every mood. "If you will forgive the impertinence," he said, "you do not look as if you needed further contribution to a restless night."

In his eyes Jenny saw only concern. He did not seem to demand her confidence, but with a delicate sensibility revealed his openness to listen. Oddly enough, Jenny did feel an urge to let spill some of the questions churning in her breast, questions she could not reveal to her only confidante. Much though she loved Sukey and respected her hard common sense, Sukey belonged to another world. In the world of cutpurses and footpads, she had been the best of guides. The world of London society was no less treacherous, inhabited by a different class of rogues—captain sharps, fortune-hunters, and rakes—and here Jenny had no guide. To whom could she turn? Nate who used flattery to prevent serious conversation? Richard who refused to respond seriously, thinking life a jest?

But Richard had been serious enough this afternoon, if somewhat misguided. Two strong arms to defend her? How much faith they could place in Nate seemed to be in question, and Richard had seemed to realize it. Jenny could only assume that he felt Nate could respond with strength where he could not with cunning.

Having waited too long to easily dismiss the accusation of worry, Jenny admitted at last, "Something Sir Richard said this afternoon disturbed me. Or confused me, I should say."

"Confused?" Yves stepped closer, sounding a little surprised by her choice of word.

Indeed she was confused. Everything she had held secure now shifted and moved like quicksand beneath her feet. The man she knew to have committed the cruel and despicable act of deliberately sending an innocent man to prison stood before her, so gentle and caring in appearance that Jenny's heart ached to see him. Were circumstances different, Jenny thought she might have sought and trusted the counsel of this man who could so easily destroy her. Compared to the mystery of Yves, the others were almost nothing. Almost.

Her confusion and anxiety demanded voice, as forcefully as Yves demanded an answer, yet how could she explain?

"Someone I had admired has evidently behaved in a manner that is, to say the least, disappointing," she said at last, speaking slowly, carefully choosing each word, Nate and his avoidance of any discussion of her plight very much on her mind. She laughed, but without mirth. "And a person I had believed without conscience has, by the same account, behaved exceedingly well." If she were honest, with herself as much as with Yves, there were two gentlemen of dubious history who had of late impressed her with their kindness, and one of them stood quite close.

She looked away, embarrassed. Would he realize that her statement referred to him? Very quietly, she added, "I feel lost. I don't know what to believe any more."

After a moment, he placed a hand on the back of her chair. "It is never easy to judge or understand people," he said softly. "No one is quite what they seem. Not I, not even you."

She trembled. How, she wondered, did she appear to Yves? The idea that he should see her as a deceitful impostor was surprisingly unpleasant.

"Each of us has hidden strengths, faults, desires ...," he continued in an earnest tone. Kneeling next to her, so close Jenny could almost feel his breath upon her cheek, he pointed to his aunt. "Take my beloved Tante. What do you see when you look at her? A kind and gentle widow, full of homely virtues, sedate, a little shy?"

Jenny nodded, hesitantly, more aware of his presence than that of the sleeping widow.

"Look again," he said, shaking his head in denial. "She could have married a prince. Would have—it is what my grandfather intended for her.

Instead, at age twenty-three—just a few years older than you are—she eloped with one of the merchants of the town. She did this knowing she would be abandoned by her family, utterly cast off and repudiated by parents, brothers, sisters . . . because she had committed the unforgivable sin—she had fallen in love. For love she gave up everything—family, fortune, position—all. And willingly."

Ignorant of the conversation on the other side of the room, the older woman still dozed peacefully. Jenny looked at her and tried to picture the passionate young girl she must have been. Yes, the hints of prettiness and the same inner fire remained, dimmed but not extinguished.

"I would not have seen that in your aunt," Jenny confessed after a moment, "but, now that you have told me, I can easily believe it, because I know how warm and generous a nature she has. But when one hears something that does not fit what one already knows," she said, looking into his brilliant blue eyes, "how do you decide what to believe? Whom to trust?"

"Reason may guide us to measure actions against words, may tell us what is likely and what is not."

He was very close, his eyes, clear and direct, on a level with hers, his hand almost touching hers.

"And sometimes, beyond reason, or even in spite of reason, the heart simply knows," he said. "Sometimes the heart just knows."

Chapter Ten

Yves' counsel was no doubt excellent, but it left
Jenny more confused than ever. Her heart, which
he seemed to advocate as judge, was behaving in
a most peculiar manner, especially when he was
near, and was certainly not to be trusted. Judge
by a man's actions, he said. Yet his own actions
were hardly consistent. To her he had been often
kind, yet sometimes cold as ice. His treatment of
Nate was loathsome. She knew he inspired many
with fear, yet some, too, with devotion. There was
an answer to be found somewhere, Jenny sensed,
but how or where to find it remained hidden.

Worst of all, there was no time to stop and
think, no time to put these troublesome thoughts
in perspective. To have half an hour alone with
Sukey, the only person she could talk to freely,
had become a luxury. Either Mrs. Mueller or Lady

Pertwee always seemed to rush in for a few minutes during the important process of the toilet, to give or ask for advice.

At least she had been able to impart Richard's warning and offer of help to Sukey, although their conversation had only deepened her sense of anxiety. Contrary to expectation, Sukey had not reacted with a smiling confidence in Richard.

"Damn. Damn it," she cried, setting down the brush she had been using to dress Jenny's hair.

In the mirror Jenny could see the hurt and anger on the girl's face. She reached back to take Sukey's hand.

"I liked it here," Sukey confessed. She bit her trembling lip. "I thought maybe . . . we could stay like this till you gets the money. Then you'd get yourself a little place in the country, like you said at first, and I'd be your maid and companion. All nice and respectable. Funny, ain't it. Me—Sukey, the diver? I like being respectable."

"We'll be respectable, Sukey," Jenny promised. "If not here, someplace." Someplace, she hoped, where she would not have to pretend to be anyone other than Jenny Wilde.

Sukey sighed and resumed her task, coaxing the auburn curls into place. "Seems like all my life I been on the run one way or t'other. Now I'm tired of running. Never stood still long enough before to find that out."

Later, dressed in a green and white striped *robe à l'anglaise* over a flounced petticoat, Jenny still thought of her friend's stricken face as she listened to a remarkably silly attempt at versifying at Lady Wetherby's soirée. The *bouts-rimés* were as embarrassing as Richard had predicted, but left

Jenny free to reflect. Looking around the ornate drawing room, from the painted faces of the guests to Yves' austere countenance, she wondered how much longer this world would be hers.

A sudden ache pierced her heart at the thought of leaving. Trap or no, there had been a sense of home with Yves, a home she must lose regardless of other outcomes. That home belonged to Jean-Marie Beauchamp, a girl who did not exist, not Jenny Wilde.

Ever attentive, Yves must have seen some momentary shadow cross her face, for he touched her arm gently and asked after her well-being. Before she could answer, however, Yves suddenly tensed. Jenny did not need to turn around to know who had provoked such a reaction. It could only be Nate.

Resplendent in blue satin, he took the floor to recite his poetic offering. Pausing a moment, he scanned the room until he spotted them, then favored them with a florid salute. For her benefit or Yves'? She could not guess.

Uncomfortable at this pointed attention, she soon discovered there was worse to come.

In a dulcet voice, and with his gaze still resting warmly on her, Nate began:

> *"Amidst the pearls of London's fairest*
> *a single ruby gleams, the greatest prize—*
> *a lady, of all her kind the rarest,*
> *as rich in spirit as in beauty. Her eyes..."*

His voice went on, each word striking dread in her heart. As counterpoint to his verses, a whispered thread of gossip had clearly begun. Jenny knew what was being said, sensed it, without hearing a word of the insinuations. Behind the painted fans, the gossips peeked slyly at Jenny and conjectured as to whether she would accept Nate's suit.

And Yves, how would he react? she wondered. Even he would have to concede that Nate was brilliant. The terms of the game easily lent themselves to expressions of romantic ardor, but Nate had turned them into a passionate evocation of love, clearly directed at her, with her bright ruby tresses.

Oh, the rhymes were nothing out of the ordinary. Somehow, however, although others had used the same words, none had inspired the same effect. There was a surprising element of sincerity behind the verse—a disconcerting quality to find in Nate's work, and she suspected Yves found it so too.

In the end, the quality of the poem hardly mattered, Jenny admitted to herself. Nate might have written doggerel, yet his purpose remained clear. The gauntlet had been thrown. Nate had announced to the world that he was courting his cousin.

Yet she feared there was more in this than a challenge to Yves. *Marriage was the simplest way*, Sukey had said. Blushing fiercely, Jenny tried to ignore the whispers around her, but she could not ignore the voices in her own mind. It was true—marriage to Nate would solve her problems as well as Nate's. As Lady Vickers, she would once again have an identity, a home. Women made marriages every day based on less affection than she had for Nate. Why couldn't she?

"Perhaps you would care for some refreshment and cooler air?" Yves said quietly in her ear.

"Yes, please," Jenny answered gratefully. Unable to face the knowing smiles of Nate and his audience, she could think of nothing but getting away from them all. Nothing Yves could say in his anger could be any worse than this.

Once outside the room, she waited for the explosion, but it never came. Instead, calm as always, Yves brought her a glass of claret. He seemed sympathetic to her embarrassment, and oddly meditative, as if this challenge also held a puzzle.

"Nate and I shared the same tutor," he said mildly, "although he is five years my senior. That poem was no work of his. I wonder who wrote it?"

The idea that Nate would go to the trouble of having someone else write a love poem to her seemed distasteful to Jenny. Although the idea would not have occurred to her unaided, she did not doubt it. There was a familiar cadence to the words, but it was not Nate's voice. It almost sounded like . . .

"Do you know, I could almost hear the voice of the condemned highwayman," Yves said. "This was much of his style."

The idea was so surprising that Jenny, for once, ignored the reference to the highwayman. Richard? No, it lacked his mocking air. In any case, Jenny suspected he would not perform such a favor for Nate, not even for the sake of amusement. Not willingly.

"With his last words so widely circulated," she said, "no doubt but that the highwayman has

214

many admirers, and imitators."

"As you say," he said, dismissing the matter, and offered her his arm. "Shall we join the others in the card room?"

Jenny nodded, thankful for his silence and the support of his arm. Beneath the satin and lace she could feel warmth and strength. She might have found some comfort in that strength, she mourned silently, had she not been an impostor.

Barely conscious of her surroundings, she strolled through the reception rooms at Yves' side. How could she begin to understand him, when she could not understand herself? The prospect of being courted by a good, if weak, friend repulsed her, yet she clung to the arm of the one man who could destroy them all. Advice or answers she needed, yet instead she exchanged greetings with acquaintances and continued with Yves, crossing the crowded apartments until they reached the room set aside for those who preferred games of chance to games of words.

"I do not see Sir Richard tonight," Yves commented as they entered and looked about for their companions.

"Perchance the terrors of literary production proved too great after all," Jenny said, trying to throw off her strange mood. Calmer now, she was a little disquieted that Yves' conversation should so closely follow from Danger to Dangerfield. "When last he visited, he expressed some reluctance to endure the poetic inspirations of others."

Yves smiled, evidently intending nothing but general conversation. "An understandable reaction. They do this sort of thing better in France, but I must still applaud the attempt to introduce a more intellectual element into society, and must applaud literary merit when it is found. Ah, here is Tante," he said, sighting her at a table with friends.

Mrs. Mueller, they discovered, had now won the grand sum of two shillings from her fellow card-players and was flushed with the pleasure of victory. Since one of the players was obliged to leave for another commitment, Jenny took the lady's place with a little relief. The cards held no more than moderate interest for her, but they relieved her of much of the necessity for small talk.

Or so she had assumed. As soon as Yves left them to converse with some gentlemen who had news of the court, the older ladies began to gossip, and the subject of their gossip, to Jenny's dismay, was Lord Vickers.

"Such a handsome man, Lord Vickers," the dowager baroness began, evidently unaware of the sudden strain in Mrs. Mueller's attitude. "He always lends such an air to any gathering. I do not know another man who dresses so elegantly."

"Or so expensively," Mrs. Mueller commented, not quite under her breath.

Jenny could sense the older women observing her, looking for some sign, some reaction to the man they believed to be her suitor. "Indeed," she said at last, feeling some comment necessary, "my cousin has beautiful manners."

"He certainly does," the dowager continued, the gossip flowing so automatically from her lips that it impeded her grasp of the game not at all. "My son saw him lose a cool thousand at play yesternight. He had lost three times as much the night before, but he showed no concern, no anxiety or ill-feeling. Instead he laughed and treated the company to breakfast. Now, that is the way a gentleman should behave—always showing the same face to the world."

Four thousand lost in two nights! Jenny was astonished. Could Nate afford to lose so much? Thinking back to Richard's earlier cryptic statement, she wondered if Nate were in danger of debt once again. To someone raised in this society, gambling might well seem an easy means to increment one's income. Yet . . . Jenny's heart misgave her. Only a fool, knowing the consequences of debt and knowing that Yves would ensure those consequences, would risk debt again. The man who had just proclaimed his feelings for her in verse did not look, however, as if he feared the bailiff, or indeed as if he feared anything. In fact, she realized now, part of what had so disturbed her about Nate's performance had been a swaggering assumption of success that pervaded his attitude, if not his words.

Almost as if her thoughts had called him forth, a few minutes later Nate came into the card room. At first he merely strolled about, laughing and talking with friends, but soon he came to stand by her and advise her on her discards. His helpful comments failed to improve either Jenny's play or Mrs. Mueller's. The presence of Yves' enemy, in fact, unnerved Mrs. Mueller so that she seemed likely to lose her meager winnings.

Finding the older woman's discomfort contagious, Jenny soon manufactured an excuse to leave the table, allowing Nate to escort her back to the other room to hear Mr. Burke recite from his work. It was past time she had a word with

Nate about his behavior. No doubt he wanted to taunt his enemy, but it was callous to do so at her expense and Mrs. Mueller's.

"I wish you would not tease Mrs. Mueller so, cousin. She doesn't deserve such treatment." Jenny was very careful to address Nate as cousin now—not from the necessity of maintaining her imposture, but to keep a proper distance in their relationship. The once-easy intimacy of his given name might lead others—including Nate—to regard their connection as one warmer than the purely familial.

"Forgive me," he said. "When she looks at me as if I had two horns growing out of my forehead, I find it difficult to resist."

Despite his engaging smile, Jenny was not appeased.

"I suppose they have been wailing in your ears all day long about what a villain I have been to my tenants. No wonder that it should leave you out of temper."

"No," Jenny said, confused yet somehow afraid to hear more. She had to know, however. "Why are you a villain this time?"

"I have emptied Vickers of all his spies," Nate said with satisfaction. "Sacked all the servants and turned out the tenants. I won't keep any of Yves' men about me to stab me in the back."

Jenny's first thought was simply that Yves would never stab a man in the back; it was not his way. Then the enormity of what Nate had done truly sank in. Turned everyone out? How could he? Yet instinctively she knew that to display her aversion would be to doom all chance of persuading him of the wrongness, if not the outright cruelty, of his action. "But, Na ... cousin," she said haltingly, "*all* the servants and tenants could hardly be loyal to Lord Yves' interests. Many of them must have served Vickers from your great-uncle's time."

"Oh, they always favored Wolf, made a fuss of him because he was youngest. Do you think I mean to have him thrown in my face every time I suggest an improvement? 'But Lord Yves always did it this way,'" Nate mimicked with a harsh sneer. "Not I. And the proof of Yves' interference is that he has taken them all under his protection—promised them places on his estates. I hope it costs him a pretty penny."

For the first time, Jenny looked at Nate and saw, to her horror, a complete stranger. Where was the considerate gentleman of Newgate? Had he quite disappeared? The feelings of those servants—the people who owed their livelihood to him—meant nothing to him. His imagination could not encompass their feelings, their physical distress. Yet Yves had evidently provided for them without a second thought.

"Yves would not count the cost of such a deed," she said softly, knowing it to be true.

Something in her voice must have alerted Nate at last to her failure to endorse his action.

"Jenny, don't tell me Yves has taken you in, too. You cannot think well of such a monster."

That is what she told herself so often, but it became ever more difficult to accept.

"In this case," she argued, "I must think well of him. He has behaved with great generosity."

"Only to make me look cruel—and to make sure

none of his people should try to return and sell his secrets to me."

When Nate said it, it almost sounded plausible, but not plausible enough. In the weeks since Jenny had become Miss Beauchamp she had seen and learned much of Lord Yves. Of his intelligence, determination, and strength she would believe anything; his cunning, however, did not extend to slander. Although she knew he despised Nate, he never told tales to influence her feelings. It might have been easier for her if he had.

"Do you forget, Jenny, what he did to me?" Nate asked her, evidently appalled by her lack of sympathy for him. "Throwing me into Newgate, keeping me from my inheritance?"

"No," Jenny said, looking away. "I do not forget what he has done."

But for the first time, Jenny began to wonder if, just possibly, Yves might not have good reason for having done so.

Yves sat at the desk in his study and looked carefully over the information left him by his eyes and ears. Matters would soon come to a head, that was clear. So far Nate had been careful to meet all debts of honor, but at his present rate of loss at the tables that situation could not long continue. His creditors knew where to bring their accounts when Nate ignored them too long.

Nate knew it, too, yet he did not seem unduly concerned. Was he so very sure of winning the hand of his cousin, the heiress? Yves wondered. Did he have reason to be sure?

No, Yves refused to think it. It was far more likely that Nate had badly misjudged the girl—

Jenny. Since Tante had told him her affectionate nickname, he had not been able to dismiss it from his mind. Jenny.

She had been troubled of late. His instinctive desire to comfort her, however, had to be stifled, no matter how difficult it proved to be. And it was difficult. On the night they had talked, he had been very tempted to tell her the truth about Nate. He knew it was impossible, of course. Too well could he foresee how that would end—utter disbelief and disdain. The disdain would hurt him, but more importantly, the disbelief might hurt her, if it sent her back to Nate.

What he could not tell was how deeply Jenny's heart was involved with either of these men who wooed her and confused her. Women were wont to be charmed by Nate's good looks and graceful manner. Yves' hands clenched convulsively around the letter opener. To the world Nate was, after all, his victim, Yves reminded himself, and as such had a sure call upon her sympathy.

Dangerfield, however, remained a formidable rival, as, he was sure, Nate realized. According to Tante, Jenny did not notice the baronet's attentions, but that situation might easily change. It seemed possible, he guessed from their last conversation, that she had already begun to perceive Sir Richard in a different way, was more aware of his virtues.

Surely it was preferable for Jenny to become Lady Dangerfield than Lady Vickers, Yves tried vainly to persuade himself. Whatever the man had been before, Dangerfield was now a responsible landowner, as good a master as he had been an officer, by all accounts. In sooth, Yves had a sneaking liking for the fellow—but not as a match for Jenny.

Yves' revery was interrupted by a knock at the door, followed by the footman's announcement of the arrival of none other than Sir Richard himself.

"Bid him enter," Yves said. What did the fellow want? he wondered as he began to put his papers away. It was possible, of course, that the call was purely social—but not likely. Closing up the safe, he pondered the possibility of new developments as the gentleman entered.

"I see you take sensible precautions, milord," Dangerfield said, referring to the safe. "Everyone seems to complain about the perils of travel, the prevalence of thieves along the highroad, but for my part, I find the encroachment of these criminals into the privacy of one's home far more frightening."

Something in Dangerfield's voice drew his attention. His comment had not sounded like mere generalization. "Don't tell me you have also experienced such a theft, Sir Richard?" he asked. Was this why he had come? If so, all that remained to be seen was whether Dangerfield felt a need to question him or to warn him.

Dangerfield shrugged. "Certainly my apartments were entered and searched, but whether such an effort deserves to be called theft..."

"No valuables were taken, then?"

Dangerfield shook his head in confirmation, and offered his host a pinch of snuff. "There was little enough of any value to be found, in faith. Nought but this signet ring of my father's, a stickpin, and a watch fob or two." He held up his snuffbox of chased silver, and took a pinch himself. "And this," he added. "Since mine are only temporary quarters, I have kept but little of personal interest or value by me."

Yves would have expected no less. It must be obvious to all that Dangerfield was a careful man, not one to leave valuables or papers lying about. That the few small items of value he admitted to possessing had not been taken was very interesting.

"Yet one would not expect a thief to turn up his nose at such trinkets," Yves said, stating what he knew must be obvious to his guest. "What may be of small value to you or me may seem incalculable wealth to another."

"Why, so I thought."

Interesting indeed. From his behavior, Yves guessed that Dangerfield had no answers yet. Suspicions, however, he must have. Had he learned enough yet about the new Lord Vickers, Yves wondered, to suspect what Yves had long assumed to be the case?

"How strange!" Yves commented. "Yet even though nothing was taken, it must be uncomfortable for you. You are quite correct in saying that the victim is far more disturbed to find his very home—even a temporary home—violated. A crime with no reason, too, is more disturbing than one clearly based on greed."

"Oh, I did not say that nothing was taken," Dangerfield corrected him. "Merely nothing of value. What a thief may make of my poor efforts at composition..." He laughed, but not with amusement. "Probably he thought it was something else, and will be greatly disappointed when he finds someone to read it for him," he continued.

The poem, no doubt, and Nate had stolen it. Foolish of Nate to think Dangerfield might leave incriminating documents about—yet typical. Nate's judgment of character always had been poor. Examining the gentleman now lounging at his ease opposite him, Yves wondered again where Dangerfield would stand when the time came, as it soon must.

He shook his head. "A foolish enterprise all 'round. You must describe this odd occurrence to the ladies. Perchance they can deduce some explanation," Yves suggested, unwilling to embarrass his guest by presenting his conclusions regarding the too-revealing poem himself. Given the opportunity, Jenny would reveal his suspicions regarding Nate's performance at *bouts-rimés*. He could only hope that the revelation would help resolve any doubts Dangerfield had about Nate.

"And where are the ladies this afternoon? I had hoped to be able to pay my respects," Dangerfield said, having evidently accomplished what he meant to do.

"They are involved in a matter of great import," Yves answered, as if this subject were of equal meaning to the game the two played. "I have commissioned Mr. Joshua Reynolds to paint Miss Beauchamp's portrait. The ladies have gone to confer with the mantua-maker regarding the proper costume."

"I shall be glad to see it. By the by, I also wanted to thank you for the information you gave me. I was able to purchase a nice pair as well as the hunter from Threlfall's stable."

"Then I am glad to have been of service," Yves

said. He swiftly reviewed the news he had received shortly before his guest's arrival. Perhaps, he reflected, Dangerfield could be induced to return the favor and provide him some information. After all, there were some things his eyes and ears could not tell him, things he would like to find out from Dangerfield. Not facts, nothing so crude as that. There was little of the Newgate conspiracy he did not know by now. How Dangerfield would react when his net finally closed around Nate, however, was one thing he could not tell. If Jenny were his first concern, Dangerfield could be a formidable ally. He could also be a formidable enemy if he chose otherwise.

How to sound him out, however? Yves leaned back in his chair. The time prescribed for the ritual polite visit was past. To lose the opportunity, he had to admit, would hurt. It was not often that the two of them met privately. Either the ladies were present, or club members, or . . .

"Your service to Miss Beauchamp on the long voyage home deserves even better recompense," Yves said, rising, choosing his words carefully. "Miss Beauchamp has oft expressed her appreciation of the company of her fellow colonials. We must regret that the press of business so often keeps you from company. Your absence from Rolandi's has certainly been keenly felt. I've not found another sparring partner to match your skill."

Dangerfield laughed and also rose. "You flatter me, milord. 'Twould be more accurate to say you can find no partner to approach your own skill."

"Nay, you are too modest. I wonder . . ." Yves feigned a moment's hesitation, as if considering a sudden whim. "I wonder—since you cannot find time to visit Rolandi's, that is—would you be interested in having a little practice here?" He gestured gracefully toward the simple yet functional smallsword Dangerfield wore.

"Now?" Dangerfield looked surprised, but not unwilling. It was possible he had yet another agenda in mind, too.

Yves shrugged, as if his answer mattered little. "The ballroom would offer us plenty of space." And, more importantly, privacy, he thought.

He could see Dangerfield weighing his motives, considering what he had to gain, before deciding. "Very well. I could profit from a little exercise after so many hours spent with bailiffs and men of business."

Yves led his guest to the ballroom, which seemed cold and curiously empty without orchestra and dancers. If he were wrong about his opponent, he quickly realized, if Dangerfield were after all another such knave as Nate, this might be a very great mistake, a chance for them to be rid of him once and for all. Which of them had the greater skill was yet to be determined. It had been impossible to tell at Rolandi's.

As they removed coats, waistcoats, and stocks, Yves observed that his opponent did not seem to have grown soft from lack of exercise. After seeing his guest do so, Yves also removed his shoes. Clearly Dangerfield was not, for all his ease of manner, taking this lightly.

"Do we need to bother with buttons?" Dangerfield asked.

Fight with an unblunted point? A challenge to his daring, or something more ominous? Yves wondered. He made a few imaginary passes in the air, moving into the center of the room. Perhaps Dangerfield, too, was hoping that the need for concentration on fencing technique would loosen his opponent's command of his tongue. Was it worth the risk, however? Yves smiled. "Very well, then. As we are."

"As we are," Dangerfield echoed.

Yves lifted his blade. "*En garde.*"

They saluted, Dangerfield showing a flourish Yves now found familiar. Their opening sallies were of a testing nature. Probably Dangerfield was as unsure of him as Yves was of Dangerfield, Yves thought wryly. Certainly neither of them could be secure enough in his own skill to risk his life on the outcome. Dangerfield had ten years of soldiering behind him that Yves knew of, and at least two years of roguery in addition to that. All Yves had was the personal determination never to be beaten again, as he had been by Nate, that had led him to perfect his skill over the last fifteen years.

As Yves seemed to become more secure, Dangerfield began to take the offensive, looking for ways to break past Yves' guard. This was perfectly fine with Yves. Let Dangerfield tire himself out, he thought. In the meantime he continued to parry each thrust with consummate ease.

"I must apologize, milord," Dangerfield began, disengaging to try a new line of attack, "if my mention of your sword practice the other day disturbed your aunt. Had I realized how deeply she felt about the matter, I would never have uttered a syllable."

"I'm glad you did," Yves responded. In this, too,

he was willing to follow Dangerfield's lead. The questions he was asked should prove as informative as any responses he elicited. The answers to his own questions could wait until his opponent began to tire.

"It was past time we had a discussion on the matter. You see," Yves said, calmly maintaining pace, "once, in my green days of hot-headed foolishness, I issued a challenge, and was soundly thrashed—a humiliating experience that neither Tante nor I would care to see repeated."

Dangerfield was beginning to perspire. His choice of offense had forced him to expend far more effort than Yves, as Yves expected. "I should not think it likely now," he said.

"Thank you," Yves said, quickly parrying. "To ensure that it would not, however, Tante made me promise that I would never again, by conscious and premeditated decision, issue a challenge."

"By premeditated decision," Dangerfield repeated, pointing out the escape clause in his promise.

Yves smiled. He was beginning to get a feeling for Dangerfield's style of fencing, one that depended strongly on the compound riposte. "Naturally, if a quarrel were to be deliberately forced on me ..."

"Or if you were forced to defend your person or your honor ..."

"Or, of course," Yves said, suddenly switching to the attack, "in defense of the ladies under my care. I must act then." His blade tapped gently at Dangerfield's chest, just above the heart.

"*Touché*," Dangerfield acknowledged. He

looked a little surprised to find himself bested, Yves thought.

They separated a moment and saluted one another again. This time, Yves noted, there was a wariness in his opponent's stance. His approach was more cautious now. Well, if Dangerfield had not realized it already, he would soon know that Yves was not a man to be trifled with.

Yet, clearly, Dangerfield still had more questions, as he pressed his attack. "I am glad to know the ladies are so well protected. The lure of Miss Beauchamp's fortune might well prove too tempting for some unscrupulous gentleman," he said pointedly.

For once Yves was disconcerted. Could Dangerfield think he was after the Beauchamp fortune? Nate, he knew, would certainly have ascribed such motives to him. How humorous to think Dangerfield might be seeking the very same knowledge as he—to discover how far he might depend on the other to protect Jenny.

"Should there be any such," Yves said as he made a swift lunge forward, "I believe I can deal with any whom Miss Beauchamp does not herself handle. I have often observed that she shows a wisdom and knowledge of the world far beyond her years."

"She has seen too much of horrors no lady should know," Dangerfield answered seriously.

There was a note in Dangerfield's voice Yves had not heard before. It struck him that his opponent was taking as much care with his words now as he was with his swordthrusts. Obviously, Dangerfield wanted the importance of what he said to be clearly understood.

"Perhaps because we share some common background," Dangerfield continued, "Miss Beauchamp has confided in part her travails upon the loss of her family. Having fought in the war myself, I know, too, the kind of experiences she does not talk about, those she cannot bear to repeat. I wonder if you realize how very remarkable a woman she is."

With equal gravity, Yves said quietly, "I believe I do. It is a foolish man indeed who prefers Miss Beauchamp's fortune to her fair self."

And neither of them were fools. Yves had never doubted that Dangerfield's regard for Jenny was sincere, however, only that it might not be able to overcome his instinct for self-preservation. Would Dangerfield defend Jenny at the risk of his own life? At the risk of betrayal by Nate?

"Unfortunately, the world is full of fools," Yves continued after a moment. "I fear me that her cousin may be one of them."

"Lord Vickers?" Dangerfield parried the redoublement at the last moment, and struggled to regain his balance. "An...undependable sort, I would have thought, as much as one may gather from so brief an acquaintance. It does seem to me, though, that Miss Beauchamp does not encourage his attentions."

"Vickers is not easily discouraged," Yves told him, wondering privately how undependable Dangerfield might have found Vickers. "But he will be stopped."

If Dangerfield were still in league with Nate, Yves knew he must see the threat implicit in his words, as he was meant to do. He must be made to see that there was more peril in opposing Yves than in opposing Vickers.

The baronet, however, answered seriously, "If there is anything—anything—I can do to ensure Miss Beauchamp's safety and happiness, I beg you will call on me to do so."

Relief surged through Yves. Yes, love for Jenny, then, would outweigh other interests, other loyalties. "Without fail," he promised.

There was one more question, however, that he found he could not dismiss from his mind, no matter how he tried. "But do you not also put yourself forward as a suitor, Sir Richard?" And would Jenny's happiness continue to be more important than his own if she refused him?

"Ah, milord, if only I could." Dangerfield answered lightly enough, but his voice held some tinge of sadness, of regret. "There are some few things a man may do which will render him unfit for the role of suitor in a lady's eyes. If I could change the past..." He shrugged and engaged in tierce. "Unfortunately, Miss Beauchamp's first impressions of me were formed when I was paying conspicuous court to a woman who was decidedly not a lady. Such a strong impression, I fear, is impossible to erase."

Yves advanced, forcing his opponent back. "Yet you have won a coveted place in her circle of friends," he reminded Dangerfield.

"Miss Beauchamp is yet new in London," Dangerfield answered, trying to hold his ground, "and I am a comfortable reminder of the past. That is all. I see well enough where her affections lead her."

Yves broke through his opponent's guard this time with a remise. Once again the blade tapped

Dangerfield, and hovered a mere hair's-breadth from his throat. A sudden spurt of emotion had nearly brought it closer still. The loss of control disturbed Yves, but if it frightened Dangerfield, he thought, perhaps it had served some purpose.

"Do you?" he asked.

Jenny watched Lady Pertwee descend from the coach with a certain degree of awe. After an afternoon of choosing silks, spending endless hours deciding between two shades of sapphire blue, and then being poked and prodded by the mantua-maker, she felt exhausted. The same activities, however, seemed to have imbued her chaperone with energy.

"A very productive day," her ladyship declared as she breezed into the house and on into the small drawing room. "Now we have only a few incidentals to purchase for your ensemble."

More? Jenny winced at the thought. Following Lady Pertwee and Mrs. Mueller into the room, she immediately sought the comfort of the large wing chair.

"What you wear for your sittings is immensely important," Lady Pertwee reminded her, having caught her look of dismay. "How you appear in this portrait is how you will be remembered in the future, for many generations to come."

Jenny looked away, embarrassed. The whole idea of having her portrait done made her self-conscious and ill at ease. What could such a picture represent? Not Jean-Marie Beauchamp—she did not exist. In her place stood a fraud, an impostor. This was not how Jenny wanted to be remembered; it was not how she wanted to think of herself.

"At Vickers, all the Beauchamps are painted for many generations," Mrs. Mueller explained, an explanation that only made Jenny feel worse. "Is good you should have likeness done. I only wish Wolfram would do so. Many times to persuade him I try, but always he refuses."

The mention of Yves' name seemed to further mobilize Lady Pertwee. "Where is his lordship?" she asked the footman who appeared at her call. Since the ball, Jenny had noticed that her ladyship lost no opportunity to put herself forward in his company.

"I believe his lordship is still with Sir Richard in the ballroom, my lady."

Was it Jenny's imagination, or did the footman seem slightly uneasy delivering this information? What could the two men have to discuss in the ballroom, in any case?

"I'll ask them to join us for tea, shall I?" Jenny said, springing up. Probably Lady Pertwee would put down her sudden spurt of energy to an eagerness to see her admirer, but that could not be helped.

It was not until she had reached the door of the ballroom that she became aware of the sound of voices, and a metallic clash that could be nothing but the meeting of swords. Frightened, she hurled open the door and rushed inside.

The two men were locked in close combat. In the heat of their exertion they had stripped to their shirtsleeves, and the untrammeled freedom of their movements had caused the shirts to open further. It only took a moment for Jenny to recognize the note of laughter in their voices. Both were obviously enjoying their sparring match immensely, and seemed, in spite of their attempts to skewer the other, to be fully in accord with each other.

What horrified and affixed Jenny to the spot was the sight of Yves' bared chest, lean and tightly muscled, branded with a cruel slash that crossed from side to side.

It was a moment before she realized the gentlemen had noticed her arrival and stopped their fight. They could also plainly see that she was staring. Quietly Yves restored his shirt to its usual order, enabling Jenny to find her tongue at last.

"You terrified me, both of you," she admonished from the top of the ballroom stairs, her hand resting over her heart. "From the noise you made, I expected to find the floor drenched with blood. I begin to appreciate why Mrs. Mueller finds the thought of swordplay so distressing."

"However, you must see now that your fears were baseless," Richard responded, reaching for his own waistcoat. "As you see, we are both unhurt—only out of breath." He seemed to be trying to reassure her on another level as well.

Assuming a calmness she did not feel, Jenny said, "And thirsty, I dare wager, after so much exertion. Mrs. Mueller has rung for tea and asks if you gentlemen would care to join us."

"Yes, certainly, as soon as we have made ourselves fit for ladies' company," Yves said, his expression cool and blank. There had been an open pleasure in his face, an uninhibited enjoyment of the pitting of skill against skill, in the moment before Jenny interrupted them that she was sorry to see disappear. "Thank you, Miss Beauchamp."

Jenny knew her cheeks were flushed when she returned to the drawing room, knew what the others must suspect, but could not help herself. Throughout tea, she remained quiet, answering only when addressed directly. She had to remind herself not to stare at Yves. The sight of that scar haunted her. Although he sat clad once again in his customary sober garb, she saw only the image of his bared chest. No wonder Mrs. Mueller had blanched at the very mention of swordplay, if this were the result.

A distressing thought crossed her mind. Yves was hardly the man to be drawn into pointless quarrels. As a courtier, he was a man who believed first and foremost in the efficacy of words in solving problems, and in dissolving tense situations. Surely this could not be the result of his duel with Nate.

No, impossible. From Nate's story, Jenny had assumed that he had barely escaped with his life. Nevertheless, the thought would not be dismissed.

It was inevitable that Yves would notice her abstraction, even though her chaperone and hostess did not. When they returned to their separate occupations after tea, he detained her for a moment, blocking her exit at the doorway. His movement was graceful, but nonetheless effective.

"I am sorry you should have been distressed by what you saw today, Miss Beauchamp," he told her quietly.

"I feel foolish now," she confessed, knowing her embarrassed countenance could attest to the fact.

"But, in sooth, at first I thought you were about to kill each other." It would be better, she thought, to pretend that that was all that had distressed her.

"Appearances are so often deceiving," he agreed. "I was not referring to our swordplay, however, but to my scar. It has been so long, I forget how shocking it must seem."

So he would not let her take refuge in polite untruth. Yet his response was an obvious lie, Jenny realized, the first she had ever caught him in. However he had come by that, it was not something he could ever forget. She could see it in the set of his jaw.

Of course, she thought, it was the mark of failure he hated. His pained expression, however, immediately told her otherwise. It was the scar itself—the disfigurement to his person—to which he was sensitive. It had not occurred to her before that her opinion—or indeed anyone's—of his appearance could matter to Yves. That, even more than the scar itself, made him seem vulnerable all at once.

She had to say something, anything, to erase that wounded look from his eyes. "If I seemed shocked, my lord," she answered carefully, "it is because I have seen scars like that before, although not often on the living. What vicious cruelty may be expected in a land where savage bands of Indians roam is all the more horrifying when found in civilization." It was terribly important now that he understand that it was not the ugliness that shocked her, but the cruelty behind it.

"Such savagery, I fear, exists everywhere,"

Yves said, more relaxed. "It may be hidden in civilization, but not erased."

"And your practice with the sword," Jenny asked; "is not that part of the same savagery?" Yves and Richard might be on good terms, but all that skill and energy must surely be directed toward some end—the shedding of someone's blood. She was afraid now. Perhaps, like Sukey, she had been pretending to herself that their situation could continue like this, but clearly it could not. Yet she longed to hold back the tide, keep them all safe. All of them. Even Yves.

"Savagery? Why, no, the sword is the most honest and equitable of weapons." Yves leaned against the door jamb, considering his words. "A man with a sword in his hand is in control of his own destiny. There's no secrecy in a sword—it's no weapon for backstabbing. Nor can it be used in hiding, or from a distance, like a pistol. No, a man with a sword must meet his opponent squarely, face to face; he cannot avoid the consequences of his action." He looked at her and she knew that whatever came, he would not be dissuaded. "What more can a man hope for than an honest and fair fight?"

"No fight at all," she beseeched, even though she knew it useless.

He shook his head, sadly. "Ah, that civilized we have not yet become. Besides, I am not sure that situation would be preferable. There are things a man ought to value highly enough to fight for— loved ones, justice, honor, truth . . ."

Angry at Yves' clear determination to seek revenge and stung by his continual harping on the virtues of honesty and truth, Jenny exclaimed,

"Truth, milord? Truth is too frequently a weapon of cruelty, as I have seen. I would not defend so wholeheartedly a virtue which is so often misused."

Surprisingly, Yves laughed and agreed. "You are right, of course. Not only is it cruel, but it is often the greatest deceiver of all. What is it that Congreve says? 'No mask like open truth to cover lies, As to go naked is the best disguise.'"

He sounded as if he were laughing at a private joked, and that angered her too. "Then what is this honesty you value so much?"

He hesitated, as if he looked within for an answer, then stepped closer. "Honesty with oneself," he said at last, looking at her, "and honesty in friendship."

So it was as Jenny had suspected when she first saw Yves and Nate together at Newgate. The greatest—the unforgivable—crime was the betrayal of friendship.

There was another message here as well. Honesty with oneself, he had said. Jenny thought she had faced some fairly brutal truths without flinching in the last few months. Her sojourn at Newgate had hardly encouraged illusions. Yet she suspected that Yves felt she was nourishing illusion—in her cousinly regard for Nate, she supposed.

Again Jenny wondered what Nate could have done to Yves to have earned such enmity. How had he deceived? How had he betrayed their friendship?

And, since honesty with oneself was to be the order of the day, how had she?

Chapter Eleven

No matter what Jenny tried to put her mind to that day or the next, the image of Yves' scarred chest was always before her. She wanted desperately to solve the mystery of its origin, but dared not question Yves and had no opportunity to privately quiz his aunt. Her hopes then for a quiet family dinner on Sunday—and a chance for a quiet tête-à-tête with Mrs. Mueller—were dashed by the visit of the pastor from the village nearest Vickers' estate.

Even disappointed as she was, Jenny had to concede that the Reverend Dr. Warren, a sprightly octogenarian, was charming. A slight gentleman with a tonsure of pure white, he had taught the young scholars of the nearby noble houses and tended still to see his former pupils as children. The great and powerful Lord Yves, a man with immense influence at court, was to him still a shy and studious young boy. His treatment of his noble host might have provoked Jenny to laughter—had his discourse not centered on his other student and the source of so many of Jenny's worries.

"Nathaniel simply must listen to reason," the old man declared, not for the first time, at dinner. "You have done a kind, a noble act, Wolfram, by taking his tenants in and providing for them—which is no less than I would expect of you."

For a moment Jenny was surprised to hear anyone other than Mrs. Mueller speak of Yves in such benevolent terms. The elderly cleric, however, seemed so innocent, so bewildered by harshness, that she presumed he saw all men as basically good. Then, too, perhaps the young Wolfram had been that kind and good, and Dr. Warren had simply never seen the changes in his former pupil, she supposed.

"But it is no answer," he continued, pressing his point. "These people want to return to their own homes. Why, there have been Partridges at Vickers since the glorious days of Good Queen Bess. Young Walter—he was named after the late earl, you know—was in tears as he packed up his things. Now, tell me if you can, what new butler could know Vickers as well as he who was raised there from a boy?"

Jenny, equally appalled, knew not where to look. At the head of the table, his expression dark and his eyes like ice, Yves responded with surprising calm. "You may find it difficult to gain an appointment even to speak with Vickers," he said, not coldly but as if he wanted to soften the blow.

"He is exceedingly busy of late and seldom to be found at home."

It might have been more to the point, Jenny thought with some bitterness, to say that Nate was never available when one wanted him. And when one did find him, he was expert at eluding uncomfortable subjects. She hated to admit that Yves might be right in anything, but if he meant to warn the pastor that Nate would inevitably slip through his fingers, his assessment was probably all too accurate—and that was more worrying to contemplate than even Nate's misdeeds.

Yet Dr. Warren was not to be so easily shocked, evidently. "Oh, I know, I know," he said. A twinkle in his eye suddenly made Jenny reassess her opinion of his experience of the world. "Coffeehouses, clubs, and gambling dens—when he's not chasing some . . ." He coughed as if he had swallowed the wrong way. "Er . . . I quite forgot what I was about to say."

He may have forgotten, but Jenny could easily guess the rest. Was this truly Nate's reputation at home—a gambler and a rake?

Hiding a hint of a smile, Yves answered, "Vickers has many social obligations."

"He has other obligations as well, and he must be made to face them." The reverend's passionate outburst was followed by a sheepish look of apology. "I ought to save my speeches for Nathaniel and not harangue the innocent."

"You might do well, sir, to ask Miss Beauchamp to intercede on the tenants' behalf," Yves said, leaning back. Immediately suspicious, Jenny watched him out of the corner of her eye, but could gauge nothing of his intent. "Her cousin favors her with his attentions," he continued. "As a suitor, he should be anxious to please, eager to prove his devotion."

Full of hope, Dr. Warren turned to Jenny, looking to her for a response. Embarrassed, she looked down at her plate of roast swan in currant jelly sauce. The conversation was rapidly destroying her appetite. "When Lord Vickers told me of his actions," she said at last, "I expressed my strong concern and disapproval—to no avail, I fear. For some reason I do not understand, he seems to feel that all these good people were criticizing and spying upon him."

"Isn't that just like Nathaniel," Dr. Warren said, to her surprise. "Do him a kindness and he will look for hidden motives. Just like the old earl. That would be your great-great-grandfather, m'dear," he told Jenny. "A very unhappy man, I remember, always needing to be in control."

"I never knew him," Yves mentioned, "but I heard many tales of his temper. People still cross themselves upon hearing his name."

"A most unhappy man indeed," Jenny agreed. "For I was told that he had driven away all his children." She did not say by whom. The lies made her feel lessened somehow, and she avoided them when she could.

"Indeed he did." The reverend gentleman shook his head at the thought of so much misery. "The late earl was the most fortunate—he was able to escape to London, but the others . . ." He shook his head again. "Since your letter, Wolfram, the family has been much in my mind," he continued. "I've not had much success at the task you set me. The people who cared for the Lady Eugenia during her last days may have emigrated. But my search has revived many memories, many memories."

In alarm, Jenny clutched at the napkin in her lap. What was Yves up to now? she wondered with increasing anxiety. Searching for a child? If only she knew the rules of inheritance, the terms of the late Lord Vickers' will, better. Surely a son of Lady Eugenia's, even if legitimate (which seemed doubtful), would not displace Nate's claim?

Such a son, however, might provide an heir should Nate die without issue, she realized.

Jenny shivered. The pastor, however, only chuckled softly to himself, amused by some ancient memory and clearly quite unaware of the undercurrents he had stirred. "I've often wondered where Wild Jack finally washed ashore," he said. "That was your great-uncle, my dear," he said to her. "The family disgrace, but a charmer. And a good friend, once."

"But surely, sir," Yves said, his interest obviously piqued, "he was lost at sea."

With his eyes twinkling, the cleric answered, "So they say, so they say. But Jack was ever an unpredictable rogue. He had the facility of being lost exactly when he wanted to be." Chuckling again over some remembered prank, the old gentleman drank some of his wine.

"Could a man leave his family and never look back, never send word?" Jenny asked, knowing Yves would expect her to show interest. After all, this was supposed to be her family. Inside, however, she quailed. A legitimate son or grandson of Wild Jack Beauchamp *would* displace Nate as earl, and would leave her still trapped.

"Miss Beauchamp feels deeply the loss of her family," Yves said, as if that explained his own interest in finding other family members.

"As is to be expected," Dr. Warren remarked, smiling at Jenny. He considered Yves' question a moment. "I daresay Jack may have felt it safer for all concerned to disappear completely. His connection with the smugglers, you know ... The Lady Eugenia, poor soul, would probably have kept in touch regardless, but she died soon after."

Jenny could see the wheels and gears turning behind Yves' intelligent eyes. Suddenly she realized that his search for another heir might well be a good thing—if it prevented him from taking more violent measures in the meantime. If such an heir were found, however, it would mean that she had stolen part of his inheritance. Perhaps Yves would even allow her to return the money to someone other than Nate.

And Nate? He might well be returned to debtors' prison. Considering how poorly he handled his responsibilities, he deserved to lose his position, but not, she thought, to be sent back to Newgate. Afraid, she realized she could no longer guess what Nate might do or not do to preserve his status—and his freedom.

Jenny could pay little attention to the conversation, or the course of sweetmeats, after that. It was a relief when Mrs. Mueller finally gave her the signal to withdraw, and they left the gentlemen to their port. In the drawing room, the two women drank tea together, silent and companionable, while Jenny doggedly persevered with her needlework. A piece of tatting kept Mrs. Mueller's hands busy, but her mind was obviously concerned with other matters.

"Jenny," she said at last, "do you think, if to your cousin you spoke, influence him you might?"

Looking up, Jenny saw fear in the lines of the older woman's face—the same fear she had shown when Yves' swordplay was mentioned. "I will try," Jenny said, hoping to comfort. "If Lord Vickers can be influenced by my earnest exhortation, then I will spare no effort."

"As long as the result does not in his debt too deeply place you," Mrs. Mueller said, clearly seeing the difficulty involved. "That would be as bad, I think. Oh, Jenny," she exclaimed, "what Wolfram will do, I do not know. Now he restrains himself, but how long? I ask. I wait, I wait, every day for the straw that the camel's back breaks."

"Calm yourself, dear ma'am," Jenny pleaded, hating to see the widow in such distress. "The gentlemen will be returning soon. You would not wish them to see you so discomposed."

"Pho," Mrs. Mueller said, pulling out her handkerchief from the pocket hidden in her panniers. "Those two I know of old. Like old women they gossip, only instead of the living, of ancient Romans long dead they talk."

And perhaps, Jenny thought, some Beauchamps not so very long deceased. At least her opportunity for a private talk with Mrs. Mueller had been returned to her.

"Do you know why Yves and Vickers are at enmity?" Jenny asked softly, but with no little urgency.

"No, no," Mrs. Mueller said, biting her lip. "Confide in me he will not. To keep my lips sealed Wolfram does not trust me. Friends they were once. At first all was happy stories—and then ... something happened, something terrible, and all is changed. What it was, I do not know, but I do know that to see your cousin destroyed, anything Wolf would do."

Jenny shivered and wondered how many others might be destroyed by this obsession. Putting aside her needle and frame, she crossed the room and sat at the widow's feet, as much for her own comfort as for the widow's. "My cousin told me that Yves deliberately kept him in Newgate," she said, daring at last to voice the accusation, "that he knew my ... father was dead and that as Lord Vickers all debts could be paid." *Tell me it's not true*, Jenny begged wordlessly. *Tell me he is not capable of so cruel an act.*

How cruel it was, only she could appreciate. Nate might not have experienced the horrors of the common side, but what he knew was ugly enough. Perhaps therein lay the reason for his present behavior, she thought. No one could long endure the degradation of Newgate without being infected by it. She looked to the widow hoping for denial.

Unable to comply, Mrs. Mueller pressed her fingers to her trembling lips. "Is true," she managed to say at last. "To me he admitted it, and still to explain he refused." She took Jenny's hands again. "But Wolfram's heart I know so well. Terrible it must be, this thing that pushes him to do this."

A wave of deep disappointment rushed over Jenny. To herself, she had to admit now how much she had relied on discovering Nate's accusation to be false. She wanted so much to believe that Yves was good and kind, as he so often seemed to be.

Could there be any action so terrible—even the betrayal of friends—that could deserve so very harsh a punishment? Banishment Jenny could understand, but Yves had put Nate in a living hell. According to Nate, Yves had also tried to kill him.

"I know they fought a duel," she said. At once the memory of that cruel scar came back to haunt her.

"Every day I remember," Mrs. Mueller said, almost whispering, and squeezed Jenny's hand for comfort. "So close to losing Wolf we came."

Then it must have been the duel with Nate that had marked him so horribly. Evidently Nate's account had lacked some pertinent details, details that must have been deliberately suppressed.

"Murder it would have been," Mrs. Mueller continued with sudden strength. "Wolfram was only a boy, just seventeen! Only five years older is Nate, but much difference there is between boy just finishing his books and man some years on the town, *nicht wahr?*"

Only a *boy?* Jenny's head spun. Nate had said Yves had challenged him at the earl's grave, and he had died less than eight years ago. Was there nothing in Nate's account she could believe? There must be, Jenny told herself, since his principal claim against Yves was obviously true. She looked to the older woman for more particulars.

A distant look settled over the widow's countenance as she traveled back in her memory. "Home in Hanover I was, thinking all fine. His last letter, I remember, of news was full about attempts to get pardon for friend John. Next comes word, come quick, Wolfram may die. I go and him I find..."

She shuddered. It took little imagination on Jenny's part to guess why.

"Is said Wolf to London drives to find his friend," Mrs. Mueller continued, her voice barely audible, "and then in middle of club he insults him, many times, until challenge is given. At once they fight. Would not you think older man might the cool head keep, might the hot-headed youth excuse? But no, what he did defense was not. If you had seen..." She wept quietly.

What Jenny had seen must have been nothing compared to the original wound, still open and unhealed. Even now, Jenny thought, after so many years, the scar was painful to see. Such a vicious wound could not have been made solely in the cause of self-preservation, she knew. Nate could not be blamed for starting the fight, but clearly once he had entered it, no considerations regarding the youth, inexperience, or emotional state of his opponent had stayed his hand.

Instead of answers, all Jenny had managed to do was stir up more questions, but she dared not continue quizzing the widow any further. Their good fortune in finding a quiet moment to talk could not last much longer. In any case, she hated to increase the widow's distress, as a continuation of this topic was sure to do.

"Come, come," Jenny said, wiping the widow's tears with her handkerchief. "If Yves finds you in tears, he will scold us both. And how will it look to our visitor?"

Taking the linen square, Mrs. Mueller dabbed at her eyes once more. "Fine I am now. Maybe if here in the shadow I sit, Wolfram will nothing notice."

"You know he notices everything," Jenny said in a playful tone.

"I notice things too," Mrs. Mueller said quietly, in a voice so serious Jenny blinked in surprise. She leaned over and took Jenny's face in her hands, gently smoothing a vagrant strand of hair away from her brow. "Worried you have been. Here and here you make lines appear. Do not let this difficulty with your cousin too much trouble you."

Genuinely touched, Jenny experienced a new pang of guilt. How deceitfully she repaid such kindness! "I have much to think about," she confessed, looking away; "much to turn over in my own mind."

The widow nodded wisely. "Sometimes one must ponder long and by oneself. But sometimes to tell another is helpful. When to talk you need, come to me. I know, Wolfram does not my tongue trust, but . . ." She winked. "Everything he does not know. Even from him I have some little secrets. Remember this, ja?"

"I will remember," Jenny promised.

Jenny remembered. She remembered too much. Late at night, listening sleeplessly to the distant strains of Bach coming from the music room, she had little to do but lie in the big curtained bed and think and remember. Her first meeting with Nate, the story that had so engaged her sympathy—it was all still clear in her memory. The picture he had sketched was so vivid— two men at the grave of a beloved friend and uncle, a sudden quarrel, the challenge given and accepted. So very vivid a picture—and it was all a lie.

No, not all a lie, Jenny reminded herself. Mrs. Mueller had confessed she knew Yves had deliberately kept Nate from his inheritance, kept him in prison. Had done it knowing exactly what sort of hell he was condemning his former friend to. There was no escaping that one terrible fact, no matter how Jenny tried to reason her way around it. What he had done to Nate was no different from what Mrs. Ransome had done to her, no less horrible or unjust. Her nightmares of the madness of the Women's Hold and memories of Deems and his threats were a continual reminder of the enormity of his offense.

That Nate was obviously not the man she had thought him to be made no difference. The realization was painful, but that too was a fact impossible to avoid. What most tormented Jenny was remembering how easily she had been taken in. So kind, so much the gentleman, he had seemed, but her angel of Newgate had been tarnished, fallen. She could not even blame Newgate for the kind of man he proved himself to be, since it was clear from Dr. Warren's account that Nate had always been weak.

All this was no excuse for Yves' behavior, however. It was no reason to effectively disinherit Nate. Even though Nate had betrayed her friendship, Jenny would not condemn him to a living death in Newgate. She simply wanted to be free of him and of the deceit he had lured her into.

Often now she thought of the option Richard had offered. Every moment she stayed enmeshed her more deeply in the trap of her imposture, she knew. How could she leave, however? To go meant suspicions must fall on those who had escorted her—Richard and Sukey. If she ran, she would force them to do the same. Richard, like the proverbial cat, would always land on his feet, she supposed, but the retirement he had so carefully planned as the respectable baronet would be destroyed. As for Sukey, she had already confessed to Jenny her longing for quiet respectability and the freedom to stay put.

There was more to her decision to wait upon events than a desire to protect her friends, she had to admit. She needed to know what happened between Yves and Nate. To leave and never know the outcome, to wonder ever after if Yves' intrigues had led to the shedding of blood, perhaps his own—this she could not bear.

So instead of fleeing, she allowed herself to be guided through the intricate maze of London Society. She sat for her portrait, where she had even more time to consider her predicament. While Mr. Reynolds' studio was often full of visitors—indeed it was almost as much salon as workplace—Jenny found she could often detach herself from the conversations flowing around her.

It was a strange feeling—to be primped for hours in order to sit, formally gowned, in silence while ladies and gentlemen stared and talked, often about her. Sometimes Jenny felt as much a part of the background as the various canvases that lined the walls. To pretend all day, every day, to be someone else had already given her a sense of unreality; now it was intensified. What was worse, however, was that the longer she sat and thought, the more she began to fear that she would never be able to escape, not even with Richard's help.

The portrait was well advanced when one day Sir Richard came to inspect its progress. In her corner of the salon, Mrs. Mueller jumped up anxiously, then resumed her seat upon recognizing the new guest. After a bow in Jenny's direction, Richard turned to kiss the widow's hand.

"I am hurt, ma'am, that you should look so disappointed to see me," he said in jest.

His gentle teasing brought a pleased flush to Mrs. Mueller's cheeks. "Oh no, not disappointed," she said. "Only waiting for Lady Pertwee I am. At two o'clock she promised to come sit with Jenny, and now already twenty past it is. Elsewhere I am expected already."

"I understand you hate to keep your friends waiting." Richard brushed his tricorne against his boots, hesitating a moment. "Ma'am, my carriage waits below. I would be happy to have my man take you to your destination. No doubt Lady Pertwee will appear in five or ten minutes. Can it be so very improper for Mr. Reynolds and I to chaperone each other for these few minutes until she comes? Mr. Reynolds' sister is below to maintain respectability as well," he persuaded.

Mrs. Mueller looked undecided, but Jenny knew she was anxious to meet her friends—members of the German community that were not part of their usual social round. At last she said, seeking reassurance, "Lady Pertwee would understand? Nothing improper would anyone think?"

"In Mr. Reynolds' studio?" Richard asked, as if the question itself were ridiculous. "Impossible!

But if you are in the least concerned, of course you should wait. What can another ten or fifteen minutes matter?"

The length of the delay had grown slightly in the last few minutes, Jenny noticed.

"You would not mind?" Mrs. Mueller asked, less hesitantly, beginning to gather up her belongings.

"I should be elated to be of service." Richard bowed with a gallant flourish.

"Well, perhaps, if truly you do not mind..."

With a great deal of fuss and excuses, Mrs. Mueller left at last. Her departure had been a foregone conclusion to Jenny once Richard began his subtle maneuvering. What his endeavors had won, however, was less clear. Even Richard could hardly lure Mr. Reynolds away from his canvas.

As the artist cleaned his brush, he greeted Richard and welcomed him to look at the work in progress.

"Is your model allowed to speak today?" Richard asked.

"She may chatter like a magpie," the portrait painter said in his loud voice, "as long as she does not move her hands."

Richard took a seat on the side of the room and lounged at his ease. "And what do you think of Mr. Reynolds' work?" he asked Jenny.

Peeking at the artist intent on the canvas, Jenny considered how to answer. The portrait was beautiful—but it was not she. This elegant creature in the azure *robe du cour* with its wide panniers, this jeweled woman sitting against the background of classical pediments and columns, was a stranger.

"Mr. Reynolds' work is always superb," she

said, trusting that the artist would not recognize her statement as equivocation.

Richard, of course, was not fooled. Smiling, he said, "Not the way I'd have you painted, though. I'd paint you like a doxy, in black velvet with a gold petticoat and trim—the gown you wore the day Yves came to the cell in Newgate—lounging decadently."

"Richard!" she cried out in alarm, losing her pose. How could he speak so in front of another?

The artist immediately threw down his brush and advanced upon his model with less than his usual amiable expression. "Miss Beauchamp, I must insist that you remain still," he said to her astonishment, completely ignoring Richard's improper suggestion. Was he so focused on his work that nothing else mattered? "Talk if you like, but leave your hands as they are. And you—" he pointed to Richard, "—if you cannot behave like a gentleman, out you go and I will have one of the maids sit with us."

Behave like a gentleman? Was that all he had to say? Jenny wondered at the artist's attitude.

"So sorry, sir," Richard said, speaking quite slowly. "I'm afraid Miss Beauchamp was unduly surprised by the news of a friend's engagement."

To her confusion, the artist replied mildly enough, "Well, well, do not surprise her again."

"Hadn't you realized?" Richard asked, a moment later when Mr. Reynolds had resumed his concentrated effort. "Unless you shout in his ear, Reynolds can hardly hear a thing. I suppose he must read lips fairly well, but he cannot see me, and he's not watching your face."

"And what if Lady Pertwee should appear?"

Jenny asked, annoyed at him for giving her such a fright.

"Oh, I don't think she will come quite yet. You know, it occurs to me now that she may have mistaken the hour, for we met only a few minutes ago," he said, much too innocently.

"I would not be at all surprised." Despite herself, Jenny could not refrain from smiling. "Wretch."

"Now that's more like it, that's my arch dell. You've been looking far too sad, Jenny. You must laugh at the world. Remember how you felt when you left the solicitor's office? Hold on to that feeling."

"I can't, Richard," Jenny said, her smile swiftly disappearing. The situation had changed too much. "I hate lying to Mrs. Mueller and to the world. Nothing is the way I thought it was anymore, and the conviction that sustained me for so long—the belief that we were doing something noble and good—is shaken."

"Nate."

"Yes." She sighed. It was a relief to admit it out loud. "Oh, I know it was true enough that he was unjustly imprisoned by Yves, but for the rest . . ." Suddenly it occurred to Jenny that perhaps she was not the only person affected by Nate's deceit. "Richard, has Nate repaid your investment?"

Richard stretched his long legs. "He stalls, but he does not refuse. That he dare not do. I am, after all, not without friends. It has occurred to me that he means to pay me with your inheritance."

"Mine?" Jenny shivered. The arrogant assumption of success she had seen at Lady Wetherby's went deeper than she had thought, evidently. Nate must truly believe that she would wed him. "I see," she said quietly.

"Foolish of him. You would think by now he would have realized that he cannot win you. And that he would have seen how well protected you are."

Richard's words from their last private meeting came back to her. "You said I had two protectors." A note of accusation crept into her voice. How could that be true, if Nate could not be trusted?

"So you have. I think you may trust that Yves and I will keep you safe."

"Yves?" The mention of his name in such a context caused Jenny to start. Tut-tutting under his breath, the deaf artist stepped forward and rearranged her hands along the silken folds of her gown. After one last severe look, Mr. Reynolds resumed his work.

"You would trust him to help me?" Jenny asked. "After what he did to Nate?" It was important to her to know. Richard was one of the few who truly understood the depth of Yves' cruelty in condemning Nate to Newgate. Could he forgive such an act?

"Jenny, Jenny, we cannot know what has passed between those two." He leaned forward, turning his hat between his hands. "Sometimes people are driven to desperate acts, but that does not mean that they enter into them lightly, or that they are without honor."

Such reasoning might apply as much to Richard as to Yves, Jenny realized. The transformation she had once considered impossible—from soldier and country gentleman to gentleman of the road—now seemed more than probable. Richard sneered at the world and its follies as if he took no part in them, but she knew now that there was often genuine kindness behind that mask.

As she had seen kindness in Yves. Perhaps understanding the motives of one would help her understand the other. After a moment's silence, Jenny decided to be bold.

"Why did you take to the road, Richard?"

He seemed surprised that she had connected his speech to his own situation, surprised and perhaps a little embarrassed. For a moment, it looked as if he would shrug off her question with a flippant reply, but in the end he opted for honesty.

"I came home after the war with the French with some of my men. My uncle is generous, I told them; he will find places for you all. They were injured, you see, maimed, not whole—they'd not have found work easily if at all. But there was no home. My all too generous uncle had been ruined by all his fancy London friends. They'd taken his money and abandoned him. He was dying then, and so was the estate."

He refused to look at her as he continued. The hirsute growth that had once masked his face had also masked his emotions, Jenny realized. Now he was obliged to turn his face away to hide his depth of feeling. He could not mask the hurt and anger in his voice, however. The highwayman who supposedly cared for nothing had obviously loved his uncle, and his home, very deeply indeed.

"There were hundreds whose lives depended on that estate," he said, "and now it couldn't keep them. I wrote at first trying to find help, but the government didn't need its soldiers anymore. And my uncle's friends did not care to be reminded of their debts—both of friendship and of honor. So I decided to collect them myself."

"I see." All his roguery had been designed to protect and care for the people under his protection. After all her cynicism, Jenny was surprised to realize there was a touch of Robin Hood in Lord Danger.

Sentimentality was, however, clearly abhorrent to Richard. The softened tone of expression caused him to look up at last, and his lip curled at the sound of it. "Don't romanticize my actions, Jenny. Leave that to the ballad-singers. In the end I stole from them all—the innocent as well as the guilty."

"Don't worry, Richard. I'm cured of any romanticizing." Yes, Nate had certainly cured her of that. "Thank you for telling me, though." She could not offer him her hand, but tried to convey the same feeling in her smile.

"Ah, well, I had to say something so you would know you could trust me if the need arose." He stood, nervous, and pretended to examine some of the other canvases about the room. Clearly he was anxious to drop the subject. His back to her, he added very softly, "You might trust Yves, too, I verily believe."

Jenny simply shook her head. The cases were not the same. For all his bravado, Danger had harmed no one. The money he had stolen had mattered little to those who forfeited it. One might well trust one's life to such a thief. But not to a man whose thirst for revenge could be satisfied with nothing less than a life destroyed.

Yet there was a more cogent reason than that

for not confiding her trust in Lord Yves. That he was capable of kindness and generosity she knew. That he could forgive such a deception as hers, she would never believe. The knowledge struck her heart like an arrow, but she did not flinch from it. No longer would she turn away from the truth, however painful.

As best she could, Jenny tried in the following days to appear more cheerful, to enjoy this time as a frivolous interlude, as Richard advised her to do. Too many people had noticed her abstraction, and she was not in a position to endure much scrutiny.

If she succeeded better at hiding her anxieties, however, she failed to dismiss them from her thoughts. Indeed, it seemed to her that her concerns grew rather than abated.

Richard had reminded her again of her ability to escape when necessary. Evidently he was quite unaware that his revelations had made it all the more difficult for her to accept his generous offer of help. How could she run now, knowing that the life he had so carefully rebuilt would be seriously endangered by the investigation that would inevitably ensue upon her disappearance?

Richard counseled her to wait and to keep the money. That Nate had given it to her freely, he was witness, he reminded her. That Nate would misuse the inheritance, they both knew. Therefore he considered that she should have no compunctions about keeping the fortune. After all, she had more than earned it.

The truth was, Jenny wanted no part of it. She certainly did not like to consider how she had earned it. Everything about their scheme, which had once seemed so noble in its purpose, now made her feel defiled.

The kindness and attention of Yves and his aunt only increased her sense of guilt. Every day, every evening, Jenny felt herself in their debt for some small consideration, some trifling act of kindness and affection. Seeing them and seeing the contrast with Nate's behavior, she was constantly and painfully reminded of her foolishness and impetuosity. She was ashamed now that she had ever admired Nate.

Of late Nate's courtship had become increasingly blatant and distressing. Nothing Jenny said or did seemed to restrain him. If it were not for Yves, who kept close guard and made sure that few opportunities were open to Nate, she did not know what she would do or say.

As always, it was Yves who remained at the center of her thoughts, and her worries. Sometimes, when they were dancing, or at home just talking, she forgot the awkwardness of her position, the need to be wary. These moments frightened her later.

She tried to tell herself that it was the incisive power of his intelligence, not his sensitivity, that allowed him to understand her moods and taste so well.

It was he, she knew, who made sure she found pleasure in her many social commitments. With Richard, he introduced her to the community of American colonials. Through Mr. Joshua Reynolds, he saw that she was introduced to the great lexicographer, Mr. Samuel Johnson. And, as he had once promised, Yves himself escorted her and

Mrs. Mueller to Chelsea to meet the child prodigy, Wolfgang Mozart.

The family had been in London for almost a year now, Jenny had been told, their departure delayed by the illness of Herr Leopold Mozart. Recovered now, however, Herr Mozart welcomed them warmly. Relaxed by the atmosphere of familial affection, Jenny looked about her with interest.

In company such as this it was difficult for her to recall her first picture of Yves—cold, full of hate, toying with his enemies. To Herr Mozart he was charming, talking of mutual acquaintances. The children, Wolfgang and his sister Nannerl, she observed with amusement, treated him with the respect they accorded their elders, but with no touch of awe or fear. Perhaps children who had played for the French king and queen could not be expected to find a mere English baron very impressive, but Jenny suspected that Yves had the more imposing presence.

The conversation, conducted both in German and French, was not particularly interesting to Jenny, concerned as it was with people she knew nothing about. But the music . . . Jenny had some experience of child performers, and had been prepared to be mildly entertained. Instead, she was enthralled.

Caught in the music's spell, it was a few minutes before she noticed Yves' response. It was the only time she could recall seeing him utterly off guard, vulnerable. His body was quite still, not tense but at rest. The austere lines of his face were smoothed. Seeing his profile like this, Jenny was reminded again how handsome he was, not in the pretty way of Nate with his powder and paint, but in a way that was more powerfully masculine.

He turned to look at her then, and smiled, a smile of friendship and sincere pleasure. It was as if he had said to her, "I knew you would share this delight with me."

His smile sent a hot wave of pleasure through her. Jenny felt as she had when they danced at her ball, but the connection between them seemed stronger now, more permanent, than the link of his hand holding hers. It was a feeling she could not name, one beyond friendship, yet not quite kinship.

Jenny returned his smile wholeheartedly, glad to see him so content. Such felicity was as rare for Yves, she suspected, as it had been for her of late. Sometimes in the quiet of the evening, when the three of them were alone at home, she had seen hints of this side of him, heard the occasional flashes of humor, but these glimpses were all too rare. Too often he seemed—not cool, she knew him better than that now—but lonely. Yes, that was it. Yves was lonely.

He had turned slightly away now, still content under the music's enchantment. As he listened, she observed him unashamedly. She saw how his golden hair rose from a brow of considerable height, ample evidence of the intellect resident beneath. A sapphire gleam shone warmly from his eyes, so often changeable. His hands rested against the satin of his breeches, still and relaxed.

This would be how she would remember him, Jenny thought, when she had at last won free of this coil and was far away from London and deception.

There was something in this thought that made her inexplicably sad, a feeling she could not shake off. In the coach returning to Hanover Square, she was able to explain her silence and air of abstraction as simple fatigue. Certainly the press of engagements recently made this claim believable.

Yves, as usual, examined her face closely. What he saw there Jenny could not tell, but he said nothing beyond encouraging her to retire early.

There was no rest for Jenny, however, even after she had gone to bed. The heavy brocaded bed curtains could no more keep out unwelcome thoughts than they could keep out the faint strains of music from downstairs.

It was the same melody as the young Mozart had played, slowly, haltingly reconstructed. The gentle swell of the andante movement brought back the memory of Yves' smile with crystalline clarity. Again, too, with his image before her, she experienced the same sense of sorrow, of loss.

It must be this house, Jenny decided. It was too luxurious, too comfortable. Like Sukey, she had been seduced by its warmth, lured by the easy acceptance of Mrs. Mueller, into thinking of this place as home. She could no longer imagine any home beyond here, beyond these people, even though she knew she must leave. It was the thought of saying goodbye to all this forever, no doubt, that made her so sad. Yves was merely the symbol of all that would be left behind, she insisted to herself.

Jenny rolled over and thumped her bolster. He was the center of all her thoughts, her fears for the future, her confusion over the two sides to his character, his twisted and torturous relationship

263

with Nate. Everything came back to Yves.

It was he, no doubt, who sent Mrs. Mueller to the harpsichord almost every evening in search of some serenity, Jenny thought. The poor widow was as aware as she was that Yves and Vickers were heading inexorably to a critical impasse. Yet, knowing what she did, Mrs. Mueller's concern was all for her nephew, Jenny realized. Whatever Yves had done to Nate, his aunt still believed in him.

Even Richard had said she might trust Yves, she remembered, and had reminded her that people may be driven to desperate acts. Was it not so in her own case? she admitted. She had been wrong about Nate, and about Richard. Had she misjudged Yves as well, basing her whole estimation of his character on a single action?

Throwing back the covers, Jenny gave up the futile attempt to find sleep. She groped for a tinder box and managed to light a bedside candle. Perhaps reading someone else's thoughts would bring her some respite from her own, she thought, donning a wrap to cover her deshabille. *Mantelet au lever de l'aurore* the mantua-maker had called it, but she could not wait for Aurora to rise this morning.

Jenny took her candle and walked downstairs, following the sound of the music. It was not really a book she was seeking, she admitted to herself outside the music room door. Mrs. Mueller had told her before that she would be ready when Jenny needed to talk. Now that time had come—not to talk of her deception, her place in the conspiracy to restore Nate's title and privileges. That was not her secret to tell, but perhaps she could unburden herself of some of the confusion in her heart.

She pinched out the light of her candle and slipped into the room. Stepping forward quietly, she set down the candlestick, a little hesitant to disturb the flow of music. Clutching her wrap close about her, she advanced a few more steps until she could see better. The light of a candelabrum atop the harpsichord cast a soft glow over the figure at the instrument and sent strange shadows playing against the gilt paneled walls.

Jenny's hand clutched at her wrap, at the spot where her heart beat so loudly she was surprised he could not hear it. Before her at the harpsichord sat none other than Yves.

Chapter Twelve

All along it had been Yves creating this beautiful music, Jenny realized, haunting her nights as he haunted her days. His golden head was bent over the keyboard. A few strands had escaped the ribbon of his queue and brushed against his high cheekbones. He was relaxed, dressed in his shirt-sleeves, the stock around his neck slightly loosened. His hands, Jenny saw now, were the hands of a musician, strong and flexible.

Without turning away from the instrument, he said to her, "I have been trying to reconstruct the melody young Mozart played for us today, with but moderate success, I fear. Did I disturb you?" He faced her now, but Jenny knew he had recognized her from the moment she stepped into the room.

"No," she said softly. "You play beautifully.

Please don't stop on my account."

"After the performance we heard this afternoon, I think it very kind of you to say so. If it please you, then, to hear my poor efforts, I will go on—but with something I know better. Is there anything you would care to hear?"

"Something from the Anna Magdalena notebook?" she suggested hesitantly. She did not care what he played as long as she could stay here by his side.

"Very well," he said, as his fingers moved into the familiar patterns.

Jenny snuggled into the large wing chair, pulling her feet up onto the seat and tucking them beneath her. It was not a ladylike pose, but Yves would not care. Resting her head on the cushion, she watched him play. Such amazing sensitivity he showed, she thought. How could she ever have thought him cold, unfeeling? The emotions that he blocked from his countenance flowed from his fingertips—sadness, loneliness, anger—but joy and humor, too.

After a while Yves finally stopped and turned to her. "Are you cold? Tante has left a shawl here." He tucked it around her shoulders and settled himself on a stool at her feet.

"Do you know what amazed me most this afternoon?" he said as if continuing a conversation. "Herr Mozart's pride in his son. Already the boy matches his father's talent—and he is only nine years old! That piece he played was of his own composing—had you understood that? Yet his father feels nothing but delight in his accomplishments and even adjusts his life to promote his son's welfare."

To Jenny there was nothing odd in such paternal affection and sacrifice, but she realized there was to Yves. Even Nate, she remembered, had commented cynically on the way Yves' parents had left him alone to the care of servants and tutors. She remembered, too, Yves' tale of how he had met her "father," Lord Quarles. How very lonely he must have been, she thought, and then corrected herself. How very lonely he must be.

"Your aunt would do as much for you," Jenny said after a moment, wanting to remind him that he was not alone after all.

"Tante? Oh yes," he admitted. "I suppose she would." He bent to stir the dying embers of the fire.

For some reason Jenny was unwilling to let the moment end. Yves so rarely revealed anything of himself, of his past, but tonight he seemed curiously amenable to more personal discourse. Perhaps she could still learn something of him that would help her put her troubled thoughts in order.

"You told me once that your aunt had been disowned by your family," she said hesitantly, unsure if questions would break the tenuous atmosphere of companionship. "How did you meet, then, and become so close?"

He smiled, bringing a very engaging and youthful gleam to his eye. "Summers were spent in Hanover," he said, and paused a moment. Jenny noticed the impersonal construction. Even then he must have been on his own.

"One day I heard the servants gossiping about an aunt whose name I had never even heard before, and I made them tell me about her. It was the summer after I'd met John and Lord Vickers, so I had become marvelous brave. I marched into Herr Mueller's shop and demanded that he produce my aunt at once. He knew who I was, of course. He looked me up and down for a bit, and then he brought me upstairs to meet Tante." His voice softened with affection. "She was in the middle of baking bread, I remember, but she set everything aside and took me in her arms." He looked down a moment, embarrassed—whether at the personal nature of the revelation or at the emotion he could not hide, Jenny could not tell. Then he looked up and laughed. "I had the devil of a time explaining later how I got flour all over my coat."

Who else, Jenny wondered, had ever embraced him with such affection? Had there been anyone else in his life who would automatically set everything aside for him?

"And you've kept in touch ever since?" she asked.

Yves nodded. "Tante insisted we keep our friendship secret, so as not to upset the family, but I managed to spend most of my time in Hanover with her and Onkel Carl."

"A home away from home," Jenny commented, noticing how the light was reflected in his eyes and hair. She had to hold onto the chair to stop from reaching out to brush aside the wayward strand falling against his cheek. Somewhere in these stories must lie the clue to his character, she knew, but she could not yet quite grasp it, sensing some revelation just beyond reach.

"My only homes," he corrected her, "were Tante's in Hanover and Vickers' in England. Until now." He looked at her, and Jenny was aware suddenly of the same intoxicating warmth she had felt earlier today at the house in Chelsea. "Since you came, this house has suddenly become a home."

Hoping Yves would take her heated cheeks to be the result of sitting too close to the fire, she said, a little breathless, "If that is true, it is surely your aunt's doing."

"No, no. Tante has done much, but until you came she hid herself away, too shy to entertain or even to meet new people. I did not like to push her into doing what she so plainly found uncomfortable," he said, "but as a result, this place was quiet as a tomb until you came to us."

"You might as well give the credit to Lady Pertwee then," Jenny said, embarrassed by his praise and the warmth of his gaze.

"Not so. It is you who have brightened our lives. You have brought us both out of our shells, and I am grateful for it."

Jenny could think of nothing to say in response, stunned by the solemn sincerity in his voice. Her consciousness of her own deception weighed heavily on her mind. It would be nice to think she had managed somehow to give them something in return for their kindness, but that gift, she knew, must be shattered by the discovery of what she had done.

"I fear, however, we have failed to replace the home you left behind," Yves added after a moment. "Despite your brave facade, I have seen the sorrow behind your smiles, and I have wondered if it is because you long for your homeland?"

Jenny closed her eyes for a moment and remembered her home as it had once been, and how she had last seen it. What was there left for her in America? Cousins, if they lived, who had never met her?

She shook her head. "My family made it home, not the land. All the people I care for are here now."

Jenny met his sympathetic gaze. In recognizing the truth of her statement, she realized at last the reason for all her confusion and worry, the reason she could not bear to leave this new home, the reason that took her breath away and made the blood course hot through her veins. She had fallen in love with Yves—passionately, irrevocably, and hopelessly in love.

Of all the foolish, impetuous acts she had ever rushed into, this was surely the worst.

To her surprise, Yves reached forward and brushed an errant curl away from her forehead. Her skin felt singed by the light contact of his fingertips. "Poor Jenny," he whispered. "I wish there were something I could do to help."

Jenny was trying to control the urge to cry, but her head snapped up at this. At the same moment they both seemed to realize what he had called her.

"I'm so sorry," he said at once. "Tante always speaks of you as Jenny, and I have caught it of her. I did not mean to be bold."

Bold? Jenny was suddenly, painfully, aware of the negligence of her costume, the quiet solitude of the night. The circumstances could hardly be more intimate, yet she knew herself as safe as if she sat surrounded by all of London society. Even if Yves were attracted to her, if he were to return her affections as passionately as she might desire, she would still be safe, because he was a gentleman. He would never take advantage of a woman living under his protection, in his very household.

Her name had sounded very sweet on his lips, she thought, too. "Miss Beauchamp seems very formal," she said, letting him read gentle encouragement in her voice. She would be glad to dispense with the name that was not rightfully hers. To allow her relationship with Yves to grow closer, as by the simple use of her given name it must, could only bring pain in the end, she well knew, but it was a pain she gladly welcomed for now.

"So is milord," he reminded her. "I would be very pleased if you would call me Wolf." His voice was hesitant, almost as if he feared to be rebuffed.

"Wolf, then," she said, and saw his eyes light up. Wolf. Once that name had stood for the beast she thought he was; now it reminded her of his loneliness. It was now a symbol, too, of friendship accepted, a friendship she had already betrayed.

"Come," he said at last. "It is late. I'll light you back to bed."

Following meekly, Jenny accepted his arm as they ascended the stairs. Would she ever sleep again? she wondered. Her doubts were resolved at last. Although she knew no more now than before of what had caused the rift between Wolf and Nate, with the realization of love had come trust. Like Mrs. Mueller, she had to believe that there was good and cogent reason for the actions Wolf had taken against Nate.

There were other things she had to face as well. She, too, had betrayed the man she loved, betrayed beyond hope of forgiveness. Her love was doomed from the start.

Jenny's newly found knowledge did not bring her any joy. The company of Yves—Wolf—was exquisite torture to her. It was not in her nature, however, to repine over past mistakes. To do so would be a useless exercise, she knew, and bent her thoughts instead to seeking remedies for her present misfortune.

Unfortunately, such remedies eluded discovery. Jenny cared little for what might become of herself now, but so entangled were the members of their conspiracy that to endanger one would be to endanger all.

How much Nate deserved to be protected seemed uncertain. He had the right, Jenny kept reminding herself. Even Mrs. Mueller had admitted his fair right of inheritance. Yet with her trust now given to Wolf, she could not help wonder, and fear, what crime of friendship had been so dreadful that Wolf's revenge would be satisfied with nothing less than Nate's imprisonment or his very life.

Jenny wished with all her heart that Wolf would simply tell her what it was that Nate had done, but she dared not upset the tenor of their relationship by asking. Since the evening of their talk, Wolf had seemed so content, and had behaved to her with unusual sweetness. That she was living in a fool's paradise, she knew in her heart, but she could not bear to destroy the illusion one moment before she must.

The problem of Nate, however, could not be set aside. Further observation of his behavior only served to increase her dismay. What she had once taken for true nobility and kindness in Newgate, she now saw was merely a veneer of elegant manners. That was enough, evidently, for London society. Nate might, as many another, risk his patrimony at cards, incur debts he had neither the ability nor the intention of meeting, keep low company, and pursue women of great fashion and no morals—all this he might do, and still be considered a gentleman.

That he failed to live up to her own definition of a gentleman, Jenny was soon convinced. Even if she had not Wolf's shining example ever before her, she would soon have had to face Nate's lack of character. She could not avoid him—indeed she dared not do anything that would upset the delicate balance between him and Wolf. In public, then, she danced with him, endured his heavy-handed courtship as best she could, and usually prayed for someone to interrupt them. In this, Wolf rarely failed her, and Richard could also be depended upon to help.

On the night of the Ardmores' rout party, however, Wolf was deep in conversation with an old friend of his father's, obviously buttonholed without hope of escape without giving offense. Richard was absent entirely, a fact Jenny had not noticed until she began to look about for rescue.

As none was forthcoming, Jenny took Nate's arm, splendid in burgundy satin, and allowed him to lead her toward the buffet table in the next room.

Nate, too, had evidently observed that circumstances had contrived to relax for once the strict supervision placed on her. "Why, Jenny," he said,

the use of her given name grating upon her ears,
"I believe your protectors are all engaged elsewhere. It seems we shall have some privacy for
once."

Jenny sincerely hoped not. Unconsciously, Nate
had used all too accurate a word to describe those
who stood between her and Nate, she noted. How
much, she wondered, had those two gentlemen
protected her from already?

Of a sudden, Nate pulled her through a narrow
hallway and into a small antechamber, a pretty
room probably used as a withdrawing room for
the ladies during smaller gatherings.

"There now, that's better," he said, satisfaction
ringing in his voice. "Now we really can talk without worrying that one or another of your chaperones might come upon us unawares."

Jenny walked firmly to the door, although her
heart quailed. Leaning against it, Nate calmly refused to let her pass. A cold fear began to pervade
her limbs, but she determined to treat the matter
lightly. As if speaking to an unruly child, she said,
"Nate, don't be foolish. Do you want to ruin my
reputation?"

"Not a bad idea," he said, laughing. The sound
of his laughter sent a chill down Jenny's spine.
"Yves could not afford to dismiss my suit then.
But no, I just wanted a few minutes alone with
you. It seems I can hardly say good day to you
without one of your hawk-eyed chaperones appearing like a djinn out of a bottle."

Since Jenny could no longer believe anything
Nate said, it was not odd that she should find his
claim to desire only conversation dubious. "You
did not find their intervention so irksome when

275

it was I who needed to speak with you," she said with biting criticism. "Indeed, whenever I have looked to you for help or advice on how I might escape my dangerous and difficult position, it seems to me that you have been mighty glad of an excuse to avoid an interview." Her cheeks flushed with indignation, but annoyance swiftly turned to alarm as she noticed the admiring way Nate watched her.

"Gad, but you're beautiful like this, Jenny," he said, typically avoiding her complaint. His words were very like Richard's, she noticed, but the gleam in his eye told her he did not speak to tease her.

Raising her chin a little, Jenny told him, "You need not go to the trouble of flattering me, Nate. Yves isn't here to be annoyed by it." She had almost said Wolf, but caught herself at the last moment.

"Jenny, I am hurt. Do you think I only praise you for Wolf's benefit? You're wrong, you know," he said warmly. Jenny stepped back a pace. "From the very beginning I knew you were special."

"But not special enough to deserve the truth," she reminded him, determined to turn the conversation from its present course. "Not special enough to be warned of or saved from the consequences of your simple little plan."

The bitterness in her voice, unfortunately, did not seem to disconcert him much. As always, he had an excuse ready. "I wanted to tell you, Jenny, truly I did," he said. " 'Twas Dick who would not let me. You know how carefully he watched over us—almost as bad as Yves."

Had Richard been protecting her from Nate even then? Jenny wondered. There was a time when she might even have believed Nate, she remembered with distaste, but no more.

No words were needed to tell Nate what she thought of his paltry defense. He took a deep breath, as the realization that she no longer trusted him must have sunk in. "I see," he whispered. "So Dick has made good use of Yves' acceptance. At first I was glad he was able to give you some support, since Wolf would hardly allow me near you, but I see how he has repaid my friendship. I suppose this is what he had in mind all along—to gain control of the Vickers fortune."

Jenny walked away from him, anxious to put some space between them. To listen to Nate's subtle lies was almost more than she could endure. "Since he cannot get what he was promised from you?" she suggested, her voice chill as ice.

A hurt look, as if he had been deeply offended, descended over Nate's countenance. Such a handsome face, Jenny thought again, wondering how many lies it had covered.

"So he has even sunk so low as to traduce my honor before you," he said. "Perhaps I should never have expected better of a highwayman, but I did. I honestly did." He pleaded with Jenny, his beautiful eyes eloquent, but she turned her face from him. She could not block out the sound of his voice, however. "You believed in me once, Jenny. I even dared to think you were beginning to care for me. Don't let vicious rumors pull us apart."

With her back to him, Jenny had not noticed how close Nate had ventured to her. Now she could feel his hot breath on her neck and shoulders. He took her arms and forced her to face him.

"Everyone in London knows I love you, Jenny. I had hoped when you heard my poor effort at poetry that you would begin to understand yourself."

The touch of his hands made her cringe. She was frightened now to hear him speak so glibly of a poem he had almost certainly stolen. If it were at all possible, however, she longed to avoid a confrontation. Trembling, she schooled her face to appear calm, and pleaded with him. "Nate, you must stop this foolishness. You know it's impossible. Yves would never permit—"

"Wolf can be managed. You'll see," he promised, pulling her even closer. His words as much as his action dismayed her. "As a courtier," Nate continued, "Wolf is particularly vulnerable to the pressure of public opinion. Even if you and I were caught before we reached the border, he could do little to prevent our marriage."

Jenny began to struggle as he tried to kiss her. His aim fell awry, the kiss falling upon her brow rather than her lips. Evidently Nate considered her refusal merely maidenly shyness, for he paid no mind to her attempts to get free. "Just say the word, Jenny," he said, "and we'll be off. Tonight, if you like."

Breathless, Jenny complained, "I'll not go anywhere with you if this is how you behave." She wanted still to maintain a facade of friendly argument, but could feel her control beginning to snap. "Let me go, Nate."

"Don't be such a prude. Surely you saw enough at Newgate—enough with Dick—to know how a man shows a woman he likes her. And you like me too, don't you, Jenny? I could see it in your eyes when we were together in the cell, wishing Dick would take himself off so we could be alone."

The horrible thing was she *had* come near to caring for him then, had certainly wished Danger at the devil many a time. It sickened her now to think of it, almost as much as it angered her to see Nate's calm assumption of her acceptance. He was clearly oblivious to the look of loathing now in her eyes and had decided to press his advantage.

Backing her against the wall, he began to fondle her. Behind the caress she could feel nothing but lust and greed, but she knew Nate would not expect her to know the difference between his coarse embrace and the touch of love. He probably did not know there was a difference. Her struggles and pleas meant nothing to him, she realized with horror. Impervious to her vehement response, he toyed with the lace at her bodice, and bent his mouth to the exposed skin of her breasts. Her arms strained to keep him away, but her strength was as useless as her pleas.

And then he laughed. With that laugh the last vestige of Jenny's control forsook her. She no longer cared that Nate would realize how far her feelings had changed toward him. It mattered not at all that he would know her now as an enemy, nor that she might actually be risking her freedom by antagonizing him. All she cared for was winning free from his intolerable embrace. Every stratagem she had ever been taught in self-defense—by her grandfather, by Sukey and Richard—she used now.

At last Nate drew back when her fingernails raked his pretty face calling forth a few drops of blood. "Bitch!" he called her, before he collected himself.

Jenny stopped him before he could apologize. From Sukey she knew that his insult had been greater than she would have considered it as a colonial. To have called her a whore would have been more polite. Already she could tell he was looking for ways to recover the ground he could see he had lost. In her raging fury, however, she wanted no more of his hypocrisy.

"You must think me a complete fool," she said, her voice taking on a rapierlike edge. "No more, Nate. No more."

"What do you mean?" he asked, trying to restore the mask of good breeding. "Jenny, I humbly beg your pardon for allowing my passions to reign unchecked. I suppose I've simply been away from civilized society too long. Damn it, Jen, you nearly gouged my eye out," he complained, pouting like an infant. "What if this leaves a mark?" A genuine sense of injury entered his voice, but Jenny was not sympathetic.

"If you ever come within arm's length of me again, Nate, I'll make sure I do. That's all you care about, isn't it? How things seem. It's a beautiful performance you give, Nate, I'll grant you, worthy of Garrick. But it's not enough for me anymore."

"I knew it," he cried, evidently still intent on playing his role. "It's Wolf and Richard. They've been telling you lies about me, turning you against me."

Jenny laughed, a harsh, humorless sound. "No,

they've said nothing. You've encompassed your own ruin, Nate. How blind did you think I could be to your conduct? Did you think I would find excuses for all your misdeeds? You're not very flattering."

For a moment he was silent. Jenny could almost see him trying to decide how to handle this unexpected development.

"You don't trust me, Jenny," he said at last. "I suppose I deserve to have forfeited your regard. After so many years of exile, London has gone to my head. But, Jenny, you must believe that what I told you in Newgate is true. For all our sakes, don't be taken in by Wolf, or we'll all end up back in Newgate if not on the gallows."

At the slur on Wolf's character, Jenny became further incensed. Her jaw muscles tense, she admitted quietly, "I know what Yves did to you. As far as I know, that is the only claim you have made with any measure of truth in it."

"That is the claim that matters, though, isn't it?" Sneering, he leaned casually against the door. The pose of apology and affability was dropped now. Nate had evidently seen that persuasion was futile, and had decided to be direct.

"Luckily for you, it is," she admitted. "You may also count yourself blessed that I feel obliged to return to you the fortune I inherited by this deception—not only because I can no longer accept any profit from my dishonesty, but because I am aware that I had virtually promised its return to you." Cynically, she shook her head and laughed. "You could not believe that, could you, Nate? That was your mistake. Had you trusted my word better than you trusted your charm, we might never have come to this." She looked at him directly. "I would never have married you, never."

That hit him hard. His self-assurance could accept the passion of her disgust, seemingly, but not the cool dispassion of her dismissal. Now he was angry too, his fists clenched in a manner that reminded Jenny forcibly of her own physical vulnerability. After all, no one as yet had come to her rescue.

"Never is a long time," Nate said, his voice silky with menace. "I find there are few decisions in life that cannot be changed. It is all a matter of finding the right persuasion."

Trying to hide the trembling of her fingers, Jenny set her gown back in order as best she could. His tone, as much as his words, terrified her, but she refused to let him see it. Facing him squarely at the door, she waited until at last he stepped aside to let her pass. Without looking back, she stopped a moment at the open door.

"You are quite correct, Nate," she said, matching his tone. "There probably are circumstances that would make me change my decisions. For your sake, then, we must hope that I never discover why Yves had you thrown into Newgate in the first place."

Even as Jenny hurried down the hall, she knew she had been abysmally foolish to make such a veiled threat. Damn. She had been so determined to crush that arrogant confidence of his that she had not cared how it was accomplished.

Shock halted her headlong rush back to the reception rooms. She paused, leaning weakly against the wall and holding her waist tightly. A passing glance at a mirror across the hall showed a hectic flush on her cheeks. Even more disastrous, she now noticed that although she had rearranged her costume, the love-knot on her bodice had been torn sometime in her struggle. With his keen senses, Wolf would notice it immediately, she was sure, nor would it take him long to discover how it had happened.

That had to be prevented at all costs, Jenny decided. Discovery of Nate's conduct to her might be all the excuse he needed to challenge his old enemy. Having seen the result of his first meeting with Nate, she dared not trust to the chance that he might fare better now. Wolf would always suffer a grave disadvantage in fighting Nate, she realized, because Wolf would fight fair.

Seeing a footman pass nearby with a tray of empty glasses, Jenny hailed him and sent him for Mrs. Mueller. Perhaps he had mentioned something of her demeanor, because the widow came with all speed. Only a look was needed to convince her that to depart instantly, without alerting Wolf, was the best remedy. At Mrs. Mueller's suggestion, they left word that Jenny had become indisposed but that they did not care to disturb his enjoyment of the evening.

They managed to return home without occasioning remark. To Jenny's surprise, her absence from the rout-party had gone unnoticed. Although it seemed to her that her struggle with Nate had lasted forever, it had only been a few minutes.

Those few minutes, however, might have changed everything, Jenny realized as she reviewed the events in her chamber. How could she have been so foolish as to offer that final taunt? Oh, her mother had been right. Her impetuous actions would be the ruin of her. Her only hope of safety lay in Nate's trusting to the unlikelihood of her ever discovering the root of his quarrel with Wolf—and the certainty of her fulfilling her pledge. If once Nate doubted that she would return the Beauchamp fortune to him, she knew not what he might do.

The sound of music—Scarlatti tonight—drifted up from the room below. And what of Wolf? Jenny wondered. If by her folly she had endangered the man she loved . . . She pulled her knees up under the covers and hugged her arms close about her. At all costs, Wolf must be kept safe. At all costs.

It was only after the intricacies of the music had chipped away at the sharp edge of his anger that Wolf realized that his contemplation of the tortuous workings of his enemy's hand had drawn him unconsciously to the complicated fingering of Scarlatti. Nate would pay for what he had done. Tonight's mischief only added to the long score he kept. The debt between them was great, and payment was long overdue. He would not wait much longer.

If he had guessed sooner what had transpired tonight it might have been finished already. When he had seen the marks on Nate's cheek, however, he had merely assumed them the gift of Nate's latest amour—until Tante's guilt gave the secret away. Evidently he had given Nate too much credit in assuming he had the cunning, if not the instincts of the true gentleman, to assume a proper character with Jenny.

A sudden discord accompanied the thought of what Nate must have done to drive her to such extreme measures. Damn Sir Frederick and his interminable boring stories! If not for him, Wolf would have seen, would have protected her. He should have been there!

His eyes strayed to the ceiling, as if he could see through to where she slept. Was she listening again? he wondered. Or had she cried herself into a restless sleep? No, he realized, Jenny was not one to seek refuge in useless tears. She would fight and claw her way out of her difficulties first. Smiling, he changed to the more gentle rhythms of Vivaldi. Those scratches on Nate's face had given him considerable satisfaction.

There was relief, too, in knowing that Jenny must finally have seen through that handsome, well-bred facade. Even to himself he could hardly bear to admit how deeply he had feared Nate's winning her affections. If the break between the two had been as deep and irrevocable as he hoped, however, Nate would be as much her enemy as his.

There was a remedy for that, of course. He might with a well-placed thrust settle his account and put Jenny's fears to rest. It might come to that sooner or later. Yet he would much rather find another way—and not only because of his promise to Tante. Without answers, Jenny would feel forever trapped. Worse, she might simply disappear one day, leaving everything behind. Leaving him.

He shuddered. By chance his glance fell upon the chair where she had sat with him the other night. She had looked so surprised, he remembered, when he had tried to tell her how much she had brought to his life. If only she knew! Over

the years he had learned to maintain an air of
self-assurance, but he had never acquired that fe-
licitous knack of making friends easily. What little
he knew of the warmth of friendship and family
he owed to old Lord Vickers and John, and to
Tante. He had never really learned how to talk to
women, however. Although there had been
women in his life, briefly from time to time, never
had he known the grace and charm of female companionship—not until Jenny.

Before Jenny, he could never have imagined
that there would be a woman who could sit curled
up in the chair, quite unself-conscious, and listen
to him play, simply enjoying the moment without
feeling any need to fill the silence with chatter.
Talking to her had been easy then, almost too
easy. He felt foolish now, remembering how he
had talked. At least he had held his folly in check
to some degree, even though he had not been able
to stop himself from reaching for her soft, bright
curls, just once.

Obviously things could not long continue as
they were, neither between him and Nate, nor
between him and Jenny. The facts that would set
them all free were so close, he could almost feel
them in his grasp. It would only take a little more
time, just a little more.

Time, however, might be the one thing he did
not have. He needed answers *now*.

Chapter Thirteen

Jenny waited anxiously for some disaster to follow her quarrel with Nate. None came, but she did not permit this circumstance to lull her into complacency. Somehow Nate would make sure she paid for her threats and insults. Her only hope was that he would wait until she had first returned the Beauchamp fortune to him—and that his revenge would extend to no one else.

Further thought had convinced her not to tell Richard what had happened. While his reaction was not likely to be as violent as Wolf's would surely be, he would undoubtedly favor Nate with a few threats of his own. Such an action would then list Richard forever among Nate's enemies, she knew. It was true that Richard must surely have greater resources for his own protection, but, she realized, it was also true that he of all of them was the most vulnerable should his identity be exposed. No, she dared not risk setting Nate against anyone else.

At least she had not revealed the depth of her feeling for Wolf, she thought with relief. If Nate knew she loved Wolf . . . The very thought was enough to bring on nightmares. How Nate would delight in being able to hurt her through the man she loved!

A shiver ran down her spine. The way he had talked of Wolf frightened her. It was almost as if the success of their conspiracy had made Nate drunk with power, and now he looked upon his old enemy as negligible, merely an inconvenience.

To think of Wolf in such a fashion was patently absurd. Love had not blinded Jenny to the fact that Wolf could also be a man to beware. Nate of all people should know that. He did know it—yet he thought he could best that remarkable intelligence. How? Jenny agonized. What did Nate think he could do?

It was not until the night Jenny was promised to go to the theater with a Mr. Rhys, one of her suitors, and his mother, the Lady Lonsdale, that she began to have a taste of where Nate's machinations might lead. Despite her usual enjoyment of the theater, she had not looked to find much pleasure in this evening's outing. Lady Pertwee, however, evidently eager to claim acquaintance with the viscountess, insisted with unusual force of manner that she should accept the invitation. The knowledge that she looked her best in a new gown of *gorge de pigeon* trimmed in *gaze de fantaisie* did nothing to raise her spirits. Since Wolf could not join them, it did not seem to matter where she went or what she did.

It did matter, however. Once arrived at Drury Lane, Jenny soon discovered that she and Lady Pertwee were not the only guests. Of the elderly gentleman who waited upon Lady Lonsdale she knew nothing, but the other member of the party was Nate.

"Cousin," he greeted her with a smile she found unpleasant. "How charming to see you again. I had begun to wonder if you had not gone from town, it has been so long since we met."

Unwillingly Jenny gave him her hand, but she could not prevent her fingers from clenching into a fist as he pressed a kiss upon them. In turn, he squeezed her fingers until it hurt. "How can you say so, milord?" she said, refusing to give him the satisfaction of letting him see her pain. " 'Tis you, I think, that must have forsaken your usual haunts for Whig assemblies." Under her breath, she added, "Not everyone frequents the cockpits and the bawdy houses, cousin."

"No," he whispered in her ear as he led her to a seat in the front of the box, "but you would be surprised at the number of acquaintances I have found from Newgate."

The name of that dreadful place had obviously been spoken loudly enough to be overheard by Mr. Rhys. Pulling a seat close to Jenny, he remarked with an air of polite interest, "Oh, are you familiar with tonight's piece, Miss Beauchamp? It's an old work, of course, but I did not know whether it had received much interest in the colonies."

Confused, Jenny set her fan in motion. Had the boy heard Nate or not? Perhaps he was just being

Mary Butler

courteous, ignoring a reference he would think referred only to Nate's incarceration for debt. "My cousin was just beginning to explain it to me," she said hesitantly. In truth, she had no idea what the play was, except that, knowing Lady Pertwee's tastes, it was not likely to be Shakespeare.

"An odd conceit, is it not?" Mr. Rhys continued, seemingly unaware of Jenny's tense reaction to her cousin, "to set an opera in Newgate prison." He smiled at her shyly. "The characters, you see, are all rogues—highwaymen, receivers of stolen goods, and the like. Even the jailers, whom one would expect to be honest men, are in league with the thieves."

Not a very subtle reminder of the past, Jenny thought, but a powerful one nonetheless. Steadfastly she refused to turn and look at Nate, sitting behind her and chuckling quietly. "Thieves and cheats, Mr. Rhys? I fear me your *Beggar's Opera* cannot set a very moral tone. If none of the characters are admirable, how may they engage the sympathies of their audience?" she asked, waving her fan in slow, steady strokes. Her own performance rather pleased her. No hint of anxiety could be seen, she was sure.

Jenny's erstwhile suitor looked suddenly crestfallen. His expressive dark eyes looked back at Nate, as if pleading for help. "I thought . . . that is, your cousin said you were sure to be pleased."

So it had been Nate's idea from the beginning to bring her here, Jenny realized. Ignoring him, she concentrated on reassuring the disappointed Mr. Rhys. "I am sure I will be. The work must have some extraordinary merit to have survived so long, no doubt."

"The music is charming," Mr. Rhys hastened to assure her. "You will probably recognize some of the songs. New lyrics were set to popular tunes. None of that horrible caterwauling you get with Handel."

Jenny, who quite liked the operas and oratorios of Handel, merely smiled and prepared herself for an evening of misery.

All through the first two acts, she wondered what Nate had to gain by this. Certainly he had reminded her of where she had come from, where she could be returned. The existence of both a Jenny and a Sukey in the cast of characters did indeed give her an uncomfortable feeling in the pit of her stomach. On the whole, however, Gay's picture of Newgate was too pretty for those who had known the real thing to induce much fear. His jailer was merely a greedy businessman. Compared to Deems, he appeared harmless. Clearly, the author had never seen the Women's Hold, Jenny thought, although he had captured the system of bribes, "perquisites" he called them, to perfection. Yet Nate might have reminded her of all this by any number of means.

Whether by his intent or not, the performance did chill her, in a way that she suspected Nate would not understand. The opera's biting satire depicted a world where dishonesty and self-interest governed virtually everyone, and those moved by genuine affection were fools, used by the unscrupulous and then discarded when their usefulness had been outlived. It was the way Nate saw the world, she realized, a place where "In all the employments of life, Each neighbor abuses his brother."

Not for her such a view of life—an outlook that ignored the existence of good people like Mrs. Mueller and Wolf. Once, in Newgate, she had almost fallen prey to that cruel philosophy, but never again. Even in prison she had found hope and kindness in the person of Sukey. Perhaps there was hope for her now, Jenny thought, because that was the one thing Nate had left out of his calculations—the possibility of genuine kindness.

His manipulation of Mr. Rhys, however, was calculated to a nicety, Jenny had to admit. After the second act, as if on a signal, Mr. Rhys rose and hurried the rest of his party out to visit an acquaintance in another box, leaving Nate and Jenny alone. After all, it was perfectly proper. Nate was not only supposed to be her cousin, but twenty years her senior.

Looking out at the multitude in the stalls below, Jenny reminded herself that they were not really alone. There were thousands to see if Nate tried to take advantage of the situation. Nonetheless, she shuddered with distaste when he leaned over to whisper in her ear.

"Mr. Rhys," he said, sounding amused, "convinced of our familial affection, has begged me to use my influence in favor of his suit. Yes, I thought it funny, too. This indication of his deplorable lack of perception should, I hope, sufficiently discourage you. If not," he added in a more pointed manner, "I am sure I can provide further inducements to persuade you against such a match."

Jenny sighed, determined to show no more than

weariness before Nate. "You and I will both be much happier, Nate, if only you can convince yourself that I will not marry anyone—anyone at all—as Jean-Marie Beauchamp."

"I intend to make very sure you don't," he said, obviously missing her point. "Except, of course, me. My offer still stands. Despite what has occurred between us, I am willing to forgive and forget, as long as you don't make me wait too long. I think you would find me a reasonably complacent husband—providing, of course, that you behave with a modicum of discretion."

This offer repelled Jenny even more than his previous one, which had been based at least on a pretense of affection. It was no use, she realized. Nate was incapable of understanding any motives but his own selfish greed. "What is it you want, Nate?" she asked, closing her eyes against his ugly hints. "I assume there is a point to this silly demonstration."

"I have told you what I want, Jenny dear," he said. "To enjoy my fortune—all my fortune—in safety and comfort, which, I fear, can only be accomplished to my satisfaction by our marriage."

Jenny opened her lips to argue with this conclusion, but he stopped her, taking her by the wrist. "The point, I would have thought, should be abundantly clear," he continued. "The point, dear coz, is that your guardians are nothing to me. I cannot be kept from where I want to be, by Wolf, Dick, you, or anyone." He let her go and waved a graceful hand over the large audience. "Where are your heroes now? Do you see them anywhere about? Yet here I am, alone with you, just as I planned."

A cool breeze swept in as the door to the box opened to readmit the other members of their party. Jenny shivered as she smiled at Mr. Rhys. The curtain was about to rise for the final act. Leaning forward, Nate whispered one final taunt. "There is nothing Wolf or Dick can do to stop me from doing as I please. Remember that, Jenny. Nothing."

Jenny did not believe that, not really, but she could not fail to admit that despite the vaunted protection of her two cavaliers, Nate had been able to secure not one but two private interviews with her. As she and Lady Pertwee were escorted home in the Lonsdale coach, Jenny wondered how much her chaperone had contributed to the ease of these meetings. That her ladyship had fallen prey to Nate's good looks and charm seemed very likely.

However many years Nate had spent in Newgate, he still knew how to use society and its rules to his benefit. Naturally. Like Lady Pertwee and the rest of society, he played the same game, shared the same concern for maintaining appearances. Listening with half an ear to the clip-clop of the horses and the rhythm of the gossip within the coach, Jenny admitted to herself that she was a mere babe at that sort of game. And so was Wolf. Although it was one of the things she loved about him, she realized that Wolf's lack of patience with the common pretenses of society placed them at a severe disadvantage.

As long as Wolf was unwilling to make an open break with Jenny's "cousin," Nate would be able to approach her whenever and wherever he wished. At a word from her, Wolf probably would make that break, she knew. The results of that break, however, would be more than social embarrassment, she saw all too well. One of them would die, and that one might possibly be Wolf. It was a chance she could not take.

Returned to Hanover Square, Jenny looked in upon Wolf and Mrs. Mueller playing a quiet game of silver loo. As he looked up at her greeting and smiled at her, she swore to herself that whatever happened she would not allow him to be hurt. If anyone had to pay for her foolishness in once believing in Nate, it must be she, no one else.

She stayed and took a cup of tea with them, but said nothing of her unpleasant encounter with Nate. If he had done nothing else, Nate had reminded her all too clearly that time was running out. All too soon she would have nothing left but memories such as this. So she stayed up a while and chatted, before she kissed Mrs. Mueller good night, wishing all the while that she might do the same to the gentleman sitting opposite, just to save a few moments against the unhappy time to come.

How soon that time must come was a question Jenny needed to take up with Sukey. As she readied herself for bed, she watched Sukey setting things to right with a graceful touch. There was nothing left now of the pickpocket from Newgate, Jenny thought, except perhaps in those nimble fingers. With her dark hair dressed neatly and plainly under her frilled cap, Sukey looked to Jenny very much like the fashionable ladies' maids who so intimidated her.

Sukey's warm heart was still the same, Jenny

knew very well, but her dreams had changed since the day they met in the Women's Hold. What she had to tell Sukey now, she recognized sadly, was likely to dash those dreams to the ground.

"Sukey," she said, trying to screw up her courage. "I have done a very foolish thing."

Arms akimbo, Sukey tossed her head back. "Well, I was wondering when you'd get around to telling me," she said, to Jenny's surprise. "As if I couldn't see you were half mad with worry and unhappiness. Come, out with it. What have you done?"

Jenny recognized the scolding tone as meant to put her at ease. Her news, however, was not such as could be so easily dismissed, she feared. Taking a deep breath, she confessed at last, "I've quarreled with Nate. Quite seriously, I'm afraid."

"How seriously?" Sukey asked, sitting on the edge of the bed.

The agony of her struggle with Nate came back to her in painful detail. "I tried to scratch his eyes out," she said.

"That's serious, all right," Sukey agreed. Shrewdly she examined Jenny. "He got a little out of hand, did he?"

"You might say so." Pulling a wrap round her shoulders, Jenny sat next to her friend on the bed. "But that's not the worst of it."

Sukey looked at her in surprise. No wonder, thought Jenny. How much worse could things get?

"I'm afraid things deteriorated after that into an exchange of unspecific threats."

"Well?"

In response to Sukey's impatient gesture, she

admitted at last, "I told him he had better pray I never discover the reason Wolf put him in prison."

Jenny was not even aware that she had used Wolf's given name, until Sukey pointed it out. "Did you call his lordship Wolf to Nate?" she asked, obviously horrified at the thought.

"No, no, I'm sure I did not," Jenny hurried to add, equally frightened at the thought that she might have given herself away so badly. "That much of a fool I'm not." A silly claim, she thought, as if loving Wolf were not the greatest folly of all.

Oddly, Sukey did not seem the least surprised at this sudden indication of intimacy with one whom they had all considered the enemy. Instead she seemed to be concentrating only on Nate's reaction.

"That's good," she said. "Although things is bad enough. I guess he knows now you ain't marrying him."

Jenny almost laughed, remembering how strongly she had expressed her refusal. Then she remembered his repetition of the offer tonight. "He said he needed to find the right persuasion," she said, quietly afraid. "He said neither Richard nor Wolf could prevent him, that he could reach me whenever and wherever he liked."

"Then he's crazed," Sukey declared with comforting assurance. "Thinks because he's got his title now he can't be touched. Thinks he don't need us anymore. Well, if he's not careful, he'll find out what we can do."

"Be serious, Sukey. What can we do?" Jenny held out her hands in a gesture of helplessness. "We cannot take any action against him without putting all of us in danger—you, me, Richard."

"Nor can he," Sukey insisted, getting up and facing Jenny to emphasize her point. "His whole claim is based on your being Jean-Marie Beauchamp. Do you think he dare have that questioned? Not paying no mind to what his lordship might do—and he's not a man I'd disregard, I can tell you—one word about our conspiracy and he's a dead man." Jenny could see she meant that literally. "If Nate so much as mentions the name Danger, he'll have the whole gang onto him."

There was another option Nate might try, however, Jenny had realized. It was a thought that robbed her of any comfort Sukey's last statement had given. "And if he tries abduction?" she asked, her voice hushed with fear. "Nate seems to think he can force me into marriage, even force Wolf into condoning it. Although I cannot imagine that Wolf would permit Nate to get his hands on the Beauchamp fortune, even if he did . . ."

Jenny could hardly bear to complete the thought. Her honor lost, would she have the strength to refuse Nate's offer? Would Wolf and Lady Pertwee let her? "In any case, he could not touch the money until I came of age—not if I married without my guardian's consent—and I have promised to return it to him then anyway."

Sukey had been pacing the room, but she stopped now, as if she too had considered something unpleasant. "Maybe he can't wait until then," she said, clearly unhappy with the thought. "I know, he wouldn't be able to touch your fortune before then anyways, but he'd have the security of it, do you see?"

Jenny shook her head.

"Listen," Sukey said, trying to explain. "If Nate is known to be betrothed to you, then the money-lenders will advance him money on the strength of his coming into the fortune when you marry. It's the same as if they loaned to a young lord who ain't come into his money yet, but will as soon as he comes of age or his old man goes off. They knows he's good for it eventually. It's the same with the shops. They'll give him credit, because they know he'll pay when he comes into his money, your money. But if he ain't got no expectations, y'see . . ."

"Yes, I do see." She saw more than Nate's need, however. With painful clarity she realized that she might not even have the few months she had hoped for with Wolf. Despite the risks Sukey had listed, Nate would try something, she knew. He would have to, and then Wolf would take action at last.

All she could do was pray that it would not involve the sword he wore at his waist.

She closed her eyes, trying to control the ache inside her. "Sukey, we had better be prepared to move quickly, just in case."

"I know, Jen," Sukey said as if she realized how much it would cost her to leave. "I've got bags packed for both of us, ready to go. And the makeup we used when you were Danger's doxy, I've got that ready too, so we can disguise ourselves."

Sadly Jenny nodded.

"Jen," Sukey said softly, taking her hand. "Did you ever think maybe his lordship knows the truth—and don't care?"

"Because it suits him to keep that much of the Beauchamp fortune out of Nate's hands? Oh yes,

I thought of it. There were times in the beginning when I felt sure of it, sure that he knew everything and was just playing with us."

"Well then?"

It was kind of Sukey to try to find some hope for her, but Jenny knew better. She had gone over this so many times in her mind. "I am the person who set his worst enemy free. If he knew that, he could never treat me as kindly as he has," she said.

In sympathy, Sukey patted her shoulder. "We made it this far, didn't we? We'll make it the rest of the way too."

Jenny touched her friend's hand and smiled, but in her heart she knew better. With luck they might well survive the next year, their secret unexposed, but there would be no happy ending for her. All she could hope for was a chance to leave before the discovery of her perfidy killed all the warmth of Wolf's friendship. Either way, she must leave him. It was only a matter of time.

Despite his threats, Nate seemed willing to bide his time for the nonce. He made no more attempts to separate Jenny from her chaperones, nor did he press his luck by trying to command too much of her attention in public.

This circumspect behavior, Jenny realized, might well be influenced by the fact that Richard had clearly set someone from his gang to follow and watch over her, or it might be due to even more pointed interference from that quarter that Richard had not bothered to disclose to her. While she had hesitated to involve Richard in her quarrel with Nate, Sukey proved she had no such compunction. That Sukey had revealed the story to Richard, Jenny only discovered after the fact, when the young maid informed her of the identity of her shadow. No amount of her questioning, however, could persuade Richard to tell her exactly what had occurred between him and Nate, but she was sure it could not have been pleasant.

Whether Richard was the only one, other than Sukey, to know of her encounter with Nate was something Jenny could not decide. She almost suspected that Wolf knew what had occurred at the ball, but that he had made no overt move against his old enemy. Could it be that Wolf would refrain from issuing a challenge that might make her the subject of gossip? In any case, she could see very plainly that Wolf had become even more protective, more determined to keep Nate from her side. From a slight coolness between him and Lady Pertwee, she suspected too that he had confronted her ladyship and reminded her of her duties and responsibilities as chaperone.

These circumstances should have comforted her. Nonetheless, she did not feel safe, except when at Wolf's side. She knew she had not been pardoned by Nate, only given a temporary reprieve.

While she was reprieved, however, she meant to take full advantage of her time with Wolf, storing up memories against the time when they would be all she had of him. It seemed to her, too, that he spent more time with her and was less concerned with business and matters of state. Sometimes now of an evening he would play for her and his aunt. If they went to a ball, he would always claim two of her dances. As the weather grew warmer, he took her riding.

In her heart, Jenny knew he did this to protect her from Nate, but she could not help but feel that he found some pleasure in her company. Surely it was not just her imagination that he seemed more relaxed and at ease? Often enough Mrs. Mueller commented on his changed behavior, how he no longer hid himself for hours in his study. The widow had been amazed that Wolf included Jenny in his audience when he played now, citing that as an instance of his contentment and his affection for her.

Affection. It was a pale word for what she felt for him, yet she would be glad to think she had won even a slight place in his regard. Further than that Jenny could allow no hope. Sometimes in the night she dreamed what it would be like to be loved by such a man, but always the dream turned to nightmare. Wolf's affections, however strong, could not survive the knowledge of what she had done.

She ought to pull away, Jenny told herself, to stop torturing herself with glimpses of a joy she could never know. To do so, however, proved impossible. As long as she could stay by his side, she must stay, no matter the cost to her later.

There was another reason Jenny wanted to hold fast and stay by his side. As long as she remained with Wolf there was some chance that she could keep his enmity with Nate from erupting into bloodshed. She could give Wolf the time to find another Beauchamp to disinherit Nate, and then perhaps he would not feel the need to do more than put Nate back in Newgate. No longer did she worry how such a discovery would affect her. As long as Wolf remained safe, nothing else mattered.

Although Jenny had not put such thoughts into words, she did think that Nate, when he acted, would move against her or Wolf. They were the two who kept his fortune from him. Believing this, however, she was unprepared for the threat when it finally came. She should have remembered that Nate knew other ways to hurt her.

It was luck that placed her on the gallery overlooking the main hall when the butler opened the door to three officers of the law. She had gone upstairs to fetch a book she had left in her chamber and was about to return to the drawing room when she was distracted by the noisy entrance of the three men. By their accents, she could tell immediately they were not gentlemen, a circumstance that immediately raised alarums in her head. Wolf's butler was not apt to open the door to anything less than gentry; tradesmen would have gone round to the rear of the house, she told herself. Waiting silently, just out of sight, she did not have long to wait for the reason for their visit.

"Information has been received," the largest of the three, evidently the leader, announced pompously, "that an escaped criminal, name of Sukey the Diver, has taken refuge in this house, probably having disguised herself as a servant of some sort, a lady's maid perhaps. We are here to apprehend this dangerous criminal."

Jenny could not see the butler's face, but she knew exactly how he would look, his eyebrow raised in disdain. His voice she could hear, rich with contempt. "I will see if his lordship will see you. If you would please wait here?"

Not waiting to hear their answer, Jenny ran to the sewing room where she had last seen Sukey trying to repair the damage done to her gown by Nate when he had attacked her. Breathless, she said quickly, "Come quick, Sukey. Nate's peached on you."

Sukey's reactions had evidently not been slowed by the ease of her life in this house. Immediately she set her work aside. "Are they here already?" she asked.

"Yes," Jenny said. "Looking for a maidservant." In the few minutes it had taken to reach Sukey, she had had an idea. "They may already have gone round to watch all the exits. You'd never get past them, not even with Richard's man to help."

Following Jenny back to her chamber, Sukey was quick to catch her idea, but less sure of her ability to carry it off. As Jenny helped her remove her servant's dress, she whispered, "They'll never believe I'm a lady, Jen. Not the way I talk."

"Then don't talk," Jenny advised. "They won't expect a lady to take any notice of them. If they so much as peek in on us, I would be very much surprised. Here, let me help you with these panniers. This white quilted petticoat will do, and the azure gown."

"Not the blue," Sukey said automatically, her professional instincts evidently aroused at last. "Give me the cherry striped one Lady Pertwee would have you get, even though anyone with half an eye could have told her it wouldn't go with your hair. The paints is hidden in that drawer there. We'd best have that too."

The two women moved quickly and efficiently

to effect the change from lady's maid to lady. In Newgate they had helped each other often enough with their costumes, so that now they merely fell into familiar rhythms. Sukey was still applying maquillage when the door to Jenny's chamber burst open to admit Mrs. Mueller.

With a single glance she took in the preparations before her. Jenny waited anxiously to see how the widow would react. Her first words confirmed that Jenny could place all reliance in her kind heart. "Ach, already you know. Wolf, he sends me to gather all the women servants to appear before him and these fellows in the study, but I think to hurry is not important, ja? Good, good," she said, looking Sukey over. "One more thing is needed. Something...I know. Wait, please."

Mrs. Mueller ran out again, and returned a moment later carrying a large cone and a bellows to powder Sukey's hair. With Sukey wearing a cape and holding the cone to protect herself from the powder, the widow went to work, changing the young maid's dark curls to fashionable white. A patch, cleverly placed to accentuate her flashing dark eyes, completed the effect. Sukey the lady's maid, once Sukey the Diver, had been changed into Susan the lady. But only as long as she held her tongue.

While the widow went at last to gather up the servant girls, Jenny and Sukey slipped down to the drawing room unobserved. Handing Sukey her needlework to hold, Jenny gave the girl's hands a comforting squeeze. "It will be all right, Sukey, I'm sure of it."

Sukey smiled wanly. "I know. At the worst,

Danger's man would rescue me before they got me back to Newgate. But I'm on the run and alone again." As Jenny expected, however, Sukey would not long let herself give way to what she would call mawkish sentimentality. "Awh, I'm just feeling sorry for meself. Don't you pay me no mind," she added. "I'll miss you, though. You been good to me, Jen."

"I've been good to you?" Jenny said in surprise. "Sukey, you saved my life and my sanity. You kept me going when I thought I could do no more. 'Tis I who do not know what I will do without you to advise and scold me."

Sukey shook her head. "I told you before. You're stronger than you know, Jenny Wilde. And I think maybe you underestimate—"

Both of them looked up suddenly as the door opened to reveal Wolf with the officers of the law. His face showed only boredom, but Jenny knew he must recognize Sukey, even behind the layers of paint and powder. If nothing else, he would recognize the gown as hers. Would he give them away?

"These are the only other ladies in the house, constable," he said as if wearied by their importunities. "My ward, Miss Beauchamp, and Fräulein Neuman, who is staying with us while she awaits passage to Hanover. If you insist, you may search the house for your fugitive, but I fear you have been misinformed from the start."

The officers seemed to be showing some doubts on that account already, but the leader was obviously not going to let go so easily. No doubt there was a large reward attached to Sukey's capture, and he intended to win it. "May we ask some questions of the ladies, my lord? They may have some information that would be of help to us in tracking this criminal."

"You may ask Miss Beauchamp what you like. Fräulein Neuman has only been here a day or two and she speaks only German." At this point, Wolf appeared to recall his manners and embarked on what seemed to be a long explanation in German of the officers' quest. As no one but Wolf spoke a word of that language, he might as well be reciting poetry. His intonation at the end, however, was clearly indicative of a question. He looked pointedly at Sukey and waited.

"Nein, Herr Baron," she said smoothly, shaking her head in innocent ignorance. Jenny was impressed. The clever girl had obviously picked up a word or two from Mrs. Mueller.

"As you see, gentlemen, the fräulein cannot help you. Miss Beauchamp, you must be wondering what all this is about, too. Evidently these men feel that there is a criminal lurking in the house in the guise of lady's maid. That is why I was forced to call my aunt away to help us. I hope you have not had too difficult a time trying to communicate with the fräulein."

For her alone his voice warmed to sympathy. It was going to be all right, Jenny knew then. Wolf might have protected Sukey from the law solely to protect the honor of his house, so that neither he nor anyone else would be compromised for having sheltered Sukey. His smile told her now, however, that far from being angry with her for trying to rescue Sukey, he was proud of her.

Later she would have to consider what his knowledge of Sukey's past meant to her position, but for now she must keep up the pretense. She shrugged. "Fräulein Neuman has been showing me her needlework. Without Mrs. Mueller to translate, I fear we could accomplish little of real conversation. But I don't understand this ridiculous claim about criminals among the staff," she said. "If that were so, this household would certainly offer much of value, but not so much as a farthing has been misplaced."

"A very pertinent remark, Miss Beauchamp," Wolf said, then turned to the officers. "Gentlemen, I cannot help but think that this false information was laid for one of two purposes—either to inconvenience this household for some imagined slight one of the servants may have made, or to deliberately lead you officers out of the way to assist some criminal to escape your vigilance. You will, I hope, be able to question your informant again?"

"Unfortunately, my lord," the leader was forced to admit, now very much embarrassed, "this information was provided anonymously."

"I see," Wolf said, in a way that was clearly designed to make the constables even more uncomfortable. "Will there be anything else, officers?"

They could hardly escape fast enough now, practically falling over their feet trying to apologize and back out the door at the same time. It might almost have been amusing, if she and Sukey had not been so nervous. Even though the officers seemed to have left, they dared not relax, not yet.

Mrs. Mueller entered the drawing room a moment later, caught between annoyance and laughter. "Those three! All the servant girls they have upset. Cook in an uproar is. What kind of dinner we shall get tonight, I do not know. But they have gone. Boots down the street followed them, until they were well on their way. Arguing all the time, he says."

"I'm not surprised," Wolf said. " 'Tis a pity, but they probably do not know who provided the information. I would like to see that person pay as much as they would."

He did know who had informed on Sukey, however, as well as Jenny did, she realized. There was no time to consider the implications, at least not yet, not until Sukey's future had been discussed.

Wolf came and sat next to Jenny, facing her erstwhile lady's maid. "Well, fräulein," he said, "I am afraid that you will have to set sail for Hanover on the next tide."

"Hanover?" Sukey repeated, obviously dismayed. She had no choice, though. What Wolf decided at this point would be what they had to do.

"Only temporarily," he assured her. "It will be safest if we follow the tale I told those three bunglers. From Hanover you may set forth for where you will. I would suggest you take ship for the colonies, for America, but it shall be as you choose."

Sukey seemed a little embarrassed to be facing Wolf like this, dressed in fine clothes, sitting in his drawing room. Smiling a little, she said, "Transportation at last. I should have known it would come to that. You're right, of course. At least they speaks English over there."

"You'll be fine, Sukey," he assured her with a

kindness that touched Jenny as well. "I'll give you some letters to take to my business contacts in Williamsburg in Virginia. They will help you find a good position. By the time we next hear from you, I expect to discover that you have either married the Lord Governor or have become the owner of one of the large plantations."

"G'arn," she said, then covered her mouth with her hands, astonished at her own effrontery.

"Go on with you, then," he answered in turn. "You've much to do to get ready, no doubt."

"Yes, milord," Sukey said, bowing. At the door she hesitated for a moment, then turned back. "Thank you, milord. I don't know as anyone else, any of the lords and ladies, I mean, would do for me what you done."

"Don't be silly, Sukey," he said, reaching out to take Jenny's hand. "Of course you do. Now hurry."

"Aye, milord," she said, and then she was gone.

Wolf was still holding her hand. "You will miss her, I think," he said.

"Very much," Jenny admitted, more conscious of his touch than anything else. Some explanation of her closeness with a servant girl, especially a servant girl who had proved to be a criminal escaped from Newgate, must be expected, she realized. "When I first arrived in London," she said slowly, carefully considering her words, "Sukey was one of the few people to show me kindness, to treat me with friendliness. Whatever she did in the past, she was never dishonest in her dealings with me." Jenny looked down. She wished she could say as much about her dealings with Wolf.

"You don't have to explain to me," Wolf said. "Loneliness is something I understand too well. I only hope you will recognize that you have many other friends now, and need not be alone."

There would be no one else to whom she could admit the truth, however, Jenny thought sadly. Wolf's obvious desire to comfort warmed her nonetheless. "I cannot tell you how greatly I appreciate your kindness in this."

"If I have pleased you," he said, "then I am happy. But I am concerned," he added. "I have no proof, I admit, but I believe I know the author of this attack against Sukey."

"My cousin," Jenny said, holding her breath. Could Nate have toppled their entire construction of falsehood by this single move? To have Jenny's maid revealed as a Newgate convict must encourage Wolf to wonder about the rest of them.

"So," he said, "you are not so surprised after all. You know that Lord Vickers was imprisoned in Newgate for debt, and would have the opportunity to meet Sukey there. Somehow he must have learned of your arrival as soon as you reached these shores. Sending Sukey to win a place as your servant, he hoped to gain inside knowledge of your activities, where you went, what you did, what suitors you favored. Unluckily for him, Sukey did truly become your friend. I can only assume that this is his revenge for her failure to provide him with the information he wants."

Stunned, Jenny hardly knew how to respond. Here was an explanation handed to her on a salver. Of itself, it was a logical enough premise, but too facile, and from one who rarely explained himself at all. Yet it did seem plausible. "The respect and affection I felt for my cousin," she admitted, "has been forfeited by what I have seen of his behavior. But to scheme in such a way... Do you really think it possible?"

"That it was your cousin behind this, I feel certain," Wolf said, "although I confess I have little but my reason and instincts to support such an assertion. As for the cause behind such behavior, can you tell me any other reason why he would do this?"

Jenny looked into his sea-blue eyes, wishing she dared confess her fears. "No," she said sadly at last. It was not a lie, after all. She simply could not tell him.

Chapter Fourteen

An hour before dawn, Jenny crept from the solace of her bed to make her final adieux to Sukey. The newly christened Fräulein Neuman looked frankly terrified at the thought of leaving. As Jenny watched her transformed friend pace from one end of the morning room to the other, obviously too nervous to eat, she remembered how calmly Sukey had faced the ugliness and degradation of the Women's Hold. That was part of a world Sukey knew, though. In making her journey to the colonies, she would be entering a new world in more ways than one.

"Will I have to fight Indians?" she asked Jenny at last.

Laughing in spite of herself, Jenny shook her head. "You may never see any. Sukey, you cannot judge all colonial life by my experiences during

313

Mary Butler

the war with the French. There are towns, you
know. Oh, nothing so grand as London, I grant
you, but with the same amenities. We have shops
and taverns and even playhouses."

From Sukey's expression, she seemed skeptical
nonetheless. "His lordship give me a letter for his
friend. He says maybe I could take a position in
one of the shops, since they ain't much need for
lady's maids," she said without enthusiasm.

"Won't you like that?" Jenny asked.

"Oh, aye, I'd like it fine. Do you think they'd
take such as me in one of the fancy shops, though?
Even if they don't know I'm a Newgate bird, they
can see for themselves I'm just a girl from the
rookeries."

So that was it. "Sukey," Jenny said earnestly,
"your past is behind you now. I think you'll find
Americans much more concerned with what you
are now, with what you can do. Wolf was right,
you know. You'll probably end up a wealthy busi-
nesswoman, with your own dress shop and a
dozen girls working under you."

Sukey smiled at that finally, then pulled at Jenny's arm and whispered to her confidentially. "He
give me a hundred pounds, Jen. To help me get
settled properly, he says."

This instance of generosity on the part of the
man she loved warmed Jenny's heart, but it reminded her of her own inability to do much for
her friend and companion. "You deserve no less,"
she said. "I only wish I could help contribute
something as well. Nothing I have here is really
mine, not mine to give. Except for this."

She pressed a small package into Sukey's hands
and watched while Sukey opened it to reveal the

embroidered fire screen she had labored over with such determination. "A more useless present I can hardly imagine," Jenny said, embarrassed by the poverty of her gift, "but it will, I hope, at least serve as a reminder of a friend who will miss you more than you know."

Sukey bit her lip, as if to stop from crying, and gazed wordlessly at her gift. After a moment's silence, she said at last, "I never had a fire screen. Now I really shall think myself a fine lady."

At the gentle touch of Jenny's hand on hers, Sukey's control seemed to snap and she fell weeping on Jenny's shoulder. Near tears herself, Jenny put comforting arms around her. "Listen, Sukey," she said, struggling to remain strong, "maybe I can offer you another sort of gift. I've an uncle who moved to Virginia before I was born. My mother took him in dislike and cut off communication, but if you tell him you're a friend of mine, I am sure he would help you. His name was Walter Wilde and he settled around Jamestown, I believe. If ever you are in difficulties, you must find him, or his sons, and tell them you're a friend of Eugénie Wilde, John's daughter, from the Mohawk Valley in New York. They'll see you are taken care of." She drew back so she could face Sukey directly. "And when I am finally free of this dreadful lie, I'll come and join you there."

Sukey accepted her handkerchief, but denied the comfort of this promise. "You could never go back now, Jen. I can see that even if you can't. Never see his lordship again? Never even have word of him?" She shook her head. "You've got spirit for most anything, but that would cut the living heart right out of you."

As she heard the words, Jenny recognized the truth of them. Her heart would indeed wither, separated from Wolf, but she had hoped no one else would see it so clearly. "Is it so obvious?" she asked.

"Only to me," Sukey said, "and maybe Richard." She appeared to hesitate a moment, as if considering how much more she dared say. "He's a good man, his lordship is," she added at last. "It don't seem to me as he'd be so harsh or unforgiving if you was to tell him the truth."

Now it was Jenny's turn to sadly shake her head, denying hope. This was something she had considered too often and too long, and always the answer was the same. "There are some things you can forgive of anyone *but* a friend. We've grown too close for my actions to seem anything less than betrayal to him. So you see, my heart will break whether I go or stay."

They stood there a moment, silent, and then embraced each other one last time. Already sounds in the hall presaged the moment of departure. Jenny, feeling far from ready, turned a pleading face toward the door. *Not yet*, she prayed, *just a few moments more*.

Time, however, as Jenny had once been told, waited for no one. A knock sounded at the door and a footman, impassive as always, announced that the coach was ready for Fräulein Neuman. Not by so much as a blink of an eye did the lad reveal that he recognized Sukey. Jenny would have loved to know what the rest of the household thought of all this, and what Wolf had told them, but doubted she would ever find out.

And now her dear friend had to leave. Behind

Sukey's tear-filled eyes, Jenny could see the spark of the girl's indomitable spirit and a touch of humor, reminding her of how she had first seen her, picking Deems' pocket.

"You remember when we first met, Jen?" Sukey asked, her mind obviously following the same path. "And you asked my name? It looks like I finally got one now."

"So you do," Jenny said, achieving a smile for this final farewell. Firmly she reminded herself that Sukey's last memory of her should not be weak and tearful. Last memory. For all her plans, this might well be the last time she saw Sukey. Certainly the events of the last few months had shown her how little faith could be placed in the plans of men. There was so much she would have liked to say, and now she could not find the words.

A cough at the door reminded them, too, that they did not have the time. Gathering up her belongings, Sukey paused a moment and looked back one more time, after checking that the footman had moved on. "I learned a lot from you, Jen," she said. "More than you'll ever know. But you gots a lot to learn too, especially about people. Maybe when you're making up your mind that nothing can go right for you and him, you might think about that. You been wrong before."

"I was right about you," Jenny whispered, but the room was empty.

Sukey's thought was kindly meant, but Jenny could not find comfort in that belief. She had indeed been wrong about Wolf when she had considered him their enemy, a cold and cruel villain who would destroy them all without consideration—the sort of man that Nate was quickly proving himself to be. Whether the wrong she had done him in undertaking this imposture deserved the same harshness as Nate mattered little; it was sure to cost her the warmth of his regard, and that was punishment enough.

His attentions told her that she had won some place in his affections, however small. That he should stand patiently by her side now while she pondered the merits of one cap over another could not be due to mere protectiveness. Recognizing this, Jenny glowed with a fragile happiness. What was cause for pleasure now would be all the more cause for suffering later, she knew. Nonetheless, she allowed Wolf to distract her, determined to enjoy every minute she had with him.

The appearance of Richard, seen through the shop window, reminded her again how very little time there might be. Did he know what had happened? His watchman must have seen the constable leave empty-handed, even if he had not discerned Sukey's transformation and escape.

"Miss Beauchamp, my lord, well met," he greeted them with his customary easy grace. "How do you both this fine day?"

"Perplexed," Jenny answered, trying to attain the same easiness of manner. "Mrs. Mueller's birthday is in three days' time and I am trying to decide on a gift, but I cannot make up my mind."

Richard came and looked over her shoulder. "Ah, I thought those caps rather matronly for you, Miss Beauchamp. Now I understand. These are charming, but I am sure Mrs. Mueller will appreciate anything you choose for her."

"So I have told her myself," Wolf added, smiling. He seemed rather pleased that Richard had joined them. *My two protectors*, Jenny thought, looking at them together like this.

"And you, my lord, are you too in search of a present for your aunt?" Richard asked.

"I'm afraid I have shown a deplorable lack of originality and purchased a box of marzipan candies, of which my aunt is inordinately fond, yet again. No, I am here merely to keep Miss Beauchamp company, and, I hope, to provide some relaxation and relief after the uproar we experienced yesterday. Perhaps you heard some word of it about town?"

Jenny looked at Wolf suspiciously, startled to find that he should bring up the very subject she needed so very much to discuss. Surely he would want to have the story of their adventure kept secret? Then she realized what he was doing—he was warning her other protector of the danger from Nate.

"There was some talk of you having the law at your door," Richard admitted, "but no one paid it any heed. It was so patently ridiculous. Are you telling me it was true after all?"

Nate had been at work again, Jenny realized, remembering what he had said of the vulnerability of Wolf's reputation as a courtier. She noted, too, that Wolf had been prepared for it.

"Oh, yes," he admitted, "in search of Miss Beauchamp's maid, who they *claimed* was a criminal escaped from Newgate. They turned the whole house upside-down searching for the poor girl."

"And never found her?"

Wolf cast a casual glance toward the clerk that sent him quickly wrapping up Jenny's purchases.

"No, never. I cannot say that I am sorry she escaped, either, for it seemed to me the girl was trying her best to live an orderly and respectable life."

His words earned him a penetrating look from Richard. No doubt the former highwayman was wondering, as was Jenny, how far Wolf's forgiveness might extend. "How is it that the girl was traced to your home, do you know?"

Gathering up Jenny's packages, Wolf led them outside again. "Evidently an anonymous letter was left with one of the magistrates. Odd, would you not say? Especially as there must be some reward attached to the poor girl's capture."

"Very odd indeed," Richard admitted. "And now Miss Beauchamp is left without a maid."

He might as well have said Jenny was left without one of her allies, for that must have been Nate's purpose. What ought they to do now was what Jenny longed to know. How she was to gain the privacy to hear Richard's advice was merely another question she had no idea how to answer.

The city street outside the mercer's shop was alive with sounds and movement. A coach rattling by drowned out part of Wolf's response, but Jenny heard him say, "But if *you* know of someone in search of a position, do send her over. Otherwise, we think it best to wait before we advertise. Miss Beauchamp depends less than most ladies on the services of a maid, so for the present my aunt's woman can give her all the assistance she needs."

"Well, I am sorry that this trouble should upset your household," Richard said, obviously looking for some means to prolong the conversation. "Whoever it was who placed information on the girl should at least have had the courtesy to wait until the Season was over."

"Yes," Wolf said dryly, "clearly this informant was no gentleman."

Although his words were mild enough, the tone of Wolf's voice alerted Jenny to a deeper resentment. Nate might have aimed this petty piece of vengeance at her, but he had struck at Wolf's household, and that was something that would neither be forgiven nor forgotten. Looking up at the beloved profile, Jenny was reminded again how dangerous Wolf could be when threatened, when betrayed.

His words, upon seeing her fearful expression, also reminded her that she must take more care. For Wolf to discover how deeply her affections were involved seemed to her now almost as terrible a consequence as his discovering the truth of her identity.

"I meant to distract Miss Beauchamp, and now I have done nothing but discuss our troubles," Wolf said, his eyes full of sympathy. "Come, Sir Richard," he continued, "I ask your assistance. What would you suggest to raise a young lady's spirits?"

"The promise of an outing, perhaps?" Richard suggested. "I had meant to propose such a diversion to the ladies to return your gracious hospitality. An advertisement for a masked ball at Ranelagh next week caught my eye, and I wondered if all of you would be available."

"A visit to the pleasure gardens at Ranelagh would be an excellent notion," Wolf agreed. "You may recall my telling you, Miss Beauchamp, that young Mozart gave a benefit concert there last year. The music there is often fine, but I fear a masked ball would not be suitable. As you are new to town, you would probably not be aware that such events tend to attract the less desirable elements. Some of the more adventurous ladies do attend, I believe, but my aunt is rather old-fashioned in matters of that sort."

"You're quite right," Richard answered. "I had not considered. Let me think."

A small placard set in one corner of a shop window, however, had already provided Jenny with her answer. Smiling, she told Wolf, "If you desire to please me, my lord, I know a way that will also provide your aunt with a birthday present she will treasure always."

"Miss Beauchamp, I am at your service as always. How may I perform this gallant deed?" Wolf asked.

For her answer, Jenny pointed to the placard, which read, "Profiles Taken." "Mrs. Mueller told me she has often begged you to have your portrait done but that you never seemed to have the time. This should take but a few moments."

The request had clearly taken Wolf by surprise. Hesitating, he seemed almost embarrassed. Jenny had originally looked upon the sitting as a chance to talk to Richard, but now she wanted the profile itself, for herself as much as for Mrs. Mueller. If she were careful, she might trace the profile with no one the wiser. Then she would have some image of him to keep, to treasure when she could no longer gaze at the original.

"Very well," he agreed at last, "but only if you will join me and have your own done."

"You have my portrait," Jenny reminded him.

"That was for posterity," Wolf said. "I want this one myself." Holding the door open for her, he said, "Will it amuse you to observe us, Sir Richard?"

Jenny hardly paid heed to Richard's response. It was a good thing, she considered, that the profile would reveal nothing of color or expression. Her face must be flaming. That Wolf should want a likeness of her—for himself!

The sadness on Richard's face, however, quickly reminded her that such a remembrance would cease to be treasured soon enough when Wolf knew the truth of her imposture. No wonder Richard pitied her. Like Sukey he had recognized her love for Wolf, but having more knowledge of the world, he realized its hopelessness.

Sitting first, Jenny refused to dwell on such thoughts and concentrated instead on the cleverness of the artist. Once before, Wolf had described the way profiles might be drawn by tracing the person's shadow as reflected on a piece of paper pinned against the wall. This lady, however, cut her profiles from life, her scissors as quick and nimble as her eyes were perceptive.

Jenny's profile was quickly done, and pronounced a remarkable likeness. As Wolf took his place on a small dais, Jenny almost wished she could watch, but the alcove allowed no space for onlookers, and the time, she remembered, could be put to better use.

"Sukey's safe, then?" Richard asked at once. Standing casually in the shop's outer room, he appeared without care.

"In Hanover by now," Jenny answered, "and then on her way to the Virginia colony. Oh,

Richard, you should have seen how wonderful Mrs. Mueller and Wo—Yves were. They helped pass her off as a German guest."

"Clever," Richard admitted, "and very kind. I am glad Sukey fared so well, but sorry for you. You'll miss her."

"I do already." Keeping her voice low, Jenny begged, "Richard, what are we to do about Nate? I'm frightened. I keep wondering where he'll strike next."

"My estate," Richard answered dryly. "Oh, he did not do any real damage," he hastened to assure her, "but he succeeded in getting me to send more of my people into the country, leaving us less well protected here in town. Now that I and my men have turned respectable, I confess I hesitate to have him killed."

Such a possibility had never occurred to Jenny. Despite Nate's actions, the thought of cold-bloodedly setting a man to murder him appalled her.

"Somehow I thought you'd not like that idea," Richard confessed, obviously reading her expression aright. "To tell the truth, I've become rather enamored of the idea of letting Yves have his way with him. I fancy his revenge will be more thorough than anything we could devise."

"I think he hopes to find another heir to the earldom, one that would disinherit Nate. Surely, after so many years, he must have investigated all possibilities before, though?"

"Perhaps he has only recently discovered some new information," Richard pointed out. "I know this much—Yves does not look to me like a man who despairs of accomplishing his revenge. Im-

324

patient he may be to finish it, but he knows it will be finished. It is just a matter of time."

Jenny peeked into the other room at Wolf, carefully holding his head still for the artist. How much time did they have? That was the question that haunted her day and night now. "And what do we do about Nate in the meantime?" she asked urgently. Nate was not likely to permit Wolf's plans to develop naturally, in their own time. One move on his part and all their plans could be set to naught—even Wolf's.

"I think . . . I think you should write a confession," Richard advised, to her great surprise. "Don't worry. You should be able to do a reasonably complete job of it without naming me as your accomplice."

"How can I do that? We've claimed that you came over on the ship with me."

"That is not a problem. There was enough time—just—after your release to sail to Boston and back. I told you, don't worry about me. With luck you will never need to use the confession, but you will have it. Or rather your solicitors will have it. And," he held up a finger for emphasis, "Nate must know that they have it and that they will deliver it to Yves if anything should happen to you. Anything."

"I see," Jenny said, preparing to admire Wolf's profile as voices announced his approach. "And if that doesn't work?"

With his usual engaging smile, Richard said beneath his breath, "Then, I fear, you must reconsider whether you think Nate's life worth the loss of your own—or of someone else's."

* * *

The Cocoa-Tree was not a place to which Wolf would usually turn for an evening's amusement, although he found the coffeehouse pleasant earlier in the day. Risking large sums of money on the throw of a die or the fall of a card seemed to him at best foolish and at worst culpably irresponsible. The facilities of the Cocoa-Tree for such questionable pursuits, however, made it one of the best places to get word of Nate. And to combat the insidious rumors he had started.

Indeed, other than dropping a few hints among cronies, Nate seemed to have remained very quiet of late. Either he was already trying to avoid some of his more pressing creditors or he was merely taking care that no one should be able to tie him to the anonymous tip that had sent the constables to Yves' home. That episode must have disappointed him, Wolf thought with satisfaction. The small amount of gossip-mongering Nate was able to effect after the fact must be poor consolation for the devastation he had clearly expected. Wolf was almost sorry that Nate was not here tonight, so he could enjoy his discomfiture.

But Nate would not be discomfited, Wolf reminded himself. If Nate had not accomplished all the mischief he intended, he had done harm enough. The rumors he had set in motion might be only a mild annoyance, but it would be foolish to ignore them. Better far to nip them in the bud lest they become dangerous.

Perhaps the world might be a little less willing to take Nate at his own estimation, too, Wolf thought, looking around him. For so many years Nate had been accustomed to using his personal charm to make his way in the world, to good effect. No wonder Nate expected public support of his courtship of Jenny!

This time, however, Nate was wrong, dead wrong. Wolf smiled as he walked through the rooms, greeting the occasional acquaintance. More than one gentleman stopped him to inquire about his lovely ward. Yes, far too many rivals were anxious to win Jenny's hand for Nate's rejection to be greeted with any feeling but relief. And too many others looked to Wolf for his influence or patronage to risk offending him. Sympathy Nate might have, but support seemed mighty unlikely.

Not that it would avail him aught. If Nate thought any force under heaven could make his old friend accept a match between Nate and Jenny, he little understood the matter. Even if Jenny had not come to mean so much to him, Wolf thought as he stopped to observe a hand of piquet, he would never release her into Nate's clutches. Now because she did mean so much ...

Nate might think himself happy to return to Newgate, he pondered, rather than risk what vengeance would demand for any harm to Jenny.

One young gamester, evidently led by the sight of Yves' visage to reconsider his choice of amusement, rose and left a place at the table. Joining the game, Wolf was quick to turn the conversation to his own advantage. Stories of having the law, or the bailiff's men, at his door had already circulated in a suitably vague fashion.

Wolf declared himself enraged at the insult to his reputation. In a voice that carried clearly across the room, he described the constables and their search for Sukey in no flattering terms. "Had they come to arrest me for some imagined slight to the crown, I had been unmoved," he told his fellow gamesters, "but to imply that I might harbor a fugitive from justice—unaware of the girl's criminal past! Accuse me of deviltry, if you will, but no man dare accuse me of ignorance. That were past forgiveness."

Laughter greeted his tale, as he intended it should. Much of society might not know what to think of him, finding him odd, a little foreign— but no one denied him the respect due his intelligence. The idea that a criminal might hide under his very nose was clearly ridiculous, so they all agreed. No one seemed to give the least thought to the possibility, Wolf noted, that he might have been very well aware of Sukey's criminal past and sheltered her nonetheless.

With only half his attention claimed by the fall of the cards, Wolf remembered how close he had come to blundering on that matter. Should he have shown more surprise at the allegations against the maidservant? he wondered fruitlessly. Quick thinking had provided him with a probable excuse, but he sensed that Jenny found it suspicious. To blame Nate openly was out of character, he saw now. What was he to do, though? He dared not admit his knowledge of Sukey's past. That would bring him too close to Jenny's own unhappy experience, and he feared too much the consequences of her discovering all he knew. Even if she consented to stay, which was doubtful, the delicate balance of their relationship was bound to be destroyed.

A cold wave of fear coursed through him. He shivered, blaming it on the poor quality of the wine. While the footman fetched another bottle, he played another hand and won. The applause and congratulations of the other players meant nothing to him. Neither wine nor winnings could ease his troubled heart, not until the game between him and Nate was played out.

The stakes involved in that game were too high to be taken lightly. Once Wolf had thought that all he had to lose was his life, but he saw now he had been mistaken. All the lessons of the past, too, reminded him that Nate was a formidable opponent—and that he would destroy anything that stood between him and the Vickers' title and fortune.

Jenny was the key to that fortune now. Obviously, however, the marriage that Nate had so desired and taken for granted had been most definitely refused. Remembering the scratches that had decorated Nate's face for more than a week, Wolf smiled. The red Beauchamps had always been noted for their tempers and their stubbornness.

Yet now that Jenny's consent could clearly not be won by conventional courtship, Nate would not hesitate to use any means that presented itself. Had not hesitated. The attack on Sukey, Wolf had to confess, had been a shrewd move. It was in her affection for her friends that Jenny was most vulnerable, he knew. Threats against her own safety were only likely to touch off her temper. What Jenny would do to protect a friend was another matter entirely.

Tonight at least, he assured himself, she was safe. He had escorted his aunt and Jenny home himself before setting out again. While he, and

Dangerfield, could guard her physical safety, however, they could not guard Jenny against her own better nature.

Sighing, Wolf collected his winnings and took his leave. He would not be missed—his place was immediately filled—and he had accomplished all he could do here tonight. A glance at his timepiece gave the hour as three in the morning. It seemed he was always conscious of the time lately, time slipping through his fingers, time rushing ahead toward disaster.

Hoping the coolness of the night air would clear some of the cobwebs from his brain, Wolf prepared to set forth. At the door, the porter stopped him for a moment.

"Still here, m'lord Yves? I thought you had already gone. You keep such regular hours, unlike so many of our customers, that when a gentleman asked if you were here, I assured him you had left some time since. Sir Richard Dangerfield, it was."

"Is he within?" Wolf asked, wondering what Dangerfield could want.

"No, m'lord, he left but a moment ago. If you walk briskly you may very well catch up with him by the next street."

"Thank you." Outside the doors, Wolf waved aside the services of a pair of sleepy chairmen. In the darkness ahead he could barely discern the light of a linkboy's lantern guiding a solitary pedestrian home—by the shape of him, Sir Richard. Taking the light for his own guide, Wolf followed.

Despite the fact that his natural pace was somewhat quicker than most, especially after an evening at the tables, Wolf did not catch up with Dangerfield by the next street, where, oddly, the pair turned. *Surely Dangerfield's route did not lie in that direction,* he thought, instantly wary. Automatically his hand went to his scabbard. When the linkboy's light suddenly disappeared, he did not wait for sounds of alarm but rushed forward, his sword drawn.

He found Sir Richard ranged against three attackers. The linkboy, obviously one of the bully crew's confederates, had already made his escape. Of the three ruffians who threatened Sir Richard, one at once discovered to his cost how well the former highwayman wielded a blade. Two yet remained, however. No, Wolf realized, seeing another figure in the shadows, there were still three. While the swordsmen had come forward to engage Dangerfield, one waited with a cudgel to finish him off.

With the flat of his sword, Wolf tapped the hidden watcher on the shoulder. "Really, sir, is this fair? Is this gentlemanly?"

Dangerfield was not the only one to reassess the situation at the sound of his voice. Whoever wielded the cudgel must be the leader of the gang, Wolf guessed, because one of the swordsmen quickly switched his attack to Wolf in order to leave the man with the cudgel free.

"How nice to see you, my lord," Dangerfield greeted him easily, as if they had met on the promenade in the park, and continued to parry his attackers' thrusts. "I do apologize for the behavior of the rest of the company. You are quite right in declaring them no gentlemen. Do you know, these fellows had not the courtesy to even ask me for my purse before they attacked? I should not have given it to them, of course, but I do believe the formalities should be observed.''

The attackers might have no manners, but they had more than the rudiments of swordplay at their command, better, certainly than most of their kind. Four of them should have been able to dispatch Dangerfield, Wolf thought, even though not all would survive the attempt. And Jenny would be minus another one of her protectors.

Renewed anger against Nate spurred his attack. "Gentlemen, I give you one opportunity," he offered coolly. "By now you must realize that you have failed in your purpose. The person who has set you on this foolish and fruitless errand can offer you little by way of remuneration, if indeed he is willing to pay anything for such a botched job. Put down your weapons, and give me the information I want, and you may live unharmed.''

From the shadows came the voice of the leader, deep and rough. "I don't see as we've failed yet, your lordship.'' He made a sweep of his cudgel at Wolf, and caught a fist in his middle which knocked the breath out of him. The other, hoping to take advantage of the distraction thus provided, made a lunge for Wolf's heart and found himself instead spitted on the end of his sword.

"They never listen," Wolf said sadly, and turned to face the renewed onslaught of the gang's leader. The fellow was big, almost as big as Wolf, and quick on his feet. But not quite quick enough.

A move designed to put Wolf flat on his back enabled him to do the same to his attacker. Although the ruffian still held the cudgel, Wolf used it to deliver a few telling blows to the body. Finding his attacker suddenly still, Wolf looked over to find Dangerfield on one knee and looking extremely disgruntled.

"Damn," Sir Richard said, "I've killed him. Any of them left alive?"

They needed one alive to confirm what they already knew—that Nate had set them on to kill Dangerfield. Unfortunately, Wolf discovered as he looked down at his last assailant, he had fared no better. In their last tussle, the fellow's head had fatally struck one of the cobbles of the street by accident. A muted groan from a dark recess gave them one last hope—the first man to fall under Dangerfield's blade.

"Your friends would not listen," Wolf told him amiably, kneeling by the man's side. Without his sword and his fellow bullies, the man looked pathetic. He cringed under Wolf's close examination. The fellow's sword arm had been pierced, a nice clean wound that would effectively keep him from undertaking similar work for some time. "I hope you mean to be more cooperative," Wolf added.

"I don't know nothing," the man hurried to explain. " 'Twas Jenkins who made all the arrangements. Some nob as wanted to pay back another for a-ruining of his sister."

Wolf did not look pleased. "You cannot have been such a fool as to accept a story like that," he said.

"What do I care why one nob wants to get rid of another? Maybe it was the other fellow who ruined the girl, what's it to me? The pay was good."

"Was it indeed? I would be very much surprised to hear that you had received one farthing before the fact. Don't repine, though. It is highly unlikely that you would have received any after the fact either." Wolf sighed and rose. As he retrieved his sword, he asked a grim-looking Dangerfield, "Do you think he knows anything else?"

Still kneeling, Dangerfield shook his head. "I doubt it. Would you trust a fool like this with important information? But he may yet be of service to us. Listen to me, fellow," he said, pulling the man close by the scruff of his collar. "I want you to put out word among all the canting crew. Tell them all—the rufflers, the upright men, anglers, rogues, the priggers of prancers, the palliards, fraters, jarkmen, the whip jackets, drummerers, drunken tinkers, swadders, and abrams—tell them all that no one touches Sir Richard Dangerfield or anyone of Lord Yves' household. You understand? Lord Yves' household is not to be touched."

"Yves?" The man looked up, startled. Evidently Wolf's reputation had carried further than he realized.

"That's right. So maybe you'll believe me when I tell you that if something should happen to me or any member of his household, the two of us will hunt down the ones who did it. We will find them, too. If your imagination cannot carry you further than that, remember this." Dangerfield leaned forward and whispered in the man's ear. What he said, Wolf could not catch, but the result upon the wounded bully was astounding. Quivering in fear, the fellow burst into tears.

"I didn't know," he cried, "I swear I didn't know."

"Well, you know now," Dangerfield said. "Now

go on with you and spread the word."

"I will, I will," he promised. Running and clutching his arm, he hurried into the dark night. In his haste to be off, the man even forgot his sword.

Without rising, Dangerfield looked up. "I have to thank you for your assistance, my lord. Tonight you have assuredly saved my life." He smiled ruefully. "I told Miss Beauchamp that you would be a good man to have beside one in a fight."

"I thank you for the compliment," Wolf responded. "And return it. I can think of no one I would rather have fight beside me." He regarded the results of the fray with distaste. "You know, of course, who was responsible for this."

"I know," Dangerfield admitted. "At least after this he should find fewer pawns to do his bidding. This may force him into the open."

"Yes, he'll have to try another ploy next time. This one has certainly failed."

Dangerfield shrugged. His expression seemed troubled. "That depends on what he meant to accomplish. Oh, I remain very much alive to trouble him, but . . . there is one slight problem."

"What's that?" Wolf asked. Had Dangerfield risked the secret of his past in warning off his attacker? he wondered. Would Jenny's other protector have to disappear?

"You'll have to help me up," Dangerfield said in a grim voice. "I think I've broken my ankle."

Chapter Fifteen

A broken ankle! The most notorious criminal of the age felled by a cobblestone! If the attack were not so frightening Jenny might almost have found it laughable.

According to Wolf's account, Richard certainly found the indignity of it all the worst feature of the attack. Clearly he would have preferred a clean swordthrust through the body to appearing foolish and clumsy. The injury to his pride must hurt him more than any wound to the flesh ever could.

Despite the fact that Wolf had made an amusing tale of the episode for them the morning after, Jenny was not fooled into thinking it a harmless or merely diverting encounter with a few rascals. Servants' gossip told quite another story, a story of a coat heavily stained with blood, and of a calm request to see that three bodies were removed from the vicinity of St. James.

Mrs. Mueller had evidently heard the same gossip. Fear clouded her enjoyment of her birthday celebration, although she made a brave show of pleasure at their gifts. The profile of Wolf was a great success, Jenny was happy to see. A posy sent from Richard also brought a shaky smile to the widow's lips.

The posy brought more than a smile to Jenny; it brought information she so ardently needed. In bringing the flowers, the servant had managed to pass her a note unseen. All through dinner she felt it rustling in her pocket, reminding her of its presence. To have retired early on such a night would have caused considerable notice, however, so Jenny was forced to contain her impatience until she could be alone.

Late at night, by the light of a single candle, Jenny finally read Richard's news. Like Wolf, he clearly intended to spare her the worst details (as well as, she guessed, the most embarrassing), but he dared not deny the significance of the attack.

His use of Danger's old password worried Jenny, even though it probably meant they were safe from hired ruffians. At the very least it might lead to rumors of Danger's escape from the gallows. It might be true, as Richard insisted, that such tales would be taken for sheer romance by the authorities. She certainly hoped so.

Nate's loss of hirelings did not mean that he would be helpless, Richard admitted, but it did mean that Nate would have to act himself, and that Nate would face the consequences of being caught. The likelihood of being caught was high, too, for Nate was followed just as she was.

But he had been followed before, Jenny knew, and that had not prevented his hiring thieves and assassins or his informing on Sukey. Somehow, he would find a way to get to Jenny. It was all very well for Richard to promise that she would be safe, and to counsel patience, but Jenny knew better now than to believe that Nate could be contained so easily.

The answer was clear, and unpalatable. She was not ready to leave. How could she bear to lose even one more day that might be spent at Wolf's side? Every moment they were together was precious to her. Tonight when Mrs. Mueller had cried over his profile, he had looked up at her with such warmth in his eyes. For that one moment they had all forgotten Nate and his schemes.

No, she could not give up one moment more than she had to. Yet, obviously, something had to be done to keep Nate in check. An appeal to his better nature would be useless. He did not believe her promises. Some of his own medicine might do the trick, however, Jenny decided as she burned the torn remains of Richard's note. Yes, she might even enjoy that. Richard had already shown her the way; now she would set the plan in motion. It was about time Nate knew the taste of fear.

That night Jenny struggled over the first step— the confession Richard had once again reminded her to write. The difficulty, she soon found, was not so much in avoiding any implication of Richard's involvement, but in finding a way to say goodbye to Wolf. Despite the lure of music from downstairs, despite the tears flowing down her cheeks, however, she finished it.

Over the next few days, as she completed her arrangements, Jenny discovered how much she had learned in Newgate. Once, she would not have thought herself capable of such intrigue, but now it came easily to her. One excuse brought her and her confession to the solicitors. Another helped her make her escape alone from the Spencers' ball. By then she had already arranged for Richard's guard to deliver a letter to Nate making the assignation with an anonymous informant, to buy her a domino, and to escort her to the masquerade ball at Ranelagh.

Jenny donned the dark wig of Danger's arch dell, as well as the enveloping crimson domino, in the coach. With her face masked, painted a fashionable white, and sporting a patch or two, she felt secure that no one would recognize her. She only hoped her costume would hide her fear as well as it hid her identity.

Once she arrived, the pleasure gardens themselves attracted little of Jenny's notice. To her eyes, accustomed to the wild grandeur of the colonial forests, these English gardens seemed too prim, too genteel. Tonight, however, her attention was fixed on one purpose and would admit of no distraction.

A careful reconnaissance of the crowd making its way into the famous Rotunda failed to reveal Nate, but did ease some fears raised by Wolf's comments. The merry-makers, however high-spirited, seemed respectable for the most part, she was glad to see. If she took care to leave early, she should face no danger other than the one for which she had prepared.

Inside the Rotunda, Jenny's guard slipped back to follow a few paces behind. It would not do for Nate to realize that his incognita had a protector in tow. Even when she herself lost sight of his black domino, however, she knew he was there. Although she had never learned the fellow's name, she had recognized him as one of the men who had assisted in Danger's escape from the gallows. Any man that close to Richard, that trusted, would be more than capable of handling Nate if he got out of hand, she felt sure.

Jenny made a circuit of the elegant room. Now that she was here, she was beginning to have second thoughts about her daring plan. The place, so large and full of people, was daunting. In addition to dominos of every color, there were sylphs and spirits of all description, shepherds and shepherdesses who had never seen a sheep, ladies and gentlemen in costumes from days of yore—all masked. How was she to find Nate among so many?

He might be anywhere—in the richly painted alcoves taking refreshment, in one of the private boxes in the gallery, around one of the four pillars taking tea, on the dance floor performing the steps of the cotillion, or like her, merely wandering where he chose, where he could best view the gorgeous spectacle.

If Jenny had not found Nate yet, others were beginning to notice her. She had avoided a few attempts to strike up conversation, but eventually she permitted one gregarious youth to lead her onto the dance floor for a set. There seemed to be no harm in the boy, if perhaps a bit too much wine. At least her acceptance prevented his making a scene, which must be avoided.

As she took her leave of her dance partner, luck at last favored her. There before her was the man she had been looking for, Nate.

He, too, was dressed in crimson, in the style of a Restoration dandy. The very prettiness and extravagance of his costume, with its petticoat breeches trimmed with ribbon loops, made her think of Nate at once. Examining his face, she was sure. Even a mask could not conceal his cold, heartless beauty.

In a manner she hoped was mysterious and intriguing, she tapped him on the shoulder with her fan.

He turned and smiled, prepared to exert his charm. "Crimson domino, at last we meet. I had almost despaired of finding you. You write a very elegant hand," he said, holding up her note.

The voice Jenny adopted was slightly lacking in breeding, like a shopkeeper's daughter who had been well schooled. "I've an elegant way in many things, sir," she said, "including the gathering of information."

"Softly, softly, my dear," Nate said, casting a quick glance around him. Did he know he was followed? she wondered. "Best to talk where it's more private. Perhaps one of these lovely boxes . . . ?"

Hiding a smile, Jenny took Nate's arm as they walked up to the gallery. This was exactly as she had hoped. After she stepped into the box, she took a moment to look out at the glittering throng with a feeling of satisfaction. There were enough people here tonight to ensure her safety.

"Now this is more like it," Nate said. "Now, my

beautiful crimson domino, you say you know something to my advantage. If you do, tell me, and it shall be to your advantage as well, I promise you."

"And I know so well what your promises are worth, Nate," Jenny said in her normal tone as she turned to face him.

"Well, well," Nate said as he recognized her at last. "If it isn't the highwayman's doxy. I am flattered, Jenny. That you should go to such trouble just to see me!"

"Not just to see you, Nate." Jenny nodded to her companion in the black domino, who had entered behind Nate. Somehow he looked bigger now, much more impressive and threatening, as he brought a pistol to Nate's throat. "To make a point. You've reminded me of my defenselessness often enough. It's time you thought seriously about your own safety."

Nate laughed, but she could see the glint of fear in his eye, a drop of sweat on his brow. His voice was steady, however. "Do you mean to make me believe that you would order my murder and stand by to watch? Be sensible, Jenny."

"I am very sensible to the delicacy of our situation, Nate. Shall I enumerate some of the facts? Some you seem to have forgotten, some perhaps you do not know."

"Do you mind if I make myself comfortable first?" he asked. "I have the feeling this may take a while."

"Please," Jenny said, trying to act as nonchalantly as her victim, and gestured to a chair. Her guardian in the black domino was more forceful, however, and pushed Nate into the chair in a manner far from gentle.

The exhibition of force seemed to alarm him a little, but not unduly, she noticed. After all, it could never go too far. Not in front of her. It was a pity he knew her so well in that respect, she thought.

"Do proceed," he said. "I'm all attention." Jenny noticed, however, that the black domino standing in the shadows behind him seemed to have distracted him a little.

"Good," she said. "Let me first bring your attention to the fact that, regardless of what steps you have taken for your own protection, you sit here with a pistol to your back."

"I had noticed," he said dryly. "I had also noticed that there are a number of people in the near vicinity who would hear a pistol shot."

"They would not hear a knife," she reminded him, deliberately blunt. "And when at last it was discovered that you were not just a drunken reveler, perhaps someone would remember a crimson and a black domino. Perhaps. I, of course, am not here at all. I am home with the migraine."

"I see," he said, and she began to think he did, although he responded as flippantly as ever. "I hope you recover from your headache soon."

"Be careful, Nate. You've made a number of false assumptions about what I would or would not do in the past. Let me tell you now what I have done. I have written a confession."

At this, Nate only laughed. "You expect me to believe that?"

With an effort, Jenny kept her voice and posture bold. That confidence of his had to be deflated. "Believe it or not, as you will, but the solicitors already have it in their hands—as yet unopened. Should anything happen to me—if I should be abducted, if I were to disappear, if I were to meet with serious accident—that letter will be opened and its contents divulged to Lord Yves. Don't trouble yourself telling me that is something I would never do. It is done."

That did indeed reach him, she could tell, although he covered up his dismay quickly, as did she. There was no doubt now that abduction had almost certainly been part of his plan if she continued obdurate. Still he smiled, ever the urbane cavalier. "An unnecessary move, my dear, I do assure you. I wish to marry you, not to harm you."

"Isn't it odd?" she said, suppressing a shudder of disgust. "I've an idea that marriage to you would prove very harmful to my health. Therefore I must once again decline."

"Must you, my dear? I would not be so hasty. After all, to whom else can you turn in times of trouble? Sukey has evidently gone. Richard, poor soul, is confined to his apartments with a broken ankle. I'm the only one left you can trust."

Trust Nate? Jenny shook her head. "If that is the case, then clearly I must be on my own. But I'm not the one holding the pistol, am I?" She paused deliberately. "By the by, you will no longer be able to send hirelings against us. Lord Danger's password protects us. From now on you will have to do your dirty work yourself. 'Tis you who are on your own, Nate, not I."

He must have already discovered that, for this brought no reaction, not so much as the blink of his eye. "You perceive me all aquiver with trepi-

dation, Jenny. If you are quite through, then ...
or did you wish to offer me another meaningless
promise to return my money?"

My money, Jenny noticed, not the Beauchamp
inheritance. "No, I won't waste my time with
that," she said. She knew now that she could
never allow that fortune to become his, not after
what he had done. The moment he had tried to
have Richard killed she had considered his rights
forfeit.

The memory of that attempt hardened her voice
as she continued, "I simply wish to remind you,
Nate, that loss of the Beauchamp fortune is not
the worst that might befall you. If you force me
to use that confession, you will lose everything—
the title, your freedom, probably your life. This
isn't debt, you know, it's fraud, theft. You won't
be the first peer to hang at Tyburn."

"I won't be alone, then," he countered quickly.
"The fraud is as much yours as mine, Jenny dear."

"I might prefer the gallows to marrying you,"
she answered coldly. "But I doubt it would come
to that. Danger's gang protects their own, as you
can see. Somehow I doubt they'd lift a hand to
help you, though, Nate."

He looked up at the black domino. "No, I suppose not. It's a good thing I have never depended
on them, is it not?"

Jenny sighed. Despite Nate's carefree attitude,
she had to hope her threats had accomplished
something, at the very least that she had won
herself a little more time. "Your arrogance will
be your undoing, Nate. Will you laugh, I wonder,
when you discover how serious I am?"

"Oh, I believe you, Jenny," he said. "Really, I

do. But there's one factor you've left out of your threats, a rather surprising failure, to my mind. Wolf."

At the mention of Wolf's name, she stilled. Had Nate seen, as Sukey and Richard obviously had, how deeply her heart was involved? Hoping her voice did not reveal more, Jenny reminded him, "I've said the solicitors will inform Lord Yves of the content of my letter."

"So you did, so you did," he said, and smiled. "As if it were merely part of the process of my destruction. But I know better, Jenny. That is the one thing you can't bear—to have the upright Wolf see you as you are, a Newgate bird who helped his worst enemy pull the wool over his eyes. What a charming way to pay him back for all his kindnesses!"

Oh, he was clever, and knew too well how to hurt. She lifted her chin bravely, though. "Should I repay him better by marrying you, Nate? I think not."

"But, my dear, you may then offer him a lovely opportunity for revenge. He may have the satisfaction then of seducing my wife, while I amuse myself with the knowledge that it is I who have stolen what *he* values."

Before he had even finished his sentence, Jenny's fist connected with Nate's jaw. Her guardian, only seconds slower, closed his hands around Nate's neck.

Almost immediately, Jenny was ashamed. So much for her determination to remain in control! She dared not even consider the implications of the second half of Nate's taunt. Putting a restraining hand on her guardian's arm, she turned quietly to Nate, who was dazedly rubbing his jaw. "I think you've said more than enough. Anything you do or say from now on can only drive me to use that confession. Perhaps I may after all repay Lord Yves' kindness by giving him the information he wants. Think about it, Nate."

Holding her head high, Jenny walked regally from the box. As she walked down the stairs to the Rotunda's main floor, however, she could feel her legs begin to tremble. At once, Richard's henchman offered his arm with an unusually gallant gesture, a kindness that strangely moved her. When she tried to express her gratitude upon returning home, it seemed merely to embarrass him.

Quietly Jenny made her way through the dark and silent house to her own chamber. As she disrobed and hid her costume away, she thought of Sukey and wondered where her friend was now, what she was doing. At times like this she missed Sukey most. Sukey could have helped her put her troubled thoughts in order, could have told her what to expect now from Nate. Instead she could only wait and hope, and rely on the men who guarded her so faithfully.

Outside, Jenny's faithful protector in the black domino hesitated outside the house. In the distance, a charley announced the time as three in the morning.

"All's well," the masquerader said cynically, repeating the night watchman's traditional phrase. "I fear not yet. But it will be, it will be," he promised, then walked boldly to the front entrance of the house. As he stood there, searching for a latchkey, the moonlight shone down upon

his fair head, showing an unexpected glint of
gold.

Looking back, Jenny decided Nate was probably much more worried than he had shown. The
danger, she realized too late, might be that he
would consider her threat a challenge to be met.
Nate's behavior was too unpredictable for her to
make any guesses, however. For all she knew, he
might sit back and simply let her own anxieties
drive her slowly insane.

Indeed, because she was peering over her shoulder every minute of the day and night, she was
almost inclined to think she had conjured the
sight of Caleb Deems from her deepest fears and
worst nightmares. One moment she had glimpsed
the familiar figure as she descended from a sedan
chair to make a morning call at the home of one
of Lady Pertwee's friends. When she turned at the
doorway to look back, there was no one about but
the usual street-sellers and a few servants going
about their errands.

Whether Jenny had imagined the episode or
not, it served to reawaken old fears. It kept her
sleepless most of the night, and when she did
achieve a restless slumber, it was to picture
Deems' menacing face as she had last seen it at
Tyburn.

It wasn't possible, she tried to persuade herself.
Even Nate would never send Deems after her—
he would be afraid the blackguard would demand
money, Nate's money, of her. That an accident of
chance should have given Deems an opportunity
to see and recognize her seemed equally unlikely,
however. If Deems went looking for her, he would

have looked to Covent Garden, not Hanover Square.

A talk with her watchmen eased her mind for a while. Neither of them had seen anyone else following her, or taking undue notice of her activities. Deems was known to both, so if he came near her he was sure to be spotted at once.

They did not spot him, however, when she next saw him, not at the theater, nor at the booksellers. Each time, there were enough people around to help him disappear easily in the crowd. What could she do? Jenny wondered. There was no way of alerting Richard's men to his presence without drawing the attention of her companions. With Wolf at her side, she felt safe, but Wolf could not always be at her side.

She no longer doubted that Deems was stalking her. The only thing that surprised her was that he had not informed on her yet. Perhaps he simply liked playing with her, she thought, like a cat toying with a mouse. Or perhaps he was not quite sure that his testimony to her imprisonment in Newgate as Jenny Wilde would be enough to disprove her claim to the name and fortune of Beauchamp.

In her heart, though, Jenny knew the truth. Deems wanted her humiliated, but not that way. From the beginning he had always made it clear what he wanted of her. Now he thought he had the weapon to force her compliance.

Go, reason told her. *Don't wait to find out if Deems can get close enough to carry out old threats.* Yet her heart continued to plead for more time. *One more evening of music and conversation*, it insisted. *One more day with Wolf.*

Even Jenny had to admit she could not bear much more of this strain. Wolf was kind enough to attribute the dark circles under her eyes to fatigue and insisted they cut back on the number of invitations they accepted. The fact was, however, that she was simply terrified of stepping out of the house.

It should have comforted her to know that she was never alone, never without a guard, but it did not. A reasonable man might be deterred by such obstacles, but she knew that Deems was not reasonable. He wanted vengeance, at any cost.

Every day Jenny waited to hear from one of her watchers that Deems had been caught and warned, but in vain. She was no longer even sure they believed her anymore. To tell them they had failed to notice such a dangerous character not once but three times seemed insulting.

There were times when Jenny was almost inclined to believe she had imagined the whole thing. Sitting in the cool stillness of St. George's on Sunday morning, she felt as if the horror of Newgate belonged to another world, another time. The words of the service flowed over her, a reminder of all that was sane, reasonable, and well-ordered. Outside the church, the sun shone brightly for the first time after a week of gloomy rain and fog, making everyone just a little more cheerful, more agreeable. On such a day it was easy to be at peace with one's fellow man, difficult to believe in the possibility of evil.

When Mrs. Mueller discovered the loss of her fan as they reached the church steps, Jenny did not even hesitate to offer to retrieve it for her. The fan must have been left behind on the pew where they sat. It would only take a moment to fetch, and, after all, what could happen to her in church?

Except St. George's looked a little darker, a little more ominous now that it was empty. Jenny walked quickly to the pew, aware of the whisper of her skirts in the silence of the nave. Every sound seemed unnaturally loud now—the buzzing of a fly at the window, the click of a pew door latch, the harsh rasp of someone's breath behind her.

She whipped around to find Deems close beside her. In his hands, he held Mrs. Mueller's fan. "Looking for something?" he asked, and rubbed the fan along the scar on the side of his cheek, the scar she had given him.

Frantically looking round for a way to escape, Jenny saw that she had been boxed in most effectively. Where was the man on watch this morning? she asked herself. Surely he must have recognized Deems by now.

"If you're looking for the fellow who's been keeping such a careful eye on you, you can stop. He's had a little bit of an accident, y'see."

Jenny ran her tongue over lips that seemed suddenly dry. So her one follower had been waylaid. Mrs. Mueller was waiting for her on the church steps, however. How long would she wait before looking to see what had happened to her? Five minutes? Ten? The heavy front doors, she noticed, were closed. A person could scream and scream and not a sound would penetrate that barrier. She had to stall Deems, keep him talking.

"So you've found me at last. And managed to secure a private interview. Bravo, Deems! Now, I suppose, you mean to tell me the price of your silence." The voice belonged to Danger's arch dell, not Jenny, but it was the only one Deems was likely to understand.

"Oh, I ain't goin' to peach on you, Jenny my girl. Money was never what I wanted from you." He stepped closer, his body pressing her against the pew. "I'd much rather you didn't lose your position. Always fancied having a lady for my mistress."

Turning her head away from his grinning face, Jenny tried to keep calm. If once he realized how frightened she was, all was lost. "Did it never occur to you that my guardian might use his influence to dispose of anyone annoying his ward?"

Deems made a sudden grab for her throat with one hand, while he patted his coat pocket meaningfully with the other. So he had thought to provide himself with proof. "There's some things a girl might think prudent to keep from a father or guardian. Set his lordship after me, Jenny Wilde, and I'll tell him more of your past than just your arrest. How'd you like to explain all those months you was Danger's doxy? If I was to tell him you was my mistress then as well as now, do you think he'd believe anything you said to deny it?"

Tears of pure fright filled Jenny's eyes. After her betrayal of him was exposed, why should Wolf not believe anything Deems said of her? Unable to speak, she simply shook her head.

"No? What do you mean, no? Your consent ain't needed anymore, Jenny Wilde. Come on, they'll be looking in here in a minute."

With Deems' hand around her throat, she could not utter a sound as he pulled her out the small side door and into an alley behind the church. She tried as best she could to break his hold, but found that her fashionable gown impeded her movement almost as much as Deems' strong arms. The bright sunlight stung her eyes after the dim interior of the church. How could this be happening, she wondered in horror, in broad daylight?

Deems threw her against the church wall, and hit her once, hard, evidently just for the sheer pleasure of it. Stunned by the blow, she forced herself to concentrate, to stay alert. Already his hands had begun to grope at her skirts. She had to do something to stop him, but he seemed prepared for all of her stratagems.

"G'arn, Jenny. Fight if you like. But make a noise and maybe I'll decide I'd rather see you dead than broken."

Now that her eyes could focus again, Jenny saw some broken or rotted building materials piled up in the corner. Letting her body sink to the ground, she reached toward the pile of refuse. As her fingers closed around a piece of brick, she hit at Deems with all her strength. "I'd rather be dead," she swore, pulling herself free of his hold at last.

Deems had been prepared for the blow, however. It glanced off the side of his brow and stunned him for a moment, but no more. As soon as she gained her feet, she could feel him lunge after her, grabbing for her ankles. She kicked out at him, and felt the kick strike, but he held tight, pulling her down to her knees again.

Struggling to get up, she expected to feel Deems' hands reaching out for her, but the jailer's attention was now demanded elsewhere. Help had come at last. How Wolf had happened to look for her, or to find her, she knew not, but he was here now.

Deems did not have a chance against such fury. Only when a few of the servants, following the sounds of the fight, came down the alley did Wolf at last desist from battering the vengeful jailer. Tossing him aside as if worthless, he lifted Jenny up and drew her into his arms. "Are you all right?" he whispered, his voice ragged.

Nodding, Jenny leaned into the comforting embrace. She could hear his heartbeat pounding in her ears. The touch of his hands, gently smoothing her hair away from her flushed cheeks, was as sweet as the touch of Deems' had been loathsome to her. When she looked up, his face was grim—not because of her, not yet. Once he knew, though, once Deems began to talk . . .

"Take me home," she begged. More than home, she needed to get close to Deems one last time. The jailer was beginning slowly to regain consciousness. Any moment now he would start spreading his poison, all the more venomous because part of it was true.

Wolf clearly would have stood between her and the man who had attacked her, but the narrowness of the alley did not permit three people to pass abreast—not when one of the three wore wide panniers. For once, Jenny thought wryly, fashion had come to her aid. As she sidled past, she pretended to cringe away from Deems, who had now been dragged to his feet, but instead fell forward against him for just one second as she feigned to trip on the hem of her gown.

That moment was all she needed for her nimble fingers to find the papers—Sukey had taught her well—but it was also all it took to revive in Deems the fire of revenge. He would not mince his words.

For now, though, Wolf would not stay to hear the jailer's ranting. While he took her home and saw to her care, it would be left to the servants to deal with her attacker. Nonetheless, he would hear Deems' story, and soon.

After such an ordeal, she was naturally expected to rest and recoup her strength. Once her scrapes and bruises were attended to, and Mrs. Mueller's delicate inquiries answered, she was encouraged to retire to her chamber. Rest was impossible, though, not even after she had tried to scrape the feel of Deems' sweaty palms from her body in the bath. The very thought of him made her feel unclean, even worse than she had felt when she first left the Women's Hold.

After the scalding bath, she insisted on donning a simple morning gown to wait for Wolf's return from the magistrate's office. To placate Mrs. Mueller, she lay down on a chaise longue in the morning room, darker now in the late afternoon, but once the kind widow had tiptoed out, Jenny was on her feet once again, pacing the room.

She was still pacing anxiously when Wolf at last returned. Her eyes searched his face for some sign of anger, of disdain, but she saw only concern. Could it be that he had dismissed the jailer's claims? She had been able to remove Deems' proof of her sojourn in Newgate, but she well knew that words could do untold damage without proof.

"Jenny, Jenny," Wolf said, his voice particularly gentle, "Tante told me you would not rest, but I hardly could believe you would be so foolish. Could you not sleep?"

She shook her head. Nightmares waited for her there, she was sure. "I had to know what happened."

"Very well, since you must know, I will tell you. But you must curl up here on the sofa first, like a good girl, or Tante will scold us both."

Obediently she returned to the chaise longue and waited while Wolf pulled up a chair. Safe still, she had to assume from Wolf's kindness, at least for a little while longer. Relaxing slightly, she begged again for his news.

"Which of your fears should I first put to rest?" he said as if to himself. "That fellow won't bother you, or anyone else, again. He's been taken to Newgate prison, and I very much doubt he will ever see outside again, except perhaps on the way to Tyburn."

Jenny shivered. The prisoners Deems had once mistreated so badly would now have the opportunity to return his past favors, No, it was unlikely Deems would survive to see Tyburn.

A warm hand covered hers. "Don't worry, Jenny. You won't have to see him again. The magistrate seemed to think my testimony, and that of the servants, should be enough. You can trust me to see that any sensational elements are suppressed. No touch of scandal will touch your reputation, I promise you."

That might not be so easy, Jenny thought. Taking a deep breath, she admitted, "He threatened to say the most awful things about me, as in *The Rape of Lucrece*."

"A most foolish lady, I have always thought,"

Wolf said, smiling at her. "To prefer her reputation to her virtue seems the choice of either a fool or a person who values only appearances. I am glad to see that you are too wise to make such a choice. Yes, he did try to distract us with some ridiculous drivel. Claimed he could prove it, too, but of course he could not."

How odd, Jenny thought, that Deems' very need to threaten her with visible proof should in the end have aided her. Had he left his arrest papers in the logbook, he could have sent to Newgate for proof. Now it was safe in her hands.

Jenny looked at the hands still holding hers. Wolf's knuckles were raw and cracked from the fight with Deems. He had been hurt, she told herself, because he had defended her. Because of her.

"Jenny," he said more seriously, "you know who is behind this."

Unhappily, she nodded. She had thought the risk too great, but Nate had obviously been willing to chance it. Deems could never have found and followed her so successfully without help, very knowledgeable help. "My cousin," she said. "I knew he was not . . . an admirable person, but I never thought he would go so far."

"I've wondered often lately if I should have warned you long ago, but I feared you would not believe me."

What a fool she had been then! "No, I probably would not have believed you then. It shames me now to admit it."

"No, no, there is no shame in that," he said, caressing her hand almost absentmindedly, rubbing his thumb against her palm. "Nearly everyone is taken in by Nate. He is every man's friend—

until they need his help. I thought he was my friend once."

"Is that what happened?" Jenny hardly dared ask, but she needed to know, now more than ever. "You needed his help, and he failed you?"

Wolf met her eyes, his full of remembered anguish. The pain of some memories never left one, as Jenny herself could attest. For a moment he was silent, and she began to wonder if he meant to answer her at all. Then he spoke, his voice carefully devoid of expression.

"Nate branded John a Jacobite traitor to the authorities in order to have him killed. When that failed, he searched for John in the colonies and hired a group of discontents to attack his homestead disguised as Indians. Then he came home and badgered an old man with a weak heart until he too died, and Nate's way to the title was finally clear. So you see, he has already gone too far to win the Beauchamp fortune to let anyone else stand in his way."

Chapter Sixteen

Nate had done much worse than betray Wolf's friendship, Jenny realized now; he had betrayed Wolf's friends, the people Wolf loved. To think she had once believed no crime could deserve the punishment Wolf had meted out! No wonder he had run to challenge his old friend to a duel when he had discovered Nate's perfidy.

"I can prove that he informed on John," Wolf continued quietly. "That could be defended as patriotism, you see. As for the rest ... I was witness to the way he treated the old earl, but I suppose that subtle sort of cruelty cannot be called murder either. My reports from John and my colonial agents prove only that Nate found and talked with John. The fact that the Indian attack followed so closely after, at a time when that part of the country was not yet in danger, might mean nothing.

Even the details of the attack, so unlike the raids of the local tribes, prove nothing. But I know, I know."

He paused a moment, then seemed to recollect himself. "The old earl knew it, too. That was why he changed his will. He hoped and prayed that you might still be alive, that you might save some of the Beauchamp wealth from Nate's greedy hands."

"Only now Nate is trying to get that fortune from me. Wolf, what would happen if I were to die before I reached my majority?" Somehow the existence of a letter in the solicitors' office seemed more fragile as protection than before. Offices could be broken into. Files could be stolen. Nate could even hire someone to do that, since it would not be an obvious move against the household. And what then?

"Don't even think such a thing," Wolf said, sounding horrified, although he must have considered the possibility before. "If you must know, the money would probably be held up in the courts for years and would be eaten up by the lawyers. That would not suit Nate at all."

"No, I suppose not," she said, attempting a smile. Nate would try again, though. Wolf was right—after so much effort, Nate was not about to give up.

Jenny knew, from the way Wolf looked at her, that her own terror must be obvious to him. What he failed to realize was that she feared for him even more than she did for herself.

"I can't blame you for being afraid," he admitted. "Today's attack can hardly have inspired you with confidence in my ability to protect you."

"You saved me from that monster," she protested. "In any case, it was my fault for being so foolish as to wander off alone."

Wolf would accept no excuses, however. Shaking his head, he said, "I hardly think you can be blamed for thinking yourself safe in the parish church on the very square where you live. The only danger to be found in St. George's is sometimes boredom, but nothing worse. Besides, it is my duty to see to your welfare. I have sworn to protect you," he said as if repeating a vow, "and I will do whatever it takes to keep you safe from harm."

Jenny knew then that she could wait no longer. If Wolf felt his presence was not enough to keep her safe from peril, then he would remove that peril—Nate. Whatever scheme Wolf might have for sending Nate back to prison did not seem to be ready yet. The entire household had noticed how eagerly he awaited the daily post, how disappointed he seemed afterward. She did not know what news he expected, but she knew he would not delay action any longer while waiting for it.

At first she had been afraid that Wolf would rush off immediately, that very evening, to challenge his enemy, her enemy. It was with no uncommon degree of relief that she finally remembered that there was a prizefight taking place some ways out of town. Nate would of a certainty be there, she realized. The lure of gambling, as well as the sport itself, would draw him like a lodestone. If she were lucky, he might even extend his stay in the country a few days more.

Wolf could use that time to devise a suitable

justification for his challenge, if he wished; Jenny would make it unnecessary for him to use it by giving him instead the ammunition he needed to put Nate back in Newgate, where he belonged.

The unreasoning fear that Nate might somehow have stolen the confession she had left with the solicitors would not go away as she prepared herself to leave. In the end, she decided to write another and leave it in safer hands—Richard's—since she had to write him anyway. To leave without a word of goodbye to the friend who had been so faithful and kind to her was unthinkable. Perhaps it was even better this way, she decided. This would give Richard the opportunity to read the confession for himself, and see that she had taken proper care to keep all taint of suspicion from falling on him. She could add the papers she had lifted from Deems' pocket. And she could be sure Richard would give Wolf the packet—only after she was well on the road to loneliness.

The name Richard had given her was still engraved in her memory—Sam Harkins at the Turk's Head. She peeked out the window to check. Yes, her evening watchman had taken up his position. He would be able to take her to the tavern in Fleet Street, and, she hoped, tell her what had happened to his predecessor. Despite her concern, she had not dared ask Wolf if he had heard aught of an "accident," as Deems had called it, somewhere in the square.

Her escape would be easy, she recognized, but the knowledge brought her no comfort. Closing her eyes, she tried not to think of what she had to leave behind. Think instead, she told herself, what you will accomplish. A duel between Wolf and Nate will certainly be averted. Justice will be done. Nate at last will be punished and the world will be saved from his machinations.

More importantly, the man she loved would be safe. What did it matter then what he might think of her? Perhaps by this final gesture she might redeem herself, at least to some small degree, in his eyes.

All the things that belonged by right to Jean-Marie Beauchamp she would be leaving behind. The beautiful gowns, the trinkets, the ribbons and laces would stay here, all the jewels . . . She picked up the sapphire ornaments Wolf had given her for her first ball. He had chosen them for her himself, she remembered Mrs. Mueller had said. And late that night, while they still glittered in her hair, he had touched one curl and called it glorious.

Jenny bit her lip to hold back the tears. No, later she would pick over each of her memories, treasure each minute circumstance. To think of them now, however, would only break her heart. Quickly, to prevent herself from thinking too much, she pulled out the small case Sukey had prepared earlier for her flight. Reaching into the back of the wardrobe, she retrieved the plain gowns Richard had provided for the heiress from the colonies.

It did not take long to stow away those few possessions that were truly hers. She sat on the edge of her bed and fingered the one gift she had stolen from Miss Beauchamp—the profile she had copied from Mrs. Mueller's. Then, finally, she heard the sound she had been waiting for, the soft sound of the harpsichord from the room below.

Until everyone had retired for the night, she

could not leave the house. Clearly, Wolf would be awake some time yet. Would it be so very dangerous, she asked herself, if she joined him one last time?

Dangerous or not, she had to do it. This last opportunity to see him, to be with him, seemed like a gift from heaven. The music, too, seemed to be calling to her tonight.

She was careful to change before she raced down the stairs. After all, she was supposed to have retired some hours ago. If Wolf saw her in one of her old gowns, he would be immediately suspicious. Before she left, she would have to change again, but she did not care.

Silently she slipped into the room and into her usual seat. Wolf did not look up to acknowledge her presence, but he switched immediately from Scarlatti to one of the songs from the Anna Magdalena notebook he knew she liked.

Was he remembering the night he had first played that for her, too? she wondered. That had been the night she had faced so many truths. It was hard to remember now as she watched his dear face, his sea-blue eyes intent on the music, that there had ever been a time when she had not loved him and known it.

Tonight he seemed content just to play for her. Perhaps his delicacy of feeling would not allow him to press her for confidences over today's harrowing experience until she was ready to talk. That would be like him, she thought.

After an hour, Jenny simply rose and left. If she stayed longer she might lose her courage. If he had come with her, had offered her his arm as they ascended the stairs, she would surely have clung to him and wept. She wept anyway as she gathered up her bags and stepped carefully down the servants' staircase.

Her watchman saw her at once. One look at her was obviously all it took to tell him what he needed to know. Without a word he took her bags and led her out of the empty square. No one had noticed her tearful escape from the house; no one now would hear her whisper a final farewell to the place where she had found, for such a short time, love and happiness.

It was nearly midnight when Jenny left Wolf's house. From there it had not taken them long to reach the Turk's Head, but there she was faced with a delay. What Mr. Sam Harkins and her watchman discussed in such earnest whispers, she did not know, but it had evidently indicated a prolonged wait for her.

Since her watchman left immediately afterward to bring her message to Richard, she half wondered if some word from him might be necessary, or if he would come himself to bid her farewell. She would have liked that, but although a coach finally appeared, Richard did not.

There was no one to make her adieux to, not even the watchman. Before he left, Jenny had thanked the man for his care of her, but he would hear none of it. Evidently his failure to credit her reports of seeing Deems much embarrassed both him and his injured counterpart, who, by report, was complaining more of hurt pride than a cracked skull.

The ostler reminded her that the horses were becoming restless. Recognizing that she had been trying to postpone the inevitable, she sighed and entered the coach. Looking around her, she could see that Richard was still taking very good care of her, even if he had not been able to see her off himself. The coach was very well appointed, she noticed, well sprung, and with thick squabs to lean her weary head against. He had made sure that she still had an escort, too, a man on horseback to ride alongside.

Finally the coach set off into the night, taking her she knew not where. It hardly seemed to matter where she went now, although she supposed in the end her road would carry her to Sukey and the colonies. The arrangements could be safely entrusted to Richard's people, who presumably had some expertise in arranging escapes. She was reminded of the night of Danger's hanging, how carefully every detail had been organized, and how she had gone from coach to coach, disguise to disguise.

Suddenly Jenny realized she had never thought to change her appearance. Her wig and paints were packed somewhere among her boxes, but she was not sure where. In her anguish over leaving she had not even thought of a disguise. Perhaps it was not absolutely necessary yet, she hoped. The man at the Turk's Head would surely have reminded her if it had been. At the first stop she would at least retrieve the dark wig, she decided. The coachman or the escort on horseback might be able to make some suggestions about what she needed to do, if anything.

In her heart, Jenny knew her worries were foolish, a distraction to keep her from focusing on the one overwhelming reality of her situation. She would never see him again. The rhythms of the coach wheels and the sound of the hoof beats of the horses seemed to repeat the chant endlessly. Never see him, never see him.

The first faint streaks of light eventually showed against the horizon of rolling hills. Sheer exhaustion had driven Jenny into a restless slumber for a while, but the slowed pace of the coach roused her now. A glance from her window revealed a small village. To her surprise, she realized she was beginning to feel a little hungry. After all, it had been hours since she had last dined, not since early yesterday, before the attack. Evidently life did go on, she thought without amusement, even when one's heart was shattered.

The coach stopped in front of a small inn, but no one came to open the door or to help Jenny out. Were they only stopping to change horses? she wondered. Looking out the window, she saw the escort who had ridden alongside the coach deep in conversation with the innkeeper, who seemed surprisingly obsequious.

She was just about to open the door and call out to them when the escort threw aside his muffling cloak and hat, revealing a familiar head of pale gold.

She had not escaped from Wolf at all.

In the moment before she had retreated from the window, he must have seen her. Before she had a chance to collect her thoughts, to even begin to consider what his presence meant, he was beside her.

"May I join you for the rest of the way?" he asked with his usual courtesy. "It won't be long. We're almost there already."

"Where are you taking me?" she asked, pleased that her voice was calm and even. No one would guess from her attitude the bleak despair she felt inside.

"Home," Wolf said. "After we make one short stop."

Home? Was this a cruel jest on his part? She had no home, not any more. Examining his countenance, she could find no clue to how he felt, what he thought of her now. How had he come to be here? Was it possible that he had simply followed her, and that he did not yet know the contents of her confession?

"You've known the truth all along," she said as the reality of the situation finally hit her. Sukey had been right. What a fool she had been not to see, not to recognize the truth behind all the sly hints, the taunts, the too swift explanations. Why did he do it? she asked herself. Why lead her on with kindness? Was that to be her punishment?

"I knew you could not be Jean-Marie Beauchamp," he answered her quietly. Of course, she should have guessed that from his confession today, no, yesterday. He had always known more about his old friend's life in the colonies than Nate had ever suspected.

His next words confirmed this. "John was not a great hand at correspondence, and for a long time we both feared the crown's discovery of his whereabouts, but he did write me at least once a year. When the baby was born, he wrote, full of excitement. The image of his wife's French grandfather, evidently, so the baby was given his name."

So it was as simple as that. Not a red Beauchamp at all, but a dark Gallic infant. Not a Scottish Jean either, but a French Jean. The Mediterranean habit of using Marie in boys' names had misled them all.

"My eyes told me the rest," Wolf continued. "Although what I saw of you at Newgate and at the hanging did not prepare me for the sight of you as Miss Beauchamp."

"Why?" she could not help asking. Nor could she keep the hurt from her voice. "Why did you let us do it? I suppose we suited your plans very well." Considering how they had hoped to deceive him, she had no right to be bitter, perhaps, but the feeling of having been used hurt nonetheless.

"Jenny, you gave me a hope I had almost given up on. Your appearance was a gift from Providence. But it was clear from the beginning that you had no idea how deeply you were involved, and I had no proof to show you. I still have no proof, but I am hoping you may be able to help me find it."

His words only confused her. He knew she believed his estimation of Nate's character now. Had he not seen the confession she had left behind? Surely that was all the proof he needed to send Nate back to prison.

"I don't understand," she said, weary in body and spirit. "What more proof against Nate can you need?"

"I'm not talking about Nate," he said, confusing her further. "Jenny . . . oh, we've arrived."

They had pulled up before an elegant baroque mansion of the last century. It rose from a small eminence, surrounded by acres of parkland which bore a slight air of being unkempt. There was something oddly familiar about it, although she knew she had never been here before. Wherever here was.

Wolf stepped down from the coach and then turned to help Jenny. "Beautiful, isn't it? One of Hawksmoore's earliest works. I fear, however, you are not seeing it at its best."

So this was Vickers. No wonder it had seemed familiar. Both Nate and Wolf had described it to her many times. Dazed now, she could not think to wonder why they had stopped here. When Wolf held his hand out to her, she automatically gave him hers and followed.

At the door, a soberly clad butler awaited them. "Oh, it's you, my lord. I couldn't think who would be coming up to the house, especially at this early hour," he said, greeting Wolf with a familiar respect.

"Certainly not Vickers," Wolf said with only a tinge of bitterness. "I'm glad to see you back here, but surprised. How are things?"

"Not quite as I should like, my lord, but we've been doing our best to set as much as we can to rights. I don't wonder you're surprised to see me here. Most of us have come back now. All the people his lordship hired ran off when their first quarter's wages weren't paid."

"Many losses?"

"Oh no, my lord. We had hidden most of the valuables beforehand. All they took was a bit of the silver. We could not save that."

"You've done more than anyone could expect, Partridge," Wolf said, patting him on the shoulder. "Certainly more than the present Lord Vickers deserves. I hope and pray your services may be better rewarded soon." Evidently reminded at last of his purpose, he turned to Jenny. "I'd like to show Miss Beauchamp some of the house, if I may."

"Certainly, my lord, Miss Beauchamp. Always a pleasure to serve one of the family," he said, casting an approving glance at her windblown auburn tresses. "Would you like me to escort you? Bring you some refreshments? We've not much in the kitchens, but ..."

"No, no, I don't want to put you to any trouble," Wolf assured him. "I know that no one knows the house and its history better than you, but as we can't stop long, Miss Beauchamp and I will go along on our own today."

"As you wish, my lord."

The door was opened into an immense hall with a beautiful central staircase that circled around the room like arms embracing the visitor. Another time Jenny would have been glad to admire the beauties of the house, but now she was much more conscious of Wolf. *Miss Beauchamp?* What was he up to now? she wondered. Or was she being unfair to assume that there was a plan behind his every move? She should at least be grateful that he had not exposed her fraud before the servant.

At every step Wolf seemed to become more excited, until at last he stopped at the entrance to the long gallery of the west wing. "Come," he said, "I want you to take a look at the Beauchamp family."

Utterly bewildered, Jenny walked along the hall, gazing at the portraits on the walls. They were all here, all the people whose names and histories she had so carefully memorized, from the first earl to Nate's great-uncle. Like the house, though, the faces on the wall seemed oddly familiar.

No wonder people had taken her for a Beauchamp, Jenny realized with a start. The resemblance was clear, almost uncanny. Stunned, Jenny stood before a portrait that might have been her own, but for the antique dress the lady wore.

"The Lady Eugenia," Wolf said, standing quietly behind her, as if he were waiting for something, some further reaction. "There is a picture of the whole family here." He showed it to her. "The infamous old earl with his children. My friend, then Viscount Quarles, Lady Eugenia, Nate's grandfather, and . . ."

"But it can't be," Jenny said, her hand reaching out automatically as if to caress a dear and well-remembered face. She did not remember him so young, but it was definitely the same countenance. There had been a miniature of him that belonged to her grandmother, painted when he was not much older than this. It sat in a corner of Mother's cabinet, she recalled, before fire had claimed the whole house.

"That's my grandfather," she said at last.

Behind her Wolf gave a great sigh of relief. "I thought it must be, but my agents had not yet found the proof I need, and I could not know that you would recognize him. All I could hope for was enough family resemblance to give you pause. It made sense. From Wild Jack to Jack Wilde. Eugenia to Jenny."

"Eugénie," she corrected him softly. "My mother really was half French."

"Eugénie, then. Yes, that is much prettier. Jenny," he said earnestly, "don't you see? You may not be Jean-Marie, but you are very much a Beauchamp. Unless you mean to tell me you have older brothers, which seems unlikely, you are the nearest direct heir to the Beauchamp fortune. It is yours by right. You haven't cheated anyone."

"Not because I didn't try," Jenny said, unwilling to accept the possibility that Wolf did not hate her for what she had done. "I meant to deceive you. The fact that I failed so miserably doesn't change that." She looked at him, but there was no anger, no blame in his eyes. If she had not known better, she might have thought his look admiring.

"*Did* you lie to me, Jenny?" he asked, taking her hands in his. "Other than the fable you concocted to support your claim, did you ever lie to me? When you came and listened to me play, when we talked alone in the music room, was that part of some plan to deceive me?"

"No, of course not!" she cried, stung. Those moments had been more precious to her than he could ever know, but she was not sure now how much she had been deceived in those moments.

Wolf seemed to understand instinctively what she needed to hear. "I promise you, Jenny, I never lied to you. Yes, I hid some of what I knew from you, but that was because I feared you would not believe me, and because I feared you would run away. After searching for you for so very long, I could not risk that."

The possibility, mirrored in his eyes, that things might be as they once were between them seemed too much to hope for. "But you could not have known, not in the beginning," she protested. "After having seen me in Newgate, too." Her cheeks flamed when she remembered her performance as the arch dell.

"I think you were very brave, very gallant," he said with a sincerity she could not doubt. "Remember what I told you before, Jenny. Sometimes the heart just knows." He shrugged, as if her inherent worth was obvious. "I knew."

The warmth did not fade from Jenny's cheeks, although the heat was no longer caused by embarrassment. She could feel the beat of her heart pounding against the stomacher of her gown. Somehow she was no longer sure if it was her honesty that was under discussion or something even less tangible.

"Tante knew, too. She made me promise I would see that my quarrel with Nate should not hurt you. In that, I'm afraid, I've failed you, to my shame, else you would not have felt compelled to leave my protection."

"No, no, I did not leave because I was afraid for myself." She could not bear that he should think he had failed her in some way. "I feared so much that you would challenge Nate to another duel. It was the only way I could see to prevent that. If you had my confession, I thought you could put Nate back in prison..."

"Would it matter so much, Jenny, if I were to fight Nate?"

Wolf's question hardly sank in. The full implications of her revealed heritage finally hit her full force. "Wolf," she said eagerly, "you don't need to fight Nate to protect me. He's not the heir, he's not the earl. You said, if I had brothers...My father had a younger brother, and he has two sons. One of them is surely alive, the rightful heir. Nate is as far from the Beauchamp inheritance as he ever was."

The shouts of elation she expected to greet her announcement did not come. Instead Wolf ignored it entirely. "Would it matter, Jenny," he demanded, his voice curiously intense, "would it matter if I fought Nate?" He pulled her closer, until her hands rested against him and she could feel the brocade design of his waistcoat against her fingertips.

"Of course it would matter," she said, refusing to meet his eyes. "Your aunt would be distraught."

"And you, Jenny?" he insisted. "Would it matter to you?"

Matter to her? It was the one thing that had been worse than the thought of leaving him. She had risked much to escape Newgate, but she could not let him risk his life. "You know Nate won't fight fairly," she said unevenly. "If you were to be hurt again..." Her eyes fell to his chest. Only inches from her fingertips he bore the terrible scare Nate had given him when they fought before.

"Actually I had thought of another way to protect you," he said tentatively, in a voice almost as shaken as hers. "I thought we could marry."

Trembling, Jenny fought to preserve some composure. That he should mention such a solution now seemed unbearably painful. In one sentence, he had offered her heart's desire and taken the offer back, making it clear that it would only be an arrangement for her safety. "But, of course, that's not necessary now," she said.

"No, it's not," he agreed. "Will you marry me, Jenny?" he asked in a tone that was far from casual, and far from cold.

By now, she thought nothing could surprise her, but his question did. Startled, she looked up at him at last. His face was tense, almost grim. Was it possible, she wondered, that Wolf was afraid? Too much had happened to her in the last two days, however, for her to comprehend what she had heard. "You want to marry me?" she asked, hardly daring to believe her ears and eyes.

The hope she could not quite extinguish seemed to awaken a kindred spark in Wolf. "Yes, Jenny," he said very firmly, "I want to marry you. I want you by my side always, to be my lady, my dearest companion, and my love. Will you come home with me now, as my lady wife?"

Home. With Wolf. It was all Jenny had ever really wanted. She rested her cheek on his chest for a moment. Home indeed.

With her heart so full, she felt herself in danger of becoming maudlin. Smiling, she looked up at him. "You'll have to get permission from my guardian."

Wolf had already seen the answer in her eyes. Her words were lost in the fervor of his kiss.

After a few more kisses, and a few happy tears, Jenny and Wolf left Vickers Hall and drove back to the village to seek out the Reverend Dr. Warren. Upon Richard's earnest recommendation, Wolf had provided himself with a special license, although (he said) he had felt scant hope of ever using it. The absence of Mrs. Mueller from the festivities was regretted, but Wolf assured Jenny that they had her blessing. Putting his arms around her waist, he added that the woman who had eloped against the wishes of her family would almost certainly understand their haste.

The kindly old clergyman greeted them with pleasure, almost, Jenny thought, as if he had expected their request. With his housekeeper and the verger to act as witness, he recited the words that would bind her and Wolf as wife and husband.

It seemed odd to her that so important a moment should be over so quickly. Only moments later, it was done and Dr. Warren was inviting them over to the vicarage for a celebratory drink, which became instead their wedding breakfast.

From there they drove to Wolf's estate. Someone from the vicarage, or even from the Hall, had evidently sent word to the manor, for all the staff were lined up in front of the entrance to greet their new mistress. The pomp and ceremony daunted Jenny a little. Suddenly she realized she was a baroness and mistress of a large household, with many responsibilities. There was reason here for pride, too, though, and she glowed to see how clearly Wolf was loved and respected by the people who had known him all his life.

Wolf showed her around her new home, pointing proudly to its Elizabethan foundations. All sorts of questions had to be asked and answered. When had she first begun to think well of him? Wolf wanted her to tell him. Remembering all their clandestine plotting, Jenny forced him to admit what he had known and what he had merely guessed.

Mary Butler

They talked until at last after dinner, Wolf, smiling at her a little self-consciously, offered her his hand and led her up to their bedchamber.

The room had been readied for them, the bed turned down and fresh flowers set on the dresser. It was a surprisingly pretty room for Wolf, Jenny thought, with its delicate traces of chinoiserie. There were a few personal touches that marked it as his and made it feel less strange to her. His shaving paraphernalia resided next the washstand. Within reach of the bed a pile of books, with titles in English, French, Latin, and German, lay waiting for him, she noticed with a smile.

"Would you like me to send one of the women to help you?" he asked.

"No, no," she assured him hurriedly. She knew the kind of sly hints and helpful suggestions the maidservants would subject her to. It would all be meant kindly, as part of a ritual; they would never understand her distaste. "I can manage, if you will help me."

"Certainly," he said quietly, but Jenny thought he was pleased, that he too longed to keep out the rest of the world for a while.

Her fingers felt clumsy as she undid the fastenings of her gown, and Wolf's seemed almost as bad as he fought with the laces of her stays. Freed of the stays and panniers, she stood in her shift, shivering, although there was no draft.

"Now I should be your valet," she said lightly, trying to hide her nervousness, and helped Wolf remove his coat and waistcoat.

"I can do the rest," he told her then, almost as if he too were shy. "I did not think before when you regretted Tante's absence that you might like a woman's presence or advice," he said hesitantly as she climbed into the massive bed.

Jittery, she giggled, then pressed her fingers to her lips to suppress the foolish sound. "I am not one of your protected court ladies, Wolf," she reminded him gently. "I know what happens between a man and a woman."

He slid in beside her. "Yes, I suppose you do." His hand reached out to caress her face. "I forgot something," he said, and then proceeded to pull all the pins from her hair, one by one. With each pin he took, he gave her a kiss, until her hair fell in waves about her face and she was breathless and laughing.

With the bed curtains closed, the world seemed very far away indeed. Jenny was shy of the candle's light, but she wished she could see Wolf better, see his face.

For just a moment Jenny fought the unpleasant memories of other faces, other hands. Then Wolf drew her close and proceeded to show her that she was wrong, very wrong—she knew nothing of what could happen between people who loved one another. Oh, as a farm girl she knew quite well how babies were made. In Newgate she had heard and seen the coupling of inmates, an activity that often had less to do with animal hunger than a need to forestall the hangman. What she had seen there certainly had no more to do with love than Nate's arrogant pawing or Deems' vengeful lust.

Those ugly memories and the fears they had raised faded away under the touch of Wolf's hands, his lips. He kissed the bruises left by Deems' attack, leaving her dizzy and warm and even a little bold. She laughed and asked, "And may I not do the same for you? Did Deems not get in a single blow?"

Wolf gave a low laugh, but flinched when she caressed his bare chest. Now she understood the hint of shyness she had seen—not from excess of modesty, but because of that terrible scar. "No, let me," she whispered against the puckered skin, and began to kiss the thin line. "I won't have you ashamed of this. 'Tis Nate who should be ashamed, not you."

He let her finish kissing the line of scar tissue, then pulled her tight against him. "I love you, Jenny," he said in a voice that had sunk several tones.

The rest of the night passed in a blur of sensation. If there was pain, she could never remember it later. What she could remember of her own behavior embarrassed her a little in the cold light of day, but there in the dark, alone with Wolf, it seemed utterly natural and right. He taught her that her body was capable of delights she had never imagined, and made it clear that she had given him a happiness he had never hoped to find. The words that had been spoken in the church that morning had made them one in the eyes of the law and the church; now they were made one indeed by the union of their bodies.

Later, when they rested at last, still entwined in each other's arms, replete and content, Jenny felt Wolf run caressing fingers through her disordered locks.

"You see now," he said, "why I would not have you powder your hair."

Chapter Seventeen

Jenny and Wolf were too happy in their rural retreat to allow the world to intrude on them or to draw them forth very soon. There always seemed to be too much to do to return to London yet. It was only right that Jenny should need time to become acquainted with her new home, only natural that she should wish to see every favorite spot of Wolf's youth.

Even in these secluded spaces, however, the world could not be forgotten. How could it be when every memory of the past, every happy association, led back to Vickers and to Nate? Loved as she knew herself to be, safe as she felt in the tender protection of Wolf's arms, Jenny knew they could not put the past behind them until Vickers was restored to its rightful heir and Nate was returned to Newgate.

Mary Butler

What could be accomplished by correspondence, Wolf did, and for a while she was able to hold on to the hope that it might be enough. The combined news of her wedding and the possibility of a colonial heir was enough to panic Nate's creditors. With the bailiff's men on his heels, he could not long escape his just punishment.

Somehow, however, Nate did elude their net, slipping past Richard's men as well as the bailiff's. He was free, and as long as he remained free Jenny knew there could be no peace for her or the man she loved.

So they returned to the house in Hanover Square and to the welcoming arms of Mrs. Mueller, now Tante to them both. Seeing them, she wept, clearly so excited she could barely think of the English words to express her joy. That first night home almost everything seemed comfortable and familiar, as if they had never left, except that Jenny did not lie alone at night thinking of Wolf.

All too soon, however, she began to realize how much her situation had changed. As Lady Yves, she had expected to take over the management of the house. What she had not been prepared for were the social demands now placed on her, and the hospitality she was expected to return.

Jenny suspected Wolf was glad to see her so involved in social concerns, hoping that they would distract her from worrying about Nate's continued freedom. From time to time, they even succeeded, until she would catch sight of another messenger hurrying to confer with Wolf for further instructions.

One messenger at least she was as glad to see

as Wolf. As he entered the morning room, the roguish look in his eyes so at odds with his sober attire, Jenny's spirits lifted with the reminder that they did not stand alone against Nate.

In deference to Tante, the conversation remained deliberately superficial while she was present. The unending speculation regarding Nate's whereabouts obviously worried Tante, so they all tried to spare her as much as possible. Jenny only wished she could be as successful in pushing the subject from her mind, in concentrating on the fact that writs had been issued for his arrest, ignoring the fact that he was still at large.

That fact, however, remained uppermost in everyone's minds, even while they chatted about such significant matters as Richard's healed ankle and their plans to host a musicale. As soon as Tante closed the door of the morning room behind her, Wolf turned to Richard, demanding, "Any news?"

"None." Clearly frustrated, Richard rose and went to look out the window at a suitably dismal gray morning. This was probably a new sensation for him, Jenny thought. It seemed doubtful that he had ever been balked at every turn as he was now. "Not a thing," he continued. "I'm beginning to wonder if Nate might not have left the country."

"No." Wolf's answer was decisive. "Arrive penniless on a foreign shore? Not our Nate. After all, what good is his famous charm if he cannot make himself understood?" Shaking his head, he added, "Besides, London is his milieu. This is where his resources are, his contacts. He would not go far from them."

Jenny shivered. No, he would not go far from London. From them.

"What resources has he left?" Richard questioned, still doubting. "He has no money, or only enough for subsistence, no credit. Yet he cannot be found in any of the places where he might contrive on so little. Believe me, if he were anywhere in Alsatia, I would know."

Without doubt, Richard had scoured the criminal underworld in his search. It occurred to her now, however, that perhaps that was not the right place to look.

"What is it, Jenny? What are you thinking?" Wolf asked, giving her hand a tweak to pull her out of her abstraction. At the look in his eyes, she forgot Nate for a moment, feeling her cheeks grow warm. For now, though, she would not let herself be distracted.

"You spoke of Nate's charms. Is it not possible that some misguided lady, believing his tales of mistreatment, might have given him shelter?"

She looked to them both, but it was Richard who answered first, shaking his head. "One of the first things we did was check among Nate's . . . female acquaintances. None had seen him. In sooth, I doubt he'd ask for their help without the money to buy it."

Blushing again, Jenny persevered. "You misunderstand me. I'm not referring to his 'female acquaintances,' as you so delicately put it, but about a lady. Someone like . . . like Lady Pertwee, slightly credulous and more than a little in love with him . . ."

"Someone with a large personal fortune," Wolf amended. "Yes, that makes sense. After our marriage, he would need to look for another heiress. If that is the case, I sincerely pity the poor lady."

Still, Richard remained skeptical. "It cannot hurt to investigate, but it seems unlikely to me. Oh, I grant you some foolish lady might well have advanced him some funds, thinking he meant to either pay his debts or flee the country. What's the point in hiding him? He can have no expectations for recouping his losses now that the new heir is expected soon."

"But don't you see?" Jenny rose and walked quickly across the room until she could control her nervousness. "Nate doesn't believe in this new heir, I'll wager. Why should he?" She turned to Wolf, looking for understanding. "After all, if he was able to fool the solicitors with an impostor, why shouldn't you? He knows you will go to any length to keep him from his inheritance."

Afraid to say more, she held her tongue. The urgency of her fears was obvious even to her own ears. Immediately, Wolf followed her and took her hands in his.

A silence fell on the room. They all knew quite well what Nate was likely to do, Jenny thought, but they would not say so before her. Instead, as Richard parted, the two men exchanged meaningful glances.

As soon as their guest had gone, Wolf gave Jenny a little shake and put his arms around her. "What is it you fear so, love? Whatever else we may think of Nate, he has never taken risks just to indulge his own spite."

"It wouldn't be just spite," Jenny insisted, terrified. "The one obstacle between Nate and the Vickers title and fortune has always been you. Not me, or the new heir. It's you who have stood in his way from the very beginning."

"I see," he said quietly. For a moment he was silent, then he kissed her furrowed brow and answered. "There was a time, not so long past, when I would not have cared much what happened to me if I could see Nate pay for his sins. But not now. Life has never been so sweet, so precious to me as it has been since I met you, since I knew you loved me. You may be very sure that I will be very cautious indeed about what risks I take."

Resting her head against his shoulders again, she slipped her hands about his neck and waited for the inevitable conclusion.

"But," he said, as she knew he would, "there are old debts still to be paid. I promise you I will take no more risks than absolutely necessary. I cannot promise that there will be no risks. You know as well as I do that Nate cannot be left free to hurt anyone else again."

"I know. I do know that," she whispered. Part of what she loved in Wolf was his sense of honor, of responsibility. There was no use repining now that it would place him in danger. "It's just that I've been so happy ..."

"I, too," he said, his voice deep, his lips brushing against her hair. "And we will be happier still when Nate can no longer worry us. He shall not take this happiness from us," he vowed.

Despite the warmth in his voice and in his embrace, Jenny shivered. Yes, he would be careful. For her sake and for Tante's, he would force himself to be satisfied with Nate's imprisonment, although Nate's crimes cried out for greater punishment.

No scruple or call of affection would influence Nate, however. Would he be satisfied with anything less than Wolf's blood?

As much as the search for Nate oppressed her thoughts, Jenny could not let it interfere with her social duties. She did not need Lady Pertwee's strictures to remind her that as Lady Yves she had a certain position to maintain. Her behavior would reflect on Wolf, on his position at court, and while the world's opinion of her meant little, it was deeply important to her that Wolf be esteemed as he deserved.

She hoped, too, that the musicale she had planned would bring him pleasure. In the lulls of conversation between greeting their guests, she cast a critical eye over the disposition of the ballroom. This was not the small, intimate affair she had hoped to hold, but it would do well. Even crowded with chairs for the evening's concert, the ballroom looked impressive.

Knowing that her own appearance, in a gown of embroidered silk, could not be faulted helped to bolster her sense of confidence. Around her neck, rested another reminder of Wolf's affection, a sapphire and diamond necklace, chosen to match the gems he had given her for her ball. It was the sapphire gleam in his own eyes, however, telling her how much he loved her that lifted her spirits more than any jewel, and was more dear to her.

With Wolf at her side, the evening progressed more smoothly than she had hoped. The music, thanks to Wolf, was excellent. His court connections had gained them the appearance of His Majesty's music master, Johann Christian Bach, as well as that of some performers from the Opera House. Listening to the lively strains, she could feel herself begin to relax. She knew, of course, that many of her guests were only waiting for an intermission and the chance to sample some of the wines from Wolf's cellars, but they did not matter. In Wolf's eyes she could see his enjoyment, and that was enough.

At the end of the selection, he rose and crossed to the dais to introduce a young soprano, but the expected words of praise never issued from his lips. His attention had been called to the gallery, from which point the sounds of an altercation could clearly be heard. In seconds it had grown so loud that half the audience began to turn in their seats, whispering and looking back to see what the matter could be.

As she turned, however, Jenny did not wonder with the rest. Even before Nate burst through the ballroom doors, she knew. Was this not what he had done before, arriving at her ball uninvited? This time, his sword was already drawn, pointing menacingly at one of the servants who had tried to stop him.

Jenny looked at the sword with anguish. All her hopes for a bloodless resolution to this quarrel would clearly go for naught. Those elegant blades, so casually worn these many weeks, were about to be used at last—and not for practice.

More than anything, she wanted to go to Wolf, to stand by his side, but she knew she would only distract him now. For just a moment, his eyes met hers in silent apology, then he quickly signaled the servants to move back.

"Yves!" Nate shouted from the landing at the top of the stairs. "You have tried to ruin me for the last time." Calling out to the astonished guests, he begged them, "Listen to me, all of you." Pointing an accusing finger at Wolf, he continued in ringing tones, "For years, as well you know, this man has been my enemy. 'Twas he that sent me to Newgate, hiding the fact of my cousin's death to deprive me of my rightful inheritance. Now that he can no longer hide this truth, he means to dupe you all with an impostor, the supposed grandson of a man who is known to have died unwed!"

The whispers flowed around Jenny as Nate continued to ridicule the facts, but she could not concentrate. All she could see was the flashing blade in Nate's hand and the determined look in his eye. She had been proved right, but it gave her no comfort, no comfort at all.

Her attention was called back to Wolf, who held up a hand to quiet the audience. With an apparently languid air, he addressed his guests. "My apologies, ladies and gentlemen, for this rude disturbance. Mr. Beauchamp is naturally distressed by the recent news. So distressed, evidently, that he has failed to remember his manners or his reason. Else he would recognize that the new Lord Vickers must assuredly be able to prove his claims to the satisfaction of the courts."

"Oh, yes, he'll have proof, no doubt of that," Nate said, his voice laden with sarcasm, as he walked slowly down the stairs. His movement drew Wolf from the dais. Advancing slowly through the seated crowd, Wolf nodded to Richard, evidently giving some sort of signal.

"Do you hear, Yves?" Nate continued loudly, for the benefit of all. "I'm calling you a liar and a cheat. Is that sufficiently clear? Meet me now and defend your honor—or let everyone in this room know you have none." At the foot of the stairs, he waited, obviously feeling sure of himself.

Jenny was vaguely aware of the cries of the ladies, alarmed now by his words. Some of them rose, clearly wishing to run from the room, but there was no place to run except past him and his sword. Suddenly she remembered to look for Tante, who had moved to talk with Lady Pertwee. Pale, the widow sat quite still, looking, no doubt, as terrified as she did herself. Jenny would have liked to comfort her, or hold on to her for comfort, but she could never reach her through the crowd, not now.

The growing disturbance behind him did not seem to reach Wolf's notice. "If that is a challenge," he answered, "I believe it gives me the choice of place and time." There were, after all, rules about this sort of thing, Jenny thought with a brief flash of hope. One did not duel in the middle of a ballroom.

But apparently Nate did. "Of course, ask for delay, if you wish," he said. "Call the bailiffs to arrest me! When I am taken to Newgate before we can meet, then everyone will know you are not only a cheat and a liar, but a coward, too!"

Wolf shrugged. "Then name your second." It was obviously a last attempt on his part to prevent the inevitable, to keep his promises. Without seconds, they could not meet, and it seemed unlikely that anyone would be so rash as to support Nate in this madness.

Yet someone did step forward. As Richard moved forward to join Wolf, suddenly they began.

There were no preliminaries, and only the sketchiest of salutes. Now that Jenny saw them duel in earnest, she could see how pallid and tame had been the practice that had once so frightened her. The memory of Wolf's scar, legacy of their previous encounter, rose to haunt her. Would this be a repetition of that terrible time?

Nate was good, that was clear, and he was desperate. Although Jenny knew from the talk she had overheard that he had not been seen practicing at Rolandi's, obviously he had not neglected this skill. In the years since he had fought Wolf, too, he had learned a few gutter tricks that a gentleman would not be prepared for.

A quick slash left a bloody trail on Wolf's arm. Stuffing her fist into her mouth, Jenny bit down to keep herself from crying out. It was only a little cut, she tried to tell herself. *He will be fine.*

With renewed vigor, Wolf took the offensive, pushing Nate back against the rows of chairs, sending terrified guests scurrying frantically into the open spaces behind the encircling pillars. Trying to trip Wolf up, Nate thrust one of the chairs against his legs, but this time Wolf was ready for him.

Was it her imagination, Jenny wondered, or was Nate beginning to slow down? All his late nights of debauchery could hardly have improved his constitution, she told herself. Yes, his breath seemed ragged, too, more labored, his defense more frantic.

At last the quick thrust of Wolf's sword sent Nate's spinning out of his grasp. Defeated, Nate fell to his knees, apparently spent.

"Take him away," Wolf said in disgust, calling to the timid servants. Turning away, he looked for her, and Jenny began to push her way through to his side.

Before she had taken two steps, she saw Nate begin to move slowly—and he was not disarmed! He must have had a dagger hidden up his sleeve all along. Rising from his knees, he held it ready to strike at Wolf's exposed back.

"No!" Her cry echoed through the ballroom. Wolf must have seen the warning in her eyes even before he heard her cry. As Nate advanced upon him, he turned, his sword still before him. It was the blade, then, not Wolf's back, which Nate met as he made his final mad rush.

Ignoring the screams around her, Jenny hurried into her husband's arms. He was safe, she assured herself, touching his face, his poor cut arm.

"It's over now, love," he affirmed, holding her close. "You'll never have to worry about Nate again."

It was considered best that they remove to the country while the scandal of the duel finally died down. The young king was known to hold strong views against dueling, and while His Majesty privately conceded that Lord Yves had had little choice, he could not appear to condone such behavior, especially in his advisor on German affairs. A short absence from the court was definitely called for.

Since this was precisely what Jenny and Wolf wanted, they submitted to this advice with extraordinarily good grace.

"Won't you come with us?" Jenny begged Tante once more as they were about to set off.

"Soon," Tante promised. "Soon. Some time alone together you deserve now. That I have not forgotten, you see."

"Soon, then," Jenny conceded, and kissed her on the cheek. "We will be waiting for you. And we expect to see you soon, too," she said to Richard, who had come to see them off. "Dangerfield Hall is not so very far away."

To her surprise, Richard was noncommittal. "It's time I saw to my own estate," he reminded her. "That should keep me busy for quite some time to come, I imagine." At her look of disappointment, he added, "If you should need me, either of you, I will come, and at once. You know that."

"I know," Jenny said, and dropped her voice to a whisper, for his ears alone. "Danger takes care of his own."

Gallantly, with the bow she always remembered as the highwayman's, he kissed her hand, then silently clasped Wolf's. Behind her the horses were becoming restive. There was no more time for farewells. Looking back one last time, she entered the coach. As soon as Wolf joined her, he gave the order to proceed, and they were off.

Examining the sky, Wolf told her, "If the weather continues clear, we should be home long before nightfall."

"Home by nightfall," Jenny repeated. "I like the sound of that." It conjured up visions of an intimate dinner, with just the two of them. No social duties, no interruptions. Smiling, she leaned her head against her husband's shoulder.

To her surprise, Jenny found herself suddenly imprisoned in his arms, leaning back against his lap. Evidently he too had been thinking longingly of home. After returning his kiss with enthusiasm, she asked breathlessly, "I am yet unaccustomed to London ways. Is this how the fashionable ladies behave in coaches with their husbands?"

"With their husbands? I doubt it," Wolf said. "But we don't mean to be a fashionable couple, I hope. I don't want you to feel you always need be a lady with me. I remember a girl from Newgate prison," he teased, "a highwayman's doxy, with a fire in her eyes. Will you be my doxy, Jenny?" he asked, with a definite glint in his own blue eyes.

"I always knew you were a rogue," Jenny said, kissing him again. Oh yes, fire there was in her, and not only in her eyes. Settling herself comfortably within the compass of his arms, she treasured the feel of him, his strength, his warmth. "Would you like to see me lounge decadently?" she asked.

NORAH HESS

Best Western Frontier Romance
Award-Winner—*Romantic Times*

In the rugged solitude of the Wyoming
wilderness, the lovely Jonty Rand lived life as a boy
to protect her innocence from the likes of Cord
McBain. So when her grandmother's dying wish
made Cord Jonty's guardian, she despaired of ever
revealing her true identity. Determined to change
her into a rawhide-tough wrangler, Cord assigned
Jonty all the hardest tasks on the ranch, making her
life a torment. Then one stormy night he discovered
that Jonty would never be a man, only the wildest,
most willing woman he'd ever taken in his arms.
__2934-0 $4.50

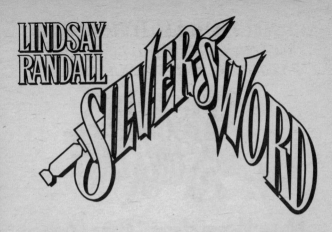

by STEF ANN HOLM

To lovely young immigrant Kristianna, the virgin Wisconsin land was the perfect place to carve a homestead. But arrogant trapper Stone Boucher disagreed violently. Stone wanted nothing to do with encroaching civilization, yet he couldn't resist Kristianna's passionate hunger. And once she was in his arms, she discovered that Stone was as exciting and untamed as the land itself.

__2983-9 $4.50 US/$5.50 CAN